# WELL DONE GOD!

*Also by B. S. Johnson*

NOVELS

Travelling People

Albert Angelo

Trawl

The Unfortunates

House Mother Normal

Christie Malry's Own Double-Entry

See the Old Lady Decently

POETRY

Poems

Poems Two

SHORT PROSE

Street Children (*with Julia Trevelyan Oman*)

Statement Against Corpses (*with Zulfikar Ghose*)

Aren't You Rather Young to be Writing Your Memoirs?

ANTHOLOGIES
(*as editor*)

The Evacuees

All Bull: The National Servicemen

You Always Remember the First Time

# WELL DONE GOD!

Selected Prose and Drama of
B. S. Johnson

Edited by Jonathan Coe, Philip Tew
& Julia Jordan

PICADOR

First published 2013 by Picador
an imprint of Pan Macmillan, a division of Macmillan Publishers Limited
Pan Macmillan, 20 New Wharf Road, London N1 9RR
Basingstoke and Oxford
Associated companies throughout the world
www.panmacmillan.com

ISBN 978-1-4472-2710-6

A CIP catalogue record for this book is available from the British Library.

Printed and bound by CPI Group (UK) Ltd, Croydon, CR0 4YY

Visit **www.picador.com** to read more about all our books
and to buy them. You will also find features, author interviews and
news of any author events, and you can sign up for e-newsletters
so that you're always first to hear about our new releases.

*Turner the painter turned a Welsh corner*
*which revealed a view of the Vale of Clwyd*
*so fine that he stopped and yelled . . .*

> Buffalo-humped, bent, next to no muscle
> substance on any limb, her face pale where
> it is not grey-yellowed at the temples,
> sunken where it is not puffy under
> the eyes; her step hammertoed, hesitant:
> even a trivial fall may snap off
> the frail neck of a femur; no eyebrows,
> hair sparse except on upper lip and chin;
> her skin with unsuntanned sunspots, her pulse
> slow and temperature low, the genital
> tract become bloodless, unmoist, atrophic;
> her eardrums are in retraction, a sluice
> of cataracts lapses before her eyes;
> she is querulous, forgetful, unclean,
> distressing to others; and to herself.
> > . . . *Well done God!*

'Little Old Lady'
from *Poems Two*
by B. S. Johnson

# Contents

# Contents

# Acknowledgements

The editors owe a great debt of thanks to Virginia and Steve Johnson, who have represented B. S. Johnson's desire for the integrity of his work to be always respected with passion and honesty, and have balanced this sensitively with a desire to restore these texts to a wider readership. Thanks too go to Paul Baggaley and Kris Doyle at Picador for their enthusiasm and imagination in bringing this project to fruition, Diana Tyler of MBA Literary Agents, and Tony Peake of Peake Associates. We are also grateful to Alan Brownjohn for his help. The staff in the British Library Manuscripts Reading Room dealt with us with forbearance and efficiency, and particular gratitude goes to the British Library's Jamie Andrews, Rachel Foss and Helen Melody. Finally, we would all like to thank our editorial assistant Christopher Webb for his exemplary work, particularly his faithful transcriptions of an immense amount of archival material.

# Preface *by Jonathan Coe*

February 5, 2013, marks the eightieth anniversary of the birth of Bryan Stanley Johnson. The present anthology is being published, in part, to celebrate this fact. We have arranged it in three sections. First we have a facsimile reproduction of *Aren't You Rather Young to be Writing Your Memoirs?*, the collection of shorter prose pieces Johnson himself compiled shortly before his death in 1973. This is followed by a selection of plays, written either for the stage or for television, three of which have never been published before. Finally, out of the mountain of Johnson's journalism published between 1963 and 1973, we have cherrypicked the pieces which seemed to us the most worthwhile: whether they find him delivering an especially feisty piece of polemic aimed at the publishers, film producers, writers or writers' organisations he found lacking, or whether they just offer some flashes of insight into the theoretical thinking, autobiography or historical interests of this perennially fascinating man.

With the appearance or reappearance in print of these pieces, a good chunk of the Johnson canon is now readily accessible – much more so than in his lifetime. All being well, it seems that a comprehensive DVD release of his film work will not be far behind, either. But there remain some significant gaps. *Travelling People*, his exuberant, picaresque first novel, remains out of print: in the 'Introduction' to *Aren't You Rather Young* . . . he gives his reasons for this self-imposed prohibition, one which his estate continues to respect. His final completed novel, *See The Old Lady Decently*, the first volume of a projected trilogy, also remains a problematic item for any interested publisher, and his two volumes of poetry (Johnson considered himself first and foremost a poet) are likewise currently out of circulation.

In the meantime, we hope that *Well Done God!* will do something to plug the remaining gaps, and that readers will emerge from it with a more rounded and more nearly complete sense of Johnson the writer than has been previously possible. Before the editorial process started in earnest in 2012, I had not seen most of these pieces since my work on Johnson's biography a decade earlier. In the closing paragraph of that book I had signed off, over-optimistically – or perhaps just bad-temperedly – with the sentence 'Those are the last words I intend to write about B. S. Johnson'. I had probably hoped that completing the book would give me closure on my interest in a writer which many people, I suspect, considered to border on the obsessional. But my interest, or obsession, has not gone away in the intervening ten years. I still find myself returning again and again to Johnson's writings for inspiration and (just as useful) provocation.

To me, looking at the contents of this new anthology as a whole, two major themes stand out: Johnson's dogmatic insistence (articulated most famously in his 'Introduction' to *Aren't You Rather Young to be Writing Your Memoirs?*) on the incompatibility between truth and fiction; and his horror at the vulnerability of the human body and, in particular, its inevitable propensity to decay. In my biography I took repeated issue with both of these positions, but now, while I still consider his mantra that 'telling stories is telling lies' to be an unhelpful over-simplification, a decade's further submission to the ageing process has been enough to convince me that, on the second front at least, Johnson definitely had a point. *You're Human Like The Rest of Them*, which for a long time I never really 'got', today strikes me as a most courageous act of squaring-up to the unpalatable truth; and Johnson's hitherto-unpublished continuation of Büchner's *Woyzeck*, *One Sodding Thing After Another*, far from seeming derivatively Brechtian, as I once thought, now feels like a lively and probing excursion into his recurring preoccupations. As for *Compressor* . . . well, best to let readers themselves make up their minds about that one. At the very least, in its combination of playful obscurity with the most massive existential themes, it shows Johnson's art, towards the end of his life, moving onto a new and intriguing level.

In its diversity of content, we tried to bring this anthology close to Johnson's original conception of *Aren't You Rather Young to be Writing Your Memoirs?*. His hope for that book, at first, had been to persuade a publisher to include a wide variety of occasional journalism, ranging from book reviews to football reports. In the end, however, he had to settle for a very much slimmed-down volume, concentrating mainly on what it would be convenient to call 'short stories', even though he of course disliked that term very much. And in the event he slimmed down the selection even further himself: having a ready-made assembly of nine early pieces to hand in *Statement Against Corpses* (1964), the volume he had co-authored with his friend Zulfikar Ghose, he nonetheless turned his back on all but two of them. Unless newness itself was the criterion, it's hard to see why he would have admitted as slight (and damp) a squib as 'Instructions for the Use of Women', for instance, when from the earlier book he could have chosen 'Sheela na Gig', a truly compelling piece of autobiography with a supernatural twist. But there you have it: the selection was his own; and Johnson's choices were never less than clear and emphatic.

In any case, *Aren't You Rather Young . . .* contains at least two of his finest pieces of work in any medium. 'Mean Point of Impact' brilliantly juxtaposes the building of a cathedral in medieval France with its destruction by aerial bombardment in the Second World War. 'Everyone Knows Somebody Who's Dead' proceeds from a similarly contrapuntal device: extracts from a banal handbook for aspiring writers are interleaved, contemptuously, with an account of the events leading up to the death by suicide of an old student friend. The despised tropes of popular fiction are mercilessly contrasted with what Johnson felt to be their formal and moral opposite: a reminiscing authorial voice which stretches after truth with the same anguished urgency we also find in his great, novel-length threnody *The Unfortunates*.

For a writer to 'tell a story', to do anything other than leave things 'untied, untidily', was to be unfaithful, Johnson believed, to the chaotic realities of life. 'Everyone Knows Somebody Who's Dead' shows him putting this credo into practice. The 'Introduction' to *Aren't You Rather Young . . .* meanwhile, shows him trying to convince us by argument. It was an argument he rehearsed again and again. Trawling through Johnson's archive, we lost count of the number of similar articles we came across, dating from the early 1960s onwards: articles in which he repeated, in almost the same words, that Joyce was the Einstein of the novel; that novel-writing was a relay race and most British writers had dropped the baton; that Beckett was the only person worth listening to; that writing neo-

## Preface

Dickensian novels was as silly as trying to write Elizabethan blank verse drama.

Putting together a readable collection of his journalism involved setting aside many of these pieces: with some regret, for all of them provided incidental, glancing pleasures. There was a good deal of sometimes animated editorial discussion about what to put in and what to leave out. But the three of us remained united by our admiration for Johnson and our determination to achieve a selection which represented him (we hope he would have approved this word) honestly. For their work and their company over the last few months, I'd like to express my gratitude to my fellow-editors. On which subject, this is a probably a good moment for me to step down, and allow them to have their say.

# Foreword *by Julia Jordan*

> I hate these women who only want bits of me. I offer her the enormous totality of me, and she says, yes, I'll have the conversation bit, and the company bit, but not the bed bit, nor even the handsonmybigtits bit. I hate the partial livers. I'm an allornothinger. (*Albert Angelo*)

B. S. Johnson, like the protagonist of his 1964 novel *Albert Angelo*, was an 'allornothinger'. The writing collected in this volume seeks to represent 'the enormous totality' of the prolific Johnson; if, in the recent past, his novels have been the only widely disseminated part of his oeuvre, here the editors offer an encounter with a broader variety of Johnson's eclectic range of forms. We say 'yes' to all his 'bits'. This anthology seeks to recover some of these long inaccessible pieces of work and to deliver them to his – recently reinvigorated – readership. While we could not include all of his unpublished and out-of-print work, the editors hope that his spirit of capaciousness has been recreated here: included are the major plays, for television and stage; the short prose collected in *Aren't You Rather Young to be Writing Your Memoirs?*; journalism; essays; literary criticism; auto-biography; single-issue polemics. These pieces throw new light onto the novels and poetry for which Johnson is best known, and show him 'in progress', in the process of working out the concerns to which he would return throughout his career.

The sheer bulk of Johnson's output demands the principle of selec-tion. A man with serious affection for objects – a collector even of paperclips – Johnson is driven, like his Customs Officer in 'Instruc-tions for the Use of Women', by the 'desire to see objects declared'. So, walking down Bournemouth's arcades, one Johnsonian narrator scrutinizes the 'locked, mahogany and brass' advertising cases, look-ing through their 'angled glass' to read 'hand-lettered posterpaint showcards for hairdressing and tinting, dancing, restaurants, the Bournemouth Casino (members only), two discotheques, theatre and cinema', itemizing 'pictures advertising the Foot Clinic and the Public Baths Department'. The exhaustive nature of Johnson's depiction is both generous and inclusive, and yet unavoidably selective. To collect is, by necessity, to select, and to omit.

Selection, in turn, necessitates interpretation: the aim has been to include the pieces of Johnson's writing that are significant in relation to his major themes. Indeed, the reader can trace Johnson's lifelong preoccupations: the slippery distinction between truth and represen- tation; the proper role of the author; fictionality and storytelling; the accuracy of memory and the importance of memorialisation; the vagaries of chance, contingency, and randomness. In the establishing of these themes we see repetition itself emerge as a characteristically Johnsonian rhetorical device: for Johnson, certainty is achieved through accumulation, through the testing and extension of his ideas. Johnson's repetitions display him in the act of gaining certainty through these accretions – a certainty which inevitably reveals itself to be precarious even in its vigour and appetite – and many of the works here are the results of the creative alchemizing of these fundamental literary precepts. The editors' explicit goal was to give a sense of the trajectory of his literary development, and to this end a sense of the chronological order of the pieces has been main- tained where possible in order to uncover changes of style and tonal shifts.

At times it seems that Johnson is at open war with the very notion of fiction. 'Telling stories is telling lies', he declares, declining to per- form such cheap party-tricks: as he writes in *Albert Angelo*, 'fuck all this lying'. Consequently, Johnson's subsequent refusal to delineate between 'truth' and 'fiction' informs the organization of this anthol- ogy, which distinguishes only between the dramatic works and the shorter prose, allowing the autobiographical to sit alongside the imag- inative. For Johnson, these genres cannot remain hermetically discrete; it is in their interaction that the line between 'telling stories' and truth-telling is effaced. 'There's a lot of me in this house', as the protagonist of *What is the Right Thing and Am I Doing It?* admits: 'Literally, when you think of it. I've spent thirty years here, and most of the skin I shed in that time must be in the dust, in the crevices, in

the air'. The reader of this anthology, and of Johnson's work in general, will feel the corporeal presence of the man in his writing; his
autobiographical dust is in the air throughout this anthology. This
intimacy is there, too, in Johnson's feel for the material stuff of life –
for food, for sex, for objects – for consuming and being consumed.
Indeed, an almost uncomfortable proximity to the physical pervades
these texts; the confines of the body and its demands press down on
his characters and on his readers. Naked women in the play *One Sodding Thing After Another*, the 'Nudies', are evoked by the image of
'skinless sausages', as Woyzeck is starved by military doctors in the
name of science. A stage direction in *One Sodding Thing* . . . reads,
tellingly: 'then he returns to his preoccupation with food: hold this as
long as it will bear.' Similarly, both *Down Red Lane* and *Not Counting the Savages* are plays that portray corpulence and compulsive
eating as correlatives of the generous capaciousness evoked elsewhere. Johnson asks us to 'bear' gluttony frequently, as indicative of
a visceral self-loathing and as a marker of compassion. As the diner
of *Down Red Lane* admits: 'I do know I have suffered from my
appetite, my grossness, my peculiarity.'

Johnson does not flinch in the face of the gross, or the peculiar.
Yet at the heart of his governing authorial injunction – to tell the truth
– lies a perceptible trace of uncertainty, a concession of unease: while
attesting a belief that truth can be represented, Johnson betrays his
fear that it may be a mirage. Truth is an opaque thing, and Johnson's
anxious attempts to fix it to the page are palpable in the works collected here. His is a poetics of frustration: his prose fluctuates
between cohesion (certainty) and fragmentation (the failure of representation to do its work). The demand for truth and contempt for
artifice inform Johnson's desire to abolish the distance between
author and reader. Indeed, to read Johnson is to find oneself in active
struggle for control over the text, negotiating with a confrontational
author, who seems at times to be let down, disappointed by our read-
erly shortcomings. As he says in 'Holes, Syllabics . . . '

But my character is something like Shandy's father, who
had—'...such a skirmishing, cutting kind of a slashing way
with him, in his disputations, thrusting and ripping, and giving
every one a stroke to remember him by in his turn – that if

there were twenty people in company – in less than half an
hour he was sure to have every one of them against him.'

In his various direct addresses, his cajolements or confrontational
indictments, his flirtatious asides – these elegiac calls into the void –
Johnson articulates a kind of mourning for the reader's presence. The
pleasures of the text, for him, are a resolutely consensual matter, and
must be negotiated via constant dialogue: 'you can provide your own
surmises or even your own ending, as you are inclined'. 'For that
matter', he continues, 'I have conveniently left enough obscure or
even unknown for you to suggest your own beginning; and your own
middle, as well, if you reject mine. But I know you love a story with
gunplay in it'.

The central principle of absolute fealty to truth is also an articulation of the importance of memory. Johnson's challenge to himself is
to lay bare the causes of things, by a continual dredging up of forma-
tive experience: to trace the contingency of events backwards.
Johnson's present is determined by an intrusive and insistent past.
Decisions made when young – to join the army at eighteen to make
oneself more attractive to women, for instance – will continue to
exert their influence long after they have been made: conscription
scripts. Equally, his characters feel the unremitting pressing of chance
and the random, both as paradoxically fated (it will always be *One
Sodding Thing After Another*), and as seductively liberating (it might
even '[trip] some trap of unbidden memory' in 'Instructions for the
Use of Women'). But if Johnson can be said to be reading contingency backwards, he is also concerned with its forwards trajectory;
one of his great themes could be described as a kind of proleptic anxiety, as Woyzeck articulates in *One Sodding Thing* . . . : '[it] comes
over me, Andres, a great black feeling of a disaster about to happen,
or my luck running out, something catching up with me....'

Though he hated the term, the plays are, for the most part, less
'experimental' than the prose.* In the six plays published here Johnson exhibits sustained ease and formal playfulness. Liberated from

---

* While he disavowed the term, Johnson nevertheless recognized that there was at this
time a group of formally innovative British writers, which included Rayner Heppenstall,
Ann Quin, Christine Brooke-Rose and Alan Burns, as he wrote in his essay 'Experimental British Fiction', published in 1967: 'There are not many of us, and in the English

the constrictions of the traditional novel form, Johnson seemed to find in dramatic form a ready vehicle, already able to contain a polyphony of ideas and voices. It is also in the drama, in *Compressor* (1972), that Johnson best expressed his fascination with new media and his sustained interest in the possibilities of the visual and the photographic. The play is notable for an acute enthusiasm for new forms, seeing them not as extraneous to literature but as a new way of invigorating narrative and form. As Sleeper says, 'a man taking pictures of a man taking pictures: there is something in that!' This play also demonstrates Johnson's consistent preoccupation with the ludic: from flipping coins and games of squash, to the suggestion that 'there's no doubt, too, that games are one of [God's] chief diversions'. Following the random bounce of a squash ball, its erratic movements delimited by court and wall, we understand Johnson's characters as similarly bound by their own ludic rules, bouncing chaotically around an indifferent universe. The characters of many of these pieces are aware of their own fictive natures in a classically Johnsonian way, one that is characteristic of a writer pivotally positioned between the modern and the postmodern. In *Compressor*, his characters echo and double each other uncannily: 'finally, standing together' they 'both independently but at the same time write: I am beside myself.' In *Down Red Lane* the protagonist's belly is independently wilful, just as subject to melancholy, nostalgia, depression, and humour as he is. And in all the plays published here there is a sustained problematizing of the artificiality of chronology: *One Sodding Thing After Another*, set in 'The Army. Any Time', gives us meditations on death and eternity, and as Ghent puts it in *What is the Right Thing and Am I Doing It?*: 'Life is a holiday from the great nothing, a vacation from the void — and, like all holidays, it seems interminable'.

Loss haunts Johnson's work: it is the fundamental determinism that he allowed for and conjured with. This sense of grief, though, is

way we do not form a "school". The things we have in common are mostly generalities. First of all, we object to being called "experimental" because of the pejorative sense the term bears for most English critics. We regard the novel as an evolving form in which there is no point whatsoever in doing something that has been done before [...] Our greatest debt is owed to James Joyce, of course.'

usually mingled with a clear-eyed compassion, and a desire to tot up life's losses and gains. In *You're Human Like the Rest of Them*, his play of 1967, the generosity of the title is tempered by the clear-sighted confrontation of the centrality of death:

> You are human just like the rest of them/
> And your one certainty is that you'll die — /
> Our dying is the only certainty/

Certainty is always a good in itself, even if it brings about this terrible knowledge of mortality. Indeed, throughout the pieces in this collection, Johnson returns to the virtues of certainty: of counting, of reckoning, and of calculation. Like the counting commanding officer in *One Sodding Thing After Another*, who needs to enumerate time (as he reminds Woyzeck: 'Just think of it, Woyzeck, all that time going on and bloody on', reminding him that 'Thirty years. . . .that means 360 months. . . .thousands and thousands of days, God knows how many minutes, an eternity of seconds. . . . .'), or the husband in *Not Counting the Savages* (the title of which, too, articulates the limits of enumeration) whose inability to respect the number on the calendar signals to us his moral decrepitude – Johnson's characters mediate existential anxiety through their desire to account for their lives. His will-to-exactitude often produces a note of half-comic bathos: life, for Johnson, scrupulously accounted for, is usually a disappointment. In the early play *The Proper End* (not included here, though again with a title that signals a need for clear and appropriate demarcation), Johnson explores his metaphor of existential accountancy later developed to such effect in *Christie Malry's Own Double-Entry* (1973): 'The double-entry theory of love: love automatically creates a force of hatred which is its opposite, its equal, its complement, its corollary.' The desire to count up the injustices, the pleasures, and the events that make up a life is eventually just another version of the urge to represent the truth of existence. As Johnson writes in 'A Few Selected Sentences' – it is imperative to 'Accommodate that mess.' Because, eventually, 'someone has to keep the records.'

# Prologue *by Philip Tew*

Preparing this anthology involved visits by its editors to the B. S. Johnson archive now held in the British Library on the Euston Road in London. This collection consists of a series of folders, files, boxes and notebooks that in essence are just as they were in autumn 1973 when B. S. Johnson left them, about a mile away as the crow flies, stored in the small work room he maintained at the top of his house in Islington. Their journey via Sotheby's was not a long one geographically, but potentially an important one for scholars. Certainly it allowed the production of this volume of Johnson's writing. One significant strand of our editorial work meant going through numerous lever-arch and other files containing the carbon copies of his efforts, including the journalism and short prose Johnson undertook for a variety of purposes, commissions and publications. They were often littered with notes and corrections, which is part of the joy of such material. Of course to do so we had to make a special request for this as yet un-catalogued material and each box was delivered rather portentously in large open wooden, leather-lined trays. Such ceremony! Johnson might well either have shuddered, or much more likely laughed out loud. Clearly for us as editors there was a certain thrill about such archival retrieval. But most of all it offered in complex ways certain concrete impressions of Johnson himself, as both a man and a professional writer, and in a sense that too is what the examples of his work published in this anthology seek to convey. We want Johnson to be given voice once more.

Returning to the British Library, the first impression given by the contents of each of the files is that they are exceedingly neat and efficiently organized, no doubt the product of Johnson's commercial education and experience, but perhaps also expressive of his need to maintain more than a semblance of order to defy any encroaching chaos. So despite his admission and avowal of the inchoate and ran-

Prologue

domness in his fiction, here his commercial training and instincts allowed him to stave these off, exhibiting perhaps underlying obsessional and controlling impulses. And they offer far more than this, for the contents of these varied pieces were certainly intriguing in at least one sense: the very persistence of his sense of radical annoyance and anger, a certain strident tone creeping in at times, at others a determination that people ought to comprehend the unfairness of certain of the ideological perversities of the powers-that-be, more precisely those actions of the authorities that led to diminishing freedom. Below I hope to illustrate something of the man by drawing upon work that as editors we had to omit from our final selection, and by doing so redeem certain passages that will allow our readers a glimpse at the remaining archive.

Johnson could be uncannily perceptive, almost prescient, in his political observations. In one piece written in 1971 for a regular column in his trade union journal, he sees Rupert Murdoch's motivations in a clear light, remarking that the publisher and magnate 'give[s] the impression of wanting money like normal people want sex.' Johnson adds of Murdoch's apparent proprietorial success:

> But while I'm on about the Digger, let's lay another myth: what he's done with the *Sun*, in any case, is the sort of thing that gets success a bad name. For his technique was simply to copy the *Daily Mirror* to the point (one would have thought) of plagiarism in features and typography, and therefore to exploit what we call in the trade the margarine syndrome: those idiots who can't tell one from the other. IPC could not have adopted this tactic since they also own the *Mirror*; so to say that Murdoch has succeeded with the *Sun* where IPC failed is patent nonsense. Murdoch has not increased the total readership of newspapers; he has simply altered the balance of readership by unscrupulous low cunning.

Of course Johnson saw such matters in terms of social class and not at all as an abstract issue, rather finding expressed in people's actions, inactions and instincts their class affiliations, their ideological blindness. He offers in this piece a memorable aphorism: '"Business ethics", indeed, is a contradiction in terms.' One finds other instances of his ideological awareness and commitment when he railed constantly about the unfairness of payments to authors, and the volume of money made by publishers from their efforts. In a speech he gave to the Society of Authors at their Annual General Meeting on 26 July 1973, printed on orange paper – again a piece not included in this volume – he complained that a recent survey of authors' earnings shows them lower than they were in 1965, and his motion 'questions whether the administration and leadership have been effective in promoting the Society of Authors; and recommends that all those responsible for such administration and leadership should resign forthwith.' He goes further. In his speech he complains of this governing committee 'What else have they done recently? It's easier to say what they haven't done.' This is classic Johnson in combative mode, personal and accusatory. However, the file in which this speech is contained also amply demonstrates how Johnson was both methodical and well-prepared. For this occasion he not only drafted a complete five-page script in advance word for word for his speech, but another page on white representing a concluding address with which he would wind up as the proposer. All of the above evokes a man who believed in the fights he undertook, demonstrating his commitment and his engagement, but ever the consummate professional he would draw on each effort of research and thinking more than once, regarding it as hard work but also as an investment intellectually. Some of the same material from this speech reappears in a piece (on green paper) entitled 'On Writer's Organisations' which opens with that 1965 survey again. Clearly he had developed strategies for recycling the efforts of his labour.

In 'The Revolution Ignored', an article written for *Vogue* in 1966, Johnson showed the same persistence and fervour with regard to the form of the novel, its generic requirement to adapt, to reflect on a contemporary world that had changed when compared to the nineteenth century, and to demonstrate the randomness and chaos (whatever his own organizational instincts) that characterized existence. This is a constant refrain, a set of principles and beliefs he returned to repeatedly. In this essay he complains of many of his contemporaries just 'how staggeringly un-modern are the vast majority of novelists, who forty-odd years on still write as though the revolution of *Ulysses* had never happened.' He rejects the idea that that a novel must tell a story,

insisting on a range of points that were later also made in the 'Introduction' to *Aren't You Rather Young to be Writing Your Memoirs?* (1973).
However, these essays do not simply represent examples of Johnson's
strategic recycling of ideas and efforts. In 'The Revolution Ignored'
there is at least one intriguing additional critical comment, exhibiting
the fullness and value the archive may promise for the Johnson scholar.
Johnson says, 'After all, no one asks that a poem tells a story any
longer, and has anyone ever asked it of a piece of music?' At least
implicitly this is testament to Johnson's desire that the relationship of
writers and readers toward the text be more sophisticated, and as he
indicates amply elsewhere, be more ideologically informed. Much of
the material quoted above also appeared in an earlier essay called 'Anti
or Ultra' (published in the *Bookseller* in May 1963) where he offers a
close account of the various formal problems he faced in his fiction
and he believed that he addressed, at least partially. Nevertheless, perhaps tellingly, in 'Anti or Ultra' he does add something concerning his
first novel not found quite as emphatically in his 'Introduction': he
insists, 'to make people laugh seems to me the supreme virtue any
book can have,' adding 'While by definition no other book could be
written as *Travelling People* is because no other book would have
exactly the same subject-matter . . . I still hope that perhaps it will
encourage other writers to re-think the form for themselves.'

As indicated above, many of the essays in the archive did not
make the cut for full and final inclusion in our anthology, largely
because we wanted to offer readers as diverse a range of elements by
Johnson as possible. However, I shall risk quoting just a few more
choice examples of the material we left out. In 'The Disintegrating
Novel 2' (*Books and Bookmen*, September 1970) he refers to rivals to
the novel – ones that drew upon new technological advantages – that
he felt would marginalize the book's public presence:

> And the book as a technological object is itself threatened with
> obsolescence, for the Japanese now have a miniature television
> set the size of a telephone handpiece, with cassette pro-
> grammes on tiny reels of wire: within ten years these will be as
> common as transistor radios, and the few unique advantages
> the book still has (portability, privacy, and ease of reference
> backwards and forwards) will be unique no longer.

His fears seem ironic now, given the technological fact of ebook readers such as the Kindle, which might have delighted Johnson on one level; but still he would have deplored the continuing output of neo-traditionalists, and no doubt he would have excoriated the numerous untalented amateur writers publishing their own fiction online. His kind of authenticity came at a personal cost, as he hints in 'Moment of Truth – and Birth of a New Novel' (*Morning Star*, February 1969) when he reveals of *The Unfortunates*: 'Certainly I know very well that this one cost me more of myself than anything else I have ever written.' And yet, as he concludes in 'Anti and Ultra', many of his peers failed in a formal sense to convey the essence of their world, by neglecting its contemporaneity, thus not fully capturing the life of their times: 'It seems to me absurd that writers should be governed or even influenced by conventions of style and technique which were already out of date by the end of Dickens' life, and within which the truth of the human situation in 1963 cannot be expressed at all satisfactorily.'

As the whole archive amply demonstrates, as an avant-garde and committed 'experimental' writer, Johnson resisted wilful obscurity, seeking a prose that was clear and precise, truthful and honest. What will be the effect of this volume? Our hope is that it brings its many examples of Johnson's commitments to as wide a readership as possible, and that these selections will encourage scholars who follow our footsteps to the British Library on the Euston Road – which seems a fitting location, for the study of this lifelong Londoner, rather than having to decamp to some library in Texas – to explore the many other, multiple possibilities of Johnson as both a writer and a living human being memorialized in his collected documents. Almost certainly this would have tickled Johnson's fancy, had he had an inkling of such future literary homage.

# Editors' Note

The text of *Aren't You Rather Young to be Writing Your Memoirs?*, a volume which Johnson himself prepared for publication, has been reproduced exactly from the Hutchinson edition of 1973.

The plays and journalistic pieces which follow have been transcribed from the surviving manuscripts and typescripts held by the British Library. Johnson was exacting about his writing, and resisted editorial intervention: we have sought to work in this spirit by adhering to a principle of non-interference wherever possible. The texts should, we agreed, be published as Johnson intended, whether from a published edition of a journal or newspaper, a typescript or a hand-written fair copy. This necessitated a degree of flexibility: where it is clear that the published text was Johnson's approved version we have used it; where he has indicated a preference for the unexpurgated version we have restored the original text from typescript. Johnson's original titles have been retained wherever possible; where this has not been possible – when none existed in the original, or to distinguish two identically titled pieces – we have followed convention and indicated our added titles by the use of square brackets. Footnotes have been added only where a contemporary reference or allusion would have proved distractingly opaque for today's reader. Cuts are indicated in the text by '[…]', but have been kept to an absolute minimum, and have only been made to avoid verbatim repetition, or, in the case of one piece ('London: the Moron-Made City . . . '), to remove long passages of quotation from sources other than Johnson himself. We have only corrected the text where a mistake is clearly a slip of the typewriter; otherwise, all Johnsonian idiosyncrasies of language and syntax have been retained.

# Aren't You Rather Young to be Writing Your Memoirs?

for Michael Bakewell

# Contents

# Acknowledgments

All but two of these pieces were first published in the
following:

> Covent Garden Press Pamphlets
> Encounter
> Penguin Modern Stories Seven
> Stand
> Statement Against Corpses
> Transatlantic Review
> Winter's Tales Fourteen

One was read on BBC Radio Three.

The author would like to thank György Novàk and
Philip Pacey.

# Introduction

It is a fact of crucial significance in the history of the
novel this century that James Joyce opened the first
cinema in Dublin in 1909. Joyce saw very early on that
film must usurp some of the prerogatives which until
then had belonged almost exclusively to the novelist.
Film could tell a story more directly, in less time and
with more concrete detail than a novel; certain aspects
of character could be more easily delineated and kept
constantly before the audience (for example, physical
characteristics like a limp, a scar, particular ugliness or
beauty); no novelist's description of a battle squadron at
sea in a gale could really hope to compete with that in a
well-shot film; and why should anyone who simply
wanted to be told a story spend all his spare time for a
week or weeks reading a book when he could experience
the same thing in a version in some ways superior at his
local cinema in only one evening?

It was not the first time that storytelling had passed from
one medium to another. Originally it had been the chief
concern of poetry, and long narrative poems were
bestsellers right up to the works of Walter Scott and
Byron. The latter supplanted the former in the favours of
the public, and Scott adroitly turned from narrative poems
to narrative novels and continued to be a bestseller. You
will agree it would be perversely anachronistic to write a
long narrative poem today? People still do, of course;
but such works are rarely published, and, if they are, the
writer is thought of as a literary flatearther. But poetry
did not die when storytelling moved on. It concentrated
on the things it was still best able to do: the short,
economical lyric, the intense emotional statement, depth

**11**

rather than scale, the exploitation of rhythms which made their optimum impact at short lengths but which would have become monotonous and unreadable if maintained longer than a few pages. In the same way, the novel may not only survive but evolve to greater achievements by concentrating on those things it can still do best: the precise use of language, exploitation of the technological fact of the book, the explication of thought. Film is an excellent medium for showing things, but it is very poor at taking an audience inside characters' minds, at telling it what people are thinking. Again, Joyce saw this at once, and developed the technique of interior monologue within a few years of the appearance of the cinema. In some ways the history of the novel in the twentieth century has seen large areas of the old territory of the novelist increasingly taken over by other media, until the only thing the novelist can with any certainty call exclusively his own is the inside of his own skull: and that is what he should be exploring, rather than anachronistically fighting a battle he is bound to lose.

Joyce is the Einstein of the novel. His subject-matter in *Ulysses* was available to anyone, the events of one day in one place; but by means of form, style and technique in language he made it into something very much more, a novel, not a story about anything. What happens is nothing like as important as how it is written, as the medium of the words and form through which it is made to happen to the reader. And for style alone *Ulysses* would have been a revolution. Or, rather, styles. For Joyce saw that such a huge range of subject matter could not be conveyed in one style, and accordingly used many. Just in this one innovation (and there are many others) lie a great advance and freedom offered to subsequent generations of writers.

But how many have seen it, have followed him? Very few. It is not a question of influence, of writing like Joyce. It is a matter of realising that the novel is an evolving form, not a static one, of accepting that for practical purposes where Joyce left off should ever since have been regarded as the starting point. As Sterne said a long time ago:

> "Shall we for ever make new books, as apothecaries make new mixtures, by pouring only out of one vessel into another? Are we for ever to be twisting, and untwisting the same rope? For ever in the same track—for ever at the same pace?"

The last thirty years have seen the storytelling function pass on yet again. Now anyone who wants simply to be told a story has the need satisfied by television; serials like *Coronation Street* and so on do very little more than answer the question 'What happens next?' All other writing possibilities are subjugated to narrative. If a writer's chief interest is in telling stories (even remembering that telling stories is a euphemism for telling lies; and I shall come to that) then the best place to do it now is in television, which is technically better equipped and will reach more people than a novel can today. And the most aware film-makers have realised this, and directors such as Godard, Resnais, and Antonioni no longer make the chief point of their films a story; their work concentrates on those things film can do solely and those things it can do best.

Literary forms do become exhausted, clapped out, as well. Look what had happened to five-act blank verse drama by the beginning of the nineteenth century. Keats, Shelley, Wordsworth and Tennyson all wrote blank-verse, quasi-Elizabethan plays; and all of them, without exception, are resounding failures. They are so not because the men who wrote them were inferior poets, but because the form was finished, worn out, exhausted, and everything that could be done with it had been done too many times already.

That is what seems to have happened to the nineteenth

century narrative novel, too, by the outbreak of the First World War. No matter how good the writers are who now attempt it, it cannot be made to work for our time, and the writing of it is anachronistic, invalid, irrelevant, and perverse.

Life does not tell stories. Life is chaotic, fluid, random; it leaves myriads of ends untied, untidily. Writers can extract a story from life only by strict, close selection, and this must mean falsification. Telling stories really is telling lies. Philip Pacey took me up on this to express it thus:

> "Telling stories is telling lies          is telling lies about people          is creating or hardening prejudices          is providing an alternative to real communication not a stimulus to communication and/or communication itself          is an escape from the challenge of coming to terms with real people"

I am not interested in telling lies in my own novels. A useful distinction between literature and other writing for me is that the former teaches one something true about life: and how can you convey truth in a vehicle of fiction? The two terms, *truth* and *fiction*, are opposites, and it must logically be impossible.

The two terms *novel* and *fiction* are not, incidentally, synonymous, as many seem to suppose in the way they use them interchangeably. The publisher of *Trawl* wished to classify it as autobiography, not as a novel. It is a novel, I insisted and could prove; what it is not is fiction. The novel is a form in the same sense that the sonnet is a form; within that form, one may write truth or fiction. I choose to write truth in the form of a novel.

In any case, surely it must be a confession of failure on the part of any novelist to rely on that primitive, vulgar and idle curiosity of the reader to know 'what happens

14

next' (however banal or hackneyed it may be) to hold his interest? Can he not face the fact that it is his choice of words, his style, which ought to keep the reader reading? Have such novelists no pride? The drunk who tells you the story of his troubles in a pub relies on the same curiosity.

And when they consider the other arts, are they not ashamed? Imagine the reception of someone producing a nineteenth-century symphony or a Pre-Raphaelite painting today! The *avant garde* of even ten years ago is now accepted in music and painting, is the establishment in these arts in some cases. But today the neo-Dickensian novel not only receives great praise, review space and sales but also acts as a qualification to elevate its authors to chairs at universities. On reflection, perhaps the latter is not so surprising; let the dead live with the dead.

All I have said about the history of the novel so far seems to me logical, and to have been available and obvious to anyone starting seriously to write in the form today. Why then do so many novelists still write as though the revolution that was *Ulysses* had never happened, still rely on the crutch of storytelling? Why, more damningly for my case you might think, do hundreds of thousands of readers still gorge the stuff to surfeit?

I do not know. I can only assume that just as there seem to be so many writers imitating the act of being nineteenth-century novelists, so there must be large numbers imitating the act of being nineteenth-century readers, too. But it does not affect the logic of my case, nor the practice of my own work in the novel form. It may simply be a matter of education, or of communication; when I proposed this book to my publisher and outlined its thesis, he said it would be necessary for me to speak very clearly and very loudly. Perhaps the din of the

15

marketplace vendors in pap and propaganda is so high that even doing that will not be enough.

The architects can teach us something: their aesthetic problems are combined with functional ones in a way that dramatises the crucial nature of their final actions. *Form follows function* said Louis Sullivan, mentor of Frank Lloyd Wright, and just listen to Mies van der Rohe:

> *To create form out of the nature of our tasks with the methods of our time—this is our task.*
>
> *We must make clear, step by step, what things are possible, necessary, and significant.*
>
> *Only an architecture honestly arrived at by the explicit use of available building materials can be justified in moral terms.*

Subject matter is everywhere, general, is brick, concrete, plastic; the ways of putting it together are particular, are crucial. But I recognise that there are not simply problems of form, but problems of writing. Form is not the aim, but the result. If form were the aim then one would have formalism; and I reject formalism.

The novelist cannot legitimately or successfully embody present-day reality in exhausted forms. If he is serious, he will be making a statement which attempts to change society towards a condition he conceives to be better, and he will be making at least implicitly a statement of faith in the evolution of the form in which he is working. Both these aspects of making are radical; this is inescapable unless he chooses escapism. Present-day reality is changing rapidly; it always has done, but for each generation it appears to be speeding up. Novelists must evolve (by inventing, borrowing, stealing or cobbling from other media) forms which will more or less

16

satisfactorily contain an ever-changing reality, their own reality and not Dickens' reality or Hardy's reality or even James Joyce's reality.

Present-day reality is markedly different from say nineteenth-century reality. Then it was possible to believe in pattern and eternity, but today what characterises our reality is the probability that chaos is the most likely explanation; while at the same time recognising that even to seek an explanation represents a denial of chaos. Samuel Beckett, who of all living is the man I believe most worth reading and listening to, is reported thus:

> "What I am saying does not mean that there will henceforth be no form in art. It only means that there will be new form, and that this form will be of such a type that it admits the chaos, and does not try to say that the chaos is really something else. The forms and the chaos remain separate . . . to find a form that accommodates the mess, that is the task of the artist now."

Whether or not it can be demonstrated that all is chaos, certainly all is change: the very process of life itself is growth and decay at an enormous variety of rates. Change is a condition of life. Rather than deplore this, or hunt the chimæræ of stability or reversal, one should perhaps embrace change as all there is. Or might be. For change is never for the better or for the worse; change simply *is*. No sooner is a style or technique established than the reasons for its adoption have vanished or become irrelevant. We have to make allowances and imaginative, lying leaps for Shakespeare, for even Noel Coward, to try to understand how they must have seemed to their contemporaries. I feel myself fortunate sometimes that I can laugh at the joke that just as I was beginning to think I knew something about how to write a novel it is no longer of any use to me in attempting the next one. Even in this introduction I am trying to make patterns, to impose patterns on the chaos, in the doubtful interest of helping you (and myself) to understand what I am saying. When lecturing on the same material I ought to drop my notes, refer to them in any chaotic order. *Order* and *chaos* are opposites, too.

This (and other things I have said) must appear paradoxical. But why should novelists be expected to avoid paradox any more than philosophers?

While I believe (as far as I believe anything) that there may be (how can I know?) chaos underlying it all, another paradox is that I still go on behaving as though pattern could exist, as though day will follow night will follow breakfast. Or whatever the order should be.


I do not really know why I write. Sometimes I think it is simply because I can do nothing better. Certainly there is no single reason, but many. I can, and will, enumerate some of them; but in general I prefer not to think about them.

I think I write because I have something to say that I fail to say satisfactorily in conversation, in person. Then there are things like conceit, stubbornness, a desire to retaliate on those who have hurt me paralleled by a desire to repay those who have helped me, a need to try to create something which may live after me (which I take to be the detritus of the religious feeling), the sheer technical joy of forcing almost intractable words into patterns of meaning and form that are uniquely (for the moment at least) mine, a need to make people laugh with me in case they laugh at me, a desire to codify experience, to come to terms with things that have happened to me, and to try to tell the truth (to discover what is the truth) about them. And I write especially to exorcise, to remove from myself, from my mind, the burden having to bear some pain, the hurt of some experience:

in order that it may be over there, in a book, and not in here in my mind.

The following tries to grope towards it, in another way:

    I have a (vision) of something that (happened) to me
        something which (affected) me
        something which meant (something) to me

    and I (wrote) (filmed) it
    because
    I wanted it to be fixed
        so that I could refer to it
        so that I could build on it
        so that I would not have to repeat it


Such a hostage to fortune!


What I have been trying to do in the novel form has been too much refracted through the conservativeness of reviewers and others; the reasons why I have written in the ways that I have done have become lost, have never reached as many people, nor in anything like a definitive form. 'Experimental' to most reviewers is almost always a synonym for 'unsuccessful'. I object to the word *experimental* being applied to my own work. Certainly I make experiments, but the unsuccessful ones are quietly hidden away and what I choose to publish is in my terms successful: that is, it has been the best way I could find of solving particular writing problems. Where I depart from convention, it is because the convention has failed, is inadequate for conveying what I have to say. The relevant questions are surely whether each device works or not, whether it achieves what it set out to achieve, and how less good were the alternatives. So for every device I have used there is a literary rationale and a technical justification; anyone who cannot accept

19

this has simply not understood the problem which had to be solved.

I do not propose to go through the reasons for all the devices, not least because the novels should speak for themselves; and they are clear enough to a reader who will think about them, let alone be open and sympathetic towards them. But I will mention some of them, and deal in detail with *The Unfortunates*, since its form seems perhaps the most extreme.

*Travelling People* (published 1963) had an explanatory prelude which summed up much of my thinking on the novel at that point, as follows:

> "Seated comfortably in a wood and wickerwork chair of eighteenth-century Chinese manufacture, I began seriously to meditate upon the form of my allegedly full-time literary sublimations. Rapidly, I recalled the conclusions reached in previous meditations on the same subject: my rejection of stage-drama as having too many limitations, of verse as being unacceptable at the present time on the scale I wished to attempt, and of radio and television as requiring too many entrepreneurs between the writer and the audience; and my resultant choice of the novel as the form possessing fewest limitations, and closest contact with the greatest audience.
> But, now, what kind of novel? After comparatively little consideration, I decided that one style for one novel was a convention that I resented most strongly: it was perhaps comparable to eating a meal in which each course had been cooked in the same manner. The style of each chapter should spring naturally from its subject matter. Furthermore, I meditated, at ease in far eastern luxury, Dr. Johnson's remarks about each member of an audience always being aware that he is in a theatre could with complete relevance be applied also to the novel reader, who surely always knows that he is reading a book and not, for instance, taking part in a punitive raid on the curiously-shaped inhabitants of another planet. From this I

20

concluded that it was not only permissible to expose the mechanism of a novel, but by so doing I should come nearer to reality and truth: adapting to refute, in fact, the ancients:

*Artis est monstrare artem*

Pursuing this thought, I realised that it would be desirable to have interludes between my chapters in which I could stand back, so to speak, from my novel, and talk about it with the reader, or with those parts of myself which might hold differing opinions, if necessary; and in which technical questions could be considered, and quotations from other writers included, where relevant, without any question of destroying the reader's suspension of disbelief, since such suspension was not to be attempted.
I should be determined not to lead my reader into believing that he was doing anything but reading a novel, having noted with abhorrence the shabby chicanery practised on their readers by many novelists, particularly of the popular class. This applied especially to digression, where the reader is led, wilfully and wantonly, astray; my novel would have clear notice, one way or another, of digressions, so that the reader might have complete freedom of choice in whether or not he would read them.
Thus, having decided in a general way upon the construction of my novel I thought about actually rising to commence its composition; but persuaded by oriental comfort that I was nearer the Good Life engaged in meditation, I turned my mind to the deep consideration of such other matters as I deemed worthy of my attention, and, after a short while thus engaged, fell asleep."

*Travelling People* employed eight separate styles or conventions for nine chapters; the first and last chapters sharing one style in order to give the book cyclical unity within the motif announced by its title and epigraph. These styles included interior monologue, a letter, extracts from a journal, and a film script. This latter illustrates the method of the novel typically. The

21

subject-matter was a gala evening at a country club, with a large number of characters involved both individually and in small groups. A film technique, cutting quickly from group to group and incidentally counterpointing the stagey artificiality of the occasion, seemed natural and apt. It is not, of course, a film; but the way it is written is intended to evoke what the reader knows as film technique.

The passage quoted above was deliberately a pastiche of eighteenth-century English, for I had found that it was necessary to return to the very beginnings of the novel in England in order to try to re-think it and re-justify it for myself. Most obvious of my debts was to the black pages of *Tristram Shandy*, but I extended the device beyond Sterne's simple use of it to indicate a character's death. The section concerned is the interior monologue of an old man prone to heart attacks; when he becomes unconscious he obviously cannot indicate this in words representing thought, but a modified form of Sterne's black pages solves the problem. First I used random-pattern grey to indicate unconsciousness after a heart attack, then a regular-pattern grey to indicate sleep or recuperative unconsciousness; and subsequently black when he dies.

Since *Travelling People* is part truth and part fiction it now embarrasses me and I will not allow it to be reprinted; though I am still pleased that its devices work. And I learnt a certain amount through it; not least that there was a lot of the writing I could do in my head without having to amass a pile of paper three feet high to see if something worked.

But I really discovered what I should be doing with *Albert Angelo* (1964) where I broke through the English disease of the objective correlative to speak truth directly if solipsistically in the novel form, and heard my own small voice. And again there were devices used to solve problems which I felt could not be dealt with in other ways. Thus a specially-designed type-character draws attention to physical descriptions which I believe tend to be skipped, do not usually penetrate. To convey what a particular lesson is like, the thoughts of a teacher are given on the righthand side of a page in italic, with his and his pupils' speech on the left in roman, so that, though the reader obviously cannot read both at once, when he has read both he will have seen that they are simultaneous and have enacted such simultaneity for himself. When Albert finds a fortuneteller's card in the street it is further from the truth to describe it than simply to reproduce it. And when a future event must be revealed, I could (and can; can you?) think of no way nearer to the truth and more effective than to cut a section through those pages intervening so that the event may be read in its place but before the reader reaches that place.

*Trawl* (1966) is all interior monologue, a representation of the inside of my mind but at one stage removed; the closest one can come in writing. The only real technical problem was the representation of breaks in the mind's workings; I finally decided on a stylized scheme of 3 em, 6 em and 9 em spaces. In order not to have a break which ran-on at the end of a line looking like a paragraph, these spaces were punctuated by dots at decimal point level. I now doubt whether these dots were necessary. To make up for the absence of those paragraph breaks which give the reader's eye rest and location on the page, the line length was deliberately shortened; this gave the book a long, narrow format.

The rhythms of the language of *Trawl* attempted to parallel those of the sea, while much use was made of the trawl itself as a metaphor for the way the subconscious mind may appear to work.

With each of my novels there has always been a certain point when what has been until then just a mass of subject-matter, the material of living, of my life, comes to

23

have a shape, a form that I recognise as a novel. This crucial interaction between the material and myself has always been reduced to a single point in time: obviously a very exciting moment for me, and a moment of great relief, too, that I am able to write another novel.

The moment at which *The Unfortunates* (1969) occurred was on the main railway station at Nottingham. I had been sent there to report a soccer match for the *Observer*, a quite routine League match, nothing special. I had hardly thought about where I was going, specifically: when you are going away to report soccer in a different city each Saturday you get the mechanics of travelling to and finding your way about in a strange place to an almost automatic state. But when I came up the stairs from the platform into the entrance hall, it hit me: I knew this city, I knew it very well. It was the city in which a very great friend of mine, one who had helped me with my work when no one else was interested, had lived until his tragic early death from cancer some two years before.

It was the first time I had been back since his death, and all the afternoon I was there the things we had done together kept coming back to me as I was going about this routine job of reporting a soccer match: the dead past and the living present interacted and transposed themselves in my mind. I realised that afternoon that I had to write a novel about this man, Tony, and his tragic and pointless death and its effect on me and the other people who knew him and whom he had left behind. The following passage from *The Unfortunates* explains his importance to me:

> "To Tony, the criticism of literature was a study, a pursuit, a discipline of the highest kind in itself: to me, I told him, the only use of criticism was if it helped people to write better books. This he took as a challenge, this he accepted. Or perhaps I made the challenge, said that I would show him the novel as I wrote it, the novel I had in mind or was writing: and

24

that he would therefore have a chance of
influencing, of making better, a piece of what
set out to be literature, for the sake of argument,
rather than expend himself on dead men's
work."

The main technical problem with *The Unfortunates* was
the randomness of the material. That is, the memories of
Tony and the routine football reporting, the past and the
present, interwove in a completely random manner,
without chronology. This is the way the mind works, my
mind anyway, and for reasons given the novel was to be
as nearly as possible a re-created transcript of how my
mind worked during eight hours on this particular
Saturday.

This randomness was directly in conflict with the technological fact of the bound book: for the bound book
imposes an order, a fixed page order, on the material. I
think I went some way towards solving this problem by
writing the book in sections and having those sections
not bound together but loose in a box. The sections are
of different lengths, of course: some are only a third of a
page long, others are as long as twelve pages. The
longer ones were bound in themselves as sections, or
signatures, as printers call them.

The point of this device was that, apart from the first and
last sections which were marked as such, the other
sections arrived in the reader's hands in a random order:
he could read them in any order he liked. And if he
imagined the printer, or some previous reader, had
selected a special order, then he could shuffle them
about and achieve his own random order. In this way the
whole novel reflected the randomness of the material:
it was itself a physical tangible metaphor for randomness
and the nature of cancer.

Now I did not think then, and do not think now, that
this solved the problem completely. The lengths of the
sections were really arbitrary again; even separate

sentences or separate words would be arbitrary in the same sense. But I continue to believe that my solution was nearer; and even if it was only marginally nearer, then it was still a better solution to the problem of conveying the mind's randomness than the imposed order of a bound book.

What matters most to me about *The Unfortunates* is that I have on recall as accurately as possible what happened, that I do not have to carry it around in my mind any more, that I have done Tony as much justice as I could at the time; that the need to communicate with myself then, and with such older selves as I might be allowed, on something about which I cared and care deeply may also mean that the novel will communicate that experience to readers, too.

I shall return shortly to readers and communicating with them. But first there are two other novels, and they represent a change (again!) of direction, an elbow joint in the arm, still part of the same but perhaps going another way. Perhaps I shall come to the body, sooner or later. The ideas for both *House Mother Normal* (1971) and *Christie Malry's Own Double-Entry* (1973) came to me whilst writing *Travelling People* (indeed, I discussed them with Tony) but the subsequent three personal novels interposed themselves, demanded to be written first. I also balked at *House Mother Normal* since it seemed technically so difficult. What I wanted to do was to take an evening in an old people's home, and see a single set of events through the eyes of not less than eight old people. Due to the various deformities and deficiencies of the inmates, these events would seem to be progressively 'abnormal' to the reader. At the end, there would be the viewpoint of the House Mother, an apparently 'normal' person, and the events themselves would then be seen to be so bizarre that everything that had come before would seem 'normal' by comparison. The idea was to say something about the things we call 'normal' and 'abnormal' and the technical difficulty was

26

to make the same thing interesting nine times over since
that was the number of times the events would have to
be described. By 1970 I thought that if I did not attempt
the idea soon then I never would; and so sat down to it.
I was relieved to find that the novel did work, on its own
terms, while not asking it to do anything it clearly should
not be trying to do. Each of the old people was allotted
a space of twenty-one pages, and each line on each
page represented the same moment in each of the other
accounts; this meant an unjustified right-hand margin
and led more than one reviewer to imagine the book was
in verse. House Mother's account has an extra page in
which she is shown to be

> the puppet or concoction of a writer (you
> always knew there was a writer behind it all?
> Ah, there's no fooling you readers!)

Nor should there be.

The reader is made very much aware that he is reading a
book and being addressed by the author in *Christie
Malry's Own Double-Entry*, too. The idea was that a
young man who had learned the double-entry system of
book-keeping started applying his knowledge to society
and life; when society did him down, he did society
down in order to balance the books. Form following
function, the book is divided into five parts each ended
by a page of accounts in which Christie attempts to
draw a balance with life.

I do not really relish any more description of my work;
it is there to be read, and in writing so much about
technique and form I am diverting you from what the
novels are about, what they are trying to say, and things
like the nature of the language used, and the fact that
all of them have something comic in them and three are
intended to be very funny indeed. When I depart from
what may mistakenly be extracted from the above as
rigid principles it is invariably for the sake of the comic,
for I find Sterne's reasons all-persuasive:

27

"... 'tis wrote, an' please your worships, against
the spleen! in order, by a more frequent and a
more convulsive elevation and depression of
the diaphragm, and the succussations of the
inter-costal and abdominal muscles in laughter,
to drive the *gall* and other *bitter juices* from
the gall-bladder, liver, and sweet-bread of his
majesty's subjects, with all the inimicitious
passions which belong to them, down into their
duodenums."

For readers it is often said that they will go on reading
the novel because it enables them, unlike film or
television, to exercise their imaginations, that that is one
of its chief attractions for them, that they may imagine
the characters and so on for themselves. Not with my
novels; it follows from what I have said earlier that I
want my ideas to be expressed so precisely that the
very minimum of room for interpretation is left. Indeed I
would go further and say that to the extent that a reader
can impose his own imagination on my words, then that
piece of writing is a failure. I want him to see my (vision),
not something conjured out of his own imagination.
How is he supposed to grow unless he will admit
others' ideas? If he wants to impose his imagination,
let him write his own books. That may be thought to be
anti-reader; but think a little further, and what I am
really doing is challenging the reader to prove his own
existence as palpably as I am proving mine by the act of
writing.

Language, admittedly, is an imprecise tool with which to
try to achieve precision; the same word will have
slightly different meanings for every person. But that is
outside me; I cannot control it. I can only use words to
mean something to me, and there is simply the hope (not
even the expectation) that they will mean the same
thing to anyone else.

Which brings us to the question of for whom I write. I

am always sceptical about writers who claim to be
writing for an identifiable public. How many letters and
phone calls do they receive from this public that they
can know it so well as to write for it? Precious few, in
my experience, when I have questioned them about it.
I think I (after publishing some dozen books) have
personally had about five letters from 'ordinary readers',
people I did not know already that is; and three of those
upbraided me viciously because I had just published the
book that they were going to have written.

No, apart from the disaster of *Travelling People*, I write
perforce for myself, and the satisfaction has to be almost
all for myself; and I can only hope there are some few
people like me who will see what I am doing, and
understand what I am saying, and use it for their own
devious purposes.

Yet it should not have to be so. I think I do have a right
to expect that most readers should be open to new work,
that there should be an audience in this country willing
to try to understand and be sympathetic to what those
few writers not shackled by tradition are trying to do and
are doing. Only when one has some contact with a
continental European tradition of the *avant garde* does
one realise just how stultifyingly philistine is the general
book culture of this country. Compared with the writers
of romances, thrillers, and the bent but so-called
straight novel, there are not many who are writing as
though it mattered, as though they meant it, as though
they meant it to matter.

Perhaps I should nod here to Samuel Beckett (of
course), John Berger, Christine Brooke-Rose, Brigid
Brophy, Anthony Burgess, Alan Burns, Angela Carter,
Eva Figes, Giles Gordon, Wilson Harris, Rayner
Heppenstall, even hasty, muddled Robert Nye, Ann
Quin, Penelope Shuttle, Alan Sillitoe (for his last book
only, Raw Material indeed), Stefan Themerson, and

(coming) John Wheway; (stand by): and if only Heathcote Williams would write a novel. . . .

Anyone who imagines himself or herself slighted by not being included above can fill in his or her name here:

...........................................................................................................

It would be a courtesy, however, to let me know his or her qualifications for so imagining.

Are we concerned with courtesy?


Nathalie Sarraute once described literature as a relay race, the baton of innovation passing from one generation to another. The vast majority of British novelists has dropped the baton, stood still, turned back, or not even realised that there is a race.

Most of what I have said has been said before, of course; none of it is new, except possibly in context and combination. What I do not understand is why British writers have not accepted it and acted upon it.


The pieces of prose (you will understand my avoidance of the term *short story*) which follow were written in the interstices of novels and poems and other work between 1960 and 1973; the dates given in the Contents are those of the year of completion. None of them seem to me like each other, though some have links and cross-references; neither can I really see either progession or retrogression. The order is that which seemed least bad late on one particular May evening; perhaps I shall regret it as soon as I see it fixed.

Make of them what you will. I offer them to you despite

30

my experience that the incomprehension and weight of prejudice which faces anyone trying to do anything new in writing is enormous, sometimes disquieting, occasionally laughable. A national daily newspaper (admittedly one known for its reactionary opinions) returned a review copy of *Travelling People* with the complaint that it must be a faulty copy for some of the pages were black; the Australian Customs seized *Albert Angelo* (which had holes justifiably cut in some pages, you will remember) and would not release it until they had been shown the obscenities which (they were convinced) had been excised; and in one of our biggest booksellers *Trawl* was found in the Angling section . . . .

B.S.J.
*London*
*4.5.73*

# Aren't You Rather Young to be Writing Your Memoirs?

At dusk by the old mill I was spinning for pike in the pools beyond the race.          From the parapet of the bridge.          Leaning on the noticeably bent iron railing surmounting the parapet of the bridge.

A romantic opening. But you would be unwise to give up at this point. Or to make assumptions.

One could reach this mill, I did in fact reach it myself, by way of an unmetalled track, after passing through a railway crossing at road level the gates of which had to be operated manually or pedestrially by those set on passing through with their vehicles.          The gates carried warnings as to their congruous operation. I contrived to pass my car through without incident, without transgression of the regulations interpreted as I understood them, according to my lights, whatever they are, unless one of them was that green eye which assured me no train was officially due to run me down during the period of my transcursion.          This was a source of sufficient comfort to me. As hardly less to my wife, I assumed, for she said nothing.          My wife was with me on the first occasion.

I baited the hook of the lighter rod with a lob for my wife and indicated generally where I imagined she might profitably display it in the water below the bridge.          Soon she grew tired, just as I finished baiting the hook of the second rod, of this spot and moved behind the mill to the traditionally still, flat, wide, smooth millpond before the weir which plashed and boomed under the clapboard walls of the probably seventeenth-century building.

Later still she grew tired of even this, and wandered off rodless, unrodded, into the meadows lying low towards the railway embankment, no doubt in expectation of those *objets trouvés* which come to her hand so readily and as if fortuitously. Aha?

I write this down so you may know in time of the circumstances of my first visit, which in turn led to my second visit.

I was float-fishing for roach or perch or anything (it was so long since I had last fished that I was not feeling particular, was hardly in a position to choose, in any case) with lobworms as the comehither. I had myself moved from the race to the millpond and back again to the race, and in the fading light my eyes were engaged in persuading my brain of doubtful bites as my float cocked and uncocked in the distance on the current: at which series of points, as I reeled in to assure myself that my lob was still at least nominally on duty, if not wriggling with that enticingly sinuous shimmy which represented the most I hoped from it, a splash on the surface that my experience told me could not have been made by a fish of less than half a pound in weight greatly encouraged me. And so comforted was I that I immediately floated off my bribe yet again into the race, thinking that this darkening hour must be just the time the perverse fish chose to feed.

It was now on this first occasion a man approached me from round the corner of the mill with (I could tell) the sureness of a native. I at once explained that I had asked permission to fish, and he was then friendly enough. He described the day he had caught twenty chub in this place (though he was careful not to give away the exact pool) and he told me that old one about reeling in a threequarter pound roach and having a pike twothirds swallow it a few yards from the bank. In return (what else did I have?) I told him how there had been a splash on the surface as I reeled in just before his arrival. The man expressed an opinion that this splash was caused by a small pike going for the moving float. It seemed reasonable. But so much does.

My wife returned, and it appeared that she was now more covetous of the house standing at a right angle to the mill than of any fish which might be found in either the race or the millpond behind. And indeed it was a fine house, of about the middle of that period known as Georgian, I should imagine, of apparently sound local brick, three storeys and three dormers, the latter above nearly-suppressed eaves: perhaps therefore having ten bedrooms, and with a bowed extension at the downstream end.

The man was willing to talk about anything, conversation it now becomes clear was what he had approached me for in the first place rather than to chide me for fishing in reserved waters.          His father had owned the mill house. . . .but you will not be interested in that. It was on my second visit that the thing in which I hope to interest you happened.

On this second occasion, then, as a result of the opinion expressed by the man, I was spinning for pike at dusk by the old mill in the pools beyond the race. It was not a cold evening, but I was glad of the exercise provided by the action of casting, reeling in, retrieving, and casting again. I was enjoying it, if you must know.

It was not the man I had seen on the previous occasion, but another. And he was in a car, a Hillman Husky about two years old, if I am not mistaken. He came swishing by me as I stood by the malformed railing on the bridge, the car lurching and bumping in his haste on the stone-studded road. He stoppped just over the bridge and his arrival coincided with that of two young men as they climbed a fence from the meadow in which

I hope I have established the millpond was situated.
This coincidence appeared to be intentional, to be no
coincidence, in fact. For he (the man in the car) quickly
opened his driver's side door (which was on the side
farther from the two young men) and he swung his legs
out, first one leg, and then the other leg : he had done it
many times before, I could see that from the assurance,
from the expertise, with which he did it.              Very
quickly he was round the front of his stationary Husky,
to accost the two young men, block their way, almost.
He seemed quite angry, from his movements I could tell
that, at the distance he was from me.
            One of the young men had a
shotgun, the taller of the two younger men had a
double-barrelled shotgun, the stock snugly under his left
armpit, his left hand round the barrels a few inches
towards their muzzles away from the triggerguard, in
what I took to be the classical position for maximum
sporting safety, the gun in this way pointing at the
ground so that it would do least damage if inadvertently
discharged.                              The car and
the group of three countrymen were too far away for
me to overhear their conversation, but from the situation
I posited (not unreasonably ?) that the two young ones
were poaching, or had offended in some other wise
against campestral law or custom, and that the driver of
the car, incensed with what many would presumably
consider to be justified outraged righteousness, had seen
them from afar, had leapt to his saddle, so to speak, and
cut them off near to the very spot where I had chosen to
spin for pike.

Having in my own way accounted for this event to the
furthest extent to which I was prepared to speculate, I
turned and leant my stomach back again on the bridge
rail. I wondered whether I should feel guilty that this
stomach has perhaps garnered unto itself more than a
reasonably average, or at least fair (but what is fair ?),
share of the world's produce. The extent to which the
circular-section sank into it gave rise to this serious

question. Besides, I was spinning for pike: that much is quite clear to me.

There was a gunshot.          It was the sound of the gunshot which made me turn, of course, from my pursuit of the predator of the green depths, as they say, probably, but my head was round quickly enough for me to understand what had happened almost as if I had been watching the three men all the time. The gun was still pointing at the ground, but from where it was directed there rose a small cloud of cordite smoke, of dust as well, not very far from the older man's right foot. That the foot had not itself been hit by any of the shot from the cartridge fired I assumed from the way the man stood his ground, only his face and clenching and unclenching fists indicating he was further outraged. I could not decide whether the shot had been fired deliberately or not. The fairhaired young man holding the gun did not have a threatening or warning look on his face, but, on the other hand, neither did he seem surprised nor apologetic.          As I watched, the older man came to some decision. Without saying a further word to the other two, he walked back round the front of his car, opened the door, entered, slammed the door and, shortly, reversed past me over the bridge at a speed not really compatible with safety in that disorienting direction, slewed to the left, stopped, and drove forward past the mill house out of my line of vision.          The two young men were walking off down the lane towards the level crossing gate when I next looked in their direction, the shotgun still carried in its recommended safe position as it had been all the time I had seen it.

The elements of this situation were such that further speculation as to motives, indeed, as to what had happened, were pointless, on my part, in the circumstances. It did occur to me that perhaps some felony had been committed, in which case I might conceivably be required at some future date to give an account of the incident as I had witnessed it. This did, however, seem to me unlikely.

I returned to my fishing, casting carefully to avoid the weedbeds while yet spinning my spoon close enough to attact any lurking monster (as I thought) resident therein. As usual my attention wandered, and very soon I was thinking of the provenance of colours, how Tyrian purple comes not from the inkfish or calamary, or from pulpi in general, but from the murex shellfish; of how sepia from the inkfish was used as a writing fluid, hence (how could it be otherwise?) the name of this cephalopod; whereas brown onions will give a green dye highly regarded by leather workers of the past and present-day fakers of the past.                     Soon I began to feel that since no pike showed signs of giving itself up I might just as well think about these things first as I was packing up, then as I was driving home, and finally (for that day anyway) over and after the dinner my wife (or the friends we were staying with) had, it made me slightly guilty to expect, prepared.                     The packing I did easily, some (not I) would say lazily, by unsocketing the rod into two parts and laying it in the boot after making sure that the line and hook were effect- ively clear of snags. It was this easiness, or laziness, which in fact enabled me, quite by chance, to be present at what you must be hoping for by now: an end.

Driving off easily, carefully, in a pleasant state of tiredness, towards the house that was for those few days home, I had gone about — I don't know, a mile or so, — on the metalled road in the opposite direction from the level crossing, when I came upon — indeed, I had to slow down to avoid it — the Husky of the man I had seen by the bridge not long before. He was talking to a policeman on a bicycle.                     I drove on and past.

The conclusion I hoped for was that the informed and uniformed policeman rode off, down the mile or so to the mill, over the bridge, along towards the level crossing,

40

and over it, up until the three-ply road became a metalled minor one. And failed to find the two men with the shotgun.

But you can provide your own surmises or even your own ending, as you are inclined. For that matter, I have conveniently left enough obscure or even unknown for you to suggest your own beginning; and your own middle, as well, if you reject mine. But I know you love a story with gunplay in it.

I am concerned only to tell you what appears to me to have been the truth, as it has happened to me, as it appears to have happened to me.          Why me?
That, I may honestly reply, is a good question.
Have I not interested you enough to make you want to read this far? Have there not been one or two wry moments, the occasional uncommon word?
                    Why do you want me to tidy up life, to explain?          Do you want me to explain?
          Do you ask of your bookmaker that he explain?                    Madame, I am a professional!

41

# Mean Point of Impact

CONFIRMED 0035 HRS ENEMY OCCUPATION
OF CATHEDRAL SAINT ANSELM 07364219
STOP AWAIT FURTHER ORDERS BATCOM

Elias was the man John wanted, Elias of Caen who had
worked at Amiens and Salisbury, had learnt the subtle
lessons of St. Denis (where it started) and Chartres,
Elias who was still young enough to see a cathedral
designed and built and consecrated : to see it done, to
have it finished in John's lifetime too.
John's was the initial act of will to build, build, a will
sustained through nearly thirty years, and the first
exercise of it was in persuading Elias. This he did by
trusting the mason's sense of what was now possible
and remarkable in architecture, and by offering him as if
equal partnership in the project; and he was fortunate,
too, in that Elias met and married a woman of the
village shortly after he arrived, so that John was able to
secure for him the final respect of and position in a
narrow community by making him Magister Elias.

> Have care for the comfort of your men, but do
> not sacrifice atmosphere for comfort.
> Neither atmosphere nor comfort here, in this
> dark: we might be anywhere, as well be
> nowhere.

They sank the footings thirty feet until they came to the
water table. There were those who said that this was not
deep enough, and that they should find another site
away from the river where there was bedrock nearer the
surface; others that they should build a lighter, smaller
structure, even to have no spire at all on the tower; but
Elias argued that thirty feet was enough, just enough.

So they outlined the cruciform in trenches, three
hundred feet in length and one hundred and eighty
across the transepts, and filled them with seventy
wagonloads a day of rubble from two quarries and most
of the ruins within ten miles or so.

And John stood on a nearby hill and saw the shape of
his long cathedral on the ground at last, no longer lines
on paper.

Work above ground began first on the nave, and
progressed as rapidly as John could have hoped: within
eight years it was up to clerestory height, and another
five saw it vaulted over. Work on the west front was not
far behind, and at the completion of the nave it had
been finished up to the height of the stringcourse just
above the great circular window to which Magister
Elias had given five anaconcentric thicknesses through
to the inner wall: there was no other like it in Europe at
the time.

*Map reference 07364219 . . .*
*The spire of the Cathedral of St. Anselm . . .*
*Yes.*

Sixteen years after John had first persuaded Elias to
build his cathedral there was a fire which severely
damaged the partly-built choir and chevet, and which in
its wake brought disagreement between Elias and his
assistant Nicolas over how they should rebuild. John's
will resolved the first problem by raising yet more money
from the Crown to offset the loss; and, seeing that
Elias' integral conception of the cathedral was being
threatened, successfully diverted Nicolas' need and
talent for innovation by setting him the Chapter House
to design. This he did in the new Decorated style, with
fan vaulting from one slender column, and having a
perfect echo that made the place like an extension of
one's skull; but whose acoustics could make heard
everywhere an unwary bishop whispering at a Chapter
meeting: a light, small-scale foil to the hard strength of
the main building.

46

The best travelling detailer was an atheist, a wencher, an artist. Elias employed him for his skills, not for his opinions or his morals : because he treated stone honestly, revelled in its own qualities, did not try to make it seem like wood or plaster, exploited stone for what it exactly was. The detailer's mildly ungrateful revenge on his religious patron took the form of a monkey gargoyle which from the choirmaster's room at clerestory level appeared from the back to be hunched over with its hands between its thighs ; but from the front it presented a very different aspect. By placing an oval pebble in a runnel so that it alternately held and released water the detailer contrived that during rain the monkey masturbated in passably lifelike spurts. No one except the detailer was ever in a position to see this, he was the only one who ever appreciated and laughed at it : he thought of it as art for his sake. The monkey saluted rain with fertile abandon until the middle of the seventeenth century, when runnel corrosion and wear of the pebble caused a malfunction of the simple mechanism.

*Range 8,500 yards equals elevation 21-3° on the clinometer.*

Elias had always known of the narrowness of his foundations' loadbearing margin : the certainty that the tower would never carry the spire he had planned came just before his fifty-fifth birthday, but his disappointment was tempered by the realisation that he could build to the height he wished, and perhaps even higher, by adoption of Nicolas' Decorated style for a pierced, hollow spire which would be two-thirds or less the weight of a solid one. So Elias and Nicolas worked together in great peace to build a spire that subtly changed its appearance as those on the ground walked past at various distances, being fretted and light and

**47**

delicately proportionate, the interplay between masonry and space, pierced rondels and finials.

*First ranging shot at 8,800 yards . . .*

The final act of building was to place at the very top of the spire a casket containing the holy relics of St. Anselm together with a tiny fragment of the True Cross. John was ill, and old, but could let no one else perform the ceremony. Bearing the small sealed lead container, he was hauled slowly in a chair up the interior of the spire by the same men on the great treadmill who had raised every stone of its fabric. At the top Elias and Nicolas helped him out through a specially enlarged rondel on to the temporary scaffolding erected round the point of the spire. He shook as he slid the lead casket into place, he turned, looked down, heard voices through the wind, did not look at the others, crawled back towards his chair. Elias followed, Nicolas was left to set mortar on the stone entombing the relics.

*. . . second at 8,200 yards . . .*

At the consecration the masons shuffled on the enamel, burnt glass tiles. One felt resentful that the clerics now acted as though the building belonged solely to them; worse, were ascribing it to God, not them. A friend spat and said: Let them have it, leave it to them. A third was openly grateful that it had given him a living for twenty years, had enabled him to marry and bring up a family: Where else would I have found such work, he said, for there are no other patrons. It'll be here when those bastards are dead, said another. And their bleeding god, said the first.

*. . . observe, split difference, two more ranging shots, observe, split difference, which should then give me the mean point of impact: the spire of the Cathedral of St. Anselm.*

John and Elias, old men for their time.
John said: Why do you build?
Elias said: I am a builder . . .
John said: Not for God?

48

Elias said: I am a builder. I'm not sure about God.
John said: No more am I.
Elias said: Then why have you spent yourself on this house of God?
John said: In order that others shall have a place in which it might seem possible to believe in God.

> ... Then commence firing for effect. Impossible to check further, till daylight. Range in any case affected by temperature, wear of gun, strength of propellant, weather, other factors largely unknown, I just fire and hope, it's not a science though they like to make out it is. Try to sleep now.

By the fifteenth century there was a close; by the sixteenth a small town; by the seventeenth boys of the city evolved an early form of handball against the walls and buttresses of the return to the choir from the Chapter House. The verticals were as plumb as they ever were.

> STAND BY BATTERY THREE STOP LAY ON 07364219 BEARING 109° 15′ CHECK VISUALLY FIRST LIGHT THEN COMMENCE FIRING ON ORDER BATCOM

In the latter part of the eighteenth century respect was so far absent that it was found necessary to affix a notice to the eastern wall of the north transept reading DEFENSE D'URINER; to which within a week was unofficially added SOUS PEINE DE CONFISCATION DE L'OBJET.

> .. on the bleeding spire, he says, who wants to hit the bleeding spire, what sodding use is that, it's the bleeders underneath we're supposed to hit, poor sods, though with all the wear this old cow's seen if we line up on the bleeding spire we'll be lucky to hit the city let alone the bleeding church. . . .

An access of piety (or fear about the impossibility of passing a rope through the eye of a needle) in the mid-nineteenth century led to very extensive restoration. The flaking, blackened Caen stone was cut back and an ashlar of very similar stone applied. The crockets and

**49**

finials where damaged were simply squared off and not replaced. Afterwards the cathedral of St. Anselm was recognisably the same building, but early twentieth century *Kunstwissenschaft* was misled into a considerable number of errors.

**FIRE!**

# What Did You Say the Name of the Place Was?

Bournemouth.
A mild morning in early May.
The sun shines, my scrupulous eyes need sunglasses,
again, for I break them leaning back over the driving
seat to the children, repeatedly.

Two old men running, slowly, a newsagency.
Unhelpfully one revolves the display, I choose, pay little
but enough, wait on the change.

"They're worth it for the season," he endorses my
purchase, smiling gradually, directing me the long walk
to the sea, the sea first. Outside the sun has gone in,
again I am surprised by, disappointed at the triteness of
it, life, if you like, that the cliché about buying sunglasses is made so immediately true for this instance.

The weather end of the pier, a theatre above and old
men fishing a stage below. I have never seen anything
caught from a pier:

> except my father hooking out crab after small
> crab at Southend, stamping on them and kicking
> them back for taking bait not meant for them,
> the only time I ever remember him fishing. . . .

The tidy scrub and sandy cliffs slope back remarkably
uniformly at about seventy degrees, ninety-degree cliffs
of hotels stand above them, at one point a cablecar
drops ninety feet or so, unseriously, a toy. A new church
spire, spike, the only thing modern on the skyline,

neither blends nor complements, is compromise, is
nothing architecturally.

There is dark change in the west, a squall off the
headland, I am pleased to know of rain at sea again, to
be able to name it. I move towards shelter.

Old deck chairs newly varnished for the season, newly
stretched with translucent plastic in striped traditional
designs. Two old ladies sit down, impatiently tear open
their printed horoscopes; both caw with laughter as the
first (Aquarius too, I note) reads the as if handwritten
headline THIS IS A HIGHLY PREGNANT YEAR FOR
YOU. The tide here seems most of the time to qualify
as in, neither retreats nor advances far, and does not
expose mud but very fine sand, classically sand-golden,
an excellent if unexciting beach for young children.


But there are very few children of any age to be seen
here, suddenly I am aware that most of the people
around are getting on, indeed have got on, are old,
retired, retired to Bournemouth, for the mildness, the
climate, the comfort, for reasons of their own.

The public gardens that run north from the pier seem
especially organised for the benefit of the old: being the
floor of a small valley or chine, the local word, Wessex
word, perhaps, chine, running greenly back, and dividing
the town arbitrarily, parodying the countryside.

Here are a glassed-in bandstand of no particular period
or style, a concrete minigolf course of standardly
unbizarre shapes, and sub-tropical sub-size subsidised
palmtrees, no doubt a pride to the councillors, a source
of surprise to some visitors, tatty, but undoubtedly
palms, undoubtedly included in the *pulchritudo* half of
the town's motto.

In the evergreen walks on the first slopes many well-to-do
old ladies, and gentlemen, too, though fewer, yes
well-to-do is right, sitting on benches in pairs, together,
or a yard apart, watching the pigeons mating, the
semi-rare birds in the clapboard cages, one woman
writing a postcard in careful blue ballpen, another
reading a letter on blue Basildon Bond written in
careful blue ballpen, communicating.

Others chance the gentle descent towards the
municipalised stream that gave the town its name, so
small for such growth from it, now tidied between
equidistant concrete banks and to a common depth,
but mouthless, unmouthed: forty yards from the pier it
shuffles through a grill into darkness, and there is no
debouchement on the beach. No traveller would return
from that bourne, either.

An intersection over the chine, a traffic island, the main
traffic island of the town: up the sides of the valley the
department stores mount and mount their signs in
competition, attracting business, is that the expression?
Bournemouth shops are very good, sounds like a truism,
where did I hear that? My mother-in-law?

SPECIAL DISPLAY OF
VERY FINE
HAND KNOTTED PIECES
FROM PERSIA
AND SURROUNDING DISTRICTS

with green jade figurines and (how fashionably in
negative) a blowup of the Venus de Milo.

Jewellers for one form of their savings, to be sold if
necessary, to put into something better, perhaps: in one
window centrally a single solitaire for £1,750, in
another viciously expensive ways of telling their time,
but not how much longer, how little. And so many
camera shops with displays of expensive equipment:

55

much of it secondhand, used for how long in those fragile, unsteady hands? But I begin to impose, to see nothing but the aged in Bournemouth, perhaps quite wrongly, yet they are there, begin to dominate my thinking about the place, I only record what I see, what happens, how I feel.

There are health food stores offering for their *salubritas* (to name but a few): rheum elixir, natural sedatives, formulæ for kidney, bladder, heart, liver, gall; Lecithin (provides extra protection in middle and later years); royal *gelée*; super wheatgerm oil; pilewort and witchhazel suppositories; marshmallow and slippery elm ointment; kelp tablets; psoriasis ointment; toothpaste with azulene; lettuce-leaf cigarettes (no nicotine, a really good smoke); blood purifying tablets; bee cappings (for hayfever sufferers); concentrated artichoke bouillon (transfers fat into energy); Zimbabwe yoghourt (the only genuine goatmilk yoghourt); cocoa butter; high-protein high-potency multi-vitamin and mineral supplement; and honey, the sweet natural life-sustainer, in pound jars and seven-pound tins, garnered from heather, clover, acacia, lemon blossom, orange blossom, sunflower; and honey anonymously floral, local, blended: no one cannot afford honey in Bournemouth.

More use, I would think, are the wine shops, many looking individual, hand-owned, hand-run, not combine from the outside though inside there may be branded products and factory stock: but if I had money and time some of these shops look the kind where I might find *fines bouteilles*, not rare, but uncommon, strange unfamiliar labels, genuine dust-encrusted, handled with casual love.

In the central area there are several covered shopping arcades, the best apparently also the oldest, Regency

56

or early Victorian, from the outside, bowed half-round either side of a fanlight-ended glass vault. But even this has been thirties-modernised, mucked about, only if you look up can you appreciate its composition, symmetry: at ground level it is nothing, just shopfront. And similarly inside, the semi-circular glass roof and fanlight are good, but the pillars of the porch are crudely 1930, Noel Coward and Gertrude Lawrence.

The premises of the provision merchants appear to have changed little since before the war, either war: curved brass nameplates, mahogany woodwork of the windows, marble slab working tops for sliced tongue and jellied veal, glass jars of chicken breasts in aspic, patum peperium, preserved ginger, all the rest of the traditional bourgeois goodies.

Down the centre of the arcade are angled glass advertising cases, locked, mahogany and brass again, with hand-lettered posterpaint showcards for hairdressing and tinting, dancing, restaurants, the Bournemouth Casino (members only), two discotheques, theatre and cinema (mainly and surprisingly sex films: 'I came very near to being shocked' *D. Mirror*. 'The love scenes are very frank' *Cinema*) Even more (though unintentionally) titillating are pictures advertising the Foot Clinic and the Public Baths Department: Gen. Manager and Engineer James G. Hawksby.

And one showcard that trips some trap of unbidden memory, I had

> *thought I did not know Bournemouth, but I do not know what I know, nor when I shall know. In this case it is* Burley Manor for the friendly drink in the New Forest. *Was this the hotel that she whom I have called all those names, Jenny, Gwen, Wendy, worked at all those summers ago, for the vacation before we became lovers, when she was still more closely bound up with the epileptic boyfriend?*
> *She was I think a chambermaid there, was she*

*was impressed with or remarked upon to me,
later, and no doubt at the time to him, the stains
on the sheets of one bed she changed there, five
patches in the course of one night, the night of
the highest count, a man and his secretary,
was it, I was sceptical of five times, then, put
forward the scatter principle to her as a working
hypothesis. There it was she first read* Lear, *in a
thunderstorm, romantically, she was not lodged
at the hotel but with an old lady in a cottage of
the New Forest, romantic again, would not at
least one night let the epileptic come to her
there, some form of emotional blackmail, he
would not make anything permanent because of
his deficiency, thought it would not be fair to
her, who only wished for him to lean on her,
become dependent upon her, or so I thought, I
heard it all only at secondhand, and heard then
only what she wished me to know, I was being
blackmailed too, I never met him, unfortunately,
it might have put things into some sort of
perspective. Why was he there? Perhaps he
arranged it, the vacation work, he was at
Southampton. The woman who ran the hotel
was some sort of good cook, she would be
quoted whenever we argued about food, which
was not often, as an absolute authority, scampi
I remember featuring in one disagreement. She
used to go for long walks on this vacation job,
in the afternoons, when the chambers were
made, I suppose, wrote a short story about it, or
which came out of it, the experience, that is,
about a girl (her) walking a long way across
burnt heathland towards a hill with three pines
on it, skeletal, I seem to remember but I might
be wrong, the trees, that is, and they were
stunted, naturally, burnt out even, I think, feel,
three pines on a blasted heath! Too much*
Lear *and* Journey of the Magi, *I said, probably,
possibly, I didn't like the story, said so, yet ten
years, twelve years later I still remember it, as
everything about her, perhaps not everything,
but these things come back, she had the power
over me. I stare at the rooms in the photographs,
wonder if this was the hotel, the Burley, in the
New Forest: feel sure it is, or could be, the name
too means something, ha, so I want it to be?*

58

The stoneclad but steelframed department stores, banks, insurance offices indicate that Bournemouth's most flourishing building period was during the nineteen-twenties and nineteen-thirties: buildings not particularly good of their time, but certainly of their time, unmistakably. Now this architecture seems to serve nostalgic purposes for the retired, recalling the period of the Savoy, old ladies in touch again with the pleasures (or perhaps what they saw from a distance as the pleasures) of their youths: it means something that they again have them, although once more at a distance, ironically at another remove.

But at least in Bournemouth the buildings are real, honest, indifferent quality though they may be: not like the London Hilton, whose interior decor seems to have been designed deliberately with this nostalgia for the past in mind, for the widows whose husbands died in making the fortunes they now spend in the surroundings they could not afford while they were young.


*The Dancing Years* at the Pavilion.

Coachloads of old ladies and the occasional gent arriving from wherever in the carpark courtyard, which is graced by a modern fountain of the kind that gets the modern a bad name. The theatregoers must call it ugly and modern, synonymously: and they are right, too. It is almost as if it had been designed for the purpose of reinforcing their prejudices, as a sop; to confirm their opinions: if we put up something ugly at this time then it must by definition be ugly and modern. As opposed to *pulchritudo et salubritas*, which is what they had then, in the past, ha.

It consists of aluminium tubes of varying heights and diameters, this fountain, which variety in no case makes

59

proportionate the tininess of the nozzle at the top of each; to these are strutted fibreglass bowls, orange in colour, which fill and spill, fill and overspill, pee weakly from a lip into a pool which is foam-covered, detergent-like.

The old ladies stand for the Queen: the one in front of me has a cardigan torn near the trapezius, perhaps they are not all well-to-do, perhaps they are just ordinary, perhaps there are also homes for the less-well-off. The more-or-less-well-off one next to me, here with her daughter, perhaps, who looks much the same (hairstyle, twin set, the eyes, the manner) hums the familiar themes of the overture; then the orchestra descends on its hydraulic platform to applause from the lined and handcreamed palms, the lights dim on the grey and tinted heads, the scene number blinks to red one on the proscenium arch, and the curtain goes up to reveal the *lederhosen*-and-football-socks never-never land of the romantic Germanic past. *Rudi Kleber is a young composer living at an inn just outside Vienna in 1911. He is poor — so poor in fact that he is being thrown out because he cannot pay his rent, and his piano, which now stands in the garden, has been sold over his head. All this has happened while Rudi was picking flowers in the early hours of the morning with Grete, the fifteen-year old girl whose aunt owns the inn. When a party of officers and actresses come out from Vienna to have breakfast in the garden, Rudi offers to play waltzes for them in the hope of raising money to buy back his piano. They are joined by Maria Zeigler, star of the Viennese operetta, who is so taken with one of the waltzes that she buys it for a thousand Kronen, and moreover persuades her lover Prince Metterling to allow Rudi to occupy an empty studio in his Palace. Little Grete is being sent to England to school. . . .*

This is theatre at its most primitive, basic — in the uncomplicated, unsophisticated sense, unreal, not like life in any meaningful way. Here they are, for instance,

60

sympathising with and sighing over the poor starving artist, but what have they ever done to support any artist? Do they even know the difference between an artist and an artiste?

Yet their attention is rapt at this illusion, they enter this world just as children used to at a pantomime, this new novel Novello world where it is shocking for a woman to be seen smoking in public, affectionate jokes are possible about England's weather and comfortably idiosyncratic people, where the fold-worn scenery and scraped furniture are not allowed to be distinguishable from what they stand for (and in certain ways they will stand for anything). The unsteady, jockstrapped ballet can only be there for some curiously remote form of stimulation, the fat women tolerated only for their doubtful voices, while the harsh crudeness of the lighting and the chorus of senior amateur citizens are equally willingly accepted by this full house.

Yet the night before my father went overseas, in the army, during

> the war, they took me to see a Novello musical, I remember bits of it, set in a large country house, some kind of shooting, flintlocks, two kinds of parting, there were Novello and two women, one I liked, one I didn't, no doubt as I was supposed to, We'll gather lilacs was one of the tunes, don't remember others, or the title, and that night I cried because they wouldn't let me sleep in their bed, and on the last night before my dad was to go away, perhaps to get killed, they wouldn't let me sleep in their bed with them. . . .

"I never have been able to come out with the words DARLING or DADDY," says the girl in her early twenties, sleeking up her furnecked beaver lamb coat yet again against the draught in this hotel's Italian restaurant, very much enjoying the control a woman of

her age has in situations with a fifty-year-old man
than whom she is in any case taller.

It has come to the point where there is no such thing
as a local speciality in the exclusive sense: for everything
is available everywhere, flown in that morning
from anywhere, with the dew and the bacteria and
insects still on it. There is no reason why the food in
Bournemouth should be any better or any worse than
anywhere else, it is merely well or indifferently or
badly cooked. And the same staff cook it: which leads
me to see that this so conservative town, this
comfort-station for the elderly, is ironically serviced by
foreigners: the Irish (though they might argue whether
they were foreign), the West Indian nurses, the
Chinese and Indians with their restaurants, and the
hotel restaurants run by Spaniards, Portuguese,
Italians.

I grow tired, my mind coasts.


I retire, move towards sleep, am only tired, not retired,
very pleased to have work in me yet.

# Never Heard it Called
# That Before

## A JOYFUL DISSERTATION UPON THE BALLS POND ROAD
*with*
## NUMEROUS CHOICE ANACHRONISMS
*and*
## SELECTED INAPPOSITE DIGRESSIONS OF ENORMOUS CONSEQUENCE

It is natural to speculate upon the identity of the posited, alleged or implied Mr. Ball, his Pond, and his Road; for these things are of perennial interest to teachers, learners, parasites, poets, readers, writers, coneycatchers, moneylosers, and round pigs in squalid holes generally. Who was he, then, the aptly-named Mr. Ball, that he should have first a Pond and then a Road named after him? For it must surely have been in that order, a Pond and then a Road, not a Road and then a Pond.

Recent research reveals him to have been a gentleman of the Caroline period, and that he delighted to exercise his creative facility freely in spelling his name Bal, Balle, Bul, Bull, Bulle, Bule, Bolle and Bole at various times during his life; that he was a man of goodly parts though somehow lesser than the sum of those parts; a faithful and regular worshipper at goatish masses; pretender to the throne of Bali; free in his acquaintance, loose in his crotch and constipated in his habits; possessed of a truly remarkable weasand, blue garters, and crossed feet; a great admirer of ecclesiastical monumental brasses and lapidary crusaders; of Albigensian leanings; having one wife,

C

whom he loved for her faults, for no man loves a perfect
woman; particular in the manner of cleansing his
podex; accustomed to shaking himself thrice, ritually,
after urination; a great devotee of backgammon for he
had chosen to be born into the Caroline period,
enormous trouble having been gone to over his selection
of suitable in every way parents; having himself
singular issue as well, a sickly infant named Jeremy
but called Bubbleguts by way of reference to his habit
of puking up his fodder continually together with
relatively small portions of his intestine (small and large,
both), his alimentary canal, and other internal organs
whose function could loosely be described as digestive,
to the slight annoyance of his parents (Mr. and Mrs.
Ball) who one day went so far as to measure the
child's intake and his output, both liquid and solid, anal
and oral, and discovered to their not inconsiderable
delight that the latter exceeded the former by no less
than 68·483%, to go to no more than three decimal
places; the child, however, could demonstrably be
seen to thrive.

But: his father, Mr. Ball of the first part lest we forget,
a gentleman of few vices and all of the virtues,
including not to say embracing levity lechery
malfeasance and suchlike, especially suchlike towards
which he manifested a great partiality, was troubled, oh
mightily, one day whilst reading (reading being perhaps
the best way he knew of sending yet another dreary
day about its awesome business) an edifying and
illuminated octavo work on a new disease but lately
come out of the New World, in the forenoon by a pain
in an indelicate-to-mention locale, as a primary result
of which he could not accomplish the well-known
process of elimination with his usual felicity.

—D Aoctor bhall se been sy me, said Mr. Ball, a
disciple of Marrowsky, that splendidly logical linguistical
cipher in which the initial letters of contiguous words
are, to their undoubted embellishment, transposed; and

also given upon occasion to inversion, a delightful trait consequent ultimately upon his having been born feet first, entering upon the world so to speak somewhat apprehensively, putting the big toe out first in an endeavour to decide whether or not to, though in truth it was merely a little big toe for so are all those of by the grace of God infants compared with big (adult) big toes unless they be mutatives, which is not so after all very unlikely; this to his wife, who, being possessed of a fine tongue and almost adequate control of it, replied:

—Yes.

The reader will be no doubt intrigued to learn that this word comprised no less than one-half of Mrs. Ball's vocabulary; and frustrated to learn further that he is not to be informed of the word which formed the other moiety.


The Doctor cocked a diagnostic little finger.

—Hæmorrhoids or piles, he said.

—Che thoice then to ye mou gre aiving? said Mr. Ball.

—You joke, said the Doctor. Cool them by immersion in water. Then they shrink.

—Jou yoke, said Mr. Ball. That when lhould s io, dn b aucket dll aay song lquat?

—Yours the method, said the Doctor, who thought, Humour the nutcase, and whose name can be Dr. Scrumeluse if you like, since he does not appear any more.

First Mr. Ball tried lustrations applied with a flannel;
then with a sponge, then with a douche; and finally
with a small polished brass garden syringe; but even
treatment with this latter, accurately aligned and
carefully discharged, had effected no noticeable
improvement after two weeks; indeed, it might almost
be said to have worsened the situation, since the strain
of the contorted position necessary for its proper
deployment resulted in muscular pains of no mean
severity.

Mr. Ball next experimented with submerging the affected
parts in water contained in various types of vessel; to
wit, saucepans, frying pans, mugs, saucers, soup-plates,
the large stone erections so unselfishly provided by the
Metropolitan Drinking Fountain and Cattle Trough
Association, jars, buckets, bottles, eggcups (Ostrich),
glasses, bowls, commodes, hats (with an impermeability
factor greater than 93%), dogdishes, scale measures,
pressure cookers, small reservoirs, the bells of suitably
large wind instruments, drawers, lightbowls, wastepaper
bins, oildrums, smelting ladles, dredger buckets,
mechanical excavator scoops, paint kettles, and many
others too numerous to mention.

The use of all these failed to improve Caroline Mr.
Ball's condition; but one day the sensible solution to
his problem came to him most suddenly. The main
cause of the inefficiency of the other methods was the
stagnant state the water assumed after a very short
interval: it was imperative to have running water, so
Mr. Ball cunningly diverted (by means of trenches) the
stream of the Fleet, which, for the purposes of this
narrative, flowed closely by, so that it ran through a
shallow pond which he built in his back garden.
Preparing for all eventualities, he also installed a
Distant Early Warning System to give him time to
apprehend the approach of any predatory pike over five
pounds in weight. Briefly, the system worked like this:
any pike over five pounds (Mr. Ball calculated that he

ran no serious risk from the teeth of lesser pike) would, several yards upstream, be forced to disturb, in penetrating, a mesh grill which was connected by thread to a subtle bell not two feet from Mr. Ball's right ear; thus warned, the patient could surface the parts undergoing treatment by means of a simple pulley and sling arrangement.

Mr. Ball would daily indulge in this treatment for perhaps four hours, usually in the mornings. Whilst so doing, he would engage his mind with speculations on possible solutions to problems like:

(1) Do the villagers of Unterammergau feel inferior to those of Oberammergau?
(2) Where does winter go in the flytime?
(3) Assuming an evolutionary continuum stretching from an amœba on the one side and man on the other, at what stage was it decided that reproduction should require two differentiated elements (male and female), which adumbrated sex in the amœba decided upon the dichotomy, and could further developments towards a multiplicity of elements be anticipated?
(4) What was the incidence of lesbianism in Persian harems?
(5) How was it possible, after æons of evolutionary research and development, that there was a distinct proneness to pustules at the extremity of the human gut?

One day, whilst actively working towards a reasonably accurate answer to number (6) above, Mr. Ball received a visit from the new Vicar.

—I look after this district for God, the Reverend Vinyl introduced himself.

—Vot nery well, said Mr. Ball.

—I beg your pardon ! said the Reverend Vinyl.

—N'm iot wery vell, said Mr. Ball.

—A man cannot live by bed alone, explained the
Reverend Vinyl, noting the evidence for Sloth implied
by Mr. Ball's posture.

—T'm irying ao tlleviate d aistressing condition, said
Mr. Ball.

—Every man needs a hobby, excused the Reverend
Vinyl, But this morning I've just dropped in for a
sweet natter about the notverymuch.

—Oh, said Mr. Ball, who regretted that Marrowsky did
not give scope to the monosyllabic grunter.

—We are all Mixed Herbs in God's Mess of Pottage . . .
began the Reverend Vinyl, only to be interrupted by the
advent of the uniparous Mrs. Ball come to inspect the
shrinkage, as she always did with her elevenses.

—Yes, said Mrs. Ball.

—Give with the reechy kisses, missus, said the Reverend
Vinyl, and, God wot, a scene of atrocious carnage
might have ensued but for the timely tinkling of Mr.
Ball's bell announcing the imminent onslaught of a
mean freshwater shark. Whereupon that gallant
gentleman operated the pulley arrangement and hoisted
himself clear of the predator's element; to first the
alarm (since he imagined himself about to be assaulted
for his forwardness) and then the mystification (for he
had never observed a similar piece of apparatus either
in or out of action) of the Reverend Vinyl. Mr. Ball
explained the mechanism and its function in palliating
his painful parts.

—There is a destiny that shapes our ends rough, said

70

the Reverend Vinyl, demonstrating for the second time his knowledge of *Hamlet*, Mystify Your Friends. But this seems a very cumbrous and complicated method of containing the water. Have you not put it in some other sort of vessel? For instance, there are saucepans, frying pans, mugs, saucers, soup-plates, the large stone erections so unselfishly provided by the Metropolitan Drinking Fountain and Cattle Trough Association, jars, buckets, bottles, eggcups (Ostrich), glasses, coconut halfshells, bowls, commodes, hats (with an impermeability factor greater than 93%), dogdishes, scale measures, pressure cookers, small reservoirs, the bells of suitably large wind instruments, drawers, light bowls, wastepaper baskets, oildrums, smelting ladles, dredger buckets, mechanical excavator scoops, paint kettles, and many others too numerous to mention.

—Yes, said Mr. Ball.

—Yes, said Mrs. Ball.

—Ah well, said the Reverend Vinyl, You're human like the rest of them, I suppose. But my beknighted brother, the good Sir Maritan, who lives at Whipps Cross, once cured. . . .

—Whipps Cross? said Mr. Ball, abandoning Marrowsky in the celerity with which he perceived an occasion upon which he thought to be witty, Sounds like a stage direction in a play written by an anti-catholic Irishman.

—My brother, went on the Reverend Vinyl very firmly, Was once cured of a most distressing pustular facial condition by kneeling with his face downwards in a bogland area not so very far from here.

—Acne Marshes, said Mr. Ball, again sacrificing Marrowsky.

Mrs. Ball sat down on the ground, saying YES and her

other word to herself, still trying to see which was better and so refine her vocabulary. In her floral pattern hessian smock she resembled, to the Reverend Vinyl, an understuffed loosecovered horsehair sofa. But there, he always was commonplace in his comparisons.

Mr. Ball regarded the behaviour of his wife before a stranger with distaste; she, he thought, will certainly not have SINEVILLAQUE on her tomb at my expense.

The Reverend Vinyl perceived that it was time to go.

—God bless you, he intoned.

—Shy whould se Htart now? said Mr. Ball.


There are several theories about how the accident which named our Pond, and thereby our Road, happened. Some will have it that a superquick pike was through the grille and had performed his grisly office before Mr. Ball had had time to lift himself clear; others swear that a pike, originally under five pounds, grew big enough over the weeks to tackle the enticing objects he saw daily dangled before his eyes; yet others are persuaded that Mr. Ball made a tragically fatal error either in the size of the pike which he imagined could do him no harm or in the estimate he made of the velocity of such a fish through water; and finally, but more fancifully, there are those who suspect that Mrs. Ball, the Reverend Vinyl, or some unknown malicious person, introduced a pike (or perhaps a small alligator or other voracious beast) surreptitiously into Mr. Ball's Pond.

The cause is open to doubt, but the result is open to none; from about this date the records of the Hackney and Islington Festal Choir note a Mr. Bull as their leading counter-tenor.

The numerical extent of Mr. Ball's losses, however, must at this remove in History remain forever an enigma. For, the Road in question running through two boroughs, the signwriters employed by the Hackney Council spell it with the apostrophe before the s, and those receiving their stipends from that of the Borough of Islington, after the s. The compilers of the best maps, and those local people ignorantly thought to be ignorant, know very well that to take sides is to invite ridicule and therefore spell it ungraced by the apostrophe in any position.

# A Few Selected Sentences

Someone has to keep the records. . . .

The Cacao is a fruite little lesse then Almonds, yet
more fat, the which being roasted hath no ill taste. The
chief use of this Cacao is in a drinke which they call
Chocholate, whereof they make great accompt in that
Country, foolishly, and without reason; for it is
loathsome to such as are not acquainted with it, having
a skum or froth that is very unpleasant to taste, if
they be not very well conceited thereof. Yet it is a
drinke very much esteemed among the Indians,
wherewith they feast Noble men as they passe through
their Country.

What are hands for, if not to hide the eyes?

Le Soixante-neuf est Interdit dans les Couloirs.

*Eight years' penal servitude.*

As a lorry driven by Croxley left the scene, the sound of
a hunting horn was heard. Was it a warning? The police
found the body of a stag in the bracken, still warm.
Later, police came across Croxley, Ryman and Straker
standing by the lorry at the place where the stag had
been. Croxley said he was birdwatching, Ryman said
his hobby was photography, and Straker, who was
carrying a crossbow, said: "I am interested in all forms
of medieval weaponry." In the lorry police found a
quiver full of arrows, a pair of binoculars, two pairs of

77

Sherwood Green tights, and five sheath knives. A broken arrowshaft corresponded to an arrowhead embedded in the dead stag. All three men said they were committee members of Bowmen for Britain, had been out seeking small vermin, and had been on a public footpath. Straker said: "I saw a squirrel and fired at it but the stag which I did not know was there ran into it."

A child left to himself bringeth his mother to shame.

I love anecdotes. I fancy mankind may come in time to write all aphoristically, except in narrative; grow weary of preparation and connection and illustration, and all those arts by which a big book is made.

The man had long white hands which he clasped tightly behind his back when not using them to eat several helpings of jellied eels. Most customers looked thoughtful.

*One year, suspended.*

All afternoon the girl threatened to jump. She said her husband had become converted to a religious sect which forbade her the use of her television. When she had wished to listen to the Queen's Xmas broadcast she had had to go into the bathroom. It was her radio. Because she used makeup her husband likened her to Jezebel, the painted woman of the Scriptures. It was accepted that he was sincere. As soon as they brought a priest to talk to her, she jumped.

Permission to laugh?

Have you heard what Cynon sang?
Beware of drunkards—
Drink unlocks the human heart.

78

The father appealed for witnesses to his son's death to come forward, not expecting to be overwhelmed by numbers. What had happened as far as they knew was that on Furse Bend he had crossed the inner edge on to the central reserve and in the resulting spill (which was not particularly dangerous in itself) the point of the clutch lever had entered his brain by way of the base of his skull. The father wished to know how designers of safety helmets had not taken this possibility into account. His colleagues said he should have had a ball on it.

But I am trying to be benign.

A rusty charlatan stated dogmatically that a discussion was an argument in which no one was particularly interested. He was reminded that every good deed is followed by the punishment of God. But, he insisted, one must have a proper regard for the ordinary.

The continuous process of recognising that what is possible is not achievable.

A man taking pictures of a man taking pictures: there must be something in that.

At a wedding reception everyone was drunk, including the children. Indeed, one of the children became so affected as to seem ill, and it was considered advisable to take him to a hospital to have him seen to, stomach-pumped if necessary. They chose the receptor who seemed least drunk to drive the child, quickly. On the way the car was stopped by a policeman on a horse, who invited the driver to puff breath into a plastic bag. Crystals in the tube attached to this bag turned a certain colour which convinced the policeman that the driver was under the influence of alcohol and he informed him that he would be charged with an offence. "Oh no," said the driver, "Your bags must be faulty. Perhaps indeed you have a batch of faulty bags. Why don't we test them by trying one out on this innocent child?"

A bard's land shall be free. He shall have a horse when he follows the king and a gold ring from the queen and the harp he shall never part with.

Do I want that to be the truth?

The Vice-Chancellor was killed when inspecting the progress of the building of Senate House. A technician was pushing a loaded wheelbarrow across a plank spanning a liftshaft. He saved himself, but the wheelbarrow was lost. The Vice-Chancellor was standing at the bottom of the liftshaft. Accommodate that mess.

Most of the time they look for things to want, schoolfriends.

Miceal and I would play snooker. He would generally win. His was always the same remark when he sank the green or the brown which would put him beyond being caught unless he gave away an unlikely number of penalty points: "Now you haven't got enough balls. You'll have to put your own up." I cannot say I laughed more than the first and second times, despite tradition. And "No points for hard luck" was another saying of his that stuck.

—Who was there?
—The usual mess, of course. Baldies, hairies, collapsed faces, fallen women, who would you think?


*Life.*


Someone has to keep the records. I may even be thanked, in time.

# Instructions for the Use of Women; or Here, You've Been Done!

Let me try to set this down with an exactness you may
or may not find curious.

The only point of precision (as distinct from
completeness, to which I feel incapable of aspiring) on
which I am undecided is the disclosure of her name.
This indecision is principally occasioned by the existence
of libel laws of a surely unnecessarily harsh character:
for I am, after all, only telling the truth as I see it now,
remembering to the best of those faculties I have what
I felt reasonably sure happened at the time. If you are
not an acquaintance of mine (which you are almost
certainly pleased not to be) her name can mean nothing
to you; and those who do know me will already be
aware of her name or be easily able, from their special
knowledge, to identify her. So how could she be
harmed? Why should our lawgivers think that she
needs protection?

But in their circumstances I shall call her Winnie, or
Rachel, or Stella, or any other name that reasonably
preserves her gender, as the mood takes me, or rather as
whatever comes to mind at the time a proper name
seems to make the rhythm of the sentence a little less of
a failure. And I shall make unthrifting use of the feminine
personal pronouns. But, whichever, no burden of
universality is to be laid upon the appellative; or on
anything else, either.

I wonder is anyone still reading?

This girl (as she then was) Millie. First eyesetting must

83

have been at our college, at some time, she was a year
or so behind me, was it two, no, she was in the same
year as Patrick, Neilsen, and all those, the heroic
young. A snobby lot, she told me, at the time I am really
writing about, which was much later, several years after
we had both become post-. I could astound you with
an amount of stunning trivia at this point, if I did not
wish to avoid boring myself. By beginning at the
beginning I am doing that, however, so how about some
sex? That I know you will enjoy: so many commodities
sold through sex testify to the stone certainty of that
truth!

At some early point in the post-college period, then, I
must have invited Daphne to count the short rosary of
my balls: one, two, one for luck, three! This must not
be misunderstood as a conceited metaphor, but read
again, perhaps more carefully. But the invitation went
unanswered for some time, and no speculation can be
more likely to show a slight profit than that this had
much to do with a boyfriend of hers who said he had
cancer. More of him later, if I can be bothered, for I am
having enough difficulty fulfilling my word and getting
to the sex soonest as it is.

How to express it?

Ah!

There blew up this very disturbing bubble under my
foreskin (for my parents did not follow the fashionable
organ-scalping of their time, for reasons into which I
have never felt competent enough to enquire). It was
after the second (I think) time that first night, and this
bubble I can only liken to that which can often form,
suddenly and almost remarkably, when a half-fried egg
is basted with overheated fat: something to do with
surface tension, perhaps, though I am no physicist, ha!
But my bubble was larger, though perhaps fingering in
the dark made it so, or seem so. Obviously it was a

84

blister, but why it should be so large worried me. The
cause was almost as obvious : Dora was dry, desiccated,
and did not let down her dew, Freda's fanny had not let
flow the sweet juices of fornication, Sonya's sluicegates
of soft desire had remained shut, Wilhemina's weirwaters
had become a wadi of waste land, waste sand — and
similar imitations of the euphemisms of the good old
pre-permissive writers.

But I am the first (and who could challenge that ?) to
admit that there was another cause, too : I was not (like
any of us) as young as I used to be. I was, indeed, as
late in the twenties as it was possible to be in those
days, and I had been, moreover (and this may come as
a shock), in an unblessed state as regards actual
penetration of a female for something approaching four
years. Not that, you must understand, I considered
myself celibate : like an athlete I had kept the appropriate
muscles in fine fettle by regular (for periods, indeed,
nightly) exercise. But no, on this occasion it was, I am
sure, or feel, the remarkably high friction quotient
generated against not an unreceptive (for it was well
enough received) but an insufficiently lubricated
receptacle for an unusual length of time. This latter
point is of major interest (for me, anyway) as this
second time, following at who knows (since it was dark)
what interval, it took me an unprecedentedly long time
to discharge my duty, if such it was, and if not it ought
to have been. Indeed, to tell all, I did not go off with
that splendid, satisfying *splott* at all, but (the method
used being timely withdrawal with Gynomin for
additional safety) dissembled by gentle histrionics. I do
not know if she was deceived ; she gave no sign. For
this only I feel guilty about the whole affair : and that
only for my own sake, certainly not on account of her.
It is the only occasion on which I have found it
necessary to feign in this connection.

But the bubble I kept fingering, after the *coitus* had
been *interruptus*, being aware of, for a long while, in

85

the dark there. Eventually I fell asleep, and when I
awoke it had almost disappeared : though the soreness
remained, so there was no dismissing it as a dream,
wet or windy, or a nightmare.

I would like it to be borne in mind during the following
attempt at description that my appearance too has not
been known to cause gasps of admiration or envy, nor
to stop traffic in even the less busy streets.

She was a big girl, Harriet, somewhat masculine, I
suspected, big except for her breasts, tits, dugs, or
mammaries, that is, which somehow protruded less than
her stomach, looked at from either side elevation. Yet
she did not appear to be fat, exactly, had a waist and
good gracile legs. It was her hips, she was very heavy
in the hip; I wish I could demonstrate for you with
some anatomical model or machinery the heavy, curious
articulation of her hips. If I had to sum her up in a cheap
phrase, and why I do so when I am under no such
compulsion causes me some surprise, I would say she
was an incipient trout, a budding if not archetypal
trout, even at her age (which at that time was about
twenty-five) manifesting distinct troutiness. And ah,
again, I would not have you thinking (if you were) that
I am envious, or even taking some kind of revenge : for
no doubt to her I also was archetypically pisciform, for
instance, perhaps clearly seen as a rock-salmon (dogfish,
*Scyllium catulus*), or as the grotesque camerafish, I am
a camerafish ! No, my only concern, as I have too often
said, is to set down what I thought, think, and
remember with some exactness. If she wishes she may
attempt to do the same : that I allow is her troutish
privilege.

Perhaps she was all that I deserved, if in spite of
everything there is justice, at that time, and I am very
pleased the time is past.

Did you find the bubble bit interesting ? I doubt you

can have read anything quite like it before. And it is true, however it reads to you. By 'quite like it' I mean anything so curiously comic and uncomic, in just that way. Or perhaps you were embarrassed? In that case it may have been good for you: have you thought of that?

Her character. She had a marked capacity for setness. She would punctiliously leave me to catch a train for no other reason than that she had at some time set her mind on catching that particular train. There was no real reason to go home then, or at all, except the setness, the execution of an arbitrary but pre-determined decision. I thought this was very near to being a mistake, but that is surely natural.

It was a wet summer, poor by popular standards, but popular with me because the number of creepy-crawlies was noticeably diminished. Or perhaps it was just that there were fewer occasions on which I was tempted to sit on the grass.

This was at her flat, in a late Georgian house facing on to Blackheath. She paid a high rent for it, for her. She was a schoolmistress. In the morning she would not let me be seen by the colleague who came to pick her up for school. I watched from an upstairs window, Morris Traveller, woman about forty, and troutlike Doris swinging in her two fine legs, never a romantic glance up at the window of her flat, smiles for the colleague, talking about something from which I was excluded. Do not imagine I did not resent it.

For the rest, or part of the rest, the notes for a failed poem of the time or thereabouts:

*Just as though nothing had happened/ Cars still crossed the rain. . . . of Blackheath/ Houses proudly primly bowfronted as day night before/ WORMS were stranded across the asphalt paths/ just as they always*

*are by heavy rain?/ a fishmonger laid out stiff*
*mackerel/ ticket office efficient/ the commuters*
*soaked and drily surly/ and the tube so packed as to*
*suggest a grotesque echo of our closeness/ Just as*
*though I had never lost my faith belief/ in loving*
*making love and you had not restored it/*

At last, you must be saying, or thinking, rather, the
point, or a possible point, at any rate: the
unsatisfactoriness of the relationship is being reflected
or refracted in what it would be a joke to call the
narrative. A suicidal point: make it as unsatisfactory as
possible for the reader in order to convey more nearly
the point of unsatisfactoriness.

There! A reward for reading this far. Another joke is
promised before the end.

There are two ways of taking what has gone so far:
your way, and my way. And you are no doubt going to
take it your way.

Mind you, in those days I used to be worried about *on to*
and *onto*, as well, ha!

Yet I have told you nothing about her, really, Anne,
Betty, Celia: nothing that could be shown to you in
any meaningful sense to be true. But at least pyrronism
may be true, paradoxically?

Shortly afterwards I met my future wife and lived
happily ever afterwards.

I am going to give up this style soon. Perhaps after this.
I mean, it is well understood that a man cannot stand
still. Change is a condition of life, I remind myself.
Perhaps the most admissible one, too.

Nor is this the piece I wanted to write.

88

But always end with a song and a giggle . . . so sing the following fescennine joke to yourself:

The usual young man was shipwrecked on a desert island. Fortunately for him he found there others, though only men, who had met with a similar but earlier fate. When he had eaten and drunk of such as the island provided, he felt recovered from his asthenia sufficiently enough to enquire into how this all-male society fared for the other. "Ah," said one of his companions-in-distress who recked not of ending sentences with prepositions, "There we are very well provided for. In the south of the island is exposed at low tide the mouth of a cave at the back of which is a vast store of dried fanny, provenance unknown but highly regarded, and you are most welcome to avail yourself of it as the need takes you." Our hero was of course at first inclined to regard the fellow as a barmecide, but, having nothing to lose, soon sought out the delitescent cave and was surprising and pleased to see that the man had indeed been speaking the truth. So, choosing circumspectly from amongst the neatly stacked piles the least hispidulous of those in the front, he was soon enjoying himself with a properly apolaustic fervour. Over the succeeding months and years he came to value this handy dehydrated convenience product so much that when the time came (as it must for the purposes of this anecdote) for the castaways to be rescued he resolved to take back a dozen or so with him: what he had in mind was to produce them triumphantly if any of his acquaintance should accuse him of gasconnading, as they naturally might. Jauncing off the boat into the Customs Shed at Falmouth, however, he met with an unexpected setback. "Anything to declare?" enquired a ventripotent Customs Officer; to which, determined to be truthful, our hero replied: "Yes. Dried fanny, as a commodity, or, if you prefer the plural, fannies." The Customs Officer did not laugh, as he found it unsettled people. Instead he expressed a desire to see the objects declared, and was immediately convinced by a glance into the sailor's kitbag. "How many are there?" he required to know, as though dried fanny were part of the everyday life of the Customs Officer. "About a dozen," hazarded the succoured castaway. "About?" queried the civil servant, "In that case I'd better count them." And, licking his enumerating finger, he began to do so. All went well to seven, mere routine, but then he paused, licked his finger again, reflected for a long moment, and said firmly: "Here, mate, you've been done: this one's an arsehole!"

# Broad Thoughts
from a Home

Robert said: A poem is a poem is a poem is a ragbag.
*Description of Robert:*

| | |
|---|---|
| Height: | 6' 8" |
| Weight: | 14 st. 10 lbs. |
| Eyes: | honeybrown |
| Complexion: | pallid |
| Hair: | fair, riotous |
| Features: | mobile |
| Collarband: | 15 |
| Disposition: | agitated |
| Bearing: | all over the place |
| Age: | twenty-two years |
| Sex: | unimportant |
| Spectacles: | worn, horn |
| Teeth: | irregular |
| Apparel: | eccentric only in colour |
| Overall impression: | long |

*Nature of statement:* exploratory-aggressive.
  Samuel said: Crap.
*Description of Samuel:* large.
*Description of description:* pithier.
*Nature of reply:* somewhat obscene.
  Robert said:  A poem is a poem is a poem is crap.
*Tone of remark:* unconvincingly flippant.
*Expression on Robert's face:* baulked-abashed.
  Samuel said: Agreed.
*Tone of reply:* sharp.
*Purpose of reply:* to end conversation, and to secure a
modicum of peace in which he might be enabled to

93

concentrate upon the effort of leaning out of the window
to observe the hour of day indicated by the clock on
the tower of Their Lady of the Assumption in Rathmines,
suburb of Dublin.

Samuel said: If I fall out of this window, you are to
inform the nearest Garda immediately.

*Tone of remark:* largely serious.

*Action on part of Samuel:* to reach out a little farther.

*Portion of anatomy poised on windowsill:* loins.

*Physical state of Samuel:* uncomfortable.

*Successful climax of action:* Samuel glimpsed the
clockface.

*Method employed:* a supreme elongation.

*Subsequent necessity for treatment:* Samuel pulled
himself in and relieved his impressed loins by gentle and
appropriate massage.

Samuel said: Twenty to five, if one can believe the
Church in oh at least this one small
particular.

Robert said: Time to eat.

*Nature of remark:* gluttonous; indicative of hyperfunction
of digestive organs.

Samuel said: You're always byourlady hungry!

*Tone of reply:* half-bitter, half-abusive.

Robert said: The trouble with our arrangement that
you cook and I washup is that *you* are
always the prime mover—I can neither
eat nor fulfil my half of the arrangement
until you have fulfilled yours; which
you do with neither punctuality nor
regularity nor seemliness.

*Verity of latter part of foregoing statement:* none.

*Grammatical felicity of latter part of ditto:* doubtful.

Samuel said: Balderdash!

*Nature of remark:* deliberately archaic, with superior
class overtones.

Samuel continued: I am a very fine cook, and you are
very well satisfied with the arrangement.
You would else be sustained by bread,
milk, and cheese.

94

*Slight literary influence on last sentence:* William Shakespeare (decd.).

Samuel said: At the moment, in any case, I am thinking of an altogether different sort of prime movement.

*Actions consistent with foregoing words:* Samuel seized his lavatorybook from the mantelshelf, tore off a strip of paper from a small roll, and left the flat.

*Title of Samuel's lavatorybook:* ULYSSES, by the most estimable of authors, James Joyce, Dubliner.

*Location of paper:* on top of gasmeter, adjacent to spare shilling.

*Length of strip torn off:* approximately 34" ($\pm\frac{1}{2}$").

*Nature of paper:* of the crepe variety, soft but weak.

*Situation of flat:* on the third floor.

*Colour of door:* pleasantly bright red.

*Architectural period of house of which the flat formed part:* Georgian of the third rating.

*General condition of house:* less than kempt.

Robert said: If you're not quick you're dead.

*Escape at last:* Samuel thudded down the stairs to the lavatory.

*Nature of lavatory:* tending to the primitive.

*Explanatory retrospect:* By a careful and systematic exploitation of the auditory sense, Samuel had struck up an acquaintanceship with the Irish girl who occupied the basement room immediately below the abovementioned lavatory.

*Name of Irish girl:* Miss Deane.

*Posited nature of acquaintanceship:* incipiently amatory.

*Degree of success met with:* encouraging.

*Plotting and acting:* The place bringing Samuel inevitably to mind of its associated female sub-tenant, he began to plan the next stage of his campaign for the conquest of Miss Deane. After cursory thought he decided on direct assault of a literary nature: he would write an unequivocal poem to Miss Deane. In ten minutes he had created his poem and written it, on a page left conveniently blank by the aforesaid James Joyce, with a pencil expressly carried for such a purpose.

95

*Type of pencil employed:* black, graphite, stubby, of the
2H quality of durity.
*Title of poem:* "Ode to a Basement Lodger".
*Foul-paper copy of poem:*
> My dear Miss Deane:
> Were I the King, and you the Queen,
> (Divine, entrancing, just nineteen),
> I'd do you all day long—with meals between.
> But as it is I haven't a bean:
> I'm not the King, you're not the Queen,
> But still I'd like to . . . you know what I mean,
> My dear Miss Deane.

*Dashing of hopes of the Filthy-Minded:* "Foul-papers"
were manuscripts originally so-called by hard-pressed
printers.
*Ascension:* In which Samuel and stairs were inseparably
conjoined.
*Manner of his going:* selfpleased, anticipatory.
*Pride in achievement:* Joyfully, he announced to Robert
the crystallization of the latest stage of his campaign,
and read the poem to him.

    Robert said: Crap is crap is crap is crap!


*Situation outlined:* Samuel sat patiently on the steps
leading down to the garden.
*Purpose of sojourn:* to keep a rendezvous with the
Miss Deane mentioned above.
*Type of steps:* of the steeply-inclined variety, rough
timber construction, treated two coats of creosote
(cheap quality).
*Horticultural description of garden:* splendid crops of
woundwort and teazel, bindweed and eyebright,
sowthistle and coltsfoot, agrimony and heartsease,
catseye and goatsbeard, chickweed and toadflax,
dandelions and viper's bugloss, dock and thyme,
marjoram and sneezewort, silverweed and vervain,
matricary and pignut, bryony and burnet, cinquefoil and
fleabane, keck and loosestrife, nipplewort and navelwort,

yarrow and oxeye; at the end of the garden three mullein raised their proud yellow columns four feet above the earth.

*Note:* the foregoing is botanically improbable, to say the least.

*Non-horticultural aspects of garden:* DUSTBINS and tinskipperboneseggshellsboxescheeselemonandorange peelsweetwrapperspapertowelscorrugatedironbroken bricksstoutbottlesslimbottlestoenailcuttingsrasherrind puffkinpacketsnewspapersoldpapersragspostcardsburnt toastglueandsoinfinitelyon scattered amongst the abovementioned herbaceous vegetation; clothes, drying on a line, none of an intimately female character.

*Other participants in the rendezvous:* two small Irish cats; wild; grey and black respectively.

*Unusual knowledge:* Samuel was waiting for Miss Deane to finish her lunch. He knew that she would have done this when a trickle of dirty washingupwater ran along the rut to his right into the drain at the foot of the steps upon which he was sitting. He was reading his stepsbook.

*Title of Samuel's stepsbook:* one of the SPEAK TO ME, FATHER, ABOUT . . . series, entitled . . . HELL.

*Reward for patience:* Samuel had just decided that Hell, as described by Father, was a most interesting place, well worth the day trip, when a gurgle from the drain informed him of the imminent approach of Miss Deane. It could not be said, unfortunately, that the concinnation of Miss Deane was of the highest order.

*Dictionary definition of* CONCINNATION: sb. Now rare; 17th C.; (f. Lat. concinnat—; concinnare, *neatly put together*). The state of having been fitly put together.

*Explanation of dictionary definition:* sb. = substantive; C. = century; f. = from; Lat. = Latin.

*Description of Miss Deane:*

| | |
|---|---|
| Height: | 5' 7⅝" |
| Weight: | 9 st. 3 lbs. |
| Eyes: | icy |
| Complexion: | tending to ruddiness |
| Hair: | black, short |

```
Bust:              31"
Waist:             31"
Hips:              31"
Features:          manly
Disposition:       uncertain
Age:               twenty-four years
Sex:               female
Spectacles:        not worn
Teeth:             passable
Apparel:           usual-uncasual
Overall impression: lumpish.
Samuel said:       Miss Deane!
```
*Tone of address:* theatrical enrapture.

```
Samuel said:       Miss Deane, Miss Deane,—or may
                   I call you Devilla?
Miss Deane said:   Devilla? Why? No.
Samuel said:       Ah, and I know why not: because
                   it isn't your name!
```
*Quality of joke:* poor in the extreme.
*Nature of Samuel's laughter:* forced, histrionic.
*Purpose of joke and laughter:* to establish an atmosphere of pleasantry in which serious questions of a sensual nature could be posed with the minimum of offence.
*Reaction of Miss Deane to joke:* simple pleasure.

```
Miss Deane said:   Have you written any more poems?
Samuel said:       No. Five days have passed their
                   weary lengths since I thrust the last
                   one beneath your prayerbespattered
                   door, Miss Deane, since when I
                   have been unable to concentrate
                   upon further creation of a poetic
                   nature, as I am far too preoccupied
                   in awaiting your reply.
Miss Deane said:   You know very well that I didn't
                   understand it.
```
*Purpose of last remark:* to gain time to think.
*Miss Deane's thoughts:* He's rather nice a bit flabby though must like his food I'd feed him all right wouldn't I would he keep me though you never know with college students there was that one the theological

98

young one you'd never have thought it he was worse than although they do say but I promised myself I'd forget that now it's over four years ago a Jesuit too this one reminds me of him in some ways nice eyes and hair he has full lips too not a very interesting face on the whole still a girl can't pick and choose very much what with all the men emigrating but I'll never unles she becomes a Catholic and confesses it decently like everyone else and promises to marry me and keep me and the children children oh that's awful no nice the children must be Catholics Father taught me that can't remember how early must be very careful as he's not a Catholic.

Miss Deane said: Have you heard anything from the Man Up There? That's your answer!

*Biological Note:* the female will instinctively tend to ensure economic provision against the birth of issue before committing herself to the act in which such issue may be procreated; in Miss Deane's case, such economic reflexes were inseparable from religious conformity, and therefore her religious question masked the economic one.

Samuel said: No, being interested only in the women down here. But I have been trying to see if either can manage a message.

*Nature of visible proof provided:* the stepsbook mentioned earlier, in which Father attempted to speak to him about . . . HELL.

Miss Deane said: Pah!

*Accompanying physical reaction:* Miss Deane turned and walked away.

*Speed of rotary motion:* approximately 14·0 r.p.m. ($\pm 0\cdot 5$).

*Distance walked:* a comfortably revocable three-and-a-half yards.

Samuel said: But Miss Deane! I adore you!

*Nature of cry:* theatrical-passionate.

*Purpose of cry:* to appeal to Miss Deane's romantic instincts.

*Result of cry:* momentary hesitation on part of Miss Deane.
*Victory prematurely assumed:* Samuel grinned,
triumphantly.
*Result of grin:* abrupt departure of Miss Deane.


Samuel said : So, all I've got to do is to become a
convert and send my prayers for Miss
Deane care of the Virgin Mary.
*Position of Samuel:* inert, upon a short sofa, his legs
dangling over the end.
*Physical state of Samuel:* too lazy to do anything about
physical discomfort.
Robert said : You must experience a kind of
apocalyptic fit, in fact.
*Position of Robert:* inert, upon a bed.
*Short-term lessee of bed:* Samuel, tenant of the first part.
*Physical state of Robert:* comfortable.
*Occupation of Robert:* consuming cheese.
*Nature of cheese:* of the Irish Co-operative Dairies
processed brand, orange in colour, solid in texture.
Samuel said : You know what she told me today? We
were very late back from this dance last
night, and I asked her if she had slept
well. Yes, she said, she was so tired she
nearly fell asleep saying her prayers! I
was very proud indeed of my constraint
of the ensuing risibility.
*Literary influence on last sentence:* Samuel Johnson,
bookseller's son, of Lichfield.
Robert said : Well, what do you expect if you send
the girl *verse* invitations to
concupiscence? She'll assume at once
that you have money and could
therefore raise her class status, so she'll
hold out for marriage. For Christ's sake,
the girl doesn't know a trochee from
the Trocadero !
*Purpose of last remark:* to use up a witticism Robert had
100

saved up for some years, awaiting only a suitable occasion upon which to use it.

*Relevance of witticism:* somewhat marginal.

*Construction of witticism:* alliterative; the yoking of unlike ideas together; somewhat akin to that figure of rhetoric called by the ancients *oxymoron.*

Samuel said: So now I await Godsent consent, do I? Do I, hell!

*Tone of remark:* immoderate.

*Nature of remark:* irreverent.

Robert said: You surely don't expect a relationship born in the flush and roar of the waters to be furthered by poesy, do you?

*Intention of remark:* to ridicule Samuel.

Samuel said: Get your cheesebesprinkled corpus off my byourlady bed, then! You've got a byourlady cheek!

*State of Samuel's feelings:* wounded.

*Purpose of remark:* partly retaliatory; partly to change the subject; partly to avoid sleeping that night in patches of emollient cheese.

Robert said: And the Mummybear said "Who's been sleeping in my porage?"

*Tone of voice employed:* feminine, bearbaiting.

*Quality of joke:* fair.

*State of status quo:* stable.

*Posture rapidly assumed by Samuel:* minatory.

*Speed of assumption:* 19·735 ft/sec.

Robert said: Promise to feed me soon, then.

*Tone employed:* mock-plaintive.

Samuel said: All right, then, just as soon as you stop feeding yourself on my bed.

*Happy outcome:* On these terms a truce was concluded, and the conversation reverted to the subject of Miss Deane.

Samuel said: What then must I do to be saved?

*Literary influence on the last sentence:* the King James authorised version of the Holy Bible.

*Occupation of Samuel at time of speaking:* preliminary preparation of a meal.

101

*Nature of meal:* rudimentary.
*Constituents of meal:* eggs, small; bacon, scraps;
potatoes, large, King Edward's; *pisum sativum,* hardy
climbing annual.

>Robert said : How far has she accepted your sensual
>advances?
>Samuel said : Not very far. I had no difficulty
>persuading her to come up here for a
>coffee or tea or something after the
>dance, and she accepted my chaste
>kisses readily enough. And then. . . .
>Robert said : I heard sharp words through the
partywall. . . .

*Explanatory note regarding construction of partywall:* of
two layers of plasterboard, low grade, separated by
battens two inches square, at either end; papered both
sides in a dunbrown floral pattern wallpaper.
*Noise penetration factor of partywall:* better than 80%.

>Samuel said : You foul, long third party: what right
>have you to listen to my intimate
>susurrations with Miss Deane?
>Robert said : You shouldn't susurrate so loudly. And
>in any case you're telling me now.
>Samuel said : But by eavesdropping you rob me of
>choice.
>Robert said : What were the sharp words about
>anyway?
>Samuel said : Oh, that was when I attempted a little
>gentle earchewing. This was so grossly
>sensuous to Miss Deane that it took all
>my diplomacy to quiet her. And she has
>such lovely ears to chew, as well.
>Robert said : No farther?
>Samuel said : No farther. So must I be converted ere
>I achieve another step.

*Literary influence on last sentence:* any one of the
following deceased playwrights of the Elizabethan
and Jacobean periods; the choice being left to the
reader.

>BeaumontandFletcher

Chapman*
Dekker
Ford
Greene
Heywood
Jonson
Kyd
Lyly*
Marlowe
Marston*
Massinger
Middleton
NortonandSackville*
Peele*
Preston
Rowley
Shakespeare*
Shirley
Udall*
Webster

*Fairness to the reader:* the author feels it to be no less than a duty incumbent upon himself to state that he cannot recommend the choice of those playwrights above whose names are followed by asterisks.

Robert said : What place ought pleasure to hold in the rational life?

Samuel said : But a small one, surely, Socrates.

Robert said : Can virtue reside in pleasure, Philebus?

Samuel said : Assuredly, provided pleasure is kept in its true place.

Robert said : And what is its true place?

Samuel said : As long as pleasure is not allowed to possess the self so far that it prevents it from reaching its end in good, then it can be said to be in its true place.

Robert said : The case, then, against pleasure is not that it is evil, but that it is unimportant?

Samuel said : Yes, Socrates. Pleasure becomes evil when it usurps a place in the self which demands that energy be expended in its

pursuit which is out of all proportion
to its true place.

Robert said :   What, therefore, Philebus, the hell are
you chasing Miss Deane for with such
misapplied energy?

*Stage now reached in meal preparation:* crucial ;
Samuel had four pans and three gasjets.
*Date of manufacture of gas-stove:* 1884.
*State of Samuel's mind:* calmly agitated.
*Note, explanatory of hiatus imminent:* Samuel being
thus occupied with culinary matters, and Robert with
thoughts anticipatory of the results of Samuel's
occupation and being careful lest his expectations be
disappointed through disturbing Samuel, the
conversation languished, and, hardly mourned, died.


*Time:* Twenty-three minutes after one in the morning.
*Phase of the moon:* in the third quarter.
*Characters:* Miss Deane ; Samuel ; fourteen ducks ; two
swans ; seven cygnets ; sundry small waterside creatures
of the night ; pennypigs, a shillingsworth ; God, too,
for those who would rather not be without him.
*Location:* the north bank of the Grand Canal, Dublin.
*Direction of movements:* Liffeywards, as regards Miss
Deane and Samuel ; stationary, as regards the birds ;
hither (and, probably thither), as regards the
waterside-dwellers ; poundwards, as regards the
pennypigs ; in a Mysterious Way, as regards God.
*Descriptive setpiece, of a lyrical, romantic nature:* it is
always wonderful to live near water of any kind,
whether it is sea, or river, or lake : but to live near a
canal ! That is the *summum bonum* ! The nearly still
waters clear and deep, with long bright streaming weeds
swaying gently ; the shallow flow of water over the top
of the lock boiling into leafgreen foam twenty feet
below ; the banks so broken and irregular in the canal's
neglect ; the variety of the plants which flourish amidst
this decadence ; and the swans and wildfowl that grace

104

the silent surface. And the locks! The locks, great narrow tunnels under the backed bridges, shaded and sombre, quiet and mysterious, calm and religious in their disuse. And the boys who fished for roach. . . .

*Quotation from FISHING IN IRELAND:* "Roach are not found in Ireland except in one southwestern river system, into which they were artificially introduced in the late nineteenth century. Confusion often arises, however, amongst those ignorant of the fact that rudd are called roach in the Emerald Isle."

*Descriptive setpiece (continued):* . . . by the old wooden swinging arms of the locks! Samuel had watched in the clear water the tiny redfinned fish actually biting the breadpaste, had watched for hours boys at their sport with the crudest of tackle. Perhaps once a week a barge would pass through, a great event, drawing all the passersby to watch it. And Robert and Samuel had watched the lock-keeper then at his work, and many other times had talked with him, and drunk with him. But if by day the canal was a wonderful place, at night, when everything about it turned grey and silver and black under the moon, it was unsurpassed in loveliness. End of setpiece.

*Purpose of nocturnal perambulation:* to take advantage of the romantic nature of the canalbank to persuade Miss Deane to forget her religious scruples for an hour or two.

*Machinations felt appropriate:* Samuel carefully selected an act (sometimes called, by others, a *line* or *ploy*), from amongst his considerable repertoire of acts, built up by hard experience in amatory warfare.

*Act chosen:* Number 7, Mark III, the Celtic Variant (the Whyshouldn'twesincehereweathrowntogetherpassing shipsinthisCeltictwilightoflife?)

*Number of times act employed hitherto:* 47.

*Percentage successes:*

   (a) against all females: 21·42%.

   (b) against females of the Miss Deane type: 67·91%.

*Site chosen for staging of act:* a canalside bench, of the wooden variety, two reinforced concrete ends, providing comfort of minimal quality; specially designed to discourage lengthy periods of residence.

    Miss Deane said:   No, that won't do at all!
    Samuel said:       But, Miss Deane, I. . . .
    Miss Deane said:   No!

*Reaction of Samuel:* discouragement; regrouping of forces; quick reassessment of campaign, current act abandoned as a failure, new act quickly chosen.
*New act:* Number 2, Mark IV, suitable for all Nationalities (The Sweepheroffherfeetwithpassionateembracessothat shecan'tthinkquicklyenoughtosayNoagain.)
*Number of times act employed hitherto:* 113.
*Percentage successes:*
    (a) against all females: 28·35%.
    (b) against females of the Miss Deane type: 41·02%.
*Note on act Number 2 Mark IV:* a very crude act, mainly employed by Samuel in his early youth; the fact that he felt compelled to resort to it on this occasion is remarkable evidence in support of those who maintain, with some justification, it must be said, that Dublin and Guinness had had an unsettling but rejuvenating effect upon Samuel, and that his character had taken a most unexpected turn for the better, or for the worse, depending which way you looked at it.
*Site chosen for act:* the area of concrete aggregate immediately in front of the seat.
*Reaction of Miss Deane to act:* alarm; initial surrender; rapid rallying; freeing her left arm, Miss Deane pushed Samuel away with it; thus freeing her right arm, she struck Samuel hard on the side of the head.
*Nature of blow:* solid.
*Emotion felt by Miss Deane during blow:* anger.
*Consequence of blow:* Samuel half fell off the bench, lost his orientation, and sat down heavily on the canal bank with one foot in the water.
*Reaction of Samuel:* surprise; followed by prompt withdrawal of foot from canal; admiration.
*Sounds in Samuel's head:* rings and buzzes.
*Tableau:* Samuel sitting still; quietly dripping.

106

Samuel said :       And that was all the farewell when
                                I parted from my dear.
*Literary source of last sentence:* A. E. Housman, poet,
scholar, shaver.
    Samuel said :       And so farewell, Miss Deane,
                                faithful spinster of this
                                priest-overrun parish.
*Scene of the above statements:* O'Meara's Bar,
Rathmines.
*Description of O'Meara's Bar, Rathmines:*

                                The Stews,
                                Grubles Street,
                                Wicklow,
                                Wicklow.

Dear Sir,
Thank you for your esteemed order of 24th inst., for the
supply of one description of licensed premises, Irish,
situate in lowermiddleclass district of Dublin. We have
great pleasure in submitting the following which we
trust will meet with your every requirement :
    Brick-built premises ; on a corner site ; just over fifty
    years old ; outer paintwork red in colour, with gold
    lettering on facia ; all grilles, shutters, etc. necessary
    for the strict observance of the licensing laws
    constructed of steel, and in a rigid manner ; an added
    attraction are the genuine bullet holes in the
    woodwork behind the counter, a proof of the part the
    premises played in the Troubles ; complete with not
    more than three barmen, of whom at least one will be
    certified to be a "character" ; steady clientele, no
    tourists ; accommodating local Gardai ; unusual
    offices ; silver-topped pump handles ; grocery trade
    section well supported ; own stout bottling equipment
    (crown cork) ; thirty-one partially worn barstools ;
    eighteen glass-topped tables with appropriate sets of
    chairs ; the whole a very desirable property from a
    literary point of view.
We look forward to receiving your favoured remittance
within the next few days. Assuring you of our best
attention at all times,

We beg to remain,
Your obedient servants,
*Kenny & Knight* (signed)
Fact-finders to Literary Ladies and Gentlemen
Irish Atmosphere Our Speciality.

*Time the farabove statements were made:* just before the Holy Hour.

    Robert said :   Tough. It seems one has to choose between the irresistible and the unresisting.

*Tone of voice employed:* laconic.

*Immediately subsequently:* Samuel turned back to his barbook without replying.

*Title of Samuel's barbook:* THE ASSASSIN, by Llam O'Flaherty.

*New Arrival:* Just at that moment who should come in but Mick the Lock-keeper, on a spell of joint offduty from his two jobs as keeper of the lock and porter of the hotel opposite the lock, seeking to quench his thirst before the drought of the Holy Hour set in.

*Number of fingers on Mick the Lock-keeper's right hand:* three, to which must be added one thumb.

*Digit deficient:* index.

*Cause of deficiency:* a steel hawser of almost too human malevolence.

    Mick the Lock-keeper said : Hallo, Robert and Samuel.

*Tone of greeting :* warm.

*Calefaction of greeting:* 90° C.

    Samuel said :  A small one for Mick.

*Person addressed:* the barman.

    Mick the Lock-keeper said : Thanks. The Powers and the glory. To you, boys.

*Tragic development:* No sooner had Robert and Samuel and Mick the Lock-keeper toasted one another than their conversation was interrupted by the clangorous groan of the steel doorgrille announcing that those citizens who were desirous of obeying the law should leave forthwith.

*Short discussion of Irish licensing laws:*

    Robert said :   I approve of Irish licensing laws : it is

108

good and human and civilised to have
an hour's break in a day's drinking.

Samuel said: Yes: and the Holy Hour is so
conveniently timed that the afternoon
post arrives at the beginning of it and
can usually be dealt with in just the
hour.

Mick the Lock-keeper said: I would be annoyed
about the break if it wasn't everywhere
ignored. Stay on drinking, boys, I'll see
to the barman for you.

Robert said: We are creatures of habit, Mick.

Samuel said: And the post from England arrives in a
few minutes.

Robert said: And we are inveterate letter writers
and readers.

Mick the Lock-keeper said: See you at four then, boys.

Samuel said: On the dot, Mick.

*Position of letterbox:* 4' 7" above the top step.
*Type of letterbox:* long, narrow, scarcely practical; the
short side horizontal; missives despatched therein
incarcerated on verso in rectangular box of wooden
construction.
*Contents of box on day under consideration:*

(i) *For Miss Deane:* a pastoral circular warning her to
make sure that there were adequate facilities for
following her religion in any country to which she
might be thinking of emigrating; an invitation to
avail herself of Curran's Kleenkid Nappy Service;
and a letter confirming her week's booking at an
Irish Holiday Camp in a month's time.

(ii) *For Robert:* a slightly obscene personal letter from
Peewee Placent, a college friend; two letters from
rival cornchandlers, touting; and a letter from his
mother, promising to send him a food parcel the
next day.

(iii) *For Samuel:* a final demand from a library for a

109

book borrowed some six months previously; a passionate letter from a late lover, saying she had made a mistake and asking if Samuel would forgive her; a badly-taken suggestion that his Life could be Transformed through reading the Rosicrucian pamphlet ETERNAL TRUTHS FROM ANCIENT LANDS.

*Magnanimous gesture:* the reader is offered a choice of endings to the piece.
*Group One: The Religious.* (a) The quickest conversion since St. Paul precipitates Samuel into the joint bosoms of Miss Deane and Mother Church. (b) A more thorough conversion throws Samuel to the Jesuits. (c) A personally delivered thunderbolt reduces Samuel to a small but constituent quantity of impure chemicals.
*Group Two: The Mundane.* (a) Samuel rapes Miss Deane in a state of unwonted elation. (b) Miss Deane rapes Samuel in a state of unwonted absentmindedness. (c) Robert rapes both of them in a state of unwonted aplomb (whatever that may mean).
*Group three: The Impossible.* The next post contains an urgent recall to England for (a) Samuel (b) Robert (c) both; on account of (i) death (ii) birth (iii) love (iv) work.

Thank you.

# These Count as Fictions

Curly hairs are to be found embedded in the soap every
morning. I could of course buy my own soap and keep
it safely hairless in my room when I am not washing:
but the terms of my sub-tenancy are such that Linen
shall be provided and (as under similar agreements I
have heretofore entered into) the description Linen
inaccurately but legally includes soap. So why should I
provide my own? But this is the reason my lodging is
less than satisfactory: every morning there is at least
one curly hair fully or partly embedded in the green
soap. I do not know whether this depilation has taken
place to the undoubted loss of a female or of a male. It
may be that there is an immutable natural law that
male curly hair circles to the left, or anticlockwise, and
female hair *vice versa*. Or the former clockwise, and the
latter *vice versa*. If I knew this law, I could perhaps
apply it after careful scrutiny to ascertain which end
might have the bulb of what appears to be fat which
often adheres to the root of an unseated hair. But I do
not know the law even if it exists (which seems
unlikely) and I am not really interested in whether these
hairs have been misplaced by a male or a female
fellow-lodger. Nor would I be prepared to peer closely
enough at them at that hour in the morning, when I am
often near to disgust. I scrub at them with the nailbrush,
but usually this only embeds them even farther.

Every other Friday now I go down to the richer quarter
of the city, to the home of a man who gives me money.
He pays me for opening his letters, making a decision
as to whether or not certain matters in them will interest
him, and replying accordingly. He does not give me

money regularly: perhaps once every six months enough to keep me for about a month. He may soon stop doing so altogether. Every time I go I think that he may dismiss me this time; or the time after. But I am used to thinking like that. I ensure that my other occupations give me the same feeling. In this insecurity lies my security. If I knew that in a year's time I would be doing a particular thing, then I would probably suffer some kind of neurosis. At least, that is how I feel about it. I am healthy now, in my not knowing. I am very careful about such things.

He trusts my judgment, this man whose letters I open. I do not know why, but it is very pleasing that he trusts me and it makes me feel I am earning my money, however irregularly it comes. And the irregularity does not matter, for I feel I have successfully lived so far and there is just as much chance of future success: I usually have enough money for tonight and tomorrow, the rent is paid in advance, and it is therefore convenient to regard what he owes me as saving, even as investment. For he is so very good with money. He sits in a graceful chair of skilfully-wrought japanned ironwork, and strokes the Burmese cat which neatly occupies the full area of the catmat on his lap. This slight, ashgrey cat is most uncatlike in that it will without provocation attack me. Why me, I ask myself, I am not a stranger after coming to this house so many times: if it has a memory it must recognise me as the short man in old clothes who comes to open letters for its master. It is possible that cats are incapable of the concepts of shortness and age, however. Certainly the cat attacks me without my doing anything to provoke it, and I conclude it does so because of personal distaste for my presence: which is reasonable enough. I have learnt not to let a free hand dangle casually by my chair as I consider my decisions on the contents of the letters, for if I do the cat will suddenly spring and savage it quite severely. Twice this has happened, and the wounds required dressing almost until I came

114

here the next time. The motives of the cat do not interest me. The eduction and study of motives in general I find largely without point: events, attitudes, feelings, states of mind are what I am concerned with, and not with the forces which may prompt them. Given motives are too often guesses, and I have better uses for my imagination. Rarely do I ask myself Why? anything: if I do, the question is almost always rhetorical. I just keep my hands out of the way of the cat.

This man whose letters I open. Recently some crisis in his business affairs abroad resulted in far more foreign mail being sent to this address. He asked me to undertake the extra work. I was glad to do so, for I thought it would mean some little extra money. He did not say it would. It is seven visits since the crisis, now once a fortnight instead of once every three weeks before it, and fifteen since he last paid me: so I do not yet know how much, if any, more money I shall receive. Neither do I know of course when it will come. But it has never failed to come yet. The extra work at first made me feel that he could now manage less well without me than before, but recently I have begun to feel that he may well decide that there is so much work that it justifies employing someone who would be able to come more frequently than he might think I could. Rightly or wrongly, I see I preserve my insecurity. It is the better way.

The worst part of this job is sealing the envelopes which the senders enclose for notification of my decision. I have been brought up to regard the putrescent taste of fishbone glue as in some way a penance, but now that used on foreign envelopes causes a certain uneasiness, guilt almost, in me. Vanilla and Mint (both pepper- and spear-) are the commonest flavours to be tasted but there are others which are both less definable and even less welcome. My employer, I think, has no idea that I am inconvenienced

115

by these flavours; at least, there is no sign that he might provide a machine (a simple watercontainer with a roller in it, for instance) to alleviate my discomfort. I shall not ask him for such a machine. Before coming here I invariably buy a small packet of paregoric cough sweets to suck while I am working.

Generally by the middle of the afternoon I have dealt with all the mail which has accumulated during the previous thirteen days. I am then free to leave. The man has never yet failed to smile as I go in appreciation of what I have done for him. I leave by the side door of his house, turn left, and walk down a slope towards the sea: watching my footing, for the pavements here I have more than once found to be treacherous. The richer quarter of this city lies near the sea, and on these fortnightly occasions I permit myself as if to wander along the municipal promenade, surveying the overstocked flowerbeds. I do not look at the sea: it makes me apprehensive. I have constantly to adjust my gaze to the left or to the ground in order that I may not have sight of the sea. Even the quays, the sight of which would fill me with quiet pleasure in the old days, I now cannot bear. Instead, I occupy my mind with statements the truth of which interests me, such as *Form follows function,* or it might be on another occasion *Everything is merely or exactly the absence of its opposite.* Or sometimes I will tell myself *You can't have it all ways: at least at once.*

Keeping my eyes to the ground occasionally has unlooked-for advantages: once I saw a great arrow in yellow chalk on the pavement and the words TO THE MAD LADY. It was for my embellishment I felt this mark had been made, a skeleton for me to flesh, and what I loosely term my mind was not content until I had searched through my pockets and found the small piece of (coincidentally) yellow chalk I had put there (sentimentally) on my last day as a teacher and had added to the original arrow enough others to make the

116

design into a circle, a fistful, of arrows, pointing as near as the limitations of the medium would permit to all three hundred and sixty degrees of direction. If I had not grown bored I would have found some means of further extending this comment into a third dimension. But I left it there. I felt that, symbolically at least, I had done more than enough to make my point.

Such things serve to keep my mind off the sea (it is the punishment once favoured by certain islanders that has estranged me from it: placing the condemned at low tide on a rock which is covered at high tide) at least until I reach the café on the edge of the brothel quarter which is my immediate destination. I have several times remarked in other cities that the richer quarter borders upon the brothel quarter, but have avoided the obvious conclusion since on further thought I have failed to think of some other quarters which I could consider metaphorically wholesome. The insufferable suburbs and the mediocre classes. But I think I have put all that behind me now.

The café that I regularly choose to visit every other Friday is only just in the brothel quarter, being on the appropriate side of the street forming the dividing line. But it is an important difference. Here, in any case, I sit and drink (coffee) and read. I read all the morning newspapers at this time, between about four and perhaps eight. I feel I must keep up. Often when I have finished I think I have wasted my time, but on those few occasions when I have not read all the papers I have felt guilty and deprived, and more than once indeed I have missed something, have not kept up, have fallen behind. As I sit and drink my coffee and eat whatever I have ordered, therefore, I swiftly but thoroughly absorb what the morning newspapers have to offer me. In the case of most of them, this produces in me very little except dismay at the poor quality of the writing: the sports pages in particular are of a depressingly low standard. But there are three

papers which do aim higher in most things: the
deplorable right-wing one, the soft left-wing one,
and the austere establishment one. It is in the letter
columns of these three that I find the matter which
interests me most keenly: the addresses of the famous.
The establishment newspaper is the most prolific source
of addresses, for many more famous people write
letters to its editor. This might be called a hobby with
me. I put a big crayon ring round the addresses of
those people of whom I have heard, or whose titles
seem to mean something, and, when I have finished,
tear out the three pages from these newspapers and
place them in an inner pocket where they are less
likely to be stolen later in the evening. On returning
home, against the famous names listed alphabetically I
write the addresses in my card-index. It passes the
time.

I have found a brothel which does not displease me. It
is some time now since it was revealed to me that
the cant name for the female genitalia was in fact a
tetragrammaton: and the frequency of my visits to the
man and his cat accords well with my fortnightly need
to worship. I make my way to this sacrarium at about
eight, when the first rush of workers on their way home
has been exhausted and the later influx of drunken
incapables has not yet begun.

The main foyer or salon or waiting room is very
interestingly decorated. It was this decoration indeed
which led me to return for a second visit rather than
the quality of the vestals. It is as though the designer
had set himself in one room the problem of employing
logically, organically and harmoniously all the
techniques of decoration that were available to him.
Thus the walls and ceiling bear patterns carried out in
mosaics, carved and painted wood, moulded and
painted plaster, pieces of mirror (besides large mirrors
in each bay) ceramic tiles in multicoloured repeating
designs, painting (both realistic and *trompe l'oeil*),

118

gilding, fresco work, and probably others for which I do not know the technical names. The Madame has tastefully chosen furnishings which do not detract from its remarkable effect: a plain deep red carpet, gold velvet-covered sofas and chairs, and an ornate chandelier. Perhaps the furnishings too were chosen by the designer: certainly the harmony of the room is such that it is as if only one person had made the decisions.

Until recently I had for many years avoided going with the same girl more than once. I had found that if I became a regular I tended to become a favourite. This did not flatter me, and I found that the next stage was invariably their confiding in me. I developed a way of dealing with such confidences: I would drag my shirt up under my armpits and show them the scar extending from my lower ribs up to the right infra-spinatus. It shuts them up, my scar. Afterwards I would usually leave a larger tip, as a solatium, but I would not go with such again.

However, in this house (chiefly because of its architectural delights) I have broken my rule. When I had gone through all the girls once and had been magisterially refused by the Madame (who nevertheless remains friendly), I found I did not break the habit of coming here after my day with the man and his cat. And since my soul could not stomach the expense of coming here just to admire the architecture, I took the first girl again: and was surprised to find that I did not remember exactly what she was like, how I had first graded her performance: as I can remember from early years the gradings of others. But that was perhaps because I had had them so often, a dozen times each, at least, the enthusiastic amateurs, the true loves: in one case several hundred times, over a period of was it fifteen months.

My coming into this house on alternate Fridays

automatically reserves the girl next in the cycle, a
personal note of which is kept by Madame herself.
While I wait in the salon, am a forecast element in its
designer's situation, am exposed to his eccentricity
(too little allowance is made for the undoubted effect
of architecture upon people, of environment upon action
or inaction), I listen to the piano-playing of the man the
girls here call Jelly Roll. He plays an accurate imitation
of Jelly Roll Morton's style, goes like the clappers at
*Fingerbuster*, often on the breaks rises from his rotating
velvet stool and saws at his crotch with his free hand,
bass or treble, whichever one the break disengages,
for some relief, apparent in his posture afterwards if not
in his expression. I have talked with him. He is buried
in the past, his whole life is less than satisfactory
because he was not born a creole in New Orleans in
about 1880, where he might have been employed (as
JRM was) playing in a whorehouse: practising all day,
and playing all night. This brothel is the nearest he can
come to it. I do not understand why he goes on earning
a living in this manner. But there, I do not understand
anyone else's job: they all make me feel dread if I
think about them. There are some things which would
be impossible for me.

Madame herself calls me or catches my eye when the
girl for this particular evening is free, and has cleaned
and prepared herself especially for me. Perhaps I flatter
myself. It does not matter.

Unexpectedly, then, I am content with this cycle of girls
in which I find myself set. They have had careful
instructions not to confide in me ever since I mentioned
my scar to Madame one day. It was not necessary to
show it to her. She is an imaginative woman. Even
that the order was arbitrarily fixed by my fancy on the
first nine occasions of my visiting the house does not
upset me. I can see revolutions of this cycle extending
indefinitely, or at least until they decide I must be sent
to another city. I do not find it in the least unpleasant.

120

If worship is obligatory, then this is as agreeable a way as I have yet discovered. While my memory is such that I know which girl I shall be having on any particular alternate Friday, I am not yet satiated enough to recall exactly which particular kind of pleasure or chance of pleasure may that evening be mine. With some girls I do associate certain things, but they seem always to be incidental to the main business: with one, for instance, the smell of something very like, I imagine, that medieval perfume which was compounded of equal parts of camphor and powdered mummy; with another, the miniature silver corncob worn on a chain round the neck. And there are always unknowns: the influence of the moon (regularly irregular), less predictable illnesses or indispositions, and twice since I have been coming here the sudden and unexplained replacement of a girl. This is ample variety for me. Am I becoming senescent?

It is usually ten before I leave, what with one thing and the other, and I usually have a considerable appetite for nourishment by that time. I go to a restaurant near the mercantile quarter but well back from the seafront, out of sight of the dark sea, where music is provided by a lady who plays the saw. The player is a thin woman of about fifty, straightwaisted as though wearing the apparatus necessitated by a colotomy, and she sits well forward on her chair to grip the handle of the saw between her thighs. With her left thumb at one hundred and eighty degrees to her fingers on the other end she bends the saw into a graceful double curve the radii of which she alters to produce different notes. She strokes the back of the saw, opposite the teeth, with a violin bow from which a number of severed horsehairs hang. The saw is a large one, but it is impossible from my table to discern the name of the maker which I assume to be engraved on its face: I can see, however, that the saw has a non-standard wooden guard which covers those teeth which would otherwise be in contact with her thighs. She achieves a continuous tremolo by

**121**

means of a rhythmic movement of the right leg; the whole performance of a hackneyed repertoire done with great style, to an audience of honest munching trenchermen.

On my way home I pass late shops, the assistants looking weary, bored, mutinous. I do not know how they can work in such places, again, I cannot understand how people do such jobs. I could not do them. Even the thought of others doing them makes me feel unwell.

Tomorrow it is painting drumskins, delineating battle honours on regimental drums. This regiment has not fought for the last twenty years, so I have only to copy the coat of arms or other representational emblem of those two outposts where it has been stationed. These I can find in the library in the morning, and I should complete the pair of kettledrums by late evening.

I have built up my bed on crates and blocks (which also make convenient steps) so that it is within two feet of the ceiling, after I had seen convincing evidence that hot air rises. It can be cold at nights in this city.

I still make religious observances, but in bed now. My half-brother (we had a mother in common, at least) and I went to the same Sunday school. He learnt the Catechism. I learnt the Table of Kindred and Affinity. I was far more interested (you never know with my relatives) in the disclosures that a man may not marry his Mother; Daughter; Father's mother; Mother's mother; Son's daughter; Daughter's daughter; Sister; Father's daughter; Mother's daughter; Wife's mother; Wife's daughter; Father's wife; Son's wife; Father's father's wife; Mother's father's wife; Wife's father's mother; Wife's mother's mother; Wife's son's daughter; Wife's daughter's daughter; Son's son's wife; Daughter's son's wife; Father's sister; Mother's sister; Brother's

122

daughter; and his Sister's daughter. And even more taken by the ordinance that a woman might not marry her Father; Son; Father's father; Mother's father; Son's son; Daughter's son; Brother; Father's son; Mother's son; Husband's father; Husband's son; Mother's husband; Daughter's husband; Father's mother's husband; Mother's mother's husband; Husband's father's father; Husband's mother's father; Husband's son's son; Husband's daughter's son; Son's daughter's husband; Daughter's daughter's husband; Father's brother; Mother's brother; Brother's son; and her Sister's son.

I think one of my fellow-lodgers must have access to my writings. Tonight I found pushed under my door a copy of the *XLCR Mechanical Plot-Finding Formula*. Perhaps it is he or she whose curly hairs are to be found embedded in the green soap every morning.

# Everyone Knows Somebody Who's Dead

So you like the title? That is the first thing, they say
here, the *Title.*

*Conflict,* they say, as well. I should engage my reader
in a *Conflict.*

That is easy. What I have in mind is the conflict between
understanding and what does not appear to be
understandable. Few subjects could be more interesting.
Surely you must see that? I trust you, not knowing
you.

It is also the partialness in the *Soul* (not a word I have
ever used before, I think) *of Conflict* that concerns
me here.

There is *Resolution* at the end, I see, skipping ahead.
Be calm. I have written before. Trust me, not knowing
me.

This is the difference between doing it and teaching it.
Perhaps. Who am I to presume? I am (like you)
everyone to presume, there is no one else.

*Conflict,* it says here. *Of three kinds, viz.: within the
self; without the self, with other humans; without the
self, with non-human forces.* Gross simplification,
but what else is there?

One conflict is within me, certainly. Many, rather. But
what I have to write of is not a conflict within him:
indeed it is rather of that moment of perfect non-conflict,

127

in the end, of unity, unison, when his self was absolutely at one with his non-self, when the will and the act itself were in accord, at peace, were the same.

One should also start at the *Beginning*, it says here. That I could have done, easily.

I first met him at the evening college of London University, Birkbeck College. We must have sat next to one another at some lecture or another. English and Latin were what we had in common, History and I think Economics were points of divergence. Everyone had to do Latin. He was tall, angular is unfortunately the only word, smart: I was none of these. He introduced me to the *New Statesman* and his fiancée, a dumpy, curly blonde quite unlike him in almost everything, unsuited, I thought. Or perhaps think now, with hindsight. I introduced him to me, I was all I had. We joined the college rowing club together, Saturday afternoons for that Spring we would imagine the exercise did us good. I may still have a key to their locker half a generation later, they may still have in it my heavy white wool sweater. He worked in an office quite near mine, both in Kingsway. Occasionally we would meet for lunch, too. Shell was his company, Standard-Vacuum mine, oil was another thing we had coincidentally in common. His job I cannot remember, mine is . . . *Irrelevant.*

*A Plot is. . . .*

There were other things. Bengs and Joyce were also friends, at this time. We each passed our examinations. He and I went separate ways, then. We left Birkbeck, the evening lectures and steady jobs, both managed to become possessed of grants to go full-time to different colleges, though still of London University. I chose mine because I thought well of the name, he his because he admired the staff. We were both five years mature. The Registrar warned me, objecting to my full-time

128

going, that I at twenty-three would be amongst a lot of eighteen-year-old girls. That is probably also amongst the things which are not relevant.

*. . . a Conflictful Situation. . . .*

There was a party for Birkbeck friends, he and I met the curls at the Albert Hall (built as a rendezvous), the rain was heavy in a way not common in July. Probably that summer too I went once and never again to the family home, Churchill Gardens, tall flats aligned north and south so that the sun set garishly on the supper table. The conversation centred, so I remember, Bengs was there, on the way the place was warmed by surplus heat generated across the river at mighty Battersea power station, piped presumably. They were very early postwar reconstruction or development.

*. . . Exacerbated by Additional Circumstances of Increasing Difficulty. . . .*

He bought an identifying scarf for his new college. I obtusely wanted nothing of such symbols, it was more than enough that I was admitted. Though they looked warm, and the winter might be coming.

That summer also I was best man at his wedding to the unlikely curls. I was brought in late, a kind of locum, second best man. I do not know why the first choice man was not available. I did wonder then and later that he should have so few friends that I, little more than an acquaintance, and recent, too, should be honoured. But that is speculation. I am allowed a little speculation?

*. . . Proceeding to one or more Abortive Efforts to overcome the Situation.*

The marriage was at a church overlooking Brighton. The spire was said to be a blessing to mariners, as well.

E                                                    129

It was a modern church. I produced the ring without
any of the mishaps celebrated in tradition. Afterwards
in the vestry, is it called, I paid the gentleman vicar.
He kept what the other functionaries were owed and
pressed back on me his own share, saying, It is
something I do for young couples, I love weddings,
you see. You see.

At the reception I stole an epigram from Oscar Wilde,
something about a spade. My punishment was that it
fell flatter than a discus. And they probably thought I was
bent, too, all those relatives, to boot. This occasion
represents my only appearance as a best man. At
another wedding, where the best man's name was Fat
Gerald, the bride's father asked me to make a speech
because I was a writer and writers were good at
speeches. But one of the reasons I am a writer is
because I am no giver of speeches at weddings or
anywhere else, I explained to him. I do not think he
understood, he remained disappointed.

You would not be forgiven for thinking my life one long
round of weddings, the like.

The first (or Oscar) wedding reception was at a hotel
on the front. Very pleasurable, being at the seaside
with something proper to do, with a purpose, and with
friends, like Bengs, in this case. But the epigram, and
reading the telegrams, too, were almost distressing.
And so was the bill. My duties as best (available) man
it seems, included paying for the reception. Not out of
my own money, the father of the bride footed. I cast
the bill carefully and quickly, being at that time more
an accounts clerk than a student. It seemed the least I
could do following the pagan flatness of my speech.
Mine was nothing approximate to the maître's total,
differing by some fourteen pounds if I remember as
accurately as I cast. A considerable sum, even more
considerable (as ever) then. The difference was in the
favour of the maître, no surprise, or of those who

employed him. His apologies were certainly profuse, though practised and just not concealing a challenge to my sharpness. The bride's father was noticeably grateful to me. The maître must have hoped we were all too drunk by then. Perhaps more often than not that is the usual state at the end of these functions. I hardly remember the bride and groom during this wedding : only her on the church path after, him in the church as we awaited the delegation. Perhaps that is as it should have been.

*Abortive* is shortly a good word in context.

Three years for our respective degrees, ha, and we hardly saw each other. One occasion though I remember with some clearness : a Fireworks Day, one of three, by deduction. A dinner or supper with him and the curls, me and my moll, what a metonym. The streets, afterwards, of Pimlico—("Have at thee, then, my merrie boyes and hey for old Ben Pimlicos nut browne"—as it occurs first written down in News from Hogsdon, 1598. But no doubt they would frown on such a scholium as having no place.). There were fireworks in the streets, we threw them, a bonfire on a bombsite, St. George's something the road was called, in Pimlico, where one may be catered for but hardly satisfied.

Then when we had both just finished we met in the coffee bar in Malet Street next to Dillons, on purpose. We were able to tell each other what we had done in between. The marriage was just become or becoming a divorce. My moll had cast me off in favour of a sterile epileptic of variable temperament. But yes ! Now I remember exactly, ha ! We had not just finished, but were finishing, finals. One of the days we met in the Rooms, I feel they called them, arranged to meet afterwards downstairs. And thence to the coffee bar. On our way, talking at a junction, waiting, just before Euston Road, to the south, I could look it up, gazetteers are to hand, but why should I ? Am I not allowed to be

131

lazy too? Or reckless? But as we stood talking at this
junction, she who was once my moll appeared in the
long distance, walked the long way towards us, crossed
the other wide diagonal, went the long way away.
And all that while I tried to talk as though I were
unaware of her, of all that she had meant to me, of all
those things I have exorcised elsewhere. Ah.

After the coffee we made an evening of it, did the thing
most opposite to degree finals we could think of at
such notice: front row of the royal circle at the Victoria
Palace. The Crazy Gang were then tailing off, we could
have sat anywhere, at any price, they would have had
us. No doubt there were other funny things, we were
raucous with relief, but now I remember only a game
they played with a fat lady, throwing old pennies so
they landed flatly on her bare mottled old chest, briefly,
then dropped into her cleavage. There were things like
that, then. No doubt we also caught up then, though
since I was without any direction, where was he?

Robin (now I have to name him) had taken up
with a student, a girl in the year below him (before,
during or after the divorce was unclear), a Swiss who
was having an affair also with a much older man with
money, and all that went with it, a car. The curls, he
told me, had had an abortion, arranged with confounding
liberality (for this was in what was thought of as the
heyday of the backstreet abortionist) by his tutor, to
whom he had gone for help in this matter. The marriage
was virtually broken, after less than a year, and
satisfaction at having foreseen their short incompatibility
was not absent from my remarks at the death on this
occasion. But I could not have acted otherwise, in
marrying her, I am sure, emotionally, he insisted. But
there had been hints, heard over the telephone not long
before Finals, that they had parted. I was put off, easily,
working all that afternoon by indecision as to ringing
her and attempting to take sexual advantage of the
state she might or might not have been in. I did not

132

know about the heyday then, and after all I had been more or less best man.

It occurs to me now because of this and other things that I could not and cannot call myself his friend. Was he capable of friendship? I do not think so. Am I? It was more a working relationship, he was like a colleague though we had no common enterprise or ambition beyond both being working-class boys bent on an education, the illusion that that was the key to—

*Extension is always achieved by the Insertion of one or more Abortive Efforts.*

There was another occasion. Bengs and I went to a Wandsworth hill road, in the curls' time. Of more I have no recollection.

Their *Comprehensive Scheme* should deal with this *Common Problem.* But it does not.

It was another flat in which I remember him next, as it may be, in Old Brompton Road, the corner of Drayton Gardens, near the powerhouse of the literary trade union movement. Though I was then of course unaware of its militancy. And now I am quaintly aware of one of those loops in time where. . . . but you do not need me to explain that cliché of the twenties. What has happened is more important, of certain interest to me, and what has happened is that I have remembered that the girl I took to this Old Brompton Road flat Robin had was in fact the very same girl whose marriage I attended all those years later and whose father I disappointed! This can be no coincidence: a real loop in time has happened. I think I did not want to marry her myself. I was at that time between girls I wanted to marry. But it is a curious loop, though I have not wanted for more curious. And while describing it the one thing I remember is that we four (the Swiss being there too) discussed a topical tragedy in the world of politics,

Sharpeville. The reason I remember what he said is that he was shortly proved to be right: in that the Sharpeville massacre, far from being the spark which would ignite a conflagration to consume the old repressive system, was on the contrary more likely to be the flame which would harden into steel the iron resolve of the oppressors. I do not know that his imagery was as elegantly contrived as mine is, but he had written an unpublished article about the incident, for (I think) a serious weekly. But he was remarkably right! I am myself never right for anyone else but me, and not too often do I achieve that small victory. How many times have you yourself been right for other people, then? Ah.

He was at this time teaching at some South London secondary school, his writing was towards another job. If ever you want to make a lot of money, he told me, open a sweetshop next to a school, the kids are in and out all day long. As we left I told the Swiss privately I thought that what he had read to us of his writing had . . . saleability! As though I knew, it was mere politeness!

*The Solution Stage. . . .*

Perhaps it was this perceptive rightness which led him inevitably to a post on the *Evening Standard* at the City Desk.

> *. . . involves the character in either (a) overcoming his problems . . .*

How full everyone's life is! Why, I hardly knew him and here I am well past two thousand words already!

> *. . . or (b) succumbing to them.*

Later in this stage they visited me. I cannot avoid the

134

thought that he was showing me that he had arrived in the world of affairs before I had. That is, he had a car and after eating curry out he bought a whole bottle of whisky to take back to the flat I had then. I think he even told me how much he was earning; it seemed at that time I was managing adequately on about a quarter of his salary. I think he wanted not only to show me he was doing well but that his way of doing well was better than mine. My way then was simply to try to write as well as those exemplars from the past I had chosen to set up whilst at college. Neither did it escape my notice that he was ahead in the matter of a mistress, too, and a glamorous foreigner at that. All I had to show was a bound set of page-proofs of my first novel: high hopes as I had of it, I do not remember it as being sufficient to set against the car, the whisky, and the Swiss mistress.

What other news from Hoxton?

A finished copy before publication I took around to dinner at their flat, still in Pimlico, some (presumably short) while later. I do not remember what Robin said about the book on this occasion: at some time previously he had expressed great scepticism about what it was trying to do. He was right if the amount of money garnered was his criterion. Perhaps it was; or was not. Present was a very pleasant, charming and witty man of about our age called Charles, who was by way of being a printer and an actor, though not necessarily in that order. I think Robin had meanwhile made a daring leap from the *Standard* to a young, vital organ which was highly relevant and called *Topic*. Robin became either its business manager or writer on business affairs, business editor: I think the latter. Much talk of a world I did not know, very high-powered, men who were coming or all the go at the time, have since gone even further, some of them, his colleagues in print.

Have I finished with the *Abortive Effort(s)* yet?

I have recently become aware that an uncomfortable number of my contemporaries are dying before what I had imagined to be their times, simply jacking it all in, for one reason or another.

There was another, hardly remembered. The landlady of a friend with the same forename as myself. Her daughter came up to attend to the disposition of the remains and remnants. She was married to a naval officer, the daughter. My friend made (he convinced me) steamy love with her, unexpectedly, in some sort of consolatory reaction to the mother's death. She had drunk a bottle of gin and sealed the drawing-room cracks and turned the gas on. Probably for her a comfortable, euphoric occasion, making herself comfy: I imagine her not desperate. The day after, the daughter and my friend were alone in the house, the naval officer as if nowhere. She had to stay the night, it was only nature, my friend was sure. My friend was also a colleague at work in a sweet factory, and he was remarkable amongst my acquaintance in that each morning after an evening on the beer he would wake up to find the plimsols he used as slippers seeping with urine. It could clearly be no one else's but his own, though at the same time he could never remember having risen in the night to perform. He would relate each occasion to me, baffled, whenever we . . . but I digress, and the *XLCR Plotfinder* leaves me unclear as to whether digressions are permitted.

Oh, I look forward to my own deathbed scene: the thing I shall have to say which I could not say before!

The *Topic* job was a great success but the magazine collapsed, ahead of its time in some respects, I seem to remember. Robin went (though there may have been a hiatus) back to the *Standard* as full-blown City Editor. We were proud of him, Bengs and I, and others, too.

136

I meant to tear it out, I was in a foreign country, I never did.

My wife and I, newly married, visited Robin and the Swiss girl, Vivienne, something like as newly-married, now, I think, at their new small house in Maida Vale, very demure, bijou. We had a meal, supper or dinner as usual. He showed me the room that he intended to fill with his files. A comprehensive filing system, he informed me, was a major factor in the success of any journalist: one simply collected facts together from many sources, filed them under subjects, and regurgitated them in new combinations as one's own articles.

Soon we must arrive at the *Resolution* or *Point of Solution*. . . .

Not long afterwards we took him up on the offer of the gift of a large wardrobe he had made himself from battens and hardboard, collected it in the old navyblue banger of a van which was the first fourwheeled vehicle I had ever owned. He described how the wardrobe was the first thing he had made for the home in the palmy days of the curls, how it was constructed over-elaborately and uneconomically due to his lack of craftsmanlike experience. He had, unexpectedly and soon, an opportunity to demonstrate its methods of construction since it became stuck on the third flight of stairs up to our second-floor flat and we had to take it to pieces there to move it any higher. They had decently followed us in their car, a bigger car, and helped us carry the wardrobe. But there we were, unsocially stuck, we above having access to our flat, they below; it was hardly possible to pass even refreshments between. I have taken it to pieces myself since then, on moving out five years later. I reassembled it for lodgers, and then on another advent I had it in bits again, roughly, crudely, with the children. It had served us well, I burnt it in the yard. Except for one piece I shall keep, have before me for this piece, having cut a foot specially with his writing on it, in pencil, curious things that confirm how he said he made it: OSSPIECE, it says, cut off by the removal necessary for a tee-halving joint, TOP BACK. Yes, the point is in. SCREW TOP ONTO X1 PIECE. IT WILL HAVE TO BE SHORTENED BY TWICE THE WIDTH OF THIS. What writing! It was always rickety, was unsightly from the first, too, we accepted it only because we had no money for a proper one.

> ... *which can admit of a Surprise Ending.*

Mostly professional things. They must have visited us in that flat when we had straightened it; I was very careful about reciprocating hospitality in those days. We learnt at one point he had been demoted to Assistant through the return of a former City Editor, a star; this was an uncomfortable arrangement but we understood he accepted it. Not so very much later he was promoted again when the star ascended ever higher. One anecdote he told us concerned travelling in a taxi with the super star and Vivienne: a carefree cyclist overtook them, dodging in and out, glorying in his mobility amongst the impacted cars in Regent Street, until some minutes later near the Vigo Street junction he was involved in a jam of his own causing which he was unable to avoid since his brain was now distributed hither and thither.

All that time, and the only exact words of his I remember are some of those spoken in the Malet Street coffee bar on that one occasion: "Life is a series of clichés, each more banal than the last."

I certainly do not feel up to inventing dialogue for your sake, going into oratio recta and all that would mean. These reconstructed things can never be managed exactly right, anyway. I suppose I could curry a dialogue in which Robin and I argued the rights and wrongs of his *Conflictful Situation*, but it would be only

138

me arguing with myself: which would be even more absurd than trying to write of someone else's life.

The last I think I saw of him was at the home of a smart lawyer to whom I had originally introduced him. I remember feeling resentful that they now knew each other better than I knew either of them. We have diverged, I thought, arrogantly, geometrical progression cannot be unwelcome.

It must have been perhaps two years later that I attended some quiet function and met again the charming Charles. He said he was very relieved to be able to tell me that our mutual friend Robin appeared to have sorted himself out at last, after his trouble. I had not heard of any trouble, I told him apologetically. With genuine sorrow, Charles explained that Robin had become involved with another girl and Vivienne had as a result successfully gassed herself. I was equally genuinely shocked, and guilty, too, that I had not been in touch with him for the period within which this had happened. Then I shared his relief that Robin had recovered to the extent that he was living with another girl: whether this was the same another girl I do not remember Charles telling me. No doubt I could find out by ringing him now and perhaps inviting him round for one of supper, dinner, or a drink.

Patience: we are about to reach the *Solution Point*.

I was for three months in Paris at the time, and nervously keeping in touch by purchasing the airmail edition of *The Times* perhaps every third day. Thus I was again genuinely shocked to read of his death only by a one-in-three chance. I cannot at this stage remember if I read a news story and the obituary, or only the latter. I seem to know that he too employed the good offices of the North Thames Gas Board, but whether this was from the newspaper or later from the splendid Charles, or some other source, I cannot ascertain. I meant to

tear it out, the way one does, and never does. It
cannot happen with North Sea Gas, I am assured. But
certainly I read the obituary, which was without a
photograph, I think. It was not very long. After some
facts, the only opinion expressed as to how he might be
remembered, or had been in any way remarkable,
concerned the way in which he had helped to find
out what was in the minds of businessmen by organising
a luncheon club at which they were invited to meet the
press. There was more than that, but that is all it said,
all there was to say, his life summed up, the obituary,
full point.

There. I have fully satisfied the XLCR rules, I think.
Popular acclaim must surely follow.

# Six Plays

# You're Human Like the Rest of Them

**EDITORS' NOTE**

This stage version of *You're Human Like The Rest of Them* was commissioned by the Royal Shakespeare Company as part of *Expeditions III*, an evening of short experimental plays, in 1964. It was not performed at the time, but Johnson went on to direct a film adaptation, under the auspices of the BFI production board, in 1967. Premiered at the National Film Theatre on 5 May that year, the film starred William Hoyland as Haakon, and won the Grands Prix at both the Tours and Melbourne Short Film Festivals in 1968. The play finally received its stage premiere as part of *B. S. Johnson vs God*, which ran at the Basement Theatre, London, from 18 to 29 January 1971. It was published twice in Johnson's lifetime: in *Transatlantic Review*, 19 (Autumn 1965) and *New English Dramatists 14* (Penguin, 1970). We have followed the second of these versions, which incorporates later revisions by Johnson, such as the insertion of an obscene joke at the expense of long-running radio soap opera *The Archers*. The distinctive punctuation of this decasyllabic verse play, to which we have adhered, includes the insertion of a slash (/) at every line break.

**CHARACTERS**

HAAKON, *a teacher, about thirty*
PHYSIOTHERAPIST, *about forty-five*
TEACHER ONE, *about fifty*
TEACHER TWO, *about forty*
MISS HAMMOND, *gym mistress, big, about thirty*
SEVERAL OLD AND MIDDLE-AGED MEN, *hospital out-patients*
CAPON, ECKERSLEY, *and several other schoolboys*

*Darkness. Then a lantern slide punched up on a screen. It represents
a stooping human male figure, in outline from the right side, with the
spine and spinal nervous system marked in different colours from the
outline. A PHYSIOTHERAPIST stands beside the screen holding a
short pointer, with which she indicates appropriately during her little
lecture, which she has obviously given many times before.*

PHYSIOTHERAPIST:
        Here you see the spine — Your attention please/
        The spine, stretching from the base of the skull/
        To this tail or tail-like extremity/
        The spine is made up of separate parts/
        Vertebrae, we call the parts vertebrae/
        They're made of bone, the vertebrae, bone, bone/
        They move in relation to each other/
        When you bend your back, they move together/
            *(It should now be possible to see that the
            physiotherapist is lecturing to a small group of
            men aged from thirty upwards, dressed in badly-
            fitting dressing gowns and clutching fibre cases.
            They sit on stacking cantilever chairs, less than
            comfortably.)*
PHYSIOTHERAPIST:
        They're kept apart, so they don't rub or grate/
        By a cartilage
PATIENT ONE:       What's that then?
HAAKON:                Gristle/
PHYSIOTHERAPIST:
        Listen and you'll know. Cartilage is like/
        Cotton, strands of cotton, on the outside/

146

Hard, but on the inside it's not, it's soft/
It's gelatinous, gluey, it's all soft/
Now, most people seem to think that the back/
That the spine can bear any weight at all/
It can't. They bend over to pick up — Ouch!/
The spine just wasn't designed to do that/

PATIENT ONE:

How's that then?

HAAKON:                What do you mean, designed?

PATIENT TWO:                         Yes?/

PHYSIOTHERAPIST:

You're all here because you asked for too much/
You all asked your backs to bear too much weight/

PATIENT THREE:

Well, I'm eighty

HAAKON:               It's a good age

PATIENT THREE:            It's not/

It's a bloody awful age

PHYSIOTHERAPIST:       That's enough/

When you put a lot of strain on your back/
Then you may move a cartilage or disc/
You've all heard of a slipped disc, haven't you?/
You see, the spine was never designed to/
Bend over like this. . .

HAAKON:                 Faulty construction!/

PHYSIOTHERAPIST:

The muscles are too weak

PATIENT TWO:             Eh?

PHYSIOTHERAPIST:         They only/

Connect short pieces of bone together/
The correct way to pick something up is/
To bend at the knees and make use of these/
       (*indicates on lantern slide appropriately:*)
Long and very strong muscles in your legs/

HAAKON:

What I want to know is, how is it that/
Since we can obviously do these things/
But our backs can't do them properly?

147

PATIENT TWO:                                    Yes?/
PHYSIOTHERAPIST:
    The fact remains that the spine is just not/
    Designed to
HAAKON:        Who designed it, then?
PATIENT THREE:                          Why not?/
PATIENT TWO:
    Yes, why make it like that?
PHYSIOTHERAPIST:      I don't know why/
PATIENT ONE:
    Yes, why?
HAAKON:      Doctors can't answer 'why' questions/
    Any more than the vicars can
PATIENT THREE:      No
PATIENT ONE:        Why?/
PATIENT TWO
    But who designed it like this then?
PATIENT THREE:      God!
HAAKON:        Yes!/
PATIENT THREE:
    It's God's fault!
PATIENT FOUR:    Another cock-up!
HAAKON:        But whose/
    Fault is it if you don't believe in God?/
PATIENT THREE:
    Yours
PATIENT ONE:
      Your fault
HAAKON:    My fault?
PATIENT THREE:      Yes, your fault, mate, yours!/

*(Blackout)*

*Spot picks out an interior wall, with a flight of plaster ducks —
small, medium, and large — on it. Another spot picks up entry of
HAAKON. He comes in wearily, but then sees ducks, drops to the
floor in a shooting posture, and imitates shotgun firing: three shots*

148

*and a clunk as one duck falls off wall make up first four syllables of*
*first line.*

HAAKON:
　　　Bompf! Bompf! Bompf!
　　　　　　　　　(*Clunk!*)
TEACHER ONE:
　　　　　　　　　　　　Tiresome histrionics/
　　　Haakon, do you have to in the staffroom?/
　　　　　(*Lights up: a school staffroom, with at least three*
　　　　　*teachers: armchairs, tables, noticeboards:*
　　　　　*everything consistent — e.g. piled crockery, cups*
　　　　　*of tea, children's voices in playground off — with*
　　　　　*the end of lunch break.*)
TEACHER TWO:
　　　Three shots from a double-barrelled shotgun?/
HAAKON:
　　　Pedant
TEACHER ONE: And I thought your back was injured?/
MISS HAMMOND:
　　　Yes, how are you?
HAAKON:　　　　　　　　Better. Or perhaps worse/
　　　Depends on how you look at it. I'm nearer/
　　　Yes, nearer at any rate, I'm nearer/
RADIO ANNOUNCER:
　　　'From the Midlands we present the Archers,/
　　　An everyday story of count. . .'
　　　　　(*HAAKON goes over to radio, switches off*
　　　　　*abruptly at exactly this point.*)
HAAKON:　　　　　　　　　Yes, quite/
　　　Just listen to this: at the hospital/
　　　They gave us a little lecture about/
　　　The spine
TEACHER ONE: We'd like to talk about that too/
　　　The spine — or rather about spinelessness/
　　　Is what we hear about you true, Haakon?/
　　　That you were in some bank on Saturday/
　　　When a gunman attempted to rob it?/

149

HAAKON:
>He didn't attempt it — he succeeded/
TEACHER ONE:
>And you stood there and did nothing at all?/
HAAKON:
>What was I sposed to do — get myself killed?/
>Only a few months ago there was this/
>Hero who picked up this adding machine/
>And threw it at a bandit and you know?/
>The next thing the nearest little girl clerk/
>Had half her face blown off by a shotgun/
TEACHER TWO:
>Well, in my day we called that cowardice/
HAAKON:
>Well, today we call it stupidity/
>And look, whose money was it anyway?/
>You just don't think about things hard enough/
>Do you know that the banks made a survey/
>And decided that safety precautions/
>Installing alarms and traps and so on/
>Would cost too much and robberies were cheaper?/
>The amount they lost through theft was far less?/
>Did you know that?
TEACHER TWO:        That's not the point!
HAAKON:                        It is!/
>It's exactly the bloody point, you see/
>You just don't think about things hard enough/
>No, let me tell you about this morning/
>There were all these old men with back trouble/
>And the hospital wasn't any use/
>They just blamed it on to God as usual/
>But that's
MISS HAMMOND: Of course they didn't! That's silly/
HAAKON: Just you shut your little mouth, Miss Hammond/
>I'm trying to say something important/
MISS HAMMOND:
>Just silly
HAAKON:                        I know your sort, Miss Hammond/

150

Your sort draw the line at actual entry/
> (*Exit MISS HAMMOND*)

TEACHER TWO:
> Haakon! Are you not feeling very well?

HAAKON:                                        As well/
> As anyone — that's what I want to say/
> We're all rotting away, slowly rotting/
> And for some it's not even slow, either/
> We just rot, corrode, decay, putrefy/
> And there's nothing we can do about it!/

TEACHER ONE:
> That's childish rot, Haakon, just damned childish!/

HAAKON:
> Because you first realised it as a child/
> Doesn't make it childish equals useless/
> We rot and there's nothing that can stop it/
> Can't you feel the shaking horror of that?/
> You just can't ignore these things, you just can't!/
> > (*The bell signifying the end of lunch break
> > sounds. HAAKON turns away, says, much more
> > quietly:*)

HAAKON:
> You just can't ignore these things, you just can't/
> > (*HAAKON goes to his locker, takes out some
> > books, goes out: no sooner has the door shut
> > than he opens it again and stands in the
> > doorway.*)

HAAKON:
> Oh, a girl in 4B called Helen Hunt/
> Told me she found a purse in the playground/
> So if anyone's lost a leather purse/
> Will they please go to Helen Hunt for it/
> > (*HAAKON makes a theatrical gesture in keeping
> > with this old music-hall joke: and exits.*)

(*Blackout*)

151

*Enough props — desk, chair, blackboard — to indicate a classroom.*
*Enter HAAKON. Noise of kids gradually subsides.*

HAAKON:
What lesson are we sposed to be doing?/
Anyway, there's something more important/
I'm not myself today
CAPON:                      Who are you then?/
ECKERSLEY:
But why can't we have Civics as usual?/
HAAKON:
You'd rather have the usual, Eckersley?/
The usual useless information?
ECKERSLEY:                               Yes/
HAAKON:
Right then. How many halfpennies in a mile?/
Secret is to know the diameter/
One inch. More. More useless information/
Do you know how to recognize your cows?/
Now your Ayrshire is a brown and white cow/
Don't confuse with the black and white Friesian/
And here's one you haven't heard of before/
The Red Poll which as its name might suggest/
Is a deep chestnut brown not red at all/
And from the Channel
CAPON:                           Sixty-three thousand/
Three hundred and sixty
HAAKON:                      What? What?
WHOLE CLASS (*shouts*):                  Halfpennies/
HAAKON:
Capon, I shall work you one in the spud!/
Now, Guernseys are sort of soft brown and white/
And Jerseys are much the same colours but/
They have funny faces. Which reminds me/
Did you hear about the old bull who said/
'I'd like a nice tight jersey for Christmas'?/

152

*(Shocked, delighted, reproving noises from class.)*

CHILD ONE:

What's up with him today?

CAPON:                                He's not himself/

HAAKON:

Who am I then? Don't answer that. Quiet!/
You ought to be able to take that now/
We make you too many allowances/
Too many for your presumed innocence/
Too many for your snotty-nosedness/
We wrongly emphasize slight differences/
To the cost of common humanity/
For — and let's be very sure about this — /
You are human just like the rest of them/
You are human just like the rest of them/
And your one certainty is that you'll die — /
Our dying is the only certainty/
            *(Someone laughs.)*

HAAKON:

Shut up you little bastards, just shut up!/
I'm trying to teach you something real, real!/
Something that I've learnt for myself this time/
Something that has to do with all of you/
You're going to die but before then/
You're going to decay, rot, for years, rot/
Slowly your bodies are going to rot/
Slowly, mind, just slowly, for years, slowly/
And painfully, your bodies just give up/
They just stop working, function by function/
I saw old men this morning with their skin/
Cross-wrinkled like the neck of a tortoise/
Skin lined and loose like a flaccid penis/
Then, after pain, comes death, you are cut off/
Like a city street-end by the railway/
            *(Long pause.)*

HAAKON:

Only one cheer for dear old God

CAPON:                                Hooray!/

153

CHILD ONE:
> He's off his squiff

CHILD TWO:                    Mad, mad

CAPON:                                        Straight round the twist/

HAAKON:
> Already you cover up like adults/
> Know you can live only by illusion/
> You must choose to believe that I am mad/
>> (*Long pause.*)

HAAKON:
> A parable, children, a true one, true/
>> (*During following speech dim all except for spot on HAAKON's face.*)

HAAKON:
> There were these lizards, at the zoo, lizards/
> In a sort of glass-fronted cage, prison/
> And they fed these lizards with big locusts/
> The lizards were about twelve inches long/
> And the locusts were about two inches/
> The locusts couldn't get away, of course/
> They had no defence against being killed/
> The only thing a locust could do was/
> To make itself an awkward thing to eat/
> By sticking out its arms and legs and wings/
> To make itself an awkward thing to kill/
> So shall I: I have to die, but by God/
> I'm not going to pretend I like it/
> I shall make myself so bloody awkward!/
>> (*By means of music and lighting a comic apotheosis of HAAKON, a complete reversal of mood, takes place: he is given medals by functionaries, presented with a loyal address, praised in dumbshow, he is exalted and gradually stands more and more upright, noble as a result of his suffering. At peak, blackout.*)

154

# One Sodding Thing After Another

## EDITORS' NOTE

*One Sodding Thing After Another* was commissioned by William Gaskill for the Royal Court Theatre, and was mostly written in March 1967. It is a free adaptation and continuation of Georg Büchner's *Woyzeck*, left incomplete at the time of the playwright's death in 1837.

Büchner's play survives in four contradictory drafts, although these were not published in their entirety until 1967, too late for Johnson to make use of them. It seems likely that he relied instead on John Holmstrom's translation (Penguin, 1963), itself based on an inaccurate first edition. In any case, his version soon departs completely from the original text.

The play was not used by the Royal Court, and has never been performed.

## CHARACTERS

WOYZECK
COMMANDING OFFICER
DOCTOR ONE (*double with MAN*)
DOCTOR TWO (*double with SECOND STUDENT*)
MARIE
JOAN
ANDRES
ROBERTS (*double with BARKER*)
BARKER (*double with ROBERTS*)
DRUM MAJOR
CORPORAL
DANCER (*double with NURSE*)

MAN (*double with DOCTOR ONE*)
FIRST STUDENT
SECOND STUDENT (*double with DOCTOR TWO*)

*Voices off*:      THREE CHILDREN
                  FIRST VOICE
                  SECOND VOICE
                  POLICE CHIEF
                  CHAPLAIN

*23 parts requiring 9 men and three women: and children's voices.*

". . .my laughter is not at *how* a human being is,
but rather at the fact *that* he is a human being:
about which he can do nothing; and at the same
time I laugh at myself because I must share in his
fate."

Georg Büchner, Feb. 1834

"Nobody really understands the human condition
unless he realises that apart from one or two
persons, there is not one soul who is interested
in whether he lives or dies."

Henry de Montherlant
in *Chaos and Night*

The Army
Any Time

*NOTES*

It is not intended that any particular period should be represented by
the uniforms worn. The uniforms chosen should be from as many
periods as possible (e.g. Roman, Persian, samurai, Boy Scouts,
commissionaires, etc., etc.) no two being the same, to create a visual
sendup of the idea of uniform.

The music for the songs should be nearer Weill than Berg.

159

## SCENE ONE

*The COMMANDING OFFICER'S room. The CO sits in a chair with a sheet round his neck being shaved by WOYZECK, who is obviously in a hurry to be finished.*

CO:                    Watch it, Woyzeck, watch it!

*Woyzeck pauses, open razor in hand, as the CO talks, impatient but not daring to begin again.*

CO:                    What's the bloody hurry? So what if you do get
                       me done in four minutes instead of five this
                       morning? I should only have to work out
                       something to do with the extra time, and my
                       life's full enough of useless activity as it is.
                       Bloody enervating, it is, too, enervating. Know
                       what enervating means, Woyzeck?
WOYZECK:               No, sir.
CO:                    Makes me bloody tired, that's what it does,
                       Woyzeck, all this working out what to do with
                       my bloody time. (*pause*) And then the Chaplain
                       talks about eternity being promised as a reward!
                       That's what depresses me about going to heaven.
                       Just think of it, Woyzeck, all that time going on
                       and bloody on, that's what eternity will actually
                       mean, just more and more time to be filled up
                       with enervating thought about even more
                       enervating actions.
WOYZECK:               Why don't you become a convert to the other
                       side, sir, then you wouldn't have to tire yourself
                       out with even the thought of it.
CO:                    No guarantee, that's the problem with this
                       religious stuff, Woyzeck, no guarantee.

160

Whichever way. . . . Why aren't you shaving me?
The bloody soap dries and then it's. . .

*CO waves his arms under the sheet. WOYZECK lathers him up
again, but cannot get started as CO begins to talk again.*

CO:               Then again, the Chaplain tells you eternity is
really only a moment, the click of the fastest
camera shutter. At the same time it's going on
and bloody on. Work that one out, Woyzeck!
(*pause*) Mind you, I can sort of understand it. It
is and it isn't, if you see what I mean. It is and it
isn't. Eternity. Beyond our comprehension. But
we're supposed to regard it as something very
much worth having, worth dying for, some sort
of reward when we die, for being good.
Whatever that means. (*pause*) The Chaplain must
know about it. After all, that's what he's bloody
paid for, eh, Woyzeck? The Army wouldn't pay
him not to know about it, would they, Woyzeck?
And you're paid to shave me!

*WOYZECK begins to shave the CO again, but repeatedly has to
break off to accommodate the CO's garrulity.*

CO:               You must have another thirty years in you,
Woyzeck. I'd say you were good for another
thirty, at least. So what are you in a hurry for?
Thirty years. . . .that means 360 months. . . .
thousands and thousands of days, God knows
how many minutes, an eternity of seconds. . . . .
So what's your bloody hurry to shave me this
morning?

WOYZECK:    It's Marie, sir, her labour began just as I was
coming out this morning. . . .

CO:               I didn't know you were married, Woyzeck.

WOYZECK:    I'm not, sir.

CO:               What's this then, Woyzeck, bringing a child into

|         | the world without the blessing of the Church, as the Chaplain would say? As the Chaplain no doubt bloody will say! |
| WOYZECK: | I don't care what he does say, sir. He's not an officer like you, sir, is he, he can't give orders about these things. |
| CO: | He can make things bloody difficult for you with God, Woyzeck, bloody difficult! No eternity for you, Woyzeck! No eternity! |
| WOYZECK: | Then I won't have your problem to worry about, will I, sir? |
| CO: | (*almost petulantly*) Yours'll be worse! |

*They are silent: WOYZECK gets on with the shaving.*

| CO: | Why aren't you married then? Too mean? |
| WOYZECK: | It only costs a few shillings, sir. But it can cost £100 or more to get divorced. |
| CO: | So you're thinking of that already! |
| WOYZECK: | No I'm not, as it happens, sir. It's just that there's so many things happen to a man without him wishing for them that I don't reckon he should pass up the chance of avoiding trouble later on so far as he can. |
| CO: | I don't quite understand that, Woyzeck. Why don't you get married like the rest of us? |
| WOYZECK: | As far as I'm concerned I am married. We love each other and that's that. No civil servant or Chaplain saying some words and charging a few bob can make it any different, now can they, sir? |
| CO: | That's not the point. |

*Pause: WOYZECK has nearly finished the shave.*

| CO: | This your first, then, Woyzeck? |
| WOYZECK: | Yes, sir. (*pause*) |
| CO: | Another thing that worries me about eternity, Woyzeck, at least I suppose it's to do with |

eternity, is the speed the world is going round at, the way it's going round – every day, round, every day, round, continuously. Oh, I know it's to do with the sun and the moon and the planets, but what's in it for me, eh, Woyzeck? What's the bloody point? And where's it all going to end? (*pause*) I get bemused, just to think about it, bemused, Woyzeck. And whenever I see anything going round it reminds me of it, usually, Woyzeck. That doesn't help my bloody concentration. (*pause*)

WOYZECK:        Sir.

*WOYZECK has finished shaving. He pulls off the sheet, and begins to tidy away his shaving things quickly but neatly.*

*The CO gets up slowly, inspects himself at length in a hand mirror WOYZECK has given him, pulls his face about masochistically.*

*WOYZECK finishes packing his things away, and stands waiting to be dismissed.*

CO:        You're a fair barber, Woyzeck, I'll give you that, yes. (*pause*) You look even more tensed-up today. Why do you always look tensed-up? I mean, what is it that constantly makes you look as though someone's going to clobber you with a meat-axe?

WOYZECK:        I don't know sir. Do I look like that?

CO:        Yes, you do, Woyzeck. Any reason for it? Conscience clear? Bowels regular? I know you're getting your oats regular – ah, but no, you're not, perhaps, since she's having a baby. But husbands are allowed some licence at such difficult times, you know, Woyzeck!

WOYZECK:        I'd never be unfaithful to her, sir. That would be the end of our. . . .marriage. It would be the end of it, it wouldn't exist anymore. . . .it couldn't. . . .

163

| | |
|---|---|
| CO: | Rubbish, Woyzeck, you're not going to tell me you haven't missed your little bit of the other. |
| WOYZECK: | Oh, I wouldn't deny I've missed it, sir, I've certainly missed it. But the. . . .sort of forced going without it has made us like. . . .brother and sister. . . .and it's a good feeling, sir, it's something more than we had before, it's extra, like a bonus, now we're that as well as being lovers. It hasn't been hard, sir. And when we're lovers again it'll be that much better, won't it, sir? |

*Pause. CO does not answer. Stares out of window. WOYZECK is clearly impatient to leave.*

| | |
|---|---|
| CO: | Appalling weather we're having. |
| WOYZECK: | Yes, sir. |
| CO: | This wind reminds me of my Aunt Sara, Woyzeck. She would never pass wind outright, my Aunt Sara, she'd just let it come sighing out, a long, soughing, susurrating sort of sigh, soft, and you'd only just pick up the sound of it halfway through. Sometimes it would be the smell which hit you first, a smell like cow-elephant droppings. Ever been in the East, Woyzeck? |
| WOYZECK: | No, sir. |
| CO: | Ah. (*pause*) A real old trouper, my Aunt Sara. (*pause: then suddenly he rounds on WOYZECK*) What worries me about you is that you've got no morals, Woyzeck, no morals at all! Or the morals of a stoat. A stoat. You know what a stoat is? Well, they've got no morals either. You ask the Chaplain, he'll tell you. I'm telling you. Your union and its offspring have not had the benefit of holy sacrament, Woyzeck! |
| WOYZECK: | With all respect, sir, don't you think that battle was fought and lost some time ago? |

164

| CO: | Watch it, Woyzeck, watch it! It may have been for some people, all these damned leftwing progressive nignogs. But what they don't realise is that there are whole areas, huge numbers of people, untouched by their so-called advances. And the Army's one of them. For some people and the Army there are eternal verities, Woyzeck, eternal verities! Either the eternal verities are eternal verities or they're not. And they are. They wouldn't be called eternal verities otherwise, would they? I mean, they wouldn't be called that, would they? Woyzeck! |
|---|---|
| WOYZECK: | Sir! (*coming smartly to attention*) |
| CO: | Say something! Answer me! |
| WOYZECK: | Yes sir! I can't understand these things as well as you can, sir, but if you say the Chaplain thinks God is annoyed that our little baby isn't going to have a few holy words said to him, then perhaps God will let me know. . . . |

*This is said so ingenuously that the CO does not know whether to take him seriously – whether WOYZECK is sending him up.*

| CO: | Well, get the Chaplain to explain some time, Woyzeck. I haven't got time to worry about every bastard's bastard in the Army, have I? What do we pay the Chaplain for? Just take it from me that you've no morals, and that that's not a good thing and won't get you into Heaven and you won't be rewarded with Eternity. You don't want to go to Hell, do you, Woyzeck? |
|---|---|
| WOYZECK: | No, sir, I suppose not, though as I said I don't really understand these things as well as you do. If Heaven's anything like what it is down here, I reckon they'll want people like me to clean out the latrines or something. |
| CO: | Of course they won't! There aren't any latrines in Heaven, you berk! That's why it's Heaven! |

WOYZECK:       Yes, sir. Thank you, sir, that makes it a little clearer.

*Again the CO does not know which way to take this.*

CO:       Don't think I'm not sympathetic, Woyzeck. I try to be. The old organ still lets me know whenever there's something worth. . . . . I mean, I'm flesh and blood as well, you know. I know what it is. . . . and I've had children myself. But I try to do the decent thing, the decent thing. (*pause*) I didn't really have an Aunt Sara, Woyzeck. I made it up to cover up for a fart I was indulging myself in. . . .

WOYZECK:       It doesn't seem important, sir.

CO:       Of course it's important! You don't hear your commanding officer confessing to a lie every day, Woyzeck! (*pause*) But there was a chap called Reynolds when I was a cadet who could fart at will. Unbelievable, he was, Woyzeck, unless you saw him at it. One afternoon we were at camp somewhere or other, and word went round that Reynolds was going for his hundred. Dozens of us crowded into that belltent and watched him, down on all fours in the so-called canine position, his face puckered and grimacing with the effort at about the half-century but later relaxed and confident as he got his second wind. You should have heard the cheer that went up from us cadets as he made it, Woyzeck, it would have made you glad to be alive! "Reynolds has done the ton!" the cry went round, and even the officers were impressed. (*pause*) Reynolds got himself killed in the war, poor bleeder. (*pause*) Shell blew an even bigger hole in him. (*pause*) But he'll live forever, that man. (*pause*) Ton-up Reynolds. (*long pause*) You see, Woyzeck, you've got to be a decent chap, and you've got to have morals. Otherwise you're sunk.

WOYZECK: Yes, sir, well, I suppose I'm not a very decent sort of chap.

CO: You've got the makings of a decent chap, Woyzeck, the makings. A very decent chappie! Don't despair. You worry too much: I can see it. You get too tensed-up. You've got me all tensed-up, too. Don't take things so seriously. Don't think so much. (*pause*) Don't take things so seriously, and think what I've said about morals, Woyzeck, stoats and morals. Right! (*WOYZECK comes to attention*) Dis. . . . .miss! (*WOYZECK breaks into a run, but before he has gone far:*) Halt! Watch it, Woyzeck, don't run! March, smartly – when I tell you! Right. Remember – no tensing-up, stoats, morals. (*pause*) Dis. . . .miss!

*Exit WOYZECK, with CO watching.*

*BLACKOUT*


**SCENE TWO**

*WOYZECK and ANDRES cross the stage at a fairly fast pace.*

WOYZECK: . . .comes over me, Andres, a great black feeling of a disaster about to happen, or my luck running out, something catching up with me. . . .

*ANDRES does not answer, but indicates they should hurry, not worry about talking of anything. Exeunt.*

*BLACKOUT*

167

## SCENE THREE

*Lights up slowly. Marie's room. A bed, kitchen table, chairs, mirror, side-table: all cheap but clean.*

*Marie lies in the bed and Joan sits by her, nursing a newborn baby.*

*Enter WOYZECK, slowly, slowly, staring, twisting his cap in his hands.*

*ANDRES follows, stays by the door to one side.*

*JOAN rises as WOYZECK comes nearer, holds out the baby to him. WOYZECK takes it, but his eyes are on MARIE.*

WOYZECK:      Is it. . .all right?
JOAN:          Of course! Perfect, a perfect baby boy! Your son!

*WOYZECK slowly looks down at the baby: then at MARIE again. MARIE smiles, holds out her hand to him.*

*BLACKOUT*

## SCENE FOUR

*The terrace of a café: indicated by placard if necessary. Sunlight. MARIE, WOYZECK, JOAN and ANDRES sit at a table: the men drinking beer, the girls coffee. The men relaxed, the girls in summer dresses, happy.*

168

*Other soldiers, students, girls, at other tables.*

FIRST STUDENT: (*sings*)    If I'm bound for Hades
                           I'll go with some ladies
                           And drive a Mercedes. . . .

ANDRES:          So then he goes and volunteers! The only one! The first thing you learn in the Army is not to volunteer for any bloody thing!

MARIE:            What is it, Franz?

WOYZECK:     An extra half-day's pay, that's what it is!

JOAN:             But what do you have to do for it? I don't see the Army giving away an extra half-day's pay without getting a weekend's work out of you!

ANDRES:          That's what I said to him!

MARIE:            But what do they want you to do, Franz?

ANDRES:          He doesn't know! They just asked for volunteers to take part in a scheme run by the Medical Corps – vivisection, probably, something too cruel to use animals for.

WOYZECK:     Don't be bloody stupid, Andres. I just know we need the money, and this is an easy way to earn it. You don't get many chances to earn extra in the Army.

MARIE:            But will they hurt you, Franz?

WOYZECK:     Of course not. (*He comforts her.*) It's probably like being a blood donor. You know, if you give blood they give you half a day off to make it up again. It'll be all right. Just think what we can do with the money!

ANDRES:          I still say don't volunteer for nothing. You don't catch me volunteering for vivisection by an Army Doctor!

WOYZECK:     How do you know what it is?

MARIE:            When will you know, Franz?

WOYZECK:     (*to audience*) Tomorrow.

*BLACKOUT*

## SCENE FIVE

*Medical Corps office. A desk, behind which sits DOCTOR ONE,*
*staring at WOYZECK, who is sitting apprehensively opposite him.*
*DOCTOR TWO stands behind and to one side. Medical charts, case*
*history files, and instruments are lying about. Scene to be taken very*
*fast.*

| | |
|---|---|
| DOCTOR ONE: | You're very lucky to have been given this chance, Private Woyzeck! |
| DOCTOR TWO: | Very lucky indeed! |
| D ONE: | A chance to help us push back the frontiers of medical knowledge. . . |
| D TWO: | Inch by inch we push back the frontiers, Private Woyzeck. . . |

*DOCTOR TWO accompanies this by a suitable inching gesture.*
*WOYZECK still looks apprehensive.*

| | |
|---|---|
| D ONE: | There are many who must envy you being given this chance to help us in this great experiment. . . . |
| WOYZECK: | Experiment? |
| D ONE: | What we want you to do is this. . . . |
| D TWO: | Just let us explain what we have in mind. . . . |
| D ONE: | In the next war. . . . |
| D TWO: | Which of course we all hope will not take place. . . . |
| D ONE: | But when it does we must be very carefully prepared. . . . |
| D TWO: | Can you blame us? |
| D ONE: | It seems likely, having regard to all the possibilities. . . . |
| D TWO: | Considering all the envisaged circumstances. . . . |

170

D ONE:          That the land will be in large tracts laid waste. . . .

D TWO:          Laid bare, largely denuded of vegetation,
                defoliated even. . . .

D ONE:          And that as a result our soldiers may be reduced
                to subsisting on the most unlikely sources of
                sustenance. . . .

D TWO:          Living off what's left on the land, Private
                Woyzeck, after being cut off from their
                cookhouse by enemy action. . . .

*DOCTOR ONE brings up a great bundle – about half a sackful – of
green vegetable matter and places it on his desk with a dramatic
gesture.*

D ONE:          Know what this is, Woyzeck?

D TWO:          Never come across it before?

WOYZECK:        Well, it looks like. . . .

D ONE:          It's moss, Woyzeck. . . .

D TWO:          Sphagnum moss. . . .

D ONE:          (*spells*) S-p-h-a-g-n-u-m. . . .

D TWO:          (*spells*) M-o-s-s. . . .

D ONE:          In the hinterlands of our enemies, Woyzeck. . . .

D TWO:          Obviously places unlikely to be regarded as
                military targets. . . .

D ONE:          Having regard to general overall strategic
                assumptions. . . .

D TWO:          As we do, of course. . . .

D ONE:          In these hinterlands, then, there are many bogs. . . .

D TWO:          Huge areas of our enemies' hinterlands are just a
                mass of bogs. . . .

D ONE:          And what do we find in bogs, Private Woyzeck?

D TWO:          What is most commonly found in bogs?

*WOYZECK is about to tell him, grins.*

D ONE:          You're right, Private Woyzeck: moss!

D TWO:          Sphagnum moss!

D ONE:          It grows all over the bogs. . . .

| | |
|---|---|
| D TWO: | The conditions suit it. . . . |
| D ONE: | The bogs are its natural element. . . . |
| D TWO: | All that water. . . . |
| D ONE: | Which our soldiers could drink. . . . |
| D TWO: | To wash down the sphagnum moss. . . . |

*DOCTOR ONE holds up a handful. WOYZECK looks at it doubtfully.*

| | |
|---|---|
| D ONE: | Try a little. . . . |

*WOYZECK takes some in his fingers, looks at it, puts it in his mouth, chews slowly: obviously not enjoying it. The two doctors stare at him expectantly, raptly.*

| | |
|---|---|
| D ONE: | You'll notice at once that this is not your ordinary moss, Woyzeck. |
| D TWO: | Not your common or garden Webb's Wonder moss, oh no. . . . |
| D ONE: | There wouldn't be any point in finding out if a man could live on that. . . . |
| D TWO: | After all, our own homegrown gardenfresh sphagnum moss is just not the same as theirs, is it? |
| D ONE: | I mean, be reasonable. . . . |
| D TWO: | Give us the benefit of the doubt. . . . |
| D ONE: | We are thorough. . . . |
| D TWO: | We are nothing if not thorough. . . . |
| D ONE: | And this sphagnum moss is the genuine article, Woyzeck. . . . |
| D TWO: | None finer. Guaranteed *pays d'origine*. . . . |
| D ONE: | (*reverently*) This moss, Woyzeck, was cut less than twenty-four hours ago in the hinterlands of our enemies. . . . |
| D TWO: | Cut with stealth before dawn broke. . . . |
| D ONE: | And flown here by channels which we are not at liberty to disclose. . . . |
| D TWO: | Under the Official Secrets Act. . . . |

| | |
|---|---|
| D ONE: | But we *can* tell you that brave men's lives were risked to see that that moss reached this desk safely. . . . |
| D TWO: | Brave men's blood may be shed before our experiment is over. . . . |
| D ONE: | But the moss will get through, never fear, Woyzeck. . . . |
| D TWO: | The moss will be here for you every day, fresh. . . . |

*They pause, look at WOYZECK intently. He says nothing for a long time, looks at them, and the moss, takes some more, looks at it, chews again, swallows hard.*

| | |
|---|---|
| WOYZECK: | Well, I suppose it wouldn't be so bad if you cooked it and had a nice pork chop and gravy with it. |

*Both doctors laugh.*

| | |
|---|---|
| D ONE: | You wouldn't get a nice pork chop in the enemies' hinterlands, Woyzeck! |
| D TWO: | Nor gravy, neither! |
| WOYZECK: | You mean I've got to eat this stuff and nothing else?! |
| D ONE: | That's it. Then we shall know if our men can survive when stranded in the bogs of our enemies. . . . |
| D TWO: | Cut off from their essential supplies. . . . |
| WOYZECK: | Nothing else? |
| D ONE: | Nothing. . . . |
| D TWO: | Only the moss. . . . |
| WOYZECK: | Christ! |
| D ONE: | You can't back out now! |
| D ONE: | You can't back out now! |
| D TWO: | We won't have you welshing on us! |
| WOYZECK: | How long for? |
| D ONE: | An indefinite period. . . . |

| | |
|---|---|
| D TWO: | See how it goes. . . . |
| D ONE: | You'll come to like it. . . . |
| D TWO: | You won't want to go back to your old carnivorous ways. . . . |
| D ONE: | You'll provide us with a good deal of invaluable information. . . . |
| D TWO: | The Army can learn a lot from you, Private Woyzeck! |
| D ONE: | The nation, as well! |
| D TWO: | You're doing it for your country, Private Woyzeck! |
| D ONE: | We'll introduce variety, of course. . . . |
| D TWO: | Poach it, grill it, braise it. . .try it all ways. . . . |
| D ONE: | We want to compare how much of the goodness is left after various methods of field cooking. . . . |
| D ONE: | See how many of the vitamins there are left after say boiling. . . . |
| D TWO: | Whether you get beri-beri if there's no B-one. . . . |
| WOYZECK: | But how do you know whether this stuff can feed a man? |
| D ONE: | We don't. . . . |
| D TWO: | No. . . . |
| D ONE: | That's the experiment. . . . |
| D TWO: | That's what we want to find out. . . . |
| WOYZECK: | But surely you can find out what's in it with all your machines and apparatus? |
| D ONE: | Too many imponderables, Woyzeck. |
| D TWO: | Too many unknowns. . . . |
| D ONE: | A test-tube is not a man, you know. . . . |
| D TWO: | We need a man to test it properly. |
| D ONE: | You're a sort of flying testbed, Woyzeck. |
| D TWO: | A kind of test pilot. . . . |
| D ONE: | The navy found a man could live on seaweed, if he had to, Woyzeck. |
| D TWO: | And we in the Army can do better than that! |
| D ONE: | Just think, you'll probably be saving the lives of hundreds of your comrades. . . . |
| D TWO: | Live to fight another day. . . . |

174

| | |
|---|---|
| D ONE: | Doesn't it appeal to you? |
| D TWO: | You'll go down in history, man! |

*Pause*

| | |
|---|---|
| D ONE: | Doesn't matter either way. . . . |
| D TWO: | You can't back out now! |

*Silence. WOYZECK looks depressed*

| | |
|---|---|
| D ONE: | (*brightly*) You can drink as much as you please, Woyzeck! |
| D TWO: | As much as you like! |
| WOYZECK: | Well at least I can get drunk enough to face the stuff, then. |

*Doctors laugh, as before*

| | |
|---|---|
| D ONE: | He's mistaken us again! |
| D TWO: | Hasn't fully comprehended our gist! |
| D ONE: | Drink as much *water* as you please, Private Woyzeck! |
| D TWO: | Feel free with water. |
| D ONE: | Our information is the bogs are full of it. . . . |
| D TWO: | Available on a plentiful scale. . . . |
| D ONE: | So a soldier could in fact drink all he wished. . . . |
| D TWO: | We won't insist on mud and other extraneous matter being added, of course, for the purposes of the experiment. . . . |
| D ONE: | That would be going too far. . . . |
| D TWO: | Far too far. . . . |

*Doctors laugh again. WOYZECK gets up to go. DOCTOR ONE puts the moss into his arms.*

| | |
|---|---|
| D ONE: | Oh, one last point regarding water. . . . |
| D TWO: | When you've finished with it, that is. . . . |
| D ONE: | We'd like it. . . . |

WOYZECK:      You'd like it?

D ONE and D TWO: (*Together*) We'd like it!

DOCTOR ONE and DOCTOR TWO:

> (*sing*) Please retain your water, Private Woyzeck:
> Don't dispose of it the customary way:
> When you feel you want to pass
> Employ this calibrated glass
> And report to us at 9 and 6 each day!
>
>         ***
>
> Do please retain your water, Private Woyzeck:
> It's so little for the Army to expect:
> But if carrying it's a fag
> Then we supply a plastic bag
> Just as long as we receive what you reject!
>
>         ***
>
> So don't fail us with your water, Private Woyzeck:
> You know we have your interests at heart:
> But if you fail us with your water
> Then there'll probably be slaughter
> So watch it, Woyzeck, watch your private part!

*BLACKOUT*

## SCENE SIX

*Marie's room: as before, with the addition of a cot. Evening. JOAN and ANDRES, eating. MARIE is cradling the baby.*

MARIE:        (*sings*) The child who sleeps in my arms tonight
                   Is child of darkness, child of light:

                   The boy who stands in his place tomorrow
                   Will already have known delight and sorrow

The man whose part he takes in turn
knows too well how to love and spurn:

The elder who replaces them last
knows all will be, and all is past:

And each child held towards the light
Is every child, on every night.

MARIE: Who's a little basket, then, and who's father's an even bigger basket? But I love you both. As long as *you* stay quiet and *he* comes home soon.

JOAN: Aren't you going to eat too, Marie?

MARIE: Later, perhaps. I don't seem to have the same appetite since Franz started this experiment. My stomach's in sympathy, I suppose.

ANDRES: Mine isn't.

JOAN: That's obvious. You wouldn't give up anything that mattered to you for my sake.

ANDRES: Why should I?

MARIE: They had the first pay parade since he started this afternoon, so he'll be bringing the extra home tonight.

JOAN: Has it been affecting him?

MARIE: I don't know. . . .he doesn't say much. He worries to himself, I know. But he's always been like that.

JOAN: He thinks too much, that one.

ANDRES: He didn't think too much about going in for this bloody experiment. . . .

JOAN: That's to his credit, you fat animal! All you think about is food and crumpet!

ANDRES: What else is there to think about?

*A tapping at the window. Marie looks questioningly at the others, then goes to window and is relieved as she sees who it is.*

*She goes to door, admits WOYZECK. He seems tired, almost distant, but embraces her warmly.*

177

MARIE:    Why were you tapping at the window, Franz?

*WOYZECK does not answer, looks at her, smiles.*

WOYZECK:   You're right, it's more important to ask
       questions. (*pause*) Than to answer them. (*pause*)
       Here!

*WOYZECK gives MARIE money. She is pleased, forgets her
question, goes across to put the money away on her dressing table.*

*WOYZECK turns towards the other table, looks briefly, sadly, at
what JOAN and ANDRES are eating, then goes to sit on the bed.*

JOAN:     Well, how are you, Franz?
WOYZECK:   Andres will tell you. Did I cut less wood for the
       CO than you did today?
ANDRES:    No.
WOYZECK:   There you are, then. (*pause*) My stomach must be
       shrinking, though. I don't feel nearly as hungry
       as I did the first few days. (*Long pause: when he
       speaks again it is directed to MARIE:he seems
       unaware of the others*) It's much worse since
       I've only been eating this. . .weed. Today, when
       Andres had gone with the wood we'd cut. . .it
       came on me again. (*pause*) It's like a dense haze,
       a great hanging pall of. . .desolation which comes
       down on me. . . .and I can't see anything else. I
       couldn't see to think of anything else at all: yet
       there the things were, all around me, the axe, the
       trees, the bright, splintered wood. It's not as if it
       were unreal — it's real enough. But (*carefully*) it
       just doesn't mean what it looks like. (*pause*) It's
       as though the world were dead, still there, still
       existing, but dead! (*pause*) While this. . .haze is
       on me, it might just as well be dead, everything,
       it's just meaningless. Nothing means anything to
       me (*looking at MARIE*) except you. And the

baby. When I think of you, then the greyness seems to lift, I can move again, moving has some meaning for me. . .again. (*pause*) You know what I'm talking about, don't you Marie? You understand? (*MARIE comes across, stands by him, cradling his head against her*). You know me, you've always known me. But just this week it's come twice, the grey pall, and it's been longer each time before I've been able to think of you, and move again, be interested in moving again. . . .(*pause*) It follows me, I carry it here. (*pause*) I carry you here with me! (*long pause*)

*BLACKOUT*


## SCENE SEVEN


*A fairground. A sideshow advertising Nudies. A Barker outside, with a showgirl next to him. During his spiel, a crowd collects: eventually it includes WOYZECK and MARIE, ANDRES and JOAN: later the DRUM MAJOR and the CORPORAL: other soldiers and students.*

BARKER: Here you are, you lucky soldier lads, all the lovely nudies you could possibly want to see, with absolutely nothing on! If they took any more off they'd be like skinless sausages. What more can you want? The show is this minute about to begin. No waiting at the nudies show. Instant nudies! Here's your own show, here are your very own nudies! This is your nudie show, get your nudies here! No connection with any other establishment. (*Pauses, nods at girl*). It breaks my heart to give something for nothing, but look at this (*taps girl with cane*) — not

179

skinless, mind you, but you boys have got
imagination, haven't you? And what you imagine
— and more! — is waiting for you!

*The Showgirl begins to dance, with the BARKER looking on.*

CORPORAL:       How about this, then?
DRUM MAJOR:     None of that tat for me, boy, I want to screw it
                not look at it!

*DRUM MAJOR gooses JOAN: she turns angrily, appeals to
ANDRES: ANDRES takes one look at the DRUM MAJOR and moves
away: JOAN angry with him.*

JOAN:           Aren't you going to. . . .?!
ANDRES:         No I'm bloody not!

*They move away: they take WOYZECK and MARIE in their wake,
thus bringing MARIE to the attention of the DRUM MAJOR and the
CORPORAL.*

DRUM MAJOR:     Here! Now that's what I call a very fair bit of
                grumble!
CORPORAL:       Very fair indeed!

*MARIE has obviously heard, but takes no notice. WOYZECK turns
his head, looks at the two soldiers: he is still enough in possession
for his look to put them off for the moment.*

DRUM MAJOR:     Just look at that arse swing!
COPORAL:        Swing-a-ding-ding!
DRUM MAJOR:     I can just tell that would be a red-hot grind!

*ANDRES and JOAN exeunt.*

CORPORAL:       I can feel the old blood rising in me!
DRUM MAJOR:     More than blood, mate!

180

*WOYZECK and MARIE exeunt.*

DRUM MAJOR and CORPORAL (*together: sing*):
>                    Crumpet! Crumpet! We're on the hunt for crumpet!
>                    Anything in skirts we see we'll hump it, hump it!
>                    We don't care what we damage
>                    When we're out on the rampage
>                    And those who don't like it — can lump it,
>                    Lump it, lump it, we're on the hunt for crumpet!
> ***
>                    Virgins, wives, widows and mothers:
>                    Younger sisters and queer older brothers:
>                    We screw 'em all, we screw 'em all:
>                    The long and the short and the tall:
>                    Our object is only orgasm
>                    For we have such enthusiasm
>                    For crumpet, crumpet, the quick bang and away
>                    To live to screw another day!

*BLACKOUT*


**SCENE EIGHT**


*Medical Corps office: as Scene Five: Two Doctors and WOYZECK (standing): DOCTOR TWO is just putting down a calibrated glass, half-full, on the table, having inspected it. He tests it with litmus paper, which turns a bright green; similar comic business, before anyone speaks, ending with a test which causes the glass to give off a flash and a cloud of smoke.*

DOCTOR ONE:     Anything on your conscience, Private Woyzeck?
DOCTOR TWO:     Conscience clear?
WOYZECK:        (*unsurely*) No different from usual, sir, doctor.
D ONE:          Go to the fair last night?

| | |
|---|---|
| D TWO: | See the Nudies? |
| WOYZECK: | Yes, sir. No, sir. |

*Long pause. Another test.*

| | |
|---|---|
| D ONE: | Sure there's nothing on your conscience? |
| D TWO: | Not feeling guilty towards us? |
| WOYZECK: | No. |

*Long pause. The Doctors look at one another significantly: then suddenly attack.*

| | |
|---|---|
| D ONE: | A usually reliable witness saw you last night. . . |
| D TWO: | At the fair. . . . |
| D ONE: | Passing water behind a tent. . . . |
| D TWO: | Urinating against the canvas. . . . |

*Pause. WOYZECK remembers, but looks defiant.*

| | |
|---|---|
| D ONE: | Pissing up against a wall, Woyzeck! |
| D TWO: | Against a canvas wall. . . . |
| D ONE: | Like a dog, Woyzeck! |
| D TWO: | A dog! |

*Pause.*

| | |
|---|---|
| WOYZECK: | I had a. . . .call of nature. . . . |
| D ONE: | A call of nature! |
| D TWO: | Nature! |

*Doctors laugh.*

| | |
|---|---|
| D ONE: | You haven't read our papers, have you, Woyzeck? |
| D TWO: | We have written papers together. . . . |
| D ONE: | One was called THE BLADDER MUSCLE AND THE HUMAN WILL. . . . |

182

| | |
|---|---|
| D TWO: | It proved beyond any possible doubt that the urinary mechanism is totally controlled by the brain, in human beings. |
| D ONE: | Nature doesn't come into it, Private Woyzeck. |
| D TWO: | Balls to nature! |
| D ONE: | Man is free. . . . |
| D TWO: | Free to pee. . . . |
| D ONE: | When *he* chooses, Woyzeck! |
| D TWO: | Not when nature chooses! |

*Pause. DOCTOR ONE drums fingers on desk.*

| | |
|---|---|
| D ONE: | Do we pay you to take part in a very serious scientific experiment. . . . |
| D TWO: | Frontiers of knowledge. . . . |
| D ONE: | Or do we not? |
| D TWO: | Inch by inch. . . . |
| D ONE: | Or do we pay you to pee up against walls! |
| D TWO: | Behind tents! |

*Pause.*

| | |
|---|---|
| D ONE: | We could have made things very much more difficult for you, Woyzeck. . . . |
| D TWO: | We have been most considerately humane. . . . |
| D ONE: | We could have put you on a diet of stewed rhubarb, Woyzeck — without sugar. . . . |
| D TWO: | (*refers to wall chart*) Only one calorie per ounce! |
| D ONE: | You would have had to have eaten a minimum of forty-five pounds a day to have stayed alive on that diet, Woyzeck! |
| D TWO: | And been permanently on latrine duty at the same time. |
| D ONE: | Or we could have put you on boiled mushrooms. . . . |
| D TWO: | (*refers to wall chart*) Two calories per ounce! |

*Pause.*

183

D ONE:          But we were good to you. . . .

D TWO:          Went out of our way. . .

D ONE:          All we asked for was your water, Woyzeck. . . .

D TWO:          ALL your water. . . .

D ONE:          Not very much to ask?

D TWO:          Very little in return for an extra half-day's pay?

WOYZECK:        What about the bloody weed!

D ONE:          You look in good shape on it, Woyzeck!

D TWO:          It must suit you!

WOYZECK:        My clothes hang on me, and I feel weaker. I was very near to fainting this morning. . . .

D ONE:          Eat more sphagnum moss!

D TWO:          Drink more water!

D ONE:          We're not hard men, Woyzeck.

D TWO:          Just scientists with a job to do.

D ONE:          We're not angry with you. . . .

D TWO:          Anger is not very scientific. . . .

D ONE:          We just don't want our project ruined. . . .

D TWO:          Isn't that reasonable?

WOYZECK:        I'm sorry that my brain just can't give the right orders to my bladder muscle. Under pressure, that is. But that's how some people are, it's their nature to be like that. . . .

D ONE:          Not that word again!

D TWO:          Balls to nature!

D ONE:          But that's an interesting symptom. . . .

D TWO:          Very revealing. . . .

D ONE:          (*making notes*) "After eight days on sphagnum moss and water the subject showed distinct signs of relinquishing control of the bladder muscle. . . ."

D TWO:          Further mental deterioration can be expected. . . .

D ONE:          That is self-evident. . .

D TWO:          Obvious. . . .

D ONE:          I must consult with my colleague. . . .

D TWO:          I am willing to give a second opinion.

*Pause while they consult.*

184

| | |
|---|---|
| D ONE: | We are prepared to forgive your lapse at the fairground last night. . . |
| D TWO: | And to allow the experiment to continue. . . . |
| D ONE: | Provided you are willing to place yourself in our hands. . . |
| D TWO: | So that the possibility of further lapses may be eliminated. . . . |
| D ONE: | In the Military Hospital. . . . |
| D TWO: | The beds are most comfortable in our Military Hospital. . . . |

*Pause. WOYZECK looks wildly from doctor to the other.*

| | |
|---|---|
| WOYZECK: | No! |

*BLACKOUT*

## SCENE NINE

*Marie's room. MARIE has the baby in her arms, and though it is obviously too small to talk or even to see much, she talks to it, shows it things. She has just taken it out of the cot when a military drum is heard. She rushes to the window holding the baby, and looks out.*

| | |
|---|---|
| MARIE: | Brrm bm bm! Hear the drums, hear the drums, babyboy! Hear them? (*pause*) And here they come! That one's the drum major! What a soldier! Thighs like trees he has! (*pause*) And look, there's your Auntie Joan — and ooh, who's that she's with? Looks like it'll be ex-uncle Andres now! So there's a new uncle for you, let's call him Uncle Corporal-to-be-going-on-with. |

*Pause. MARIE turns away from the window.*

185

MARIE:           (*sings*) Oh, how a man in battledress
                  Wins over the girl who couldn't care less. . . .
                        (*pause*)
                  Thighs like young trees. . . .

*BLACKOUT*


## SCENE TEN


*Three hospital beds. In them WOYZECK, with various wires, electrodes and other equipment attached to him and looking gaunt, exhausted, half-sitting, half-lying, propped by pillows; ROBERTS, a man of about fifty, apparently healthy, sitting up, wanting to talk; and a figure lying still in the third bed.*

ROBERTS:       You just can't tell with doctors, now can you. I mean, you know about their exams? Well, they just get a pass or fail. There's no knowing whether a man got top marks or only just scraped a pass. You can't tell, yourself. (*pause*) I mean, you just go to one and say "I've got a pain inside" and they'll say "It's so and so" or "It's such and such" without you telling them any more than that you've got a pain inside you. (*pause*) And when you think of it, as well, those who'd want to join the Army as doctors must be pretty well the lowest of the low. I mean, what goes wrong with soldiers in peacetime? Colic and VD, that's about the lot, colic and VD. And they don't get much of a chance to practice on women, now do they? So they don't have to know that bit, the women's specialities, do they? Oh, I know a lot of things must be the same as men, but I suspect anyone who wants to limit the

186

amount they have to bother themselves to learn,
don't you?

*During this speech WOYZECK has moved his head once or twice
from side to side, but has given no real indication that he is
listening: but he is not on the point of collapse, just weak.*

ROBERTS: But I suppose it means they have to put up with
a lot of boredom, too, Army doctors. Do you
remember when you had your medical to join up
there was a doctor who looked at you to see if
you had VD? Just imagine his job — sitting on a
chair while a long line of naked bastards passed
you, and peering at their privates all day long!
(*laughs; pause*) And what about the poor sods
who had to test your urine? That reminds me —
when I had my medical there was a man next to
me who just couldn't pee a drop to save his life.
But he couldn't face going back with an empty
glass either, so you know what? He had some of
mine! (*pause*) I once thought of doing it myself,
you know, studying medicine. It's a long grind,
but at the end of it you're set for life, of course.
But I could never face the grind. . . .

*A NURSE enters with three trays of food. One she gives to
ROBERTS, one she sets down on the bed of the third man: then she
turns to WOYZECK.*

NURSE: Special treat for you today, Private Woyzeck!

*WOYZECK stirs, lifts his head, struggles into a sitting position.*

WOYZECK: Oh?
NURSE: Yes: a jelly! They've made you a lovely
sphagnum moss jelly!
WOYZECK: (*ironically*) What a treat!
NURSE: Yes, isn't it? Jelly has virtually no food value, so

187

WOYZECK:         it isn't breaking your regime to give it to you.
And we thought you'd like a change.
Thank you very much.

*He downs the thing in huge mouthfuls, quickly: helping it down with lots of water from jug and tumbler by his bedside. Exit NURSE, brightly. ROBERTS does not seem very hungry, only toys with his food. No sooner has WOYZECK finished than a monstrous piece of machinery is wheeled in by DOCTOR TWO and the NURSE, and they begin to use it to carry out various tests on WOYZECK. It is intended that the exact bizarre nature of the machine shall be left to the stage designer, and the nature of the comic business in its operation to the director and actors: adlibbing if they so choose.*

*But the following song might be incorporated, in rhythm with a particularly violent piece of testing.*

WOYZECK:        (*sings*) Why is it
Whenever
You're seen by
A doctor
You lose your
(*despairing yell*) Dignity!

DOCTOR TWO and NURSE:
Power! Power! We're in it for the Power!

WOYZECK:        Why is it
So often
With doctors
You feel that
They're not on
Your side (*yells*) OOOOOH!

DOCTOR TWO and NURSE:
Patients! Patients! Patients are irrelevant!

WOYZECK:        I know that
I'm only
The patient

DOCTOR TWO and NURSE: (*stop testing for a moment to say:*)

188

|            | Good!                              |
|------------|------------------------------------|
| WOYZECK:   | But why do                         |
|            | You treat me                       |
|            | So roughly?                        |

DOCTOR TWO and NURSE:

|            | Power! Power! We're in it for the power! |
|------------|-------------------------------------------|
| WOYZECK:   | Why should you                            |
|            | Want power                                |
|            | Over such                                 |
|            | A poor sod                                |
|            | As me! Me!                                |

*Pause: DOCTOR TWO and NURSE are astounded.*

| DOCTOR TWO: | Power is its own reward!                |
|-------------|-----------------------------------------|
| NURSE:      | Power over a human being is so satisfying! |

DOCTOR TWO and NURSE:

| | Power! Power! We're in it for the power! |
|--|------------------------------------------|

*After as much as possible has been made of the testing business, the machine is removed by DOCTOR TWO and NURSE when DOCTOR ONE and the CO enter on a tour of inspection. The CO sniffs heavily.*

| CO: | Smell? |
|-----|--------|

*DOCTOR ONE looks offended, does not answer.*

| CO: | Before we go any further, I'd like to ask your advice about some little trouble I've been having myself recently. |
|-----|------|

*A look of vulturine interest comes over DOCTOR ONE's face, and he shepherds the CO downstage out of earshot of the patients. WOYZECK lies back, even weaker now. ROBERTS reads a paperback, and the third man lies as still as ever.*

| CO: | It's a peculiar sort of depression — not your |
|-----|------|

ordinary kind of feeling-below-par, you know,
but little things seem to set me crying —
weeping, man! Weeping! Me! And for no reason
at all that I can make out. Only today I suddenly
saw one of my wife's old dresses on a
coathanger behind the door, and that set me off!

*The Doctor's interest has lessened considerably.*

| | |
|---|---|
| D ONE: | Sounds as if you've got a touch of the human condition, sir. |
| CO: | Can anything be done for that? |
| D ONE: | No sir. Death is the only known relief. Some authorities even dispute that, sir. |
| CO: | You mean there are some things you doctors don't know about? That's contrary to what I've always been led to believe about the medical profession! |
| D ONE: | Ah, but there are lots of things we do know about sir! You look a very suitable subject for an apoplectic fit, sir, if I may say so, a classic case: bull-neck, purple with rich living, overweight. Let me tell you about your apoplexy, sir. |
| CO: | Damn my apoplexy! I've got melancholia! |
| D ONE: | Oh, don't upset yourself, sir, it's most probable that your apoplexy may affect only one side at first: you'll only be half paralysed then. On the other hand, you may be lucky enough for it only to affect the brain, in which case you'll retain most of your limb movements and live for years as a sort of animated cabbage. |
| CO: | Damn you! |
| D ONE: | Or think how interesting it would be if just half the tongue were to be paralysed! The experiments that would become possible! Something to look forward to, sir! |
| CO: | People have been known to die of sheer bloody terror, you know! |

190

| | |
|---|---|
| D ONE: | We weren't discussing shock. It's a different thing from apoplexy. |
| CO: | We weren't discussing that either in the first place. Come on, let's get on. Who's this? |

*They turn towards the beds, coming first to ROBERTS.*

| | |
|---|---|
| D ONE: | Roberts, sir, a most interesting case. This man came to us complaining of pain in the thorax, a sharp pain. And he yelped most realistically whenever we prodded him there. So we took x-rays of him and do you know what, sir? |
| CO: | Of course I don't know what, man! |
| D ONE: | We found he had two darning needles lodged in him! |
| CO: | No! How the hell did they get there? |
| D ONE: | He says he doesn't know, sir. |
| CO: | What! (*to ROBERTS*) How did two darning needles get into your vitals, eh, man? |
| ROBERTS: | I don't know, sir. |
| CO: | What d'you mean, you don't know! |
| ROBERTS: | If I may respectfully say so, sir, perhaps you should ask the doctor how two darning needles got into his x-ray machine. |
| D ONE: | Impossible. No one darns in the x-ray room. |
| ROBERTS: | No one darns in my dinner, either. . . .sir. |
| D ONE: | (*smiles*) Anyway, we shall be opening you up tomorrow, Roberts. However, they got there, out they've got to come. |

*As they move away, DOCTOR ONE speaks confidentially to CO.*

| | |
|---|---|
| D ONE: | Fascinating case, that. What we call the Munchausen Syndrome. Patients who deliberately swallow objects so that they can get themselves looked after in hospital. He probably wrapped the needles in cotton wool to get them down him. But we don't know which sort he is |

191

yet. There's two sorts, you see. One kind are masochists who actually want to undergo a serious abdominal operation. The other kind merely want a rest in bed at the expense of the hospital, and they almost always make a run for it as soon as surgery is mentioned. Some of them we catch, however. And operate. (*smiles*) We're pretty sure Mr. Roberts will be here in the morning, sir.

CO: But soldiers walk around with all sorts of bits of metal in them. Got a lump of shrapnel in me myself.

D ONE: Yes, sir, I was the one who left it there. . . .

CO: My god, it's Woyzeck! I hardly recognised you! You don't seem to be helping very much with this experiment, Woyzeck! Look at the state you've let yourself get into!

*WOYZECK has raised himself at the CO's voice.*

D ONE: Ah, you know this very interesting case, do you, sir?

CO: Of course I do. The new man doesn't shave me as well as you did, Woyzeck. When are you coming out?

WOYZECK: I don't know, sir. (*to doctor*) Do you have to let me starve before you can call the experiment a failure?

D ONE: (*laughs*) Of course not, Woyzeck, of course not. We're very much keener on it being a success. Just you concentrate on making the experiment a success.

*WOYZECK looks disheartened.*

CO: I'd like a chat with this man, Doctor, for a few minutes. I'm sure you've plenty of other things to do. . . .

192

*As the CO turns away he gives some indication to the DOCTOR that this is as they had planned: a glance or something which WOYZECK cannot see: or perhaps not if what comes later must seem a complete surprise?*

D ONE:    Of course, sir. I shall be in my office when you are ready to continue with the inspection.

*Exit DOCTOR ONE, The CO sits down at the side of WOYZECK's bed.*

CO:    At first I thought I'd bring you a bunch of grapes, Woyzeck, until I remembered what you're in here for. Then I was going to get some flowers, but you'd probably have eaten those. . .even.

*WOYZECK looks at him, knowing he is lying.*

WOYZECK:    I wish I'd never volunteered for this job, sir.
CO:    You've got to see it through now, Woyzeck!
WOYZECK:    I know, sir.
CO:    This is the Army you're in, you know! You do like being in the Army, don't you? (*pause: WOYZECK does not answer*) Why did you join the Army in the first place, Woyzeck?

*During the following long speeches WOYZECK shows signs of mind-wandering, of initial mental disturbance, which takes the form of fast-speaking, repetition, unnatural pauses, and so on.*

WOYZECK:    Well, because I chose to, I admit. (*pause*) I could have done all sorts of things when the moment came to choose, I suppose, when I left school, that is. I could have tried to be all sorts of other things, I know that. And when I think of it I could have done something pretty exciting, too, knowing what I know now about myself and the

193

|  | way I can do certain things. But, well, when I left school it seemed the best thing open to me to do, joining the Army. I think we always choose the best of choices we think are available to us, don't you agree, sir? |
| --- | --- |
| CO: | That's not saying very much, is it? |
| WOYZECK: | Oh, I don't mean it always turns out to have been the best choice, sir: but it seems so at the moment you have to make the decision. Well, when I had to make the choice about what to do for the next few years, the Army seemed the best thing. You know how when you're young your thoughts are dominated by sex, completely dominated — well, mine were, I don't know about everyone, though my mates seemed to think of nothing else as well, so there must be something in it, but not many people, especially as they get older, seem to realise it, or remember it: when you're seventeen or so you can be so eaten up with sex that it seems to affect everything you do. Certainly that's how it was with me — I could see that girls felt proud to be seen out with a man in uniform, of being out with a soldier, which meant you were a man, a real man. And that's really why I made the decision, sir, stupid as it may sound now. Joining the Army is such a big thing to make a decision about in a way like that. I just didn't consider the fighting bit, or that I might so easily be killed. And only when I was in it did I find out how boring it was really, and how stinking the food. . . . |
| CO: | Hrrrmph! |
| WOYZECK: | Sorry, sir, but you got me going. I've been lying here with not much else to think about the last few days but how I got myself into this state, and since you asked me I'd like to talk about it. The sex in general was why I joined, but in particular there was one special girl I wanted to impress, |

and I thought I could do it with the uniform and
appearing to be a man. . . .and so on. It didn't
work. There seemed to be other. . . .forces at
work, sir, which had forced us apart in the first
place and kept us apart even though I tried to
change things so. . . .much. . . .

*The CO shows signs of restiveness, of wanting something to be over:
but WOYZECK's fever is such that he can hold his listener: and for
some reason the CO will not use his rank to stop him.*

WOYZECK:     The man she did take up with left her with a kid
             after two or three years and I felt a kind of
             pleasure in that, sir, and I know that doesn't put
             me in a good light, but can you understand? It
             seems logical enough to me, anyway. But there I
             was, stuck in the Army, and I hadn't got what I
             thought I was going to get out of it, what I joined
             for. But I made the best of it, just as I'm trying to
             make the best of this job, sir, and I found that in
             doing that I actually got something better. Do
             you find that happens, sir? It's as though if you
             expect nothing, then anything you do get is a
             bonus. And I found after a while I actually liked
             the limitations, the regularity of everything, even
             the discipline. When your choices are limited, so
             are your responsibilities, aren't they, sir? For a
             long while the only thing irregular about my life
             has been my bowel movements. Funny, that, isn't
             it sir? As though some part of me had to revolt
             against the routine!

*WOYZECK laughs far more than the remark is worth: the CO smiles
awkwardly.*

WOYZECK:     Oh, I know it's not how you regard the Army, sir.
             To you it's a career, and you were meant for it
             like priests are meant for the church.

195

*The CO is about to say something, but WOYZECK goes on.*

WOYZECK:    But I sort of just *fell* into the Army, in any sense
            that really matters. Then a couple of years ago I
            met Marie, and everything seemed to fall into
            place. No, that's not right. What happened was
            that it didn't seem to matter any longer what job
            I did — Marie doesn't care what uniform a man
            wears, that's beside the point for her, she's not
            that sort of girl. It just altered my life completely,
            meeting her, marrying her, though not in your
            sense, sir. . . .

CO:         No. I was just going to remind you that the
            church had not blessed your union. . . .a source
            of displeasure to me, Woyzeck, as you already
            know. . . .

WOYZECK:    I know, sir. But one way or another, the church
            seems to demand a great deal in return for its
            blessing, doesn't it? And with Marie and me it just
            isn't necessary. . . .We're as much married. . . .

CO:         Yes, yes, you said that before, and it's not the
            point, though I can't exactly remember what the
            point is. You should see the Chaplain.

WOYZECK:    He hasn't been anywhere near me since I came
            in here, sir. Whereas Marie comes every
            morning. . . .

*WOYZECK grins for the first time in this scene.*

CO:         That doesn't prove anything, Woyzeck!
WOYZECK:    No, sir? All I was trying to show you was that
            Marie and me are what we are together without
            anything outside having to matter to us one way
            or the other. As soon as we came together it was
            as though a great burden had been lifted off me
            — now I could get on with the real business of
            living, now I could live. . . .

CO:         I don't see it, Woyzeck. You haven't seemed to

improve yourself in the years I've known you. You seem just the same to me — a fair barber, a worrier about nonsense.

WOYZECK: Let me put it this way, sir. Life is so bloody awful in general, the only way you can make anything of it is by having someone to help you — no, I'm putting it badly. . . . I'm losing the thread of what I'm trying to say. . . . If there's someone else who's in it with you. . . .relying on you. . . . .There's a lot to put up with. We all have to put up with it, sir. Yes, that's it, in general, sir. I'm able to deal with. . . .things since I've been together with Marie. Oh, I still get fits which come over me, I still get very depressed . . . .but now I can cope, sir, with Marie's help . . .And then there's the baby. . . .(*Long pause*) So. . . .you do know what I'm trying to say, sir? Even if it's not what you think sir, not what you'd agree with?

CO: Sometimes I feel. . . .You've made it easy for me, in a way, Woyzeck. . .A hard task. . . .But really for your own good. . . . .and that of the Army. You are still in the Army, Private Woyzeck!

WOYZECK: Yes, sir!

CO: For your own good. . . Woyzeck, your simple confidence is like a cut-throat razor on which others slash themselves, you hurt them without intention. . . .You're basically a very decent fellow, you know, Woyzeck. It's for your own good, you know. . . .

WOYZECK: What is, sir?

CO: (*Pause, then, with difficulty:*) Your. . .Marie. . . . is having it away with someone else!

*Long pause while this sinks in.*

WOYZECK: Sir, you must be having me on. . . .

197

CO:               Not me, Woyzeck, your commanding officer! I tell you she's being knocked off by a drum-major from this very camp!

WOYZECK:     (*pause*) Not a tall. . . .about six foot two, black hair. . . .? The bastard! (*recovering*) She wouldn't. . . .I know her, sir, she wouldn't. Why, she was in here this morning to see me, I know her so well, I'd know immediately if she. . . .

*WOYZECK thinks. Pause.*

CO:               Did she look you in the eyes, Woyzeck?

*Obviously WOYZECK has remembered some evidence corroborating the CO's story.*

CO:               I don't lie, Woyzeck. I'm your commanding officer!

*Nevertheless, after a long pause, WOYZECK tries again.*

WOYZECK:     Look, sir, I'm a poor enough sod as it is, and I have nothing if I don't have her. For crissake, if you're joking, tell me now. She's all there is! (*pause*) Sir!

*The CO does not answer, stares at him. Very long pause while WOYZECK cracks up. Suddenly DOCTOR TWO bursts in, highly enthusiastic, waving a pulsometer reading on a piece of paper.*

D TWO:          Bloody well done, sir! Look at this! His pulse went all over the shop as you told him, the breathing became shallow and irregular, and as for his blood temperature! I'd never hoped to see a reading that high! And we even registered the classic symptom of failure to control the sphincter muscle!

*The CO gets up, moves away, somewhat disgusted at what he has done.*

| | |
|---|---|
| CO: | D'you mean the poor bastard shit himself? |
| D TWO: | Crudely put, sir, crudely put. We do not employ such terms in science. |
| CO: | It's the same bloody thing even if you do use the Latin for it! |
| D TWO: | I wouldn't know about that, sir. My concern is with the truth of science. |
| CO: | It would be. |

*DOCTOR TWO goes over to the side of WOYZECK's bed, removes a hidden camera, detaches the remote shutter control. The CO sees what has been happening.*

| | |
|---|---|
| CO: | You even spied on the poor bastard with a camera as well! |

*DOCTOR TWO does not answer: is still triumphant: Exits. CO goes back to WOYZECK, who is lying back as if unconscious, very pale.*

| | |
|---|---|
| CO: | Look, Woyzeck, you're basically a very decent chap. (*pause*) You know I think that, Woyzeck. I've told you often enough before, haven't I? (*pause*) Woyzeck. (*pause*) It had to be done this way. It was part of the experiment. They wanted to know what your physical reaction would be to extreme emotional stress. Our men are going to be very grateful to you for this work, Woyzeck. Very grateful. . . . |

*Long pause. WOYZECK recovers enough to try for the last time to make it into a lie.*

| | |
|---|---|
| WOYZECK: | Sir. . .you mean it was just the experiment? |
| CO: | Of course. Nothing personal, you know. . . . |
| WOYZECK: | She isn't really. . . .it was all lies, sir? |

CO:     Oh no, Woyzeck, it had to be true. I can't make
       myself a party to telling lies. You must know
       that. But I only agreed to do it because of the
       experiment. The way it was put to me, it was
       made to seem my duty. You must understand
       that, Woyzeck. It was no less than my duty.
       Not only for the experiment, but for your own
       good. You should know the truth. I have the
       best interests of the men under my command
       at heart, Woyzeck. You must know that by
       now. The best interests. . . .basically a very
       decent. . . .Woyzeck. . . .

*The CO exits, silently, backwards, leaving the three patients alone,
Roberts has been looking at WOYZECK sympathetically, but the
audience should notice this only if they take their eyes off WOYZECK.*

WOYZECK:   Yes. . .and yes once more, sir. The gulf
       between yes. . . .and no. . . .the difference it
       can make. . . .Yes, sir! No, sir! tell me more
       lies, sir. . . .no lies, sir, no more! There can be
       no more. . . lies. . . .

*Slowly WOYZECK comes out of what is a state of shock and looks
wildly around. Very slowly he eases himself up his pillow, looks
around again. Eventually he notices the third man's bed: his eyes
fasten on the fact that the man's food is untouched. He looks round
once more, and again tries to lift the bedclothes: fails. Then he sees
the man's walkingstick between the two beds, reaches for it, grasps it
at the second attempt, hooks at the third man's bedrail with it.
Eventually he hooks it, but in pulling all he succeeds in doing, such
is his weakness, is to pull himself out of bed, crashing and groaning
on to the floor.*

*As he falls, ROBERTS leaps out of bed and goes round to help him.
ROBERTS lifts WOYZECK back into bed, goes back to his own tray
and gives WOYZECK what food there is on it. WOYZECK looks at it,
at ROBERTS, then falls to, ravenously. ROBERTS goes round to the*

*third man's bed and takes the tray from the foot. The he turns*
*suddenly to WOYZECK after looking at the occupant.*

ROBERTS:        Hey! He's dead! This one's dead!

*WOYZECK hardly registers any emotion: he is too busy eating.*
*ROBERTS gives him the second tray, returns slowly to his own bed.*
*After he has settled in bed:*

ROBERTS:        Eat, rest until this evening. (*pause*) I've always
                  found hospitals as easy to get out of as to get
                  into. . . .

*ROBERTS smiles across at WOYZECK, WOYZECK slowly turns to*
*look at him as he understands what he is saying. Then he returns to*
*his preoccupation with food: hold this as long as it will bear.*

*BLACKOUT*

(*INTERVAL SUGGESTION AT THIS POINT*)

**SCENE ELEVEN**

*Marie's room, she is by the cot, looking down at the baby.*

MARIE:         Yes, they sparkle and catch your eye, don't they!
                  You've never seen anything like these before!
                  Nor have I, for that matter.

*She goes across to mirror, looks at her ear-rings in it.*

MARIE:         What sort of stones are they? He said they were
                  gold, but what are the stones? Look at them flash
                  in the light!

*The baby cries. Marie turns.*

MARIE:            Off to sleep now, you! Close your eyes! They'll
still be here to sparkle in the morning. Off you
go to sleep now!
(*sings*)    Quickly, quickly, close your eyes,
Settle your head and still your cries:

The Gipsy comes by stealth and night
And takes the boys not tucked up tight

To lead them quietly by the hand
Never to return from gipsyland.

*The baby is quiet. Marie gets up, goes to mirror again. She turns her
head this way and that to see herself. WOYZECK's haggard face
appears at the window for a long time, staring: Marie does not see
him: eventually he taps, and she turns at once, gasps, goes to the door.
WOYZECK's face disappears. At the door, before she opens it, MARIE
pulls off the earrings and throws them into a vase on the table before
her mirror. Then she lets in WOYZECK. He comes in slowly, weakly.*

MARIE:            Franz!

*WOYZECK is so exhausted he cannot even speak for a moment. He
half embraces, half falls on Marie. She helps him to a chair at the
table, on which are a few scraps of cheese, bread, fruit. A long pause
as Woyzeck stares at the food. Then, very slowly, he realises that he
can have it; again very slowly he takes a piece of cheese, then bread,
fruit and anything else, in a mounting rhythm until he is eating
ravenously, not taking his eyes from the table. Marie stands watching
him. Then she pours him a glass of beer: this he drinks at one draught.*

MARIE:            They're. . . .finished with you?

*WOYZECK does not answer, goes on eating.*

MARIE:            It's good to see you eating again, Franz.

*Long pause: MARIE fetches more food: WOYZECK begins to slow.*

WOYZECK: Not too much. (*pause*) Overloading (*pause*) At first. . . .

*At length he sits more upright, begins to talk, not so much to MARIE — though she is obviously meant to hear — as to himself.*

WOYZECK: . . .for you, Marie. (*pause*) And the boy. (*pause*) Such a relief! (*pause*) You should have seen the things they did, I should tell you about the things they did to me! (*pause*) Why? (*pause, then turning to her, as casually as his condition allows:*) Did I see you had an earring on just now?

MARIE: (*flatly*) Yes. I picked it up in the street.

*Pause.*

WOYZECK: How lucky to find the pair of them. . . .

*Long pause. Abruptly, WOYZECK gets up, MARIE backs away a little. But WOYZECK goes over to the baby, looks at him, lifts him, puts him back in another position.*

WOYZECK: There, that's more comfortable for the little bastard. (*pause*) How he sleeps through anything! (*looking closer*) But he's sweating! (*turns to MARIE*) The poor kid sweats in his sleep! Already he knows what it is to work! Poor little bleeder, he's human like the rest of us.

*Long pause. WOYZECK turns very slowly and looks hard at MARIE for a long moment. Then his weariness overcomes him and he sinks down on the bed, asleep or unconscious. Another long pause as MARIE watches him. Then she goes to the table, sits down, and quietly begins to cry.*

*SLOW FADE DOWN*

203

## SCENE TWELVE

*Marie's room. The DRUM MAJOR rises from the bed, where he has obviously just been making love to MARIE. He begins to dress.*

MARIE:        *(from the bed, fiercely)* Now will you tell me!

D MAJOR:     First things first, like I said!

*He grins, keeps her in suspense as he pulls his trousers on and looks round for his shoes.*

MARIE:        Tell me!

D MAJOR:     They gave him a month's jankers, that's all. Bloody lucky it wasn't longer.

*MARIE looks relieved. She gets out of bed, dresses from this point on.*

D MAJOR:     The CO's got a soft spot for him. Sometimes I think he's bent, the CO. *(roars with laughter)* Queer for bloody Woyzeck! *(laughs again)*

*MARIE goes over to the baby's cot, checks that the baby is asleep, then turns back towards the DRUM MAJOR.*

MARIE:        I always knew this was going to happen. He's sort of haunted, Franz — no, not haunted, but fated, you know? *(pause)* It's almost as though he wants things to happen to him. I can't explain it, really. *(pause)* Because he's so taken up with the pain and things which are happening all the time to everyone, not only to him, he doesn't seem able to see anything else but pain and misery. *(pause)* He brings things upon himself. You know?

D MAJOR:      No. (*pause*) You're finished with him.

MARIE:      I'm not! You just don't do it like that!

D MAJOR:      I do.

MARIE:      You're an animal! I still have a responsibility towards him. You don't love a man for two years and then suddenly. . . .there's nothing. . . .

D MAJOR:      Yes, there is. Though I don't usually want anyone for more than a week.

MARIE:      You have a responsibility in love. . .

*The DRUM MAJOR laughs uproariously.*

D MAJOR:      Responsibility! Love!

MARIE:      The least we can do is to pass him on. . . .let him down lightly. . .I'll talk with Joan, I'll pass him on to Joan. . .she was always keen on him. . .in the beginning, anyway. . .

D MAJOR:      Pass him on to the CO!

MARIE:      You sod!

*The DRUM MAJOR laughs, and stands up. As he begins to put on his tunic MARIE rushes across to him and runs her hands under it before he has fastened it.*

MARIE:      What a man's chest! I've never felt a chest like it before! I feel so proud of that chest!

D MAJOR:      Now you feel proud! Wait till you see me on a full dress parade with my baton!

MARIE:      Conceit!

D MAJOR:      Christ, you're a woman! Already my baton's up in the air again!

*DRUM MAJOR puts hand on MARIE's left breast, pulls her to him, tries to kiss her.*

MARIE:      No!

D MAJOR:      Now who's an animal?

| | |
|---|---|
| MARIE: | Leave me alone! |
| D MAJOR: | (*laughs*) What a great fighting bitch you are! |

*MARIE continues to struggle, then suddenly capitulates.*

| | |
|---|---|
| MARIE: | Have it your way, then. (*then, straight to audience*) What's it matter, anyway? |

*Hold briefly, frozen: then BLACKOUT.*

## SCENE THIRTEEN

*The Medical Corps room, DOCTOR ONE and DOCTOR TWO come to attention as the CO enters. He motions to them to stand at ease: DOCTOR ONE sits down, DOCTOR TWO relaxes.*

| | |
|---|---|
| CO: | What are you doing about my melancholia? Have you been working on my melancholia? |

*The Doctors look at one another.*

| | |
|---|---|
| CO: | I thought you bloody hadn't. Look, it's getting worse. Now I can't even look at dirt and dust and stuff like that without being reminded that's what I am, that's what we all are. Why do I insist on wanting to be more than that, eh? Why do I feel like this? Why is anything like this? Why don't you bloody do something? |
| D ONE: | We can't answer "Why" questions. . . . |
| D TWO: | We were not trained to answer "Why" questions. . . . |
| D ONE: | "Why" questions are properly referred to the Chaplain. . . . |
| D TWO: | The Chaplain is trained to answer them. |
| D ONE: | He can refer if necessary to higher authority. . . . |

206

| | |
|---|---|
| D TWO: | Dear old God, by name. . . . |
| D ONE: | Science is our concern. . . |
| D TWO: | "How" questions are the ones we attempt to answer. . . . |
| D ONE: | In certain cases can answer. . . . |
| D TWO: | Can provide an accurate answer to within a high degree of certitude in many cases. . . . |
| D ONE: | As in the case of our mutual friend Private Woyzeck. . . . |
| D TWO: | You recall our friend Woyzeck, sir? |
| CO: | Of course I bloody do! Is that what you've got me here for? What about the poor bleeder? |
| D ONE: | (*to D TWO*) Let's have Woyzeck. |
| D TWO: | (*goes to side*) Bring in Private Woyzeck, Corporal! |

*Enter CORPORAL, with WOYZECK: the latter is haggard, greyfaced, but tired and dispirited rather than weak.*

| | |
|---|---|
| D ONE: | As you know, sir, we fed this case for twenty-four days on nothing but sphagnum moss and water. . . . |
| D TWO: | And then the case had approximately one decent meal before incarceration. . . . |
| CO: | YES yes yes! |
| D ONE: | Well sir, this corresponds to a pattern. . . . |
| D TWO: | A pattern of great military significance. . . |
| D ONE: | He has so to speak enacted for us. . . . |
| D TWO: | Acted out for us. . . . |
| D ONE: | Exactly the pattern of survival which may well be typical of our troops when cut off from their supply routes! |
| D TWO: | And then taken prisoner by the enemy! |
| D ONE: | It seems fortunate now that he had the one decent meal. . . . . |
| D TWO: | There seems a very good chance that the enemy would give him one good meal on capturing him. . . . |

207

| | |
|---|---|
| CO: | Why should they? |
| D ONE: | Private Woyzeck therefore represents, as you see him, as nearly as we are likely to come. . . . |
| D TWO: | As far as we know. . . . |
| D ONE: | To a soldier in this condition. . . . |
| D TWO: | In this state. . . . |
| D ONE: | So we now propose to carry out a searching series of tests. . . . |
| D TWO: | We shall examine him with unbelievable thoroughness. . . . |

*WOYZECK groans, nearly collapses, has to be supported by CORPORAL. CO gets up.*

CO:          (*roars*) You're so bloody concerned with your own bloody work that you never have time to read what other doctors are doing, do you?

*CO throws down on the desk a sheaf of papers he has been carrying.*

CO:          Let alone do something for me. Read that HQ Bulletin, you stupid tits! This bloody experiment has been done before! Five years ago!

*BLACKOUT*


## SCENE FOURTEEN

*Barrack-room. Two camp beds with soldiers' belongings beside them. WOYZECK lies propped up in one of them. ANDRES sits on the other, reading. WOYZECK is obviously not recovered, but he is stronger than in the last scene.*

WOYZECK:          (*looks around*) Andres! (*pause*) Sunny day!

ANDRES:         Yes.
WOYZECK:        The band will be playing. There'll be dancing on
                the terrace. . . .
ANDRES:         Uh-huh.
WOYZECK:        They'll be dancing. . . .

*ANDRES looks quickly at him.*

ANDRES:         I suppose so. . . .
WOYZECK:        Dancing together. . . .Andres, I feel ill. . . .like I
                had a great hollow where my guts should be. . . .
ANDRES:         I should think so, after what you've been
                through.
WOYZECK:        No, it's nothing to do with that. It's not that sort
                of illness. . .(*pause*) I must see them together for
                myself, I must be sure!

*WOYZECK attempts to get out of bed: ANDRES restrains him.*

ANDRES:         What good would it do? Rest, you're not well,
                you're weak, you'll be strong again soon enough.
WOYZECK:        Every day is. . .(*pause*) my head rocks. . . .
                (*pause*) This place is so hot. . . . .

*WOYZECK allows himself to be put back on the pillow, and closes
his eyes.*

*BLACKOUT*

*Lights up on same scene after just enough time for ANDRES to get
into bed. Night. WOYZECK starts up in his bed, wildly.*

WOYZECK:        Andres! I've been lying there unable to move!
                How long? I'm still alive! I had only seconds to
                live and the seconds ran out!

*ANDRES stirs, groaning sleepily.*

| | |
|---|---|
| WOYZECK: | But I'm still alive! It was a dream. (*pause*) Was it I had taken poison, had been injected? (*pause*) No, no. (*pause*) The knife, the knife, it takes time to die by the knife, shorter or longer, it takes time. Does it take time? Not the bullet, the knife. . . . |
| ANDRES: | Go to bloody sleep! |

*BLACKOUT*

*Lights up again, almost immediately. Both half-dressed, finishing dressing.*

| | |
|---|---|
| ANDRES: | Why should it be me who has to tell you? |
| WOYZECK: | You're my friend. |
| ANDRES: | What does it matter? She'll get tired or he'll get tired, then there'll be more trouble. Things are quiet now, enjoy things being quiet! |
| WOYZECK: | Tell me what you've seen! |
| ANDRES: | I haven't seen them! |
| WOYZECK: | (*fiercely*) What you've heard then! What other people have told you they've seen! |
| ANDRES: | Why? |
| WOYZECK: | I must know! |
| ANDRES: | (*pause*) They say she's shacking up with him. . . . |
| WOYZECK: | That doesn't mean he's screwing her! |
| ANDRES: | No. . . . (*pause*) |
| WOYZECK: | I dreamt last night. . . . |
| ANDRES: | I know you bloody did! |
| WOYZECK: | (*handing ANDRES a jacket*) Here. Have this. Go on, I don't want it any more. (*pause, then, with a smile*) It doesn't fit me any more. (*pause*) This ring was my mother's. You know, the last time I went to see her she didn't even look at me? The neighbour who looks after her said the only time she seems to notice anything now is when the sun comes out and she feels it on the backs of her hands. (*pause*) You might as well have the ring, as well. |

210

*ANDRES does not take it: stares at WOYZECK sadly. WOYZECK puts the ring down on his bedside table, picks up his paybook, reads:*

WOYZECK:      "Franz Woyzeck, private soldier, Third Infantry Regiment, First Battalion, Fifth Company. Born July 20th" — which makes me thirty years old. . . .seven months. . . .and twelve days. You can have that too, Andres. If you know where to flog it, you can get a fair bit for a soldier's paybook.

ANDRES:      Franz. . . .You're not well. . . .

WOYZECK:      (*long pause*) No. . . .

ANDRES:      See the doctor again. . .

*WOYZECK reacts as though he has been hit: or madly, with a nervous tic. Stares at Andres for a long time.*

WOYZECK:      When each goes out in the morning, Andres, who knows whose hearts will fail to carry them through the day, whose hearts will just stop, will not bring them home that evening?

*Long pause. Then WOYZECK moves to go.*

ANDRES:      What are you going to do now?

WOYZECK:      Report for duty. (*pauses*) But it was good, Andres, it was good!

ANDRES:      What was?

WOYZECK:      Nothing.

*BLACKOUT*

## SCENE FIFTEEN

*The street: indicate by placard if necessary. MARIE and JOAN enter, to be surprised, accosted, confronted by WOYZECK.*

WOYZECK:      I thought it would have altered you, I thought I'd be able to see it in your face!

JOAN:      What do you want with her?

WOYZECK:      (*ignoring her*) After all, a betrayal that monstrous! I thought it would have turned you into an ugly bitch overnight — to look at, as well as in my mind!

JOAN:      You know nothing about her! Leave her alone!

WOYZECK:      But your lips look as soft as ever. . .Are they bruised, Marie, does he bruise your soft mouth? How can a woman do what you've done and still be so lovely!

*WOYZECK moves as if to embrace her, obviously loving her. JOAN gets between him and MARIE, who backs away.*

MARIE:      Franz, you're not well yet!

WOYZECK:      (*points appropriately at her, shouts*) Was he *there*, woman? Was he *there*? Was he?!

*MARIE turns away, WOYZECK pushes JOAN aside, and makes as if to grab MARIE.*

MARIE:      No! You won't touch me! I'd rather you killed me than so much as touch my hand! Even my father didn't dare touch me from the time I was ten! No one touches me unless I want them to!

*WOYZECK watches as she avoids him, no longer able to find the*

212

*will to pursue. MARIE and JOAN exeunt. Hold on WOYZECK's*
*dejection as long as it will bear.*

*BLACKOUT*


## SCENE SIXTEEN


*WOYZECK downstage left, standing at ease, facing audience,*
*unmoving. Bare stage. CO next to back wall of stage, back to*
*audience. Hold for a long silence: CO turns: another silence,*
*somewhat shorter: then:*

CO:  Where's it all going to end, Woyzeck?

*WOYZECK's eyes flicker towards the direction the CO speaks from:*
*otherwise he does not show he has heard.*

*Hold for a long silence.*

*BLACKOUT*


## SCENE SEVENTEEN


*Terrace of a café: as Sc. 4. Noisy. Dancing. Music. ANDRES and*
*WOYZECK drinking sullenly. Suddenly a student leaps on a table*
*and begins preaching. Others react vociferously during his speech.*

1ST STUDENT:  (*drunkenly*) Brethren, verily, verily, I say unto
you that I am the bearer of tidings of great
moment! I have good news for you! I have been

213

vouchsafed a vision! An official communication from God! The Almighty has spoken to me of why he started it all! What it's all about! It seems it happened rather like this, Brethren. God was mooning around one day with nothing much to do, twiddling his celestial thumbs, when he thought of the idea of the Creation. He says it came to him in a blinding flash, this idea. Not very original choice of words, the Almighty! But there, he doesn't have to worry about his listeners, he's got everything going for him! The trouble arose, Brethren, when he actually came to put this wonderful idea of the Creation into practice! You see, it's one thing to think of the idea, but quite another to actually do it! He just hadn't got the right sort of power, or enough of it, to complete the Grand Design! But Brethren, and this is the good news I promised you, he does say, the Almighty told me, that he's learnt so much from the experiment! He's so grateful to us and the rest of creation for what we've taught him! He said he'll find it so useful next time! In fact, he's already embarking on a yet larger project!

2<sup>ND</sup> STUDENT: You mean he's buggered off and left us?

1<sup>ST</sup> STUDENT: Yes, Brethren, that's the final piece of Good News! He's gone, but he sends his best wishes. He's gone, we're free, free FREE!!

*General applause: the Student is pulled down, fêted. Towards the end of his speech, WOYZECK has wandered off to watch the dancing (this can be offstage, if necessary) and now he comes back to ANDRES.*

WOYZECK: They're dancing!

ANDRES: Leave it alone! It can't do you any good!

WOYZECK: I don't want to be done any good! The way he holds her! It's. . .obscene! (*pause*) I can see she

|           | likes it. . .The bastard! (*pause*) Soon it'll be done with. . . |
|-----------|------------------------------------------------------------------|
| ANDRES:   | Yes, you'll soon forget her.                                     |
| WOYZECK:  | That's not. . .                                                  |

*WOYZECK has seen the DRUM MAJOR and MARIE approaching arm in arm, WOYZECK suddenly attacks the DRUM MAJOR.*

WOYZECK:        These hands!

*WOYZECK and the DRUM MAJOR fight. WOYZECK is easily beaten, ends up in a corner nearly unconscious. Dim lights except one on him: exeunt all others except MAN who is not, however, really noticeable until after song. WOYZECK slowly stirs, bloody, dishevelled: gets up: comes forward to audience.*

WOYZECK:        One sodding thing after another:
(*sings*)     Just when you think you're set
And've won your private bet,
You expect to draw your due —
Then it catches up with you:
Life's one sodding thing after another!

It's possible to forget
You're heavily in debt;
You feel you're in control
And then it takes its toll —
Just one sodding thing after another!

Since everything's upset
The best terms I could get
Then — chaos! Nothing matters!
And I'm not finished yet
With one sodding thing after another!

*WOYZECK turns away. Bring lights up slowly to represent evening, sunset. The man sits at a café table.*

WOYZECK:        Look at that! (*genuinely pleased at the sunset, then reverts to his former mood*) Only God can piss in such straight lines through the clouds!

*WOYZECK goes purposively towards the MAN. There is a pistol on the table. WOYZECK picks it up, looks at it, puts it down again.*

WOYZECK:        It's too dear.

MAN:        D'you want it or don't you?

WOYZECK:        I haven't enough money. What else have you got?

MAN:        Ironic, it is, supplying weapons to the armed forces: How about this then?

*MAN produces a knife, puts pistol away.*

MAN:        Much quieter, of course. . . .

*WOYZECK balances the knife, feels its edge, point.*

MAN:        It'll cut more than bread, that. Cut your throat easy enough, if that's what you want it for.

*WOYZECK comes to a decision, throws down coins on table. The MAN looks at them, at WOYZECK.*

WOYZECK:        It's all I have.

*The MAN accepts by picking them up. Exit WOYZECK, concealing the knife. The MAN looks again at the coins, clinks them in his hand.*

MAN:        So I'm that much nearer becoming an armaments king!

*BLACKOUT*

**SCENE EIGHTEEN**

*Marie's room. The baby is being put to bed.*

MARIE:       (*sadly*) Here's your very first story, then. There was once a little child — a poor little girl, like Mummy was once, if you like, or a little boy like you are. But this little child had no father and no mother: they were both dead. And everyone else in the world was dead, too. But all day long the child looked for someone else, he still tried to find someone. When he was finally sure that there was no-one on earth, he looked up at the moon and thought it seemed very friendly: so up he went to the moon. How disappointed he was when he arrived! You know why? The moon was made of wormeaten wood, all soft and crumbling away! So he went to the sun. . . . .

*WOYZECK enters silently, without MARIE noticing.*

MARIE:       . . .and yet again he did not find what he had hoped for! The sun was just an old, faded sunflower, a husk after the seeds had dropped out! And when the poor little child came to the stars he saw they were only like insects stuck on blackthorn spikes by a butcherbird. (*pause*) So the little child turned back towards the earth and saw. . . .That it was empty, no more than a goldfish bowl upside down. . . .Nothing! (*Pause*) And the child saw that he was always to be quite alone, and he sat down, and he cried. And he's still there, crying, crying. . . . . . . .quite alone. . . . . . .(*Pause*)

WOYZECK:   Marie!

*MARIE turns.*

WOYZECK:   We have to go!
MARIE:    Why?
WOYZECK:   It's time.
MARIE:    Where?
WOYZECK:   How should I know?

*Neither of them moves.*

*BLACKOUT*


## SCENE NINETEEN

*A pond by the edge of a wood: establish either by placard or by lighting effect — low water rippling very slightly to one side of stage for WOYZECK to wade into.*

*Enter WOYZECK, with MARIE.*

MARIE:    But home's in that direction! And it's nearly dark!
WOYZECK:   You've time enough yet. Why don't you sit down?
MARIE:    I'm going!

*WOYZECK prevents her, throws her down roughly.*

WOYZECK:   Rest your feet! You must be tired.
MARIE:    (*cries*) What's got into you? You never used to be like this.
WOYZECK:   (*slowly*) Neither did you! (*pause*) Can you remember how long it's been, Marie?
MARIE:    (*Very slowly*) Two years. . . .nearly. . . .

218

| | |
|---|---|
| WOYZECK: | Two years next month. (*pause*) And how much longer do you think it's going to be? |
| MARIE: | I must go back to feed the baby. (*WOYZECK still restrains her*) Franz, I'm cold! |
| WOYZECK: | Cold are you, Marie! You, the hot whore, cold! That's not what I was told — "She's red-hot in bed!" they said he said, he boasted to them! Cold! (*tries to kiss her. Pause, then desperately:*) Christ! Why can't things be as they were, why can't things be still! Still! |

*Pause. MARIE tries to edge away, but WOYZECK is quick to notice.*

| | |
|---|---|
| MARIE: | Soon the dew will be. . . . |
| WOYZECK: | I don't think you'll feel the dew! If you're cold already you won't feel the cold. . . . |
| MARIE: | What do you mean? |
| WOYZECK: | What do I mean? (*pause*) Nothing (*pause*) |

*MARIE tries to distract his attention and make a run for it.*

| | |
|---|---|
| MARIE: | The moon's up. . .and it's red. . . . |

*WOYZECK anticipates her move, seizes her, takes out his knife, and stabs her again and again.*

| | |
|---|---|
| MARIE: | Oh, Franz, no, help, aaah, it's not, etc. . . . . |

*WOYZECK steps, gets up, still holding knife, MARIE still moves.*

| | |
|---|---|
| WOYZECK: | Are-you-not-dead-yet? Are-you-not-dead! Dead! |

*As he says the above, WOYZECK stabs to each word. MARIE is still then.*

| | |
|---|---|
| WOYZECK: | Dead, dead. (*pause*) Marie? So pale? (*pause*) Those red earrings (*pause*) Red. (*pause*) Your hair not. . . . (*pause*) Marie. . . . |

219

*WOYZECK rises very slowly, stares at the knife, MARIE, the blood.*

*Then, infinitely slowly, he begins to move away from the body towards the water, which he enters without appearing to notice; though his gait goes from walking to wading. He begins to go round in circles, and continues to do so for the rest of this scene until shown.*

*All the following to end of scene are off-stage voices.*

1<sup>ST</sup> VOICE:    (*Off*) Hear that?

2<sup>ND</sup>VOICE:    (*Off*) What?

1<sup>ST</sup> VOICE:    Listen!

2<sup>ND</sup> VOICE:    It's the water lapping. . .

1<sup>ST</sup> VOICE:    Long while since anyone drowned here. . . .

2<sup>ND</sup> VOICE:    It's just the water, lapping. Let's not bother. . . .

1<sup>ST</sup> VOICE:    Who's bothering?

(*Pause. Children's voices, playing, distant, then closer*)

1<sup>ST</sup> CHILD:    Where's Marie?

2<sup>ND</sup> CHILD:    Don't know.

3<sup>RD</sup> CHILD:    Come and play!

1<sup>ST</sup> CHILD:    Let's look for Marie

3<sup>RD</sup> CHILD:    No, let's play!

2<sup>ND</sup> CHILD:    I'd like Marie to tell us a story. . .

1<sup>ST</sup> CHILD:    Let's look for her, then.

3<sup>RD</sup> CHILD:    All right, let's go and find Marie. . .

*Long pause. WOYZECK is still wading round in circles, but farther and farther towards the back of the stage: so that he can disappear when necessary to get blood off his hands for next scene: WOYZECK goes: the water disappears slowly during the next few lines, leaving the end of the scene in darkness.*

POLICE CHIEF:    In all my years in the force, I don't think we've had a juicier murder than this one. Oh, yes it's been a very long time since we had a good,

oldfashioned murder like this. It's all a man
could wish for. . . .

*Pause.*

CO:                (*off*) He'll be tried by the military, of course.
POLICE CHIEF:   (*off*) No! The woman was a civilian!
CO:                You can't try her, can you? Woyzeck will be
                   tried by Court Martial.
POLICE CHIEF:   At the Assizes!
CO:                I shall preside myself.
POLICE CHIEF:   Judge Stein won't give up the chance to try a
                   beautiful murder like this!
CO                 Balls!

*End of scene.*


## SCENE TWENTY


*The CO sitting high, as though a judge presiding. WOYZECK in a
desk, guarded by two soldiers. Other officials of the court as
available: but these are not strictly necessary.*

CO:                You must explain to us, Private Woyzeck. . . .
WOYZECK:        I do not have to explain to you.
CO:                . . .so that we may understand. We are concerned
                   to understand, Private Woyzeck.
WOYZECK:        I am not concerned that you should understand!
                   It is nothing to me that you understand. (*pause*) I
                   do not understand myself.
CO:                Let us go through the business slowly. . . .
WOYZECK:        Hasn't the Army finished taking from me yet? I
                   am busy about my dying. You even take that
                   from me with your ridiculous "understanding".

221

CO:                 You were co-habiting with the woman Meissner, Private Woyzeck, until recently. . . .

WOYZECK:     What will you understand even if you discover reasons? What are the reasons! Actions are the only things that matter, don't you see? I killed her, whether there are reasons or not!

CO:                 You admit you killed Marie Meissner?

*The CO makes a note.*

WOYZECK:     Of course! Didn't I just say so?

*Long pause.*

CO:                 Any normal soldier would have gone out and found himself another woman. . . .

WOYZECK:     Let me be mad, then, sir, let me be considered mad!

CO:                 Or tried to win her back. Or at least have thrashed the bastard who'd cuckolded him!

WOYZECK:     I tried to, sir, though not with very much. . . conviction. (*pause*) What we had was. . .what we both had. . .When she went, it all went. . . there just wasn't anything else. . .nothing matters. . . . when love fails, all fails.

CO:                 Not true!

WOYZECK:     It's true for me! Damn what's true for you! (*pause*) I have all rights, and no rights. I have a right to destroy the thing itself, the thing that was love, to kill physically what is already really dead. . . .I have what I call that right, though you may call it just having the power to kill. . . .as you have the power to kill me. . . .or the power to leave me to choose to kill myself.

CO:                 What if everyone thought as you do — or acted as you did!

WOYZECK:     I can't answer that. I can only answer for myself.

I don't care if anyone or no-one does as I have done. And who are you to demand duty from me now!

*WOYZECK laughs: loudly but unhumorously. Long pause.*

CO:                 You leave me with no alternative. . . .
WOYZECK:     (*violently*) I don't want there to be an alternative!

*BLACKOUT*

*Following voices offstage to cover scene shift.*

CHAPLAIN:   (*off*) If you truly repent of your crime. . . .
WOYZECK:     (*off, contemptuously*) Carrion-eater!
CHAPLAIN:   . . .then you may be saved. . . .
WOYZECK:     If you could make things as they were, then you would be some use to me! (*pause*) Time is the criminal, time.
CHAPLAIN:   (*solicitously*) My son. . . .
WOYZECK:     (*kidding*) Daddy! (*Roars with almost hysterical laughter. Cuts off sharply. Pause.*)

*Lights up. Absolutely bare stage. WOYZECK at very front, back to audience, standing quite still with hands behind back as though bound.*

*Long pause.*

*WOYZECK begins to walk very slowly, but directly and calmly, towards the back wall of stage.*
*No sound but his footsteps.*
*WOYZECK reaches the back wall.*
*Stops, facing it.*
*Long pause, held until audience is almost bored.*

*Suddenly WOYZECK turns to face the audience, very quickly, and then he shouts at the top of his voice:*

WOYZECK:       Yes!

*Immediately a volley of shots; two or three wounds on WOYZECK's shirt (use blood-pellet guns).*

*Before he falls*

*BLACKOUT*

**What is the Right Thing and Am I Doing It?**

## EDITORS' NOTE

*What is the Right Thing and Am I Doing It?* was commissioned by ATV in 1971 for their one-hour *Armchair Theatre* programme. The script was not produced and, until now, has never been published.

## CHARACTERS

GHENT, *about fifty; handsome, fit for his age; a leader; the sort of man who usually dominates any company in which he finds himself; upright, moral, and emphatically not a criminal in the ordinary sense although he has just come out of prison*
GWEN, *his wife; early forties; still an attractive woman*
HIND, *about 28; tall, thin, intense, dedicated*
CHRISTINA, *25, blonde, highly intelligent as well as pretty*
DOCTOR (JOHN), *old friend and contemporary of Ghent; self-assured, calm, sympathetic*
NEWS EDITOR, *about 45, sharp, bald little man, Americanised*
JOURNALIST, *about 27, subservient hack, Americanised*
SACSEN, *Ghent's generation, old friend, soft-centred, vague*
ERICSSON, *about 28; sharp, clever*
YOUNG FARMER, *about 20; callow, rash*
YOUTH, *guest at party*
GIRL ONE, *guest; about 20*
GIRL TWO, *guest; outsider; about 20*
SON, *aged 5; non-speaking*
TELEVISION INTERVIEWER, *standard; voice-over only*
GUESTS, *about half a dozen, mainly Ghent's generation, non-speaking*

*Accents should be more or less standard English, with no regional variations.*

## SETS

1) *A composite main set consisting of a large living area flanked on the right by a kitchen and on the left by an open terrace or balcony overlooking a view. A large, well-modernised farmhouse in a remote, hilly area.*
2) *Main set: bedroom in the same farmhouse, first floor.*
3) *Corner: prison cell.*
4) *Corner: newspaper editorial office.*
5) *Corner: committee room of the Language Association.*
6) *Corner: doctor's study/consulting room in a rural practice.*

## TIME

*The present; May – June.*

**PART ONE**

*1. INTERIOR. BEDROOM. NIGHT*

In double bed are two forms lying apart: GHENT and his wife
GWEN.

At first, only their voices can be heard in the dark during a semi-
circular track round foot of bed. Then gradually reveal their faces.

> GHENT (*slowly*)
> You had to float. (*pause*) You had to float
> between (*pause*) events. Even the tiniest thing
> could be an event, the next thing to look forward
> to. Until then you had to float, to stay above the
> (*pause*) situation.

*FLASH INSERT*    Side shot: two-tier prison bunks, with sleeping
forms in them. End flash insert.

> GHENT
> If you didn't float (*pause*) it got on top of you.
> You learnt that very quickly. (*pause*) Rimmer
> would sometimes be up all night, three paces to
> the window, three back, all night. And all the
> time he would be rubbing his hands together
> with the same (*pause*) circular motion. (*pause*) A
> dry sound. You know?

GWEN says nothing: stares up at ceiling, listening carefully.

> GHENT
> Rimmer had been in Burma in the war. A
> Japanese soldier smashed him in the face with

229

the butt of his rifle and was about to bayonet him
when one of Rimmer's mates shot the Jap.
(*pause*) So Rimmer rubs his hands, walks up and
down and stares. (*pause*) So he told me. (*pause*)
It was his way of floating.

GWEN
Will you see Rimmer again?

FLASH INSERT    CU hands being rubbed together. End flash
insert.

GHENT
Will I see Rimmer again? (*pause*) You have to
float.

FLASH INSERT    Wider shot of hands of men walking towards
camera. End flash insert.

GHENT
Rimmer has another five years to do. At least.

FLASH INSERT    Full shot, hands, figure: as we see the face it is
GHENT and not Rimmer, whose presumable
form lies in the bottom bunk beyond. End flash
insert.

GHENT
You had to ignore so many of the (*pause*)
grievances, the causes for grievance.

FLASH INSERT    Greasy plate with uneaten food on it. End flash
insert.

GHENT
Otherwise you'd blow up. Many of them blew
up. (*pause*) Not Rimmer. You had to float to
survive. I can't put it any better than that, though

230

it's a cliché. Sometimes the use of clichés can be the only response to (*pause*) deep emotions. It's sometimes the only way they can be expressed. (*pause*)

            GWEN

But there were the poems. . . .

            GHENT

Yes, I had the poems. (*declaims*)
"Long in the lizard's green labyrinth
 Slumbered the seed of my country's grief."
(*pause*)

            GWEN

You must get them down.

            GHENT (*smiles*)

Believe me, I shan't forget them. (*declaims*)
"Moment and moment in forge and field
 Marking the hour of my country's need."

CU GWEN's face: doubtful, anxious.

*FLASH INSERT*    Prison cell: full shot: GHENT stands at far end, feet apart, hands down and slightly away from sides, fingers spread, palms towards camera. End flash insert.

GHENT turns to GWEN, addresses her directly for the first time.

            GHENT

I'm sorry.

            GWEN (*impassive*)

Patience, it will come.

*2. INTERIOR. FARMHOUSE – COMPOSITE LIVING AREA.*
*KITCHEN. TERRACE. NIGHT*

A small party is in progress: perhaps fifteen to twenty people, of
whom about half are the same generation as GHENT and the rest
younger.

As we dissolve between one group and another, overhearing snatches
of conversation here and there, it becomes evident that all these
people have something of a spirit and a purpose in common: they are
in fact part of the core of a dedicated minority nationalist movement.

GHENT is the centre of the largest group; he is relaxed, buoyant.

> GHENT
> Mind you, the cocoa was good, last thing at
> night. In fact, if our boys had come over the wall
> to get me out at cocoa-time, it would have been a
> toss-up whether I went back with them or not!

The others laugh.

*QUICK DISSOLVE TO*:

Another group including HIND and CHRISTINA.
CHRISTINA has just finished saying something in a foreign
language; clearly this particular nation's language. The others all
laugh, except for one YOUTH.

> YOUTH
> What does that mean?

> CHRISTINA (*pleasantly, but with an
> edge*)
> It's an old story about the impossible rent asked
> for a farm — a snowball in June, and a rose at
> Christmas. (*pause*) It doesn't make the same
> sense in English, as usual.

232

> HIND
> "Scorian y vall, lorian a Summass." You can hear the difference, at least, can't you?

YOUTH nods, looks embarrassed.

*QUICK DISSOLVE TO:*

SACSEN, an older generation nationalist, and ERICSSON, about 28.

> SACSEN
> D'you shoot pigeon?

> ERICSSON
> No, but when I'm in London I make a point of kicking stones at them!

*QUICK DISSOLVE TO:*

Group including DOCTOR.

> DOCTOR
> . . .for two hundred years the charts showed a depth of fifteen fathoms when there was only three at high water — generations of wreckers in that quiet little village must have been paying clerks at the Admiralty to keep the charts unchanged. Shifting sands, they'd say, but there was always solid bedrock there that would tear the keel of any ship afloat to tatters. And there they'd be on the shore, generation after generation, waiting to kill anyone unfortunate enough to avoid drowning, and then. . .

*QUICK DISSOLVE TO:*

GHENT's group, which now includes HIND and CHRISTINA: all young people as well. GHENT is now noticeably drunker: clearly he is not used to alcohol after his long lay-off.

233

GIRL ONE
It must have seemed never-ending.

GHENT
No, I could always see an end. Who was it said
we all get what we want in the end: that's the
trouble! (*laughs*)

CHRISTINA (*half-jokingly*)
Not when the end we reach is power. . .

GHENT
Especially when we gain power! What do we do
with it? Why, John Stannis and I would reach a
point — usually when we were drunk, and it was
late at night — Oh, I can see John Stannis now,
sitting there like a young Toby Jug he'd be, and
I'd say 'What are we going to do when we win,
John Stannis?' And he'd think a while, and he'd
say, 'Damned if I know, Ghent!'

GHENT roars with laughter; GIRL ONE joins in; CHRISTINA
begins to smile, then stops herself; HIND does not smile.

GHENT
Then we'd just decide to win first, and work out
then what we'd actually do with the power!

HIND (*quietly*)
We know now what we'll do when we win.

GHENT
Eh?

HIND
We've worked out a policy to cover every
important area which. . . .

GHENT
Policy! What policy can there be? How can we
possibly decide until we've won?

HIND
This isn't the right time to discuss it. We'll meet
later in the week and have a whole day to go
over everything.

QUICK DISSOLVE TO:

GIRL TWO
Is that his wife?

YOUNG FARMER
Yes. . .

ERICSSON
She worships the grass that grows under his feet.

ERICSSON wanders off as GWEN approaches.

GWEN
Hullo, you must be Calnin's son. Is the farm still
up for sale?

YOUNG FARMER (*somewhat guiltily*)
Yes. He says he can't work it on his own now
Stahl is retiring, and I'm away at college most of
the time.

GWEN
Is there no other way? Won't you come back
after you've finished college anyway?

GIRL TWO
What is there here for him?

YOUNG FARMER looks embarrassed; GWEN looks reproachful.

*QUICK DISSOLVE TO:*

Group including GHENT and SACSEN.

> GHENT
>
> You have to float, you know, that's the only way
> to. . . .

> SACSEN
>
> . . .survive? To keep going? I couldn't have done
> it, Ghent, and it might so easily have been me.

GHENT puts his arm round him.

> GHENT
>
> Ha! Yes, we kept you out, didn't we, boy! There
> was nothing they could do about it! (*hesitates,*
> *then commits a rather drunken indiscretion: but*
> *for a purpose — to exorcise*) You might say we
> kept John Stannis out, too! (*pause*) One way or
> another!

An awkward pause.

> SACSEN
>
> The poems, Ghent, what about the poems? If
> they're half as good as the novels they'll be
> marvellous!

> GHENT
>
> Ah yes, the poems.

> SACSEN
>
> Aren't you going to let us hear them this
> evening?

236

                    GHENT
          If I'm sober enough!

*QUICK DISSOLVE TO:*

GWEN and DOCTOR on terrace.

                    GWEN (*coolly*)
          It's interesting how fit he seems. You remember
          how easily he would put on weight? You once
          warned him about his heart.

                    DOCTOR
          Perhaps the physical regime of eight years in
          prison has added as many again to the end of his
          life. Perhaps even longer. I've known something
          similar happen.

GWEN's cool expression does not change.

                    GWEN
          You'll give him a complete check-up as soon as
          you can fit one in?

                    DOCTOR
          Of course.

*QUICK DISSOLVE TO:*

Another group including GHENT.

                    GIRL TWO
          I mean, everyone's entitled to an opinion. . . .

GHENT is by now very drunk, almost falling around.

                    GHENT
          Opinion! Entitled! I've decided to give up

237

opinion! What use is opinion! What does it
matter? I didn't go to prison for being entitled to
opinions, but for holding them so strongly that I
was prepared to back them up with action! With
violence! (*pause*) Without it, mere opinion is
useless — (*mimics childishly*) he holds this,
someone else holds that — what does it mean!
(*pause*) I had a long while to get used to mere
opinion! (*pause*) The 'intellectual support' is
about as useful as a truss with perished elastic!
Ha!

GHENT's voice has been raised so much that everyone in the room
has fallen silent: a certain amount of embarrassment is evident at his
drunkenness, but it is mingled with realisation that, having been
deprived of alcohol for so long, it was virtually bound to happen;
and, in any case, the occasion entitles him to a certain amount of
licence.

GHENT

What use are these intellectual theorists without
action in support of their ideas? None at all!
(*pause*) None! (*pause*) I judge people by what
they do, not by what they say! Ha!

He is now totally dominating those present; and he knows it.

GHENT

Why are you all here tonight? (*pause*) No
answer. You're here because of what I did all
those long years ago, eight years, it seems a
lifetime, eh? I am your conscience, I was the one
who did what you all wished you had the nerve
to do, the courage, the guts! (*pause*) There are
people here tonight who should have been there
instead of me, there are others (*pause*) who
should be here tonight who cannot be. (*pause*)

He is lost as to how to go on. Anti-climax. To cover up, he searches around for yet another drink; and fortunately finds one to hand; drinks; end on BCU GHENT drinking.

*3. INTERIOR. BEDROOM. DAY*

GHENT and the DOCTOR. They are clearly old friends: an easy atmosphere between them.

GHENT is pulling on a roll-neck sweater, and it is apparent that the DOCTOR has just concluded a medical examination of him. Throughout the first part of the conversation he tidies away various pieces of medical gear into a case.

> DOCTOR
> The only things I can find at all wrong with you are consistent with the hangover I know you must have after last night.

> GHENT (*clearly hungover*)
> How long will it be before I can take as much as I used to?

> DOCTOR (*smiles*)
> Depends how hard you work at it. I wouldn't advise shortening the process to less than a month. Here, I use this myself when the next morning rears its aching head.

Hands GHENT a pill; GHENT goes across to washbasin, rinses out toothmug, takes pill, drinks.

> DOCTOR (*half seriously*)
> That was one of the main reasons I became a doctor — so that I'd know what was wrong with myself and be able to treat it as quickly as possible.

239

GHENT

But what if you had something serious, really
serious — fatal, even?

DOCTOR

I'd rather know. It's true I've had to train myself
to accept that I'd know, and I tend to examine
every little twinge minutely for what larger
implications it might have. But that's how I've
chosen to live. I wouldn't have it any other way.

GHENT (*nods*)

'Choosing how to live' is something of a new
idea to me at the moment, you understand.
(*laughs*)

DOCTOR

Physically, there's no reason why you shouldn't
adjust very well — though you'll put on weight,
of course, for the first few weeks. (*pause*) Apart
from physically. . . .

GHENT (*guessing*)

Mentally, I know, it's going to be more difficult
to adjust.

DOCTOR

Some things have changed, Ghent.

GHENT (*rhetorically, rehearsed*)

Ha! You don't have to tell me about change! I
know all about change, John, change is one of
the conditions of life — and perhaps the most
important condition, too. Everything is changing
constantly. We change physically over the years,
we change our habits, our likes and dislikes —
but we don't change our characters, John, we
can't change our character!

DOCTOR

No?

GHENT

No. We are what we are. I am what I am. I don't
understand how I came to be what I am, but I do
know that I'm stuck with being what I am. Until
I die. Do you remember those long arguments we
used to have about whether Freud was right, or
the conditioned reflex theory, or. . . .oh, you
know, all that? Have your opinions changed?

DOCTOR

Well, I'm still a Freudian, though a severely
modified Freudian, I find, the longer I live.

GHENT

There! Change again! And if Freud hadn't lived
it would have been necessary to invent him! You
don't know how much I missed some form of
(*pause*) engaged, intelligent conversation. . . .

DOCTOR

I can imagine. . . .

GHENT

Rimmer had only two basic subjects, football
and crime, and I couldn't pretend to be interested
in either of them beyond a certain point.

DOCTOR

Yet you didn't ask to share a cell with someone
else?

GHENT

No, there were plenty worse than Rimmer!
Really hard men, twisted men who would
attempt any kind of malice just for its own sake.

241

The malice itself would be satisfaction enough
for them without any other gain from it. Men just
determined to prove they were living up to being
criminals. No, once I'd found I could put up with
Rimmer, then that was enough for me.

DOCTOR (*awkwardly*)
Look, there are some things I have to say. As
your friend. Adjusting other than physically may
be a lot more difficult than you think. Everyone
you know has been developing, changing in all
sorts of directions while you've been (*pause*) not
standing still, exactly, but centred, limited, if you
know what I mean. . . .

GHENT says nothing, looks serious.

DOCTOR
. . . .You mustn't misunderstand or take offence.
But many things you took for granted are no
longer (*pause*) relevant, or relevant only in a
special way. . . .

Again DOCTOR is anxious that GHENT shall understand.

DOCTOR
The most obvious example of what I mean
is. . . .Well, look, you've been living constantly
in the company of an old lag of sixty. Surely
you can see it's going to take some adjusting,
living with Gwen again?

*4. INTERIOR. KITCHEN/LIVING AREA. DAY*

GWEN picks up a tray with coffee things on it, walks from kitchen
through door to living area, across living area, and out through doors
on to terrace.

*5. EXTERIOR. TERRACE. DAY*

On the terrace GHENT and DOCTOR sit at a table in the open air. They have clearly just finished lunch.

Enter GWEN from living area. She pours and distributes coffee for the three of them throughout the following.

> GHENT
>
> I had an official letter from the college this morning. Do you know, they're allowing the years I was inside to count towards increments in my salary? So I won't be worse off financially.

> DOCTOR (*wryly*)
>
> Apart from the eight years' salary you lost, of course — no chance of the college doing anything about that, is there?

> GHENT (*laughs*)
>
> No, the Senate could never be that generous, much as they sympathised with what I stood for. (*pause*) I can never really say thank you for the way you've looked after things for me. . .

> DOCTOR
>
> You of all people don't have to.

> GHENT
>
> I don't know how you managed. . . .

> GWEN
>
> I don't know how we managed sometimes, either.

> DOCTOR
>
> When do the college want you to start again?

>           GHENT
> Not this term, anyway. They suggest the
> beginning of the new academic year, October.

GHENT grimaces on tasting coffee, helps himself to lots of sugar.

>           DOCTOR (*slightly amused*)
> You take sugar now!

>           GHENT
> Yes. Everything had sugar in it, so I took it
> willy-nilly. Now I can't do without it! That's an
> example of the corrupting influence of prison if
> you like!

GWEN helps herself to sugar, sits down.

>           GWEN (*almost smugly*)
> A question of taste. (*pause*) There are a great
> many letters. . . .

>           GHENT
> From?

>           GWEN
> People. Do you want to answer them all?

>           GHENT
> How many are there?

>           GWEN
> Dozens. . . .perhaps a hundred.

>           GHENT
> Yes, let's try to answer them all.

>           DOCTOR
> You're already becoming a Grand Old Man!

GHENT

Well, it's better than becoming a dirty old man, I suppose. If that's the choice! Is that the choice?

DOCTOR

Who knows?

GHENT

Which do you want, Gwen?

GWEN does not answer: is distinctly cool. She moves off terrace under cover of clearing away plates and so on. DOCTOR notices awkwardness.

DOCTOR

Ghent, you must have dreamed of the view from here across the valley.

GHENT

Not so much dreamed of it as held it fixed in my mind's eye. I could call up every detail at every season. . . .trouble is that now the real thing seems a poor copy of what I had in my mind! Places take on a different significance as one's centres of interest change. Think how many different things London has meant to us! It was college and Bart's for you, for me it was my first job. D'you remember warning me each Friday not to hit the kids that day as Friday night was bath night and their Mums would see the marks?

DOCTOR laughs.

GHENT

Then London became the centre of oppression, the place that stood for all we were fighting against. (*pause*) It was still that at first after the trial, but curiously enough London later became

245

chiefly the place where the Prison
Commissioners had their offices. And now
London once again seems. . . .

Enter GWEN with HIND and CHRISTINA.

> HIND (*apologetically but firmly*)
> I intended to ring you later in the week, to give
> you time to settle in, but something's come up
> which we ought to discuss this afternoon, I think.

> GHENT
> Oh?

DOCTOR rises, tactfully begins to leave, greeting CHRISTINA as
an old friend: they and GWEN go into living area and towards
kitchen.

> HIND
> I understand you've agreed to record a television
> interview in the morning?

> GHENT
> Yes.

> HIND
> What are you going to say?

> GHENT (*carefully casual*)
> I haven't thought that much about it. (*pause*) I
> shall just be myself, as they say.

> HIND
> But which self? The one that went in, or the one
> that came out?

> GHENT
> Who knows?

> HIND
>
> We were hoping you would.

> GHENT
>
> We?

> HIND
>
> The Language Association. (*pause*) The Party's
> been a lot less active since you were sentenced.
> Or didn't they keep you in touch? (*pause*) Most
> of the nationalist effort comes from the
> Language Association now. . .

> GHENT
>
> The Language Association! A lot of steamy old
> ladies of both sexes!

> HIND
>
> In your day, perhaps. Now most of the members
> are young. And very active. The old women are
> in the Party! (*pause*) If you're looking for them.

Long pause.

> GHENT
>
> I knew your father. In the Party. (*pause*) I always
> thought you'd go far.

> HIND (*smiles*)
>
> I always hoped to go too far. . . .

> GHENT
>
> Look, I'm not going to be told what to say or not
> say by the Language Association or anyone else!

Long pause. HIND gets up, stares out at view.

> HIND
>
> Of course, you never learnt our language, did you?

GHENT looks viciously at him. HIND goes over his excuses for him, almost to himself.

>           HIND
> You were one of the millions culturally deprived
> by the English. One can have only one mother
> tongue, of necessity, one imbibes it with one's
> mother milk, as our proverb has it. And your
> mother tongue was English.

>           GHENT
> No one could hate England and what the English
> have done to our country more than I do! No
> one!

>           HIND
> But your wife's mother tongue was certainly not
> English. . .

Again GHENT looks at him viciously. Pause.

>           HIND
> And how did you fill in the long prison days?

>           GHENT
> The only thing they'd let you have notebooks or
> paper for was study. Approved study. . . .

>           HIND
> And our language was not 'approved' study!

>           GHENT
> I had to write to stay sane between one slopping
> out and the next. But no, my own writing was
> not allowed: nothing could be written on their
> paper about your own life, prison conditions,
> other prisoners, methods of committing crime,
> and lots of other things, all lumped together as

the same offence. So I told them what to use
their official paper for, and what to do with their
approved courses of study, and I began to write
despite them, but in my head! And because it
was easier to remember, to keep, for the first
time since my early twenties I wrote poetry, long
poems I could thunder through my head like a
tape recording, but variable and changeable, I
could improve the poem at any point on
playback. And I was able to put in my own life,
prison conditions, methods of committing every
crime I heard about, all on purpose, all the things
they would not let me write down on their
bloody paper! And there they all are still, up
here, lying ready for. . . .(*pause*) It was the only
thing that kept me sane.

> HIND (*unmoved*)
> Why don't you just talk about the poems in this
> television interview, then?

## 6. INTERIOR. LIVING AREA. EVENING

Subdued light. Television set (black and white) on. A group watching
GHENT in an interview pre-recorded in this same room.

GHENT in MCU on set. He has no idea of television presentation of
himself; he appears bombastic, ham, overacting, far larger than life.

> GHENT (*on screen, declaiming*)
> "Night and the thundering heat on me
> Proclaim the emptiness made for one,
> Spurning the grafting hand in the dark
> And the jets that spume to the aching void
> While the tower of need goes emptied, full. . . ."

HIND and CHRISTINA sit watching.

249

CHRISTINA (*quietly, to HIND*)
Is that what I think it's about?

HIND
I'm afraid so.

CHRISTINA
Why can't his generation be straight about sex?
Instead of wrapping it up in verbiage like this?

HIND
Ask him!

GHENT (*answering question*)
Tape recorder! As though I could ever forget
them! They're here, (*taps forehead*) here!
Branded forever on the quivering flesh of my
brain by the whitehot iron of necessity! (*pause —
for effect*) Why, I remember, when I was a tiny
boy, a child in God's sight, not even a pimply
youth, going to school, an English school where
they forced those of us who spoke the mother
tongue of our country. . . .

Reaction shot: HIND.

GHENT
. . . .to wear a placard reading FOREIGNER —
yes, this in Britain, Great Britain as those
gentlemen in London call it — they called me
FOREIGNER who had never set foot outside my
native land, who had. . . .

Reaction shot: CHRISTINA.

GHENT
. . . .been brought up on the words of Stahl and
Beline, who had drunk at the shrine of St. Erling.

> Who did they think they were? What did they
> think they were doing to me? To us? Gentlemen,
> I wonder!

It is apparent by now that GHENT is either drunk again or overcome
with emotional hysteria.

Embarrassed reaction shots now cover DOCTOR, SACSEN, and
GWEN, besides HIND and CHRISTINA.

> INTERVIEWER (*voice over only*)
> The situation you found in your childhood still
> largely exists. What do you see as the next step?

Pause.

> GHENT (*flannelling*)
> The next step is obvious. . . .

Reaction shots of HIND in particular during the following:

> GHENT
> . . .Clearly, my act of defiance and the vicious
> reaction of the establishment represent only a
> beginning, they formed the vital spark from
> which has flamed the movement and reaction
> which have (*pause*) followed. The next step is
> clear: there must not be just one martyr, but two,
> and then three, and then ten, and then fifty, and
> then five hundred, and then five thousand, until
> our whole nation is seen to be so united, so
> opposed to the whole vicious idea of empire, of
> one nation dominating another, that a true
> conflict arises, an actual confrontation of a mass
> of people with another. . . .mass of people. . . .

Contempt on HIND's face.

> GHENT
> . . .this is not only inevitable
> and. . .conclusive . . . .but will be seen to be
> inevitable and conclusive!

This nonsense is proclaimed with hammy conviction: CHRISTINA, DOCTOR, and GWEN register varying degrees of unconviction.

> INTERVIEWER (*voice over only*)
> Can we turn now to your actual experience in
> prison — What did it mean to be a perfectly law-
> abiding citizen, a university lecturer with an
> increasing reputation as a specialist in medieval
> English literature, an eminently safe career —
> then this career, this security, you gave up,
> abandoned, virtually overnight, to become what
> some saw as a criminal and others as a
> nationalist hero. Simply, what did it mean to you,
> a man used to comfort, to the unhampered use of
> extensive libraries, to have to endure the
> privations of a prison designed in Victorian times
> for the accommodation of only a third of the
> prisoners it does now?

Pause on GHENT (screen) as he gropes for answer.

> GHENT (*at length, insincerely*)
> You had to. . .float. (*pause*) Float. (*pause*) If you
> didn't float, then it got on top of you very
> quickly. (*pause*) Otherwise you'd blow up.
> (*pause*) You understand?

Patently the unseen interviewer does not: GHENT sees this, but tries to conceal that he has seen it.

> GHENT
> I can't put it any better, you had to float. . .you
> had to float. . .

252

Suddenly, and almost simultaneously, the image on the screen is switched off, and the lights in the room are switched on.

GHENT stands at the door, by the TV set, in a position to have done both: his presence has not been realised until now: the five others in the room look at him.

> GHENT
> That isn't *me*! They haven't got *me* there!
> (*pause*) Have they?

## 7. INTERIOR. NEWSPAPER OFFICE. DAY

Start tight on badly-reproduced, ten-year-old newsprint photograph of GHENT.

> NEWS EDITOR (*vo*)
> Did you know he read his own obituary notice at
> one point?

Pull back to see NEWS EDITOR in his office. He is briefing the JOURNALIST who has a cuttings file before him through which he has clearly just been reading.

FX off: newspaper editorial processes in large room.

> NEWS EDITOR
> Must be a select little club, the few people
> who've done that.

> JOURNALIST
> This must have been shortly after the explosion?

> NEWS EDITOR
> Yes. Get on to him about it. Ask him how he felt,
> reading of his own death. Great angle, if he'll
> talk.

JOURNALIST
But how did they come to think he was dead?
There's nothing in the file about it.

NEWS EDITOR
There wouldn't be. The thing was that they knew
at least two of them had done the job, and there
was so much blood and guts and bits and pieces
lying around everywhere that it looked like two
of them had to have made the mess. But this
Stannis who was with Ghent was an enormous
man, twenty stone and tall with it. And the
bloody thing must have gone off as he was
clutching it to his stomach or something, because
there was one godawful scene. I was on the night
desk when Tony Druce came through with the
story, and he sounded shattered — and you know
how hard Tony is.

JOURNALIST (*nods*)
Where the hell was Ghent?

NEWS EDITOR
That's the question you should use all your
journalist's cunning up to which to lead. (*He
smiles smugly at the pedantic inversion*) No one
knows. Did he chicken out? Did he go for a leak?
There are lots of stories, of course. You'll hear
them. There's bound to be a pub near this converted farmhouse he has. It should be no hardship
to put in a bit of market research there, between
drinks. You'll hear the locals' versions then.

JOURNALIST
Did you see him on the box last night?

NEWS EDITOR
Some of it.

JOURNALIST
What did you make of the poetry bit?

NEWS EDITOR
Curious. But not for our readers. Irrelevant to the paper. It sounded a load of crap, anyway.

JOURNALIST (*hesitantly*)
I thought it was quite revealing, the way it confirmed a pattern in his life. I came across a quote by Nietzsche the other day. . . .

NEWS EDITOR (*horrified at the intellectualism*)
Nietzsche!

JOURNALIST
He said "Every man of character has a typical experience which recurs over and over again". It seems to fit Ghent very well, as far as I can judge. His 'typical experience' has been an emotional conflict which has always been resolved by an act of violence.

NEWS EDITOR
You're reading a lot into those crappy poems. And I'll bet you a fiver you don't get Nietzsche past the subs.

JOURNALIST
The point is that if there is a pattern, then it's going to be repeated. . . . .

NEWS EDITOR
Ah. . .so what's he going to blow up next?

JOURNALIST (*nods*)
Where was he when he read his own obit?

NEWS EDITOR
No one knows. On the run, somewhere. The story was in some local nationalist paper first, but it didn't say where.

JOURNALIST (*casting around*)
I wonder if he was with his wife. . . .

NEWS EDITOR
The wife. . . .(*searches for sheet of paper in file tray*) There's some dirt on her dug up by a stringer locally. (*pause*) Yes, here. The marriage had nearly broken down at the time he went inside. It seems to have been given a longer lease of life quite artificially as a result.

JOURNALIST
Any children?

NEWS EDITOR
No. The stringer says she didn't go short of it while he was a guest of Her Majesty.

JOURNALIST (*slightly disturbed*)
Ah. Look, I want a definite line on this story.

NEWS EDITOR
The paper's line is very clear and simple: we're opposed to all forms of nationalism within Britain, whether it's the Welsh, the Scots, the Cornish or the Herne Bay Freedom Movement. This is *Great* Britain, greater than the sum of its parts, diverse as they may be. And anyway, two out of the last four Prime Ministers have been Scots, the Welsh had Lloyd George — What more do they want? So you dig as much dirt as you can, right? Your methods are your methods, I don't want to know anything but the dirt. Right?

JOURNALIST
Right.

JOURNALIST gets up to go.

NEWS EDITOR
And for crissake keep bloody Nietzsche out of
your copy!


*8. INTERIOR. KITCHEN. DAY*

GHENT is standing at a working surface, cleaning half a dozen
small fresh trout. His back is to the door, and he does not look round
as GWEN and SON enter. GWEN appears more tense than before.

GWEN
So you're cooking yet again!

GHENT
Yes, the novelty's still not worn off. I took these
down the brook early this morning. It's good to
see they're still there to be caught. All this talk
of pollution assumed vast proportions in my
mind. I imagined great rafts of detergent foam
spreading like cancer on the brook I caught trout
in as a boy. But it was much the same as when
Sadkin was alive. Who's the new water bailiff,
by the way? I'll have to go and explain my little
ways. . .

He breaks off as he senses something different about the presence
behind him, and turns to see GWEN and her SON. SON clearly
resembles his mother; and equally clearly does not resemble
GHENT.

GHENT looks at them both for a long while as the relationship
becomes clear to him.

257

GHENT (*flatly*)

Your son.

GWEN

My son. His name is Anghrist. He'll be five next month.

Pause. SON says nothing, simply stands looking straight back at GHENT, close to his mother who rests her hand on his shoulder, holding him close to her.

GHENT

I gave you. . . .

GWEN

You gave me freedom to act as I chose. We both had freedom to act as we chose. I chose to have Anghrist. (*pause*) You chose to blow up the Duke of Wellington.

Pause.

GHENT

Who is the. . .

GWEN

No one you know. It lasted three years. An extended affaire. Then he went. I sent him away. He was no one you know.

GHENT

You never talked about me?

GWEN

No. He didn't know you. Oh, he knew my (*pause*) situation. Others told him, I suppose.

GHENT

We shouldn't talk about it in front of the boy.

GWEN

It doesn't matter. He can't understand.

GHENT (*quickly?*)

What's wrong with him? Is he deaf?

GWEN

No. He just doesn't understand English.

GHENT

He doesn't speak English?!

GWEN

No. It's what we believe in.

GHENT

We?

GWEN

His mother tongue. His mother's tongue, as well.

Pause.

GHENT (*violently*)

Then he can be no part of me!

GWEN

He is no part of you. (*pause*) I'm not the person you took me to be.

GHENT

No, I realise that only too well. But you certainly took advantage of my thinking you were that person.

GWEN

Perhaps I never was. Or it's different now.

GHENT is silent, turns back to his cooking. He seizes a carrot, arbitrarily, cuts it into pieces very rapidly, puts one piece in his mouth.

> GHENT (*to himself*)
> You can't hear so well when you're eating.
> (*pause*) Strange.

Pause. Then GHENT in BCU.

> GHENT (*to himself*)
> I can change, you know. (*pause; then with a little doubt in his voice*) I can change.

*END OF PART ONE* (at about 33 minutes)

**PART TWO**

*9. INTERIOR. BEDROOM. DAY*

GHENT is standing buttoning up a clean shirt, relaxed, happier-looking than we have seen him before. Suddenly he stops, undoes shirt.

GHENT

I can change!

Takes off shirt.

Goes to cupboard, takes out another, differently-coloured shirt.

GHENT (lightly)

I have the right to change, I have the will to change. . . .

Takes off first shirt, picks up second.

GHENT

. . .and I choose to exercise it. Anyone can change their life if they don't like it, if they choose to. (*pause*) I *can* change.

Puts on shirt, but before he can begin to button it CHRISTINA, completely naked, moves into shot, presses herself against him, kisses him.

CHRISTINA

You have changed. . . . .

261

In the background, the bed on which they have clearly just made love.


## 10. INTERIOR. COMMITTEE ROOM. NIGHT

A Committee Room of the Language Association.

HIND, with ERICSSON and YOUNG FARMER who were at the party; GWEN and CHRISTINA.

> HIND
> He'll never change.

> YOUNG FARMER
> We can't risk it anyway. He's a liability
> whichever way you look at it, a bloody fool.

> HIND
> No, he's not a fool. . . .

> ERICSSON (*half seriously*)
> What this movement needs is a martyr, a martyr
> on the grand scale! Can't we tell him there's still
> a job he could do for us?

> HIND
> It might be to our advantage to let people see
> what sort of hero he really is. We could arrange a
> tour of our branches for him — the very fact that
> he addressed them in English would be enough
> to put him down right from the moment he
> opened his mouth.

> GWEN
> You can never rely on people taking the effect

you want them to in that kind of situation. He's a good speaker. And he does have a certain amount of personal charm. . .

ERICSSON
What could he teach our people anyway? How to make a mess of blowing up equestrian statues of the Iron Duke?

HIND
No, you're misjudging and underestimating the man. Blowing up anything requires a lot of nerve and courage. And none of us have the same experience. . . . .

YOUNG FARMER
None of us want it, either, I should think.

ERICSSON
What *did* go wrong? That's the most useful thing he could tell us.

HIND
Has he told you any more?

This last remark is addressed to CHRISTINA. It is the first time her presence has been revealed in this scene: it is something of a surprise.

CHRISTINA (*smiles to herself*)
No. . .

HIND
There's also the question of what he did with the rest of the gelignite. Sacsen told me they had over a hundred pounds in stock at the time, all

made available to Stannis and Ghent, and they
used less than twenty pounds on the job.

> YOUNG FARMER
> What do we want with gelignite anyway? You'd
> never carry the members with you if you wanted
> to start that kind of violence!

> HIND
> I just want to know where it is, that's all. And
> while it may be politic to agree with the
> members now, I'll remind you that no small
> nation has ever succeeded in becoming
> independent without the use of some kind of
> violence.

The others are silent at this: no one argues: tense faces.


## 11. INTERIOR. KITCHEN/LIVING AREA/TERRACE. DAY

GHENT's clothes are the most noticeable change about him: but his
manner is different, too: that of a man who is confident, has made up
his mind about something important.

During this scene he is restless, moves about from living area to
kitchen, then to terrace, back again, and so on. His movements
parallel the vagaries of his moods during the conversation.

> GHENT (*expansively*)
> . . . .John Stannis could never remember his
> socks, God knows why. But he was a most
> meticulous man about washing, about keeping
> himself clean. I remember one gig we were
> doing, and John Stannis turned up just before
> we were due to go on, the sockless wonder yet
> again, and you just can't go on and have people

saying "The bass player isn't wearing any
socks" now can you, the bass player's the most
energetic, you'd see his trousers going up and
down, wouldn't you? And first we thought of
tossing up to decide who went without,
someone in a less conspicuous position, and
then we thought of all going without, as a piece
of. . . stylistic uniformity, if you like. Or two of
us handing over one sock each and keeping one
foot hidden however we could. But finally we
noticed some ink in the dressing room there,
and we painted him on a pair of blue-black
socks and dammit if anyone noticed!

It is only now that it becomes evident to whom GHENT is speaking:
the JOURNALIST, who is clearly not at ease in the interview. That
is, he is trying to be interested in the anecdotes GHENT tells, but
they are not what he came for. This is evident in his reply, which is
only partly relevant to what has gone before: but it is the best he can
do.

> JOURNALIST (*awkwardly*)
> The normal is what is done by the majority. . .

> GHENT

Eh?

> JOURNALIST
> Er. . .you were not normal in that you put into
> practice those. . .

> GHENT
> You have to feel yourself abnormal, oppressed,
> the underdog if you're a poet, or a writer of any
> sort. A real writer, that is. You must feel that
> everyone has things better than you do, is better
> off than you are, has things easier, or richer, or

longer, or bigger. Otherwise you can't cultivate a
proper curiosity, a proper ambition to put down
on paper what you see. Even if you don't feel
that, then you have to teach yourself to feel it,
to be it.

JOURNALIST
Yes, but that's not quite what I meant. . . .

GHENT looks innocent.

JOURNALIST
Since you. . . .since you and John Stannis went
out and did what others only talked about. Why?
What's the essential difference between you and
others? That's what I'm after.

GHENT
I know what you're after. I did some journalism
myself once, in my early days, in London.
Freelance, of course, part time, too, while I was
teaching. Here, d'you know, I was making some
notes for an article once, at a dance, and the local
oicks and tearaways beat me up because they
thought I was a copper? (*pause*) I could never
really fit it together, that experience. Why did I
seem a threat to them, at a dance of all places?
I could. . . .

The JOURNALIST is becoming increasingly impatient.

GHENT
. . .have understood it if I'd been outside writing
down the numbers of their motorbikes or
something, but why at. . .

JOURNALIST
But what about John Stannis?

GHENT

Oh, he didn't have a motorbike. Too scared, John Stannis was. . .

JOURNALIST

No! You persist in misunderstanding my questions!

GHENT

You persist in misunderstanding my answers!

JOURNALIST

I came here to interview you. . . .

GHENT

At your own request, without there being any noticeable advantage to me.

JOURNALIST

I came to see you as something of a hero in your own country, to give some substance to what is a pretty shadowy myth as far as I can see.

GHENT smiles, unperturbed.

JOURNALIST

As for what's in it for you, I should have thought that what you're trying to do needs all the publicity it can get in England.

GHENT

From your paper?

JOURNALIST

From any paper.

GHENT

But you've never given us a fair hearing — or anyone else's nationalism for that matter.

267

> JOURNALIST
>
> The paper stands for the large nationalism — we
> want barriers broken down, not set up. Surely
> that's logical? The bigger the nation the better,
> until it. . . .

> GHENT
>
> I haven't noticed you extending it to the blacks
> yet. . . .

Reaction shot: JOURNALIST.

> GHENT
>
> . . . .there's a barrier for your paper to break
> down! And if I remember rightly you were
> outright anti-semitic before the war, right up to a
> couple of weeks before the war started!

> JOURNALIST (*tartly*)
>
> I wasn't on the paper then. . . .

> GHENT
>
> No, but your proprietor was.

GHENT turns, goes into kitchen. He starts dismembering a plucked
duck. The JOURNALIST follows him into the kitchen.

> JOURNALIST
>
> Okay, so I'll act the bum and ask all the stupid
> questions. And you put me down each time.

GHENT says nothing.

> JOURNALIST
>
> So why did you agree to see me?

> GHENT
>
> I didn't. I can only think the arrangement was

another act of malice on the part of my wife.
(*pause*) My ex-wife. (*pause*) I let you in out of
common courtesy, or something. Wanting to
know who you were. And now I can't physically
remove you because you're younger and stronger
than I am.

Pause. Stalemate. JOURNALIST decides to try throwing himself on
GHENT's mercy.

> JOURNALIST
> Look, I've got a job to do. . . .You know what
> it's like — fall down on a big one like this and
> I'll be out.

GHENT looks sceptical.

> JOURNALIST
> . . .I beg you to help me.

GHENT laughs.

> JOURNALIST
> Will you at least answer some questions straight?

GHENT says nothing, carries on preparing wild duck soup: has
drumstick in hand as JOURNALIST goes on regardless.

> JOURNALIST (*mock-intensely*)
> What's the philosophy behind your work?
> What's the meaning of it?

GHENT smiles to himself at this stupid question, does not answer.

> JOURNALIST
> Do you still hold those opinions you did eight
> years ago?

GHENT (*tiredly*)
Yes and no. . .

JOURNALIST
What kind of an answer is that? (*pause*) Are you still a nationalist?

GHENT
I was born in this country: I can never be anything else, I can't resign from that, can I?

JOURNALIST
But will you use violence again to support your nationalism?

GHENT
You don't imagine I would tell you anyway, do you?

JOURNALIST
What was it like in prison?

GHENT
You haven't done your homework if you have to ask me that!

JOURNALIST
I want to hear it from you.

GHENT (*parodying his earlier self*)
You have to float. . .if you don't float you go under. . . .

JOURNALIST
Would you go under if you went back inside again? (*pause*) You'd go down for a long time if you blew anything else up — perhaps twenty years. (*pause*) Does this affect the strength of

your beliefs? Or your will to put them into
action? Do you think about it at all?

GHENT (*in same mood of self-parody*)
The whole of life is a prison sentence, some
people say, usually Christians. Not me. Life is a
holiday from the great nothing, a vacation from
the void — and, like all holidays, it seems
interminable.

The JOURNALIST does not know which way to take this; tries yet
another tack.

JOURNALIST
You read about your own death while you were. . . .

GHENT
No, I didn't.

JOURNALIST
My information is. . . .

GHENT
Your information is wrong.

JOURNALIST
But you *were* on the run?

GHENT
On the walk, really.

JOURNALIST
Where?

GHENT
From pub to pub mainly, as I remember.

JOURNALIST
Which part of the country?

> GHENT
>
> I don't remember that. One pub looks much like another.

> JOURNALIST
>
> Don't remember! (*pause*) Why didn't the bomb that killed Stannis kill you too?

GHENT pauses, looks up. This question has hit him, jolts him out of his former mood. The JOURNALIST sees this, presses his advantage.

> JOURNALIST
>
> You'd took off, hadn't you? You weren't going to be the patsy, you weren't. . . .

> GHENT (*exploding*)
>
> Patsy! Bloody Americanisms! Look at you, dressed up like a fancy cowboy! Have you ever thought that you live in an American colony, that you ape American fashions and American so-called culture? Have you no national pride of your own, no English national character? Who d'you think you are to talk to me about my country? We have our own language, unpolluted by Americanisms! You ought to be starting a resistance movement yourselves against that sort of corruption and pollution! Every sort! You can't know how far it's gone — I can, comparing it with eight years ago. I thought I knew English, but the extent of Americanisation that's gone on makes you more and more unrecognisable! Unrecognisable! (*pause*) Look to your own next, scum, before you foul ours!

The JOURNALIST clearly sees he can achieve nothing: is taken aback by this attack, but not moved by its validity.

JOURNALIST turns, leaves by kitchen outside door, not shutting it behind him, disappearing along side of house right (that is, in the same direction, but outside, that GHENT will presently take).

GHENT goes back to cooking, picks up duck drumstick, then looks up.

> GHENT (*to himself*)
> Meaning. . . .meaning!

Puts down knife, turns, goes out of kitchen into living area, across and on to terrace. There he leans over the parapet, waves duck drumstick wildly to (unseen) JOURNALIST presumably departing down path from house to road.

> GHENT (*triumphantly*)
> Meaning! What's the meaning of duck soup, eh?!
> Duck soup!


## 12. INTERIOR. DOCTOR'S STUDY/CONSULTING ROOM. NIGHT

DOCTOR and GHENT, very friendly, close. Clearly it is outside consulting hours, late at night, and they have been drinking. DOCTOR offers GHENT another drink.

> DOCTOR
> Another before we unlock Joanna Southcott's box?

> GHENT
> No, let's do it while we're still sober.

They both go over to where two large safes (of the kind in which a doctor would keep dangerous drugs) are standing. One looks as though it is used a great deal; the other does not. It is the latter which the two men go to. It is of the kind which requires two keys to unlock. Both GHENT and DOCTOR produce separate keys and

273

place and turn them in their separate keyholes. The DOCTOR turns
the handle, pulls: the door stays shut. Both pull, and the door swings
open. Inside there are a few phials and other medical containers,
clearly old stock and disregarded; and an old fibre suitcase.

GHENT removes the suitcase and places it on the desk. He tries the
catches but cannot budge them.

> GHENT
> Did we lock this?

> DOCTOR
> I don't even remember having keys for it.

The DOCTOR tries the catches: with a little force they give, and the
lid is opened.

Inside are neatly-arranged cartons with labels indicating that they
contain blasting gelignite. There are also smaller cartons marked as
containing detonators.

GHENT and DOCTOR are silent as they look into the suitcase.
GHENT looks up, lost in thought. DOCTOR glances at him.

> DOCTOR
> You don't still blame yourself for what
> happened, do you?

> GHENT
> No, I never did. I've always been quite certain
> that I didn't short across as I was wiring up. Did
> I tell you Rimmer was a Peterman in his day,
> amongst other things?

DOCTOR shakes head.

> GHENT
> Well, Rimmer told me that he'd known similar
> things happen. There can be a freak short —

some unsuspected current, totally unknown,
perhaps static electricity on someone's clothes.
No one knows, and such accidents are
unexplained because the only person likely to
know is dead.

Another silence.

> DOCTOR
> The longer gelignite is kept, the less sensitive
> and dangerous it becomes.

> GHENT
> Yes, so Rimmer told me. . . .

> DOCTOR
> I didn't rely on hearsay! Since I had it as a
> house-guest for so long, I took the precaution of
> looking up its endearing characteristics in a
> dictionary of chemical technology.

> GHENT
> I'm sure it didn't tell you what to do with it
> when it does get old! Rimmer told me — you
> simply use a. . . .

> DOCTOR (*still friendly*)
> I don't really want to know. It's not as though I'll
> be using it again.

Silence.

> DOCTOR
> Our initial mistake was haste, I've always
> thought.

> GHENT
> John Stannis wasn't quick enough. . . .

275

DOCTOR glances at him with just a hint of disapproval.

>DOCTOR
>
>We've read the textbook way, and we chose to disregard it. Some would say that was amateurism. I wouldn't though.

>GHENT
>
>The way we left the place was bloody professional! I'm sure you've never driven like that again!

>DOCTOR
>
>If you'd both set out the charge, and then run the cable back together, as the textbook. . . .

>GHENT
>
>Then we'd both have been blown up together. I'm positive it was caused by nothing the textbooks could have warned us against.

Another silence.

>GHENT (*suddenly*)
>
>I'm going away.

>DOCTOR (*after a pause*)
>
>This time our correspondence should be free of the need to say everything in one letter a month.

>GHENT (*warmly*)
>
>I shall write. . . .

>DOCTOR (*reciprocating*)
>
>I shall be here. . . .

## 13. INTERIOR. KITCHEN. DAY

GHENT is in the kitchen: he gingerly sniffs at some cold food: makes a pained face, moves out of kitchen door towards living area.

## 14. INTERIOR. LIVING AREA. DAY

Most of the furniture in the living area has dustcovers over it, and the room shows other signs of the house being about to be shut up for a long period.

CHRISTINA sits reading a newspaper in an armchair with its dustcover thrown back.

Enter GHENT from kitchen.

> GHENT
> Now I've got stomach trouble. I suppose it was inevitable. . .

> CHRISTINA
> Have you read this!

> GHENT (*deliberately*)
> My stomach and I have been acquainted for forty-odd years — I thought I understood it. I've never known it behave. . .

> CHRISTINA
> But it's libellous!

> GHENT
> I thought the 'Mad Bomber' bit was quite funny. . .

> CHRISTINA
> They also make you out to be a writer of

277

pornography, a lecher in general and an adulterer in particular. A liar. . . .and probably a murderer.

GHENT

I didn't laugh so much at those bits.

CHRISTINA (*distressed*)

Laugh! And what about me? It doesn't give my name, but it'll be obvious to anyone around here that I'm the woman living with you!

GHENT

'Flaxen-haired beauty' is the gem of a phrase they used, isn't it?

CHRISTINA

And that explains the phone calls! Three times this morning there were breathers!

GHENT

Breathers?

CHRISTINA

Just breathing at the other end of the line, nothing else. (*pause*) Surely you'll sue them for libel over this?

GHENT

I could do. But I'm a gaolbird, and they think they're safe to say anything about me. (*pause*) Besides, I'm going away, aren't I?

CHRISTINA

You don't seem worried by it all!

GHENT (*resigned*)

This is just the latest of a long series of caricatures of me — and in some ways it's the funniest. Barely recognisable. (*picks up paper,*

*reads aloud*) I never knew this house was a
'mountain fastness', did you? My father thought
of it as good arable hill country. 'Sex is a
marvellous idea — only God could have thought
of it.' They quote that as though I said it
yesterday!

CHRISTINA
But did you say it?

GHENT
Yes and no. It's a line out of a play I wrote years
ago, oh, twenty years ago. (*pause*) Poor Gwen
doesn't come off too well either, does she? I
should think she could successfully sue for libel.
Though they're only telling the truth about her
having the child. (*pause*) Oh, and this is a bit I
like a lot: 'Guilty secret of frightened. . . .'

Phone rings. CHRISTINA answers it.

CHRISTINA
353? (*pause*) Hallo? (*pause*) Hallo!

CHRISTINA is distressed, looks across at GHENT. He comes across
and takes the phone from her. Listens for a moment.

GHENT
You'll have to breathe harder — it's a bad line!

Smiles; waits a moment for a possible reaction, then puts down
phone. He consults a small notebook, picks up phone again, and
dials a long (STD) number.

CHRISTINA
I don't know how you can find it funny!

GHENT
I don't know how I can do anything else! (*pause*)

Laughing at other people is really only saying that they are not like oneself — which we all knew already, of course. (*pause: then to phone*) Hallo? Russian Embassy?

Reaction shot: CHRISTINA puzzled.

GHENT (*on phone*)
Hallo? I suppose I want to speak to some sort of Cultural Attaché. (*pause*) I'm a writer, a poet, Ghent. G-h-e-n-t. Ghent. (*pause*) You must have heard of me. (*pause*) Yes, yes. (*pause*) Well, I want to defect. (*embarrassed but sincere*) Defect. Choose freedom in Russia. (*pause*) Defect, don't you understand? I want to leave this bloody country to go to one where minorities are not oppressed. (*pause*)

Reaction shot: CHRISTINA cannot tell whether he is serious or not.

GHENT (*on phone*)
Think of the propaganda value. (*pause*) Ghent! Ghent? I was on television a few nights ago! Released from prison after a twelve-year sentence for political offences! Ghent! This could mean a tremendous amount of. . . .

Phone goes dead; he puts it down.

GHENT (*annoyed*)
Put the phone down on me! Must think I'm a crank — I expect they get dozens on the phone every day. I'd better go there myself when I'm in London.

CHRISTINA (*very puzzled*)
I didn't know we were thinking of going to Russia?

280

GHENT (*looking round room*)
There's a lot of me in this house. Literally, when
you think of it. I've spent thirty years here, and
most of the skin I shed in that time must be in
the dust, in the crevices, in the air.

CHRISTINA (*brusquely*)
What a curious idea!

GHENT
No, you know our skin is constantly being shed,
rubbed off and renewed? Well, it must go
somewhere, mustn't it? That's how places
literally become one with the people who live in
them a long time.

CHRISTINA looks dismissive.

GHENT
No, it's not a whimsical idea. I felt it as we were
converting the place. This section, from about
here (*indicates*) was a long barn, a continuation
of the same structure but intended to house farm
animals. I suppose what they'd left behind was
joined with what we had when we knocked the
old kitchen and the barn into this one space.
Rubbed skin, pared nails, the odd spot of blood
— there's a lot of me in this house. (*pause*)
Nothing I can't do without.

CHRISTINA
What makes you think I want to go to Russia?

GHENT (*severely*)
Nothing makes me think you want to go to
Russia!

Silence.

GHENT (*to himself*)
There was a time in this house when Gwen and I were so close that I could say about love: I *lived* up there, at night the whole of me would *live* up there.

CHRISTINA has realised that he is not going to take her with him, wherever he is going: she stands, comes across to where GHENT is now putting on his coat.

CHRISTINA (*sadly, genuinely*)
I was going to make you into a great poet, remember?

GHENT (*gently*)
Don't you see I only needed the poetry while I was in prison? (*pause*) It kept me sane. (*pause*) I'll take you back to Hind. Then you two can get on with your life's work of seeing that a decent burial is given to 'our' language. And there's something else I have to leave with Hind, too.

*15. INTERIOR. NEWSPAPER OFFICE. DAY*

Close on the fibre suitcase (last seen containing gelignite at the Doctor's house) being carried fairly swiftly up some stairs and through a door: follow it as it is swung up and on to a desk.

GHENT (*vo*)
It's the Mad Bomber!

Widen to reveal NEWS EDITOR, startled, seated at desk behind suitcase. Reveal it is GHENT who has placed it there and stands menacingly in front of him.

GHENT
Where will he strike next!?

282

NEWS EDITOR says nothing: looks petrified.

> GHENT
>
> Death is a marvellous idea — only God could
> have thought of it. (*pause*) Ha!

NEWS EDITOR starts at this — as he was meant to.

> GHENT
>
> You know, for someone who's shown such a
> deep interest in me for the last few weeks, you
> have very little to say. (*pause*) Or don't I look
> like any of the caricatures by which you think
> you know me? (*pause*) You don't mean I've
> come all this way, stropped by the London
> traffic, and you're not even going to say hello?
> 'Stropped by the traffic, stropped'. Do you like
> that? Do you think that's poetical? Don't find
> language like that in your paper, do we? Of
> course, you couldn't mention I was a poet. The
> Mad Bomber Poet. The Mad Poet Bomber.
> Doesn't sound right, does it?

NEWS EDITOR seems transfixed by the suitcase. Only very
occasionally can he bring himself to glance at GHENT's face.

GHENT goes across to a chair, sits in it.

> GHENT
>
> Perhaps you think I'm here to indulge myself in
> a confession to a total stranger?

NEWS EDITOR finally manages a glance at his office door, which is
still half-open.

> GHENT
>
> Yes, someone might come in. But it wouldn't
> make any difference. To you, that is. It might to

them. (*pause*) Tell us a joke, then. You journalists
know all the filthy jokes. It's a long while since I
had a good laugh. (*pause*) We know who your
stringer is in the village. He won't be letting you
know many more. . . .filthy jokes. Save you a bit,
that piece of information.

Silence. The two of them stare at the suitcase for a few seconds.
Then an unexpected noise outside the door makes GHENT leap
quickly to his feet and go over to the suitcase.

GHENT

This is how we set it. Watch!

Carefully, pretending precision, he clicks open both catches but does
not open lid.

GHENT

There!

This is said with dramatic over-emphasis: its intention being to
transfix the NEWS EDITOR even more.

Then GHENT suddenly makes a very quick exit from the room.

The NEWS EDITOR sits staring at the suitcase for about ten
seconds in increasing fear. Then his eyes go to the door: then back to
the suitcase: then to the window. It is clear that he thinks he stands
more chance if he throws the suitcase out of the window than if he
makes a run for the door.

Another long stare at the case: then NEWS EDITOR suddenly picks
it up and throws it through an already open window.

## 16. EXTERIOR. NEWSPAPER OFFICE BLOCK. DAY

Tight on upper floor window as suitcase comes through. The catches being undone, its contents begin to spill out as it falls: papers. Widen to follow fall.

The suitcase hits the ground, spills the rest of its contents: all papers of various sizes and descriptions.

Close on papers: it is clear that they are poems, and that they are by GHENT. There is no sign of gelignite.

Come up off papers to see GHENT on his own in middle distance walking away from camera.

Credits over last shot.

# Not Counting the Savages

**EDITORS' NOTE**

*Not Counting the Savages* was commissioned by the BBC in 1971 for the series *Thirty Minute Theatre*. It was broadcast on BBC 2 on 3 January 1972. The cast consisted of Hugh Burden (the Husband), Brenda Bruce (the Wife), Fiona Walker (Rosa) and William Hoyland (Jerry). The director was Mike Newell. The screenplay was later published in *Transatlantic Review* 45. A black and white home recording of the broadcast was recovered in 2012 and screened at the bfi South Bank on 2 December that year.

**CHARACTERS**

HUSBAND
WIFE
ROSA, *their daughter*
JERRY, *their son*
WOMAN PATIENT, *aged 60*
ANAESTHETIST
NURSE

The drawing room and kitchen of a professional-class house in (say) Maida Vale/St. John's Wood, London.

Early Evening; May

*KITCHEN*

HUSBAND and WIFE are eating at home, informally; or, rather, he is eating: she is in attendance, agitated over something she has not yet told him; indecisively moving between cooker and draining-board.

HUSBAND is coarsely feeding, finishing what remains of a huge main course. He is fat; expensively dressed, though in shirt sleeves now, tie loosened. He is ignoring the WIFE: she moves about behind him. He may have been late for dinner: he is gross, getting down to his food piggishly. He is about fifty: so is the WIFE. She is very well dressed, even for the kitchen: this more than anything else gives the professional class of the couple.

HUSBAND is an ugly, lumpish man. He finishes his course, pushes plate away from him, cutlery splayed anyhow.

WIFE tidies away plate immediately, automatically putting cutlery in the conventional closed position; then she brings a large bowl of half-a-dozen different fruits, and a cheese board just as varied.

HUSBAND cuts a whole camembert cleanly and precisely in half, eats with his fingers, messily; but is careful to wipe them afterwards on linen napkin.

WIFE pours coffee for him from an electric percolator, spilling some at first into the saucer: it is doubtful whether this was an accident or an attempt to gain his attention. She clears away both cup and saucer, fetches clean ones, this time pours successfully.

HUSBAND still gives no indication of having noticed her agitation; even her presence; reaches for the other half-camembert and eats it even more grossly. When he has finished this, he sits back and wipes his mouth roughly with the napkin. His hands are noticeable: beautifully clean, manicured, supple: totally at odds with the rest of his person, with the way he has been behaving over his food: the hand movements deft, precise, as he takes up coffee cup.

> ### HUSBAND
> Well?

WIFE looks at him with animosity.

> ### HUSBAND
> You want to say something. (*pause*) I can
> tell.

WIFE overcomes her hostility, obviously does want to talk, is relieved.

> ### WIFE
> I went out to see Georgie today. (*pause*) To see
> how the grave was looking (*pause*) after the
> winter. There wasn't much on it, it was a terrible
> winter for Georg. . .for the grave, for the garden.
> (*pause*) As you know. That moss you planted has
> done well, though, green as green, and those seed
> things on the end of their tiny hairs, stalks. . . . it's
> nearly all over the grave now, I'll have to cut it
> back to. . . .

> ### HUSBAND
> So?

> WIFE
> You know where it is. (*pause*) Two or three
> graves from the edge, from the fence. And
> there's a sort of public footpath through the
> woods on the other side. Well, I was kneeling
> down, tidying up as best I could, with my back
> to the fence, when suddenly I heard voices, two
> men carrying on a conversation. One of them
> called the other John, I think. (*pause*) I didn't
> look round, of course, but when I went round to
> tidy the other side of the grave I became aware
> of a man standing close up against the wire
> fence. (*pause*) At first I thought he'd caught his
> handkerchief or something white on it. (*pause*)
> Then I realised what it was. . . .

> HUSBAND
> What?

> WIFE
> He was exposing himself! (*pause*) Exposing
> himself! To me!

Pause. HUSBAND takes large gulp of coffee. Then hawks.

> HUSBAND
> You've seen one before.

HUSBAND takes coffee cup (but not saucer), gets up from the table clumsily, noisily, and begins to move away.

> WIFE
> But it upset me terribly! (*pause*) You can't know
> how distressed I was! (*pause*) I still am!

WIFE never quite breaks into tears: as though she never does: this is the limit of her emotion.

HUSBAND stops on his way out, cup in hand, turns.

HUSBAND

Why? You're an old woman. Why should you be upset? (*pause*) It was playacting. You're an old woman.

Exit HUSBAND

WIFE's face, from being distressed, sets into a bitter stare.

*DRAWING ROOM*

HUSBAND goes across to a calendar on the mantelpiece. The date can be changed on this kind of calendar by turning a knob at the side. HUSBAND twiddles idly with the knob, not quite changing the date (which is the 16th): then suddenly gives it a quick twirl which sends the date several days wrong, preferably ending up part-way between two numbers.

Then HUSBAND turns, coffee cup still in hand, goes across to a bow-fronted chest, puts coffee down, and from the top drawer takes out a flat object about 3' x 8" x 4" made of polished hardwood. He carries this to a table, puts it down, undoes a catch and unfolds it to reveal that it is a piano keyboard of the kind on which pianists practise when no piano is available. HUSBAND seats himself before this keyboard and launches into what appears to be a full-scale bravura performance of a romantic sonata: a professional pianist, however, would be puzzled at the exact sequence of notes HUSBAND is hitting; he would think it more an exercise of the fingers than an attempt to interpret any piece of music. Again we notice the precision and strength of the fingers as he works at the silent keyboard.

The sound of the front door opening and shutting in the hall outside. Then come up off HUSBAND's hands to see the drawing-room door facing him open and admit ROSA.

ROSA is their daughter, a striking-looking girl of about 30, fair, tall, sharp features, an air not at all butch about her but certainly she appears independent, self-contained, hard.

293

ROSA starts slightly when confronted with the sight of her father
'playing', but recovers immediately and, without saying anything,
she moves across the room past him towards the kitchen.
HUSBAND looks up when ROSA enters, but his expression does not
change and his 'playing' continues as before.


*KITCHEN*

WIFE is still sitting as last seen, staring ahead. She turns at ROSA's
entry, slightly surprised.

> ROSA
> I came as quickly as I could.

ROSA sits down at table with WIFE. During the following
conversation it becomes clear that ROSA can give her mother only
the outward, formal aspects of sympathy; she can say the right
words, make the appropriate gestures, but there is no genuine feeling
behind them.

> ROSA
> How sickening for you, mother. And you say it
> was while you were at Georgie's grave, too.

WIFE indicates she wishes to be physically comforted: after a
moment's hesitation ROSA puts her arm round her mother, squeezes.
But it is only a gesture at a gesture.

> ROSA
> Well, it's over now. Why don't we have a large
> drink together?

ROSA gets up; wife relaxes a little, stares down at the table now.


*DRAWING ROOM*

ROSA crosses to drinks cabinet, takes out decanter of whisky.
HUSBAND takes no notice, goes on 'playing' as before. ROSA

294

glances at him, almost with contempt, as she passes towards kitchen again.

*KITCHEN*

WIFE as before as ROSA comes back with decanter, takes glasses from shelf, ice from fridge.

> ROSA
> You told the police?

> WIFE
> Yes, I ran to the cemetery-keeper and told him, and he said it has happened before. He phoned the police. They said it happened before, too.

> ROSA
> The same man?

> WIFE
> Yes.

> ROSA
> Then why haven't they caught him!

> WIFE (*more upset*)
> I don't know. They seemed to treat it all as a joke. The cemetery-keeper could hardly keep a straight face.

> ROSA
> Didn't he go and try to find the man?

> WIFE
> Yes, but by the time he'd reached the other end of the cemetery he'd gone, of course. (*pause*) I was wearing my gardening gloves, and when he saw those it seemed to set him going twice as hard. "Rubber gloves, John!" he said, and as if. . .

295

ROSA (*firmly, tritely*)

Mother, you must try to come to terms with it. I know it's hard to get it out of your head, but you must realise it's no good going over it again and again. You've got to accept it and become bigger than the experience. Not let it dominate you.

WIFE looks at her daughter: it is clear that this advice is no help at all to her. ROSA sees this too, puts out her hand to touch her mother's. But WIFE removes her hand, picks up glass to cover up for the rejection, drinks deeply, stares ahead again.

ROSA

It's the police who ought to do something. And what about the doctor? Have you been to the doctor?

WIFE

No. Yes. Not mine, they sent for a doctor. He gave me those.

WIFE indicates pill container on shelf over sink. ROSA takes them down, looks at them as if professionally, then throws them suddenly and accurately into the sink waste disposer.

ROSA

A placebo! Mother, you should know them all by now!

WIFE is distressed, looks almost longingly towards the waste disposer.

WIFE

They seemed to do me some good. . . .

ROSA looks sceptical, dismissive.

ROSA

Mother: is there anything more you want to tell me?

296

WIFE is halfway to being cowed: changes direction towards stubbornness, shuts up, closes her mind.

> WIFE
>
> No. What do you mean? (*pause*) No.

> ROSA
>
> Well, what's *he* doing about it?

Exit ROSA from kitchen towards drawing room.


*DRAWING ROOM*

HUSBAND still 'playing'; with even greater concentration, dedication.

ROSA enters; stands in front of her father, having decided to try to transfer guilt for her own failure of sympathy on to him.

> ROSA
>
> What are you doing about it?

HUSBAND takes no notice.

> ROSA
>
> You fat pig!

ROSA moves closer, forces her attention on him. HUSBAND looks up but continues 'playing'.

> ROSA
>
> Can't you see she's very upset? Haven't you any sympathy for her? (*pause*) For anyone?

HUSBAND stops 'playing' suddenly.

> ROSA
>
> At least you could find out what the police are doing!

297

> HUSBAND (*quietly, reasonably*)
> What use would it be if the man were caught?
> (*pause*) Does she want him caught?

WIFE has entered from the kitchen.

> WIFE (*so hysterically it is almost comic*)
> I want him hanged! Hanged!

HUSBAND stands up awkwardly but very quickly; snaps the release catch on the practice keyboard and goes as if to bang the two halves shut violently; the two women react accordingly; but HUSBAND (his timing is perfect) holds back at the last possible moment so that the women relax momentarily: then he slams it shut with a considerable bang (but which is not as loud as it might have been) finally to startle them. In the same movement he picks up the keyboard, then crosses the room and places it carefully in the same drawer from which he took it. Then he picks up his coffee cup from where he left it, drinks most of the contents at one gulp and then tosses the remainder of the coffee grounds accurately at the roots of some exotic house plants in an imitation log trough. He then looks round to make sure that the two women are expectedly disgusted at this uncivilised act. They are.

> HUSBAND (*humourlessly*)
> Go mad for their coffee grounds, they do.
> (*pause*) Can't live without them. (*pause*) Been having them for years, years, ever since they came to live here at my expense. Reminds them of their natural habitat. All day long there the coffee beans fall off the trees. (*pause*) Happens all the time in their native equatorial. Cruel not to help them to acclimatize. (*pause*) Go mad for them they do, mad.

HUSBAND tosses dregs again: hardly any this time: close up on roots of exotic plants: HUSBAND stares at them.

298

WIFE turns away from him, showing hardly any reaction to what is
apparently his normal gross behaviour. She goes across to the
calendar and tetchily sets it correctly at 16 again.

> ROSA
> Something similar happened to a friend of mine. . .

> HUSBAND
> Similar to what?

> ROSA
> To what happened to mother this afternoon! She
> was at an underground station, going up the
> escalator, and she happened to glance up at a
> man coming down looking at the advertisements,
> and he had his. . . .

Sound of the front door bell. ROSA glances at her mother, then goes
out of drawing room to answer it for her.

Close on HUSBAND.
Close on WIFE.

ROSA and JERRY can be clearly heard talking out in the hall.

> ROSA
> Jerry!

> JERRY
> My dear sister Rosa! What's this about someone
> flashing it at the mater, then?

> ROSA
> Oh. So she phoned you too, then?

> JERRY
> Wasting his time, wasting his time. Must be
> centuries since she knew what to do with one!

Enter ROSA and JERRY.

JERRY is the couple's other child. Younger than ROSA, late twenties: tall, lean, sandy hair, sharp-featured. He is not a hippie, though there are certainly hippie elements in his clothes: e.g. a long pendant. Casual expensive suede jacket, jeans, a tee shirt bearing some such statement as Gobi Desert Sailing Club, or How Can I Fail If I'm Sincere? His accent is basically public school, though he can turn on a working-class or hippie variation for effect. On the surface he appears bright, sharp, fashionable: underneath there is little but decadence, as far as that word has any meaning.

> JERRY
> Well, well. A real gathering of the clans! Not even at Xmas is the whole family met together like this. (*pause*) Always excepting Georgie, of course.

This last remark is directly addressed to HUSBAND, who stares back at his son with just a hint of anger which he immediately controls; then he goes and sits down in armchair, takes up *Evening Standard*.

WIFE goes to greet her son, embraces him; although the two of them are poles apart in thinking and appearance, it is clear that WIFE can respond to the outgoingness of JERRY to become closer to him in a way she never could with ROSA. JERRY is over-effusive, even adopts an old-fashioned turn of phrase to communicate with her.

> JERRY
> Mummy! Poor old you! You must have gone through it!

JERRY shepherds his mother over to the sofa solicitously, and sits down with her. ROSA sits on the opposite side of the room, pretending disinterest: stares at her father, but is listening.

> WIFE
> The worst part of it was the things he kept saying. . . .

JERRY
What things, mummy? What did he say?

WIFE
Oh, I couldn't repeat them. They were dreadful,
filthy things. Ugh!

She is becoming upset once more.

JERRY
Come on mummy! It'll do you good to get it off
your chest. (*pause*) What did he say? (*pause*) I'm
over eighteen! As you well know. (*pause*) How
old was this flasher, then?

WIFE
Flasher? (*pause*) Oh, about your age, I should
think. I don't exactly know. (*pause*) It wasn't
only the words. He was talking to someone else I
couldn't see. That really frightened me. "Here's a
fair bit of grumble, John," was the first thing he
said, and this John answered in a sort of a
mumble, "Grumble and grunt, grumble and
grunt." I don't know exactly what he meant, but
from the tone it was obvious.

JERRY (*guessing*)
John? What sort of voice? Like his?

WIFE
Now you come to say it, yes, but. . .sort of
indistinct though. . .

JERRY
John Thomas! John Thomas!

JERRY roars with laughter; WIFE is puzzled; ROSA is stern,
unsmiling; and HUSBAND's expression does not change.

301

> WIFE
>
> John Thomas?

> JERRY
>
> John Thomas! He was throwing his voice to his John Thomas! Using it like a ventriloquist's dummy!

JERRY laughs even more uproariously. WIFE, to do her justice, does allow her face to break into a shy smile; ROSA does not. On HUSBAND's face there is a suggestion of a smile.

> WIFE
>
> Of course! Perhaps you're right. . . .

> JERRY
>
> But what was the conversation all about?

ROSA gets up angrily: she has not found it at all funny. She is also put out that JERRY has found a way of alleviating WIFE's distress; accidentally or not.

> ROSA
>
> Oh Jerry, for god's sake stop badgering her!

> JERRY
>
> You want to know just as much as I do! Come on, mummy, tell us what he said.

HUSBAND's eyes narrow as he listens intently.

> WIFE
>
> No. . .(*pause*) I'm feeling a little better now you're both here.

Telephone rings.

> WIFE (*cont.*)
>
> I must try to forget it, you're right dear. . . .

This remark addressed to ROSA, who then goes to sit on the other side of WIFE on sofa. JERRY is nearest the telephone, which is on a table next to his end of the sofa.

> JERRY
> Centre Point Regional Seat of Government?
> (*pause*) No. Yes. (*pause*) It was a joke. (*pause*)
> Yes, it is. (*pause*) Yes. (*to his father*) It's for you.
> They want you to go and give a talk about your
> life and work.

HUSBAND shakes head firmly, says nothing.

> JERRY
> He says he's not at home. (*pause*) What? (*pause*)
> You're a non-profit-making organisation? Well,
> that's probably because of the way you run it.

HUSBAND gets up angrily, goes across and takes the phone brusquely from JERRY.

> HUSBAND
> Yes. (*pause*) No!

HUSBAND puts down phone even more brusquely, goes back to chair.

There is an awkward pause.

> JERRY
> Don't you want to know about my latest
> cinematic epic, then?

> ROSA
He ceased to be interested in anything we do long ago.

> HUSBAND (*ambiguously*)
> No. . .

          JERRY

It's set at a fictitious Agricultural College called
Sodd Hall, and the leading character. . . .

          WIFE

You can't be serious!

          JERRY

Of course I'm serious! (*rummages in
fashionable-type bag*) Here's the script. (*pause*)
A line taken at random. A student of animal
husbandry speaking: "Girls are all very well, but
they're not like the real thing, are they?"

A single, loud belly-laugh from HUSBAND.

          JERRY

That's my audience! The dirty old men in
raincoats. Only now they tend to be wearing
crombies or sheepskin duffel coats. Want to
know how it goes on, old man, Daddy? (*pause*)
Most of the action takes place in a field, and a
nearby copse, but there's a scene in a barn full of
some very sharp agricultural cutlery—for the
sados, of course.

HUSBAND sits looking at his son: he is certainly paying attention
but from his face it is impossible to know whether he is interested or
repelled.

          JERRY

You've got to cater for the sados these days or
you're nowhere boxofficewise. . . .

          ROSA

Scum!

          JERRY

Who, me or the sados?

WIFE

Both!

JERRY

If she was in the CP, they'd call her a hardliner or a bootfaced Stalinist. But what *do* they call you, sister Rosa?

ROSA

A patriot! Patriot! Truest blue!

JERRY

Perhaps you'd like a part in my truest blue movie, then?

ROSA

Ponce!

JERRY

Tart! (*pause*) Untasted, of course.

HUSBAND gets up, moves out of this fracas towards kitchen.

JERRY

Having a bit of trouble with the title, though, we are, at the moment. *Fun on the Farm* didn't seem quite right, and *Slaughter at Sodd Hall* was not acceptable for London Transport Posters. . . .

ROSA

Sheer filth!

JERRY

Yes, that's quite good. *Sheer Filth*. Or perhaps it should alliterate—just call it *Filthy Film*? Yes. I like that. *Filthy Film*. Though I should think that some sharp operator has already registered that as a title. Did you know that you can. . .

>           ROSA
> You're despicable, degenerate!

>           JERRY
> If you go on being nasty to me, sister Rosa, I'll
> tell mummy and daddy what we used to do up in
> the railway room. . .

>           ROSA
> Ha! They know! (*pause*) He does, anyway. He
> used to spy on us.

>           JERRY
> (*pause*) Of course. Funny. Why didn't I realise
> that before?

JERRY gets up: goes towards kitchen.


*KITCHEN*

HUSBAND is eating fruit, grossly, handsful of cherries at a time,
spitting the stones out anywhere. JERRY slightly recoils at the sight
on entering.

>           JERRY
> Christ, you're even fatter! I bet you can number
> the layers of fat against the great meals you've
> stuffed down you!

HUSBAND says nothing, continues eating.

>           JERRY
> It's almost as if you're trying to commit suicide.
> Or help nature do it for you. "Died of a surfeit of
> everything," your obituary will read. Guts!

Still no reaction from HUSBAND.

306

JERRY
And since we've happily met by chance like this,
let's have another little chat about the money
Auntie Ann left me. . .

HUSBAND spits out a cherry stone.

HUSBAND
Sue me!

JERRY
I need it at once! I'm setting up this cassette
company. . . .

HUSBAND smiles.

JERRY
. . .Once you've got set up you can't fail to make
a bomb. All I need is the capital, and if I had the
bread Auntie Ann left me then I wouldn't need to
be scratching around down Wardour Street trying
to raise a few bob.

HUSBAND
I like the idea of Auntie Ann financing the
making of pornographic films!

JERRY
You'll release the money, then?

HUSBAND
No.

JERRY
Why not? Where is it?

HUSBAND
Sue me.

307

JERRY
You bastard! What have you done with it?

HUSBAND
Sue me!

HUSBAND takes more cherries, moves off towards drawing room.

JERRY
If that's the only way, I will do!


*DRAWING ROOM*

WIFE and ROSA are still sitting on the sofa. Enter HUSBAND. He goes to the calendar on the mantelpiece as before. JERRY follows as far as the kitchen door.

WIFE
. . .in such a state. Can't remember the journey home at all.

ROSA
Were you driving?

WIFE
No. . . .They brought me home. The police, I think it was. Yes. (*pause*) But I took the car—the car must still be there at the cemetery!

This thought upsets her out of all proportion to its seriousness.

ROSA
Don't worry about the car. I'll fetch it later for you. (*pause*) Wasn't Auntie Ann subjected to some similar filthy performance? How did she take it? (*pause*) In the war?

WIFE
In the war. (*pause*) Oh yes, I remember, it was in

the blackout, on her way home. You had to feel
your way along, almost, then. She said she could
tell there was someone in this doorway, and as
she approached he shone his torch on himself
(*pause*) down there.

JERRY

Ah! Hence the origin of the term 'flasher'!

WIFE

She just ran and ran. Then she bumped into a
policeman who asked her what was wrong.
When she told him, he said "That's him I'm
after!" and ran off. When Ann told us about it,
your father asked her why she hadn't hit it with
her umbrella, but how could she, it was pouring
with rain at the time.

HUSBAND is slowly turning the calendar back from 16: 15-14-13-
12, one digit at a time. The two women stop to watch him.

HUSBAND

You mustn't think I condone his action, or
approve of it: no one really approves of conduct
which is at variance with his own behaviour. . .

JERRY

Epigrams now!

HUSBAND

I myself don't need to expose myself to elderly
women in cemeteries. It's not something which
would give me either pleasure or profit. (*pause*)
The only remotely similar incident I can recall
gave me a great deal of embarrassment. I was
attending a conference in Moscow at the time,
and the sole of my shoe became unstitched along
one seam. The weather was inclement, and I'd

309

brought only one pair of shoes with me. I therefore went to the first shoe repairers' I came to and attempted to communicate my need to the lady behind the counter by hopping on one foot and pointing to the damaged shoe. But far from understanding my problem, she appeared outraged, and went to the back of the shop and fetched her husband. He was even bigger than she was. Again I did my little mime, hopping and pointing. The husband also reacted with anger, and then himself performed a little mime to indicate to me that all this time my flies had been undone.

JERRY roars with laughter, enacts his own version of the mime.

> JERRY
> I see it! I can see it!

HUSBAND returns to rewinding calendar: 11-10-9-8-7.

> WIFE
> He's never been to Moscow!

> ROSA
> Where was your interpreter? The Russians never let you out without an interpreter!

> HUSBAND
> You shouldn't believe all you read in the newspapers. Or what the Foreign Office tells you before they let you go. They put the fear of god into you about spying and being spied upon. Quite unnecessarily, in the vast majority of cases. It stops one having ordinary. . . .

Telephone rings. WIFE is nearest, and answers it. HUSBAND carefully turns back the calendar again: 6-5-4.

WIFE
611 1234. (*pause*) Yes. (*looks distressed*) It's a
woman, for you.

HUSBAND (*takes phone*)
Yes. (*pause*) No, I'm on call tonight, standby.
No. . .(*pause*) Of course, of course. I'll phone
you tomorrow. (*pause*) I said I'll phone you
tomorrow! Lunch time. About lunch time.

HUSBAND puts down phone, goes back to calendar: reverses
direction of movement 4-5, then stops.

HUSBAND
Yes, the Foreign Office must imagine half the
Russian people are trained linguists who sit up
listening to tapes of the conversations of their
foreign visitors. I couldn't even have an ordinary,
simple friendly relationship with my interpreter.
Though she was a pleasant enough girl. The
Foreign Office had warned me she would as a
matter of course be reporting everything I did
and said back to her superiors, to *them*, whoever
they were.

It should be obvious by now that long speeches by HUSBAND are
something of a rarity, an occasion: hence the others listen to him at
least out of curiosity; and he has a certain authority.

HUSBAND
What she had to report I can't think. Though
there might have been one thing. We were in the
south, at a city called Tbilisi, in Georgia. Shortly
after she'd seen me to my hotel room I was
aware of a painful irritation in my right eye. It
had happened before, and I knew that if I
couldn't remove it myself within a few minutes
then it had to have expert attention. I couldn't

remove it. And this is where the dilemma began. I'd been told that they barely spoke Russian at reception, let alone English. And of course I knew no Georgian, which is a sort of Turkish. So I was faced with the prospect of presenting myself at my interpreter's bedroom door and saying I had something in my eye. She couldn't fail to take this as the crudest of advances. I'd been warned by the Foreign Office in the most solemn way about blackmail in regard to sexual indiscretions, you see. And everything about the girl seemed to fit, if she had been put up to something. That is, she wasn't a raving beauty, or I might have been suspicious. Nor was she ugly, or obviously I wouldn't have been tempted. She was just a nice, ordinary, pleasant sweet girl, and of course I thought: That's just what they'd do! You see now what I mean about poisoning relationships before they even start?

ROSA

I don't see how it would be possible to blackmail you. Nothing anyone told me about you, however bad it was, could possibly lower my opinion of you!

JERRY

But what did you do? (*pause*) About the thing in your eye?

HUSBAND

Well, there was a further complication in that I didn't know the number of my interpreter's bedroom. All I knew was the direction she'd seemed to be taking when she left me. So I would have had to have gone along the corridor knocking at every door until I found her. You can imagine how I regarded that prospect!

ROSA

No.

JERRY

But you're so good at mime. . . .

HUSBAND

I sat down and shut my eyes to think about the situation, and suddenly noticed that the pain was eased greatly when my eye was shut. So I therefore decided to try to get to sleep. (*pause*) And fortunately I did, fairly easily.

JERRY

Is that all?

HUSBAND

Next day I told her about it, and she arranged for me to see one of their top eye men. It was a tiny sliver of glass.

JERRY

No, I mean. . . .

WIFE

But he's never been to Russia! He's never been there!

HUSBAND touches the knob of the calendar, pauses, then twirls it sharply. The calendar goes quickly through 5-4-3-2-1 and comes to rest at 0. The bizarreness of a calendar with 0 on it should not go unremarked.

WIFE

I'd have known if he'd been to Russia! (*pause*) Sometimes he frightens me!

WIFE is clearly very distressed again.

ROSA stands up, goes directly to her father.

> ROSA
> Sometimes I think the things we're frightened of
> are more frightened of us!

> HUSBAND
> Like cancer, for instance? Like cancer?

ROSA turns back to her mother.

> ROSA
> Mother, if I go to fetch the car now, will you be
> all right? I'll take a taxi, so I shouldn't be more
> than half an hour.

WIFE nods; clearly she is not all right, but ROSA staying will not
make her any better. ROSA turns to go. HUSBAND restrains her by
her arm at the door.

> HUSBAND
> If it is all chaos, then any attempt to understand
> is just useless. Don't you see? Pointless! Or even
> if it only seems to be chaos, then trying to
> rationalise about it is just so much wasted effort!
> Wasted.

ROSA ignores him, removes his hand from her arm distastefully.

> ROSA
> Mother, do you still leave the car keys under the
> front seat?

WIFE looks up, nods. Exit ROSA.

> JERRY
> She's still trying to win the Duke of Edinburgh's
> Award for Courage and Initiative.

WIFE (*slowly*)
Sometimes I feel like. . .a spectator of my own
life. . .outside. . .you know?

JERRY comes over, sits down besides his mother, comforts her.

JERRY
Yes, yes. (*pause*) Now, what did he say,
mummy?

WIFE
Who?

JERRY
The flasher, mummy. The nasty man.

WIFE
Never you mind, darling. Mummy protect you
from nasty men. Don't you bother your little
head about such things. . . .My baby. . . .

HUSBAND
My mother said. . . .

JERRY
Your mother!

HUSBAND
Your grandmother would. . . .

JERRY (*raucously but unjocularly*)
My grandmother would be a hundred and thirty-
three today if she'd lived!
　　(*sings*)
　　Happy birthday dear Gran,
　　Happy birthday dear Gran,
　　Happy birthday dear Granny,
　　Happy birthday to you!
If she'd lived, of course, if she'd lived!

Close on HUSBAND.

> JERRY
> And what about Auntie Ann?

> HUSBAND
> Sue me!

HUSBAND goes over to television set, switches it on, seats himself in front of it.

WIFE has clearly regressed to some earlier stage of her life: her voice is fainter, her eyes partly closed.

> WIFE
> We never left you alone even for ten minutes, you know. Never. There was always someone there to look after you, someone fully competent. . . .

> JERRY
> Competent. . . .

> WIFE
> Fully competent, oh yes, you deserved nothing less, you little darling. I would never grudge paying out to give you the best, the very very best. You do understand that, don't you?

JERRY has become more and more concerned about the state in which his mother appears to be.

> JERRY
> Yes, mummy.

> WIFE
> And whatever happened we always tried to do what we thought was the best for you, for. . . .

The phone begins to ring. JERRY has his arm round WIFE, is too concerned with her to answer. When this becomes clear to HUSBAND, he protestingly gets up.

WIFE (*cont.*)
. . .your future, that was all we cared about, I could put up with . . . the . . . other . . . things . . . if . . . only.

HUSBAND (*on phone*)
Yes. (*pause*) When? (*pause*).

JERRY
She's ill!

WIFE may be going through the early stages of a heart attack; or she may be faking in order to gain sympathy: it is difficult to determine which.

HUSBAND
I'll come at once.

HUSBAND puts down phone. JERRY is holding WIFE as they sit together on sofa.

JERRY
She's ill! Look at her!

HUSBAND
They want me at work now.

JERRY
It's mummy! It's your own wife!

HUSBAND
I must go to work now!

JERRY tries to get up: but he dare not for fear of worsening the condition of WIFE. He is reduced to shouting at his father.

317

                              JERRY
                          Bastard! Bastard!

Exit HUSBAND. Pause. The front door bangs.

                              JERRY
                            Bastard!


*OPERATING THEATRE*

A pair of hands being washed in a hand basin; pull back to show
arms; the forearm turns off the long lever tap. Come up to see that it
is HUSBAND with a look of seriousness, dedication on his face
which he has not shown before so far.

A NURSE hovers behind HUSBAND with gown, mask, and so on.
As she prepares him for the operation. . . .

                      HUSBAND (*voice over*)
                Yes, it is a terrible word. A frightening word. . .

Cut to file/case history: pick out key words in montage of notes,
charts, x-rays: *(1) terminal carcinoma (2) Dr. Noone (3) urgent.* The
one BCU of the patient concerned: a woman about sixty, worried,
but with an intelligent, open face.

                      HUSBAND (*voice over*)
                . . . but something like five times as many people
                are cured of cancer as die of it. . . .

HUSBAND's voice is infinitely concerned, compassionate,
reassuring: in as many ways as possible his manner is diametrically
different from his earlier behaviour.

                      HUSBAND (*voice over*)
                . . . I've had people sent to me who had been told
                "No one can save you." And I've pointed out to

318

         them that if you take away the space between
         'no' and 'one', then it spells my name. No one
         can save you, Noone can save you, d'you see?

BCU patient's face: hesitantly smiles, relieved, thankful, admiring, and so on.

BCU NOONE's face: tense, dedicated. The mask is placed over the lower half of the face.

An abdomen with broad, coloured felt-tip marks on it. A scalpel makes a precise, large incision appropriately.

BCU NOONE's face: concentration, compassion.

Montage of operating theatre details, bringing out that this man who has been seen behaving so cruelly, abominably, as an object of hatred, a failure socially and as a father, is in fact worthy of admiration and respect for the one thing at which he is superbly skilful and compassionate.

BCU NOONE's eyes: the concern, the care.

Fade in Philips BO7148: Billie Holiday/Teddy Wilson "When You're Smiling": vocal lasts for 40 seconds for end credits.

# Compressor

**EDITORS' NOTE**

*Compressor* is one of the most mysterious of Johnson's later works. The manuscript is dated May 1972, but it is not known who – if anyone – commissioned this play for television. Possibly it was intended as another contribution to the BBC's *Thirty Minute Theatre* series. It includes some speeches originally written for *One Sodding Thing After Another*, and also some material which was shortly afterwards incorporated into *Christie Malry's Own Double-Entry.*

**CHARACTERS**

PRIVATE*
SLEEPER
PORTER
WOMAN SQUASH PLAYER ONE
WOMAN SQUASH PLAYER TWO

*This part was written with the actor WILLIAM HOYLAND in mind.

Tight on a Matchbox model saloon car:
a white, battered Austin 1100.
SUPERIMPOSE title:

*COMPRESSOR*

Hand comes into shot, pushes car along
red line as if along road. Track with it,
widening slightly to show the red line is
painted on a polished woodblock floor.

*Car noises, starting and moving off,
made vocally over by PRIVATE.*

Widen further to show arm of hand is in
battledress sleeve; hold; continue
tracking along red line with car.

SLEEPER: (*vo*) You know we've always
said there were no new ideas? (*pause*)
Nothing new? (*pause*) Ever? (*longer
pause*)

Continue tracking as before, without
response or reaction.

Car reaches a tee junction on red lines:
from the 'road' at right angles suddenly
appears a large road tanker (same scale
Matchbox model) propelled by the other
hand, also in battledress sleeve. The
tanker is halfway across the road,
turning into the direction of the 1100,
when the latter is sent hurtling into it.
Hands arrange the accident more
satisfactorily: that is, tanker jack-knifed,
1100 on its side and nearer tanker than it
finished up after being violently pushed.

SLEEPER: (*vo*) Well, I think I've had a
new idea! (*pause*) Check me!

Widen to show that the man 'playing'
with the two model vehicles is a
PRIVATE soldier, dressed in his 'best' or
'walking-out' uniform of circa 1945. He

is in his mid-20s. We do not yet see his face, as camera is looking down and from behind.

Those who play the game may recognise the red line markings as being those of a squash court: to others there is no indication of the place yet.

Widen as PRIVATE reaches out to an old plumber's carpet toolbag, takes out a model motorcycle and rider, returns to point at which 1100 started and sets off guiding motorcycle fast in same direction. Just before the motorcycle is about to hit the 1100/tanker pileup, he stops:

PRIVATE lifts off motorcycle, reaches into carpet toolbag again and takes out a short length of model wire fencing. This he places carefully beside the red line opposite the upright of the tee junction. He then returns the motorcycle to first position and speeds it towards the pileup. As before, he releases it so it goes anywhere, then tidies it up: he sends the motorcycle one way, under the tanker, and the rider flying towards the fence.

SLEEPER: (*vo*) After some unspecified number of years, he decides to change the rules of the game. For this purpose he feels it necessary to split himself into three. One part stays wherever it is, but sends the second part down to insert a bun in the oven of a virgin living at the eastern . . .

PRIVATE: Damn!

SLEEPER: (*vo*) . . . end of the Mediterranean. Her husband is understood to be a very understanding man. When this child is born it turns out to be — surprise! — the third part of himself! When this third part grows up he goes around stirring up a right load of trouble, gets on the wrong side of the local law, and ends up dead. He then proceeds to join the other two parts of himself in wherever, which is now called heaven.

PRIVATE: (*to himself*) The wires cut through him like a cheesecutter.

SLEEPER: (*vo*) You don't think it's new?

325

PRIVATE indicates over shoulder to camera: for the first time his face can be seen.

PRIVATE: They've heard it all before.

BCU SLEEPER, also seen for the first time. He is about sixty, fat, bald, jovial.

SLEEPER: Like that? On the Epilogue?

They both break into loud laughter.

Full shot of set. The two men are on a squash court. A carpet bag identical to PRIVATE's and belonging to SLEEPER is in the right corner of the front wall. Cameras are generally looking at court from back wall position.

SLEEPER stands with his back against the front wall. He is dressed in a long, striped winceyette nightgown which stretches to his ankles, and is barefoot. On his head he wears a tasselled red nightcap.

SLEEPER stops laughing suddenly, is serious.

SLEEPER: I haven't been feeling mysel today.

PRIVATE: You want me to do it for you?

SLEEPER walks slowly but directly to where PRIVATE is squatting with cars, overturns tanker with bare big toe, delicately.

SLEEPER: I'm beginning to feel sad about my extremities, too, particularly the smaller ones.

PRIVATE begins packing the models away in his bag.

PRIVATE: Sometimes you treat me as

326

|  |  |
|---|---|
|  | though I'm from another planet. |
|  | SLEEPER: But you are, aren't you? |
| PRIVATE fishes in bag, brings out a book entitled *Essays: David Hume*. | PRIVATE: How about Hume? |
|  | SLEEPER: Whom? |
|  | PRIVATE: Hume. Pronounced Hume. *Of The Standard of Taste*. |
| SLEEPER takes book, opens it, begins reading. | SLEEPER: Yes. *Of the Standard of Taste*. "Men of the most confined knowledge are able to remark a difference of taste in the narrow circle of their acquaintance, even where the persons have been educated under the same government, and have early imbibed the same prejudices. But those who can enlarge their view to contemplate distant nations and remote ages, are still more surprised at the great inconsistence and contrariety. We are apt to call barbarous whatever departs widely from our own taste and apprehension; but soon find the epithet of reproach retorted on us. And the highest arrogance and self-conceit is at last startled, on observing an equal assurance on all sides, and scruples, amidst such a contest of sentiment, to pronounce positively in its own favour." |
| During this speech, establish detail of squash court: CU of corners, red lines at various levels, different material of lower board, and so on. | |
| BCU PRIVATE | PRIVATE: (*eagerly*) You mean it doesn't matter what they think of us? |

SLEEPER: No, it doesn't matter. Though it may be painful.

PRIVATE: It's all subjective opinion?

SLEEPER: Yes.

PRIVATE: So what does matter?

SLEEPER: Me. (*pause*) And perhaps you.

PRIVATE: Me! And perhaps you!

SLEEPER: Me!

PRIVATE: Me!

(*pause*)

SLEEPER: There you are, then.

PRIVATE: There *you* are!

SLEEPER: Where?

PRIVATE takes from his bag the smallest 8mm home movie projector available, sets it up to face front wall, gets up, takes plug lead towards back wall. Just before he reaches the flush door in back wall it opens: a West Indian railway PORTER hands PRIVATE a tea tray (two mugs of tea on it) with one hand while with the other he takes the projector plug and lead. Exit PORTER, door shuts.

*Immediately door opens, sound of a diesel express passing at high speed through a main line station.*

*Sound off immediately door shuts.*

328

PRIVATE puts tray down on floor, goes back to projector, switches it on. Shown on front wall is now a film of a squash court with two women (pretty, athletic, early twenties) playing squash very well.

Establish beyond doubt that the two men are on a similar court by widest shot of full set to include them, the projector, front wall and as much as possible of side walls.

*Music over: distantly, the sound of a boys' bugle band rehearsing in a tin hall.*

BCU PRIVATE watching screen as though he had never seen either women or squash before.

BCU SLEEPER calm, taking it in his stride.

SLEEPER: (*to himself*) A man taking pictures of a man taking pictures: there is something in that!

SLEEPER crosses to projector, switches it off.

PRIVATE: But what happened in the end?

SLEEPER plugs in another lead (i.e. at a take-off point), which trails from his own bag. On the other end is a miniature slide projector (e.g. Ilford Elmo CS) which SLEEPER sets up to throw on right side wall.

PRIVATE: Once more you're in the forefront of non-stop developments.

SLEEPER: It's my nature — don't crucify me for it.

PRIVATE: I wouldn't crucify you with someone else's nails!

SLEEPER smiles, settles himself,

329

punches up the first slide: which is of a Biblical pastoral scene (hills, shepherds) of the cheapest printed kind (crude colours and drawing) as given to children at some Sunday schools.

SLEEPER: The change in the rules of the game is that anyone can now gain entry to this place called heaven. The trouble is that the regulations for entry are rather obscure, and there's no way o telling whether it's worth going to anyway.

New slide: El Greco's "Christ expelling the moneylenders"

At the same time as heaven was christened, two other parts of wherever were renamed purgatory and hell. Purgatory is a sort of halfway house between heaven and hell. There is also another place called limbo, which is

BCU PRIVATE: sulking

where he has sent all those unfortunate enough to have been born between himself and the third part of himself. Residents include such all-time favourites as Moses, Job, Socrates, Heraclitus, the Unknown Centurion, and Julius Caesar. Few actual details of limbo have been allowed to seep out, but it does not appear to be as bad as hell; nothing, it was said, could be as bad as hell.

Change slide to Roman soldier, grinning foolishly

Change slide to another pastoral scene of same type as before.

To qualify for entry into any of the new places you had first of all to be dead. Then, if you had satisfied the regulation and been what was accepted as good, you were at once translated to heaven and given over to endless pleasure — whether you felt like it or not. If you ha not been good, then you went to hell, which was very painful and also withou end. If there was any doubt about whether you had been good or not good

Change slide back, as if by accident, to grinning Roman soldier.

PRIVATE begins to get restless, fiddles to change reel on his own projector.

Proper slide replaces soldier: which is of Frank Lloyd Wright's house *Falling Water*.

Change slide to still of Skylon at 1951 Festival of Britain.

PRIVATE finishes changing reels.

Silence.

When it is clear SLEEPER has finished, PRIVATE starts his projector. On front wall is now projected a film loop of a dolphin leaping out of water up towards an object held high, failing to reach it, and falling back again into the pool. Loop repeats endlessly during following conversation and until indicated.

then you did a stretch in purgatory while he sorted things out in what might presumably be called his mind. Later you would be posted either up to heaven or down to hell, though these directions, up and down, must be considered metaphorical, of course. But even if you made it into heaven, you still had to watch it: there were examples of people being chucked out for one kind of mafficking about or another.

Once you were in hell, however, you had to settle down to it: you were not allowed out, however good you tried to be through the unimaginable pain.

PRIVATE: (*proudly, indicating screen*) That's a genuine Turkish bath.

SLEEPER: The Turks overran these parts?

PRIVATE: (*nods*) Yes. They were bastards then, the Turks.

SLEEPER: (*mildly*) We've been bastards ourselves, in our time.

331

PRIVATE: Yes. Not now, though. Nor the Turks.

SLEEPER: How come there's still much bastardy about, then?

PRIVATE: Must be. . . .others. . .

SLEEPER: Other who?

PRIVATE: Other Turks.

SLEEPER tosses florin at PRIVATE in token contempt. PRIVATE picks it up, flips it high in the air, catches it, looks at it.

PRIVATE: Nineteen sixty-one! Did you know that you can read that upside down?

SLEEPER comes across to him, takes the coin back.

PRIVATE: D'you know the next year that will happen? (*pause*) Eh? The next year you'll be able to read the date upside down as well as right way up?

SLEEPER: (*bored*) No.

SLEEPER moves away towards front wall and lies down prone on his back, parallel with the left sidewall.

PRIVATE: I'll tell you, then, shall I? (*pause*) You could work it out, though, i. you wanted to. (*pause*) It's six thousand and nine. Six thousand and nine! You could guess there'd be sixes and nines and noughts in it, couldn't you?

The dolphin is still leaping unsuccessfully on the film loop; Skylon remains projected by slide projector.

Hold.

Then PRIVATE reverses his role, imitates the bearing of a high-ranking officer, maintains it as he goes over to look down at SLEEPER and asks:

PRIVATE: (*discouraged*) The stupidest thing you can do is to behave as though you were right.

PRIVATE: (*pompously*) Why did you join the Army?

SLEEPER: (*youthful persona: another reversal of roles*) Well, because I chose to sir, I admit that. I could have done all sorts of things when the moment came to choose, I suppose, when I left school, that is. I could have tried to be all sorts of other things, I knew that, sir. And when I think of it I could have done something pretty exciting, too, knowing what I now know about myself and the way I am good at certain things. But, well sir, when I left school it seemed the best thing open to me to do, joining the Army. I think we always choose the best of the choices we think are available to us, don't you agree, sir?

PRIVATE: That's not saying very much, is it?

SLEEPER: Oh, I don't mean it always turns out to have been the best choice, sir. But it seems so at the moment you have to make the decision. Well, when I had to make the choice about what to do for the next few years, the Army seemed the best thing. You know how when

333

you're young your thoughts are
dominated by sex, completely dominated
— well, mine were, sir, I don't know
about everyone, though my mates
seemed to think of nothing else as well,
so there must be something in it. But not
many people, especially as they get
older, seem to realise it, or remember it.
When you're seventeen or so you can be
so eaten up with sex that it seems to
affect everything you do. Certainly that's
how it was with me — I could see that
girls felt proud to be seen out with a man
in uniform, of being out with a soldier,
sir, which meant you were a man, a real
man. And that's really why I made the
decision, sir, stupid as it may sound now.

PRIVATE: But you stuck by it, eh?

SLEEPER: Oh yes, I made the best of it,
sir, and I found that in doing that I
actually got something better. Do you
find that happens, sir? It's as though if
you expect nothing, then anything you
do get is a bonus. And I found after a
while I actually liked the limitations, the
regularity of everything, even the
discipline. When your choices are
limited, so are your responsibilities,
aren't they sir? For a long while the only
thing irregular about my life has been
my bowel movements. Funny that, isn't
it, sir? As though some part of me had to
revolt against the routine!

PRIVATE suddenly changes role to that
of a doctor: whips out stethoscope,
listens to SLEEPER's stomach.

334

PRIVATE: (*serious*) Yes. (*pause*) Yes. (*pause*) I think you've got a touch of everything. (*pause*) Needles! I see needles! Darning needles! (*pause*) Two of them! (*pause*) At least two! (*then, as an aside, directly to camera*) What we call the Munchausen Syndrome. Patients who deliberately swallow objects so that they can get themselves looked after in hospital. He probably wrapped the needles in cotton wool to get them down him. But we don't know which sort he is yet. Yet. There's two sorts, you see. One kind are masochists who actually want to undergo a serious abdominal operation. The other kind merely want a rest in bed at the expense of the public, and they almost always make a run for it as soon as surgery is mentioned. (*fiendishly*) But some of them we catch, of course; and operate!

SLEEPER stands; rheumatically. He has reverted to role as at start of play.

SLEEPER: You don't help. (*pause*) Does it mean nothing to you, the old cliché, you'll be like me one day?

PRIVATE too now reverts to first role.

PRIVATE: It's exactly because I'm so aware I shall be something like you one day that I'm enjoying *not* being like you now!

SLEEPER rubs his scalp, removing his nightcap to do so.

SLEEPER: (*almost to himself*) Bald as a badger.

PRIVATE: Badgers aren't bald.

SLEEPER: Bald as a badger.

335

PRIVATE: Your trouble's alliteration.

SLEEPER: One of them, one of them.

SLEEPER 'pulls himself together',
moves purposefully towards the door in
back wall, collecting tea tray as he goes:
the tea undrunk.

PRIVATE: (*mockingly, with antique
flourish*) Godspeed!

SLEEPER: Has he? That accounts for
the atrocious weather we've been
having.

SLEEPER opens door. Immediately,
PORTER enters as before, hands plug
lead in to SLEEPER, takes tray in other
hand, shuts door.

*Express noise as before, sharply.*

SLEEPER drops plug lead on floor,
unplugs his own lead, goes over to his
slide projector and begins to pack it
away.

*Sound off.*

PRIVATE goes over to his projector,
begins to pack it away.

While they do so:

SUPERIMPOSE CAPTION: *The Duel
of Dictionary Words*.

Superimpose each of the following
captions over recipient's appropriate
reaction.

SLEEPER: (*venomously*) Gasconnade!

SUPERIMPOSE CAPTION:
*Gasconnade equals Boaster*

336

(*pause*)

PRIVATE: (*surprised, then hitting back*) Saurian!

SUPERIMPOSE CAPTION: *Saurian equals reptile.*

(*pause*)

SLEEPER: Dacoit!

SUPERIMPOSE CAPTION: *Dacoit equals thief.*

(*pause*)

PRIVATE: Android!

SUPERIMPOSE CAPTION: *Android equals man-like automaton.*

(*pause*)

SLEEPER: Magma!

SUPERIMPOSE CAPTION: *Magma equals dregs.*

(*pause*)

PRIVATE: Palterer!

SUPERIMPOSE CAPTION: *Palterer equals equivocator, etc. etc.*

(*pause*)

SLEEPER: Androgyne!

SUPERIMPOSE CAPTION: *Androgyne equals hermaphrodite.*

(*pause*)

PRIVATE: Hermaphrodite!

SUPERIMPOSE CAPTION: *Hermaphrodite equals androgyne.*

(*pause*)

PRIVATE: Roinish coenobite!

337

SUPERIMPOSE CAPTION: *Roinish coenobite equals scabby monk.*

(*pause*)

PRIVATE: Eccrisis!

SUPERIMPOSE CAPTION: *Eccrisis equals an excretion.*

(*pause*)

SLEEPER: (*triumphantly — role-changing again*) Coprolite!

SUPERIMPOSE CAPTION: *Coprolite equals fossil turd.*

PRIVATE opens mouth, hesitates, closes it, defeated.

SLEEPER: (*pressing home*) Coprolite, coprolite!

SUPERIMPOSE CAPTION: *Coprolite, coprolite! equals fossil turd, fossil turd!*

PRIVATE is still for a long pause, thinking.
Then he suddenly leaps up and dances a long, weird dance round SLEEPER (actor to improvise).

SLEEPER relaxes in his triumph, ignoring PRIVATE.

PRIVATE finally stops dancing, goes over to his carpet bag and places projector inside it.

PRIVATE: You know, in the twenties it was said that anyone in the second half of this century who could not use a typewriter and a camera would be a new sort of illiterate!

SLEEPER laughs; PRIVATE joins in almost immediately; until they are both laughing immoderately.

338

PRIVATE stops; at length.

PRIVATE takes out surveyor's tape measure from bag, begins measuring the squash court. Business with tape pulling each end in turns; snapping back into case; ad lib.

SLEEPER watches incuriously.

When PRIVATE does succeed in measuring a dimension he writes it in large black felt-tip characters on white side wall right.

PRIVATE: Ah well, back to work.

SLEEPER: (*straight to camera*) Streamers, we call them, I don't know why. I've known them stay two, even three years in one place, set up a home, garden, a kid. Then off they go. And when the poor girl tries to check, they can't find a trace of him before she knew him, either. Streamers. What do you say to the kid? You say, of course, now you're a child and can understand: you know you were once a baby, and now you're a child? Well, next you'll be a teenager, then a girl, then a woman, perhaps a mother, then a matron, then a lady, then an old lady, and then you'll be dead, you'll make a lovely corpse, perhaps, if all goes well.

SLEEPER goes across to front wall, starts writing with a large red felt-tip the following slogans:

*1) Never is the most terrible word.*

*2) I'm not talking metaphors, I mean the*
*lot!*
*3) Your life has been bought: steal it!*
*4) One can learn lessons from anything,*
*unfortunately.*

To avoid unnecessary boredom, jump-
cut the above after it is established what
SLEEPER is doing: and some slogans
may just pop on.

PRIVATE joins in at this point,
abandoning his measuring, with his
black felt-tip. The following are joint
efforts between the two:

*5) Change is the only constant.*
*6) We are eggs in the hands of a blind*
*juggler.*
*7) Society is a carnivorous flower.*
*8) All periods are transitional ones.*
*9) Contradiction is worth more than*
*yea-saying.*

Finally, standing together, they both
independently but at the same time
write: *I am beside myself.*

They look at one another, stare each
other out.

PRIVATE is the first to break away, rubs
elbow.

PRIVATE: I think I've got rid of my
tennis elbow at last.

SLEEPER: Yes? (*pause*) How?

PRIVATE: By not playing tennis for

three years.

The two men stare at each other again. This time it is SLEEPER who breaks. He turns deliberately, walks slowly towards front wall.

PRIVATE equally slowly walks to left side wall.

Change to full shot of set.

PRIVATE reaches side wall, SLEEPER reaches front wall. Both remain facing walls.

Then SLEEPER turns and, at the same time as he begins speaking, camera begins slow movement in on him finishing tight where indicated below.

SLEEPER: It seems he always existed, or alternatively he created himself. There's no doubt he claims to have created the world, however, which must be understood in context to mean the universe as well. Or universes. There's no doubt, too, that games are one of his chief diversions. Into this world he places various other creations, roughly inter-dependent though a certain amount of jockeying for position is evident in the early stages. Amongst these creations is Man and, shortly afterwards, Woman. He gives this couple something called free will, which means they can act as they like. If they act in a way he doesn't like, however, they will get thumped. Practically the first thing they do he doesn't like! It turns out that he knew this was going to happen, because he is (*slowly, didactically*) omniscient. It also turns out that he could have stopped it,

341

too, since he is (*slowly again*)
omnipotent. (*pause*) The couple are of
course quite baffled. But they take the
thumping in reasonably good grace, and
even go on to procreate three sons.
That's that, you must be thinking, end of
story, incest not being allowed by the
rules the family must die out. But no:
he's been making it all up as he goes
along, like certain kinds of novelists,
and he now reveals the parallel existence
of some tribes who have (*pause*)
women. Two of the sons thereupon mate
and his game can be carried on. It's
important that the game carries on. The
game is everything.

Fully tight in BCU

Suddenly, as from inside the court, the
sound of squash being played: the
explosive detonations of the ball on the
various surfaces.

Wide shot of front wall: PRIVATE has,
while camera was off him, moved up to
stand about two yards away from
SLEEPER.

Both men react to the sounds as though
the squash ball were hitting them: and as
though it were a bullet.

PRIVATE is more active, acting out the
part of a wounded man energetically,
even over-reacting.

SLEEPER does not react with the whole
of his body, only with those parts which
may be supposed to have been hit, in
turn.

Neither falls.

After between five and ten seconds of
this, fade up SUPERIMPOSITION of
two women squash players (the same
two as in the 8mm film earlier) playing
on the same court/set. The women must
mime to wild sound: use of an actual
ball is impractical in the studio since all
four walls could not be made solid
enough to produce the genuine sound. In
any case, the ball is so small and is hit
so hard that it would not generally be
seen on television: hence no coverage of
the sport.

The women are not, of course, aware of
the men since the two shots are distinct.
Both men and women mime to the same
wild, actuality sound. Both shots are
from the same wide, locked-off camera:
they can conveniently be taped on after
the other before or after the rest of the
play, and superimposed in the final
editing.

SUPERIMPOSE end credits over
continuation of above.

# Down Red Lane

A lunchtime theatre play

**EDITORS' NOTE**

*Down Red Lane* was written towards the end of Johnson's life, and first performed after his death, in a lunchtime production at the Open Space Theatre in 1974. The Diner was played by Timothy West, the Waiter by Simon Callow, and the Belly by Martin Coveney. In the later radio production, broadcast on BBC Radio 3 (5 May 2002), Timothy West again played the Diner; the Waiter was played by David Timson and the Belly by Roy Hudd.

**CHARACTERS**

WAITER
DINER
BELLY

Time: The Present

*A gastronomic restaurant.*

*A table set with good cutlery, a single flower; all in careful taste. The tablecloth reaches to the ground on all sides.*

*The WAITER, hovering, sees a guest enter whom he recognizes with a great show of pleasure. It is the DINER. He is gross, fat, enormous, but likeable; aged anything between fifty and seventy; dressed in dinner suit, but it is carelessly maintained; yet he has a certain dignity, even when he behaves grossly; he still has a human dignity.*

WAITER:           Good evening sir, how good to see you this evening, sir.

*The WAITER fusses around DINER whom he obviously knows and respects as a good customer; pulls chair out for him, seats him with no little effort. The DINER appears flushed, out of breath with the effort of crossing the room, sitting down. He slumps, hardly acknowledging WAITER.*

DINER:            (*almost to himself*) Maxim's last night. (*pause*) Canard à l'orange. (*pause*) Duck! (*pause: then with contempt*) Duck!

WAITER:           Yes, sir, well, sir, what do you. . .

DINER:            (*even greater contempt*) Duck! (*pause*) I saw it coming, too. It still hit me! (*single unfunny laugh*) Ha! Duck!

WAITER:           Yes sir, how disgusting, sir. . .

DINER:            Duck!

WAITER:             (*confidentially*) I'm told, sir, they were inspected
                    last week, and the Department found an alsatian
                    in the deep freeze. (*pause*) Jointed! Just as well
                    you didn't have the venison! The case comes up
                    at the next quarter sessions. (*short pause*)
                    Quarter. . .
DINER:              (*unhumorously cuts him off*) Ha!

*DINER settles himself.*

WAITER:             Aqua minerale, sir?

*DINER looks at him with contempt: as though he should need to
have to ask.*
*WAITER exits. DINER settles himself further, as though he were
uncomfortable, belches, slumps over the table, moves in so that his
stomach is as near as may be underneath the table.*
*WAITER returns with mineral water; pours it; presents menu; exits.*
*DINER drinks; belches visibly but only just audibly; pauses.*
*WAITER returns for order. DINER ignores him, studying menu.*

DINER:              Nothing new?
WAITER:          ˙  The classics, sir. One cannot improve on the
                    perfect. . .sir.
DINER:              Ha! (*pause*) Nothing new. . .
WAITER:             (*grossly flattering*) How could one hope to
                    presume to give a new gastronomic experience to
                    a man so justly famed for the all-embracing
                    wideness of his knowledge?
DINER:              Ha!

*DINER stares at menu. Long pause. Mouth, slavering movements.*
*Grossness business. Pulls out handkerchief, wipes forehead, neck.*
*WAITER attentive, as if bated breath.*

DINER:              (*suddenly*) You call them hortobagyi. Does that
                    mean you now have a Hungarian chef, eh?
WAITER:             (*covering up*) No, sir, but. . .

DINER:          Then they're not hortobagyi, are they, they're
                just bloody pancakes stuffed with leftover meat
                and cream and paprika. . .
WAITER:         (*on his mettle*) Fresh veal, sir, fresh cream, sir,
                gratinée. . .
DINER:          Ha!

*Silence.*

DINER:          I'll start with the hortobagyi, then. God help you
                if they're wrong!

*A long drawn-out, just-heard wince or groan from the direction of
DINER's BELLY. It can go on throughout the following exchange.
A pause.*

WAITER:         May I recommend the salmon, sir, spécialité du
                jour tronçon de saumon Philéas Gilbert.
DINER:          How?
WAITER:         Philéas Gilbert, sir.

*DINER frowns.*

DINER:          Remind me. . .
WAITER:         The cavity stuffed with a julienne, sir, of truffles,
                mushrooms, carrots and celery hearts braised in
                butter, the whole poached in sherry, sir. . .

*A louder groan from BELLY indicating some unease.*

WAITER:         . . .and served with. . .
DINER:          Who was Philéas Gilbert?
WAITER:         (*glibly*) A gentleman, sir an old gentleman.
DINER:          Did he die of it, his speciality?
WAITER:         It is not recorded, sir.
DINER:          He died of something. (*pause*) A way to be
                remembered, Omelette Arnold Bennett, giving

350

one's name to a dish, leaving something behind
to be remembered by. (*Smiles maliciously*)
Perhaps not the salmon. . .

*A sigh of relief from BELLY, who, if it is not obvious by now, is
played by an actor or actress concealed under the table.*

| | |
|---|---|
| DINER: | Are the whitebait good? |
| WAITER: | Of course, sir. . . |
| DINER: | Stow records that during the season one could lower a basket on a rope from old London Bridge and bring it up brimming alive with Thames whitebait. . . |
| WAITER: | (*laughs unhumorously*) Not now, sir, not now! |
| DINER: | Let's be simple. Whitebait. (*pause*) No, I'll have a dozen claires. |

*Alarm from BELLY; the groan assumes the drawn-out words:*

| | |
|---|---|
| BELLY: | Oy-sters! Oy-sters! |
| WAITER: | The larger ones, of course, sir? |

*DINER nods. Groans appropriate from BELLY throughout at each
new assault following.*

| | |
|---|---|
| DINER: | No, make it two dozen. It'll give me time to think about the entrée. |
| WAITER: | Certainly, sir. And the wine? The usual? |

*DINER nods. Exit WAITER. DINER settles to a further study of the
menu.*

*Groans continue from BELLY, the words blending with groans but
gradually (as he begins to become more and more articulate)
becoming more distinct. The accent should be London working-class.*

| | |
|---|---|
| BELLY: | Oysters! Cream! Veal! Pancakes! Oysters! Oysters! |

351

*Enter WAITER with white wine; sets it out; pours; DINER tastes,
says nothing; at which WAITER assumes it's acceptable and pours
full glass. DINER drinks it at once. BELLY makes brrrrr noise as
though cold.*

WAITER:        We have just nine bottles left of the Vaillons, sir.

DINER:        Keep them for me. Last about a fortnight. And
after that?

WAITER:        A good successor, sir, though as you know
yourself there's never been anything since as
good as the '67.

*Exit WAITER.*
*DINER drinks again; BELLY again shivers.*

DINER:        (*appreciatively*) Ah, yes. . .

BELLY:        Oooooooh, no, the acid, the cold acid!

*WAITER returns with first course, the rich pancakes. Flames them
over spirit stove if you can afford it. Sets them before DINER with
flourish, acting his part. Exit WAITER. DINER tucks huge napkin
into his collar, then eats quickly, grossly.*

BELLY:        Here they come, the front runners, on top of this
sour Chablis, premier cru, what does it matter, by
the time it's down here, premier nothing, for the
last thirty years, Chablis with paprika tonight,
god save us! (*groan*) (*pause*) Paprika! Paprika!

*BELLY makes short, sharp noises as if burnt.*
*DINER breaks off to take an enormous draught of wine.*

BELLY:        (*shivers again*) Ah, the old torture treatment, hot
and cold, first this, then that, no doubt the other
soon, dogs, whose dogs, slavering, (*comically
giving in*). All right, I'll tell you all you want to
know! Don't torture me any more! What d'you
want to know? Not the paprika again! No! (*as if*

*burnt sounds)* Oooooooh! I can't stand it!
Noooo! (*series of groans, coping noises;
gradually wins through, out of breath*).

*BELLY's victory coincides with DINER's completion of this course.
He wipes his mouth roughly; farts hard. Even as he does this there is
still a dignity about him; that is, he does not fart in a polite nor a
mannered way: it is simply a human function performed naturally.
DINER takes another draught of Chablis, which sets off BELLY into
shivers again, more sorrowfully than painfully.
Enter WAITER with oysters; clears previous course, refills glass.
DINER takes large draught of mineral water; belches again before
starting on oysters. He sprinkles lemon juice on a few, tosses first
back without biting. BELLY groans progressively louder as half a
dozen or so are wolfed down without pause.*

BELLY:          At least bite them first! Kill them! The buggers
are fighting each other down here! It's a right
punchup! What you don't realise is that they think
they're back in their native element down here,
you've never realised it, they get all lively, until
me hydrochloric acid gets them, and we all know
there's not enough of that to go round, you can't
go on doing this to me, let alone the others, one of
us'll crack soon, you must know what I'm talking
about, I've been warning you all these years. . .

*DINER pauses, gasps with sudden pain at gripe in stomach (this can
be co-ordinated by BELLY actor tapping shin of DINER actor).
DINER pours mineral water, swallows draught; then another.*

DINER:          Aaaaaah. . .!

*DINER swallows another glass of Chablis. BELLY makes drowning,
glugging noises. DINER resumes wolfing oysters.*

BELLY:          Two dozen he has tonight! That must be eight. . .
another sixteen to go. . .!

353

DINER:    Fifteen, actually. There's one here I don't like the look of at all. . .

*It is the first time he has answered BELLY; it ought to be acceptable by now.*

BELLY:    Small mercies. . .
DINER:    There may be more. You can't tell until you squeeze the lemon on. Sam taught me that. Only the third time I had had oysters, in my young life, and in Paris. His eyes were bad, Ginnie saw him feel for the ashtray with his little finger before tapping his ash, later he did it in the sugar bowl, we averted our eyes. I used to like oysters, he said to me, young, I used to like oysters too until once when I put the lemon on I saw the creature wince. (*pause*) If they don't wince they're no good, if they don't wince they're dead! (*pause*) Though we happily eat other. . . corpses.

*Silence.*
*DINER continues knocking back the oysters and Chablis. Mounting groans from BELLY, culminating in another stab of pain felt by DINER.*

BELLY:    Take that, you slippery sliders, you oily swine!

*DINER grunts, pauses.*

BELLY:    (*vengefully*) You're beginning to pay!

*DINER recovers, with an effort, more mineral water, finishes remaining two or three oysters, sits back with a practised satisfaction, wipes mouth.*

DINER:    Fines claires. . . so different from the fat, oily Whitstable natives I had the first time, a stall on

the front, where was it, most unlikely, I was a
young lad then, really only. . .

*DINER gulps, his gorge rising, controls himself with difficulty.
BELLY sighs with relief.*

*Enter WAITER. Begins to clear.*

WAITER:         And to follow, sir?

*DINER belches.*

WAITER:         May I recommend the venison, sir, filets mignon
                     with juniper berries, the sauce. . .
DINER:          After what you told me about Maxim's?

*WAITER clears away, in a huff. DINER studies menu. Rumblings
from BELLY. DINER finishes Chablis. WAITER returns; professional
smile.*

WAITER:         For the entrée, sir?
BELLY:          Something light! You'd enjoy something light!
DINER:          (*to himself*) It must be substantial, nourishing, as
                     mother would say. (*pause*) Now she says
                     nothing. (*pause*)
BELLY:          Something light! As a feather! Preferably
                     nothing!
DINER:          Shut up! Or I'll order a chili, in between whiles!
BELLY:          (*panic*) No! No!

*Silence.*
*DINER ponders menu. WAITER hovers, not daring to make a further
suggestion.*
*Whimperings from BELLY.*

DINER:          (*at length*) The beef, then.
WAITER:         Sir.
BELLY:          All right, then, I'll accept the beef, under protest,

|          | but nothing fancy, just plain beef, I can't take some of those sauces, nothing fancy. . . |
| DINER:   | Where's the pepper from? |
| BELLY:   | No! Nothing fancy! |
| WAITER:  | (*improvising*) The pepper, sir? Curacao, sir, I heard the chef ordering it myself, sir, only this morning. . . |
| DINER:   | Liar. |
| WAITER:  | Sir! Not from Curacao itself, of course, sir, from the wholesalers'. But I could have sworn it was Curacao he said. . . |
| BELLY:   | Don't have it wherever it came from! Not pepper! |
| DINER:   | (*pause*) You're sure he ordered it this morning? |
| WAITER:  | Yes sir, gospel sir. |
| DINER:   | So it should be fresh, wherever it came from? |
| WAITER:  | Yes, sir. |
| DINER:   | I'll take the steak au poivre, then, just sealed, no more. . . |
| BELLY:   | (*groans*) Noooo! Look, it's not only me, it's the kidneys, too. |
| WAITER:  | (*offended*) Yes sir, as usual for you, of course. |
| DINER:   | . . .with lyonnaise potatoes and perhaps a green. . .no, asparagus, yes asparagus. . . |
| BELLY:   | Sparrers arse, nooo! In butter they'll be! |
| DINER:   | . . .in butter. |
| BELLY:   | Oooooooh! |
| WAITER:  | Sir. And no doubt the Gevrey-Chambertin with it? |

*DINER nods. Exit WAITER.*

| BELLY:   | Now look, don't say we haven't been warning you for months now. I'll have a word with the kidneys. . . |

*Whispered consultations, other groans from BELLY who appears to be mediating with someone else.*
*DINER gives increasing and various signs of physical discomfort*

*from now on, though as he is a large man they are not noticeably dramatic.*

BELLY:                (*flatly*) Look, one kidney's not answering, and the other says he's had all he can take. He's up to the gills in bloody pepper as it is. Any more, and he says he's jacking it all in too. (*pause*) For good. (*pause*) Liver's not looking too bright, either. (*pause*) (*in pain*) D'you hear?

*DINER takes no notice, appears to be wrapped in thought, apart from occasional shifting of position on chair.*

BELLY:                (*in distress*) D'you hear! Your last kidney's on the blink, and Liver's asking for his cards!

*WAITER returns with burgundy; opening, sniffing, tasting business. DINER drinks whole bottle throughout entrée course following.*

BELLY:                (*as though listening*) What's that? (*pause*) Yes, they're all at it now! Spleen says he's hanging up his boots! Spleen! You know, your spleen!

DINER:               I don't know them all. Appendages, how should I know?

BELLY:                Appendages! (*nostalgically*) Appendix! Remember Appendix?

DINER:               Ah, Munich!

BELLY:                Ah, pendix! Appendix! My Appendix. How I miss her! Forty years we were together. . .

DINER:               I nearly died. . .

BELLY:                I with you. . .

DINER:               The two of us. . .

BELLY:                I with you. . .

DINER:               Both one. . .

BELLY:                Together.

*Pause. Silence. Sudden rumbling. DINER drinks deeply from glass, refills it.*

DINER:     Nearly had my. . .appendages, that dog. Must
           have been the day before I went into hospital.
           Vast beergarden in Munich, fat, ugly waitresses.
           Dog was tied to a tableleg, green, castiron, out
           in the open. I was with. . .fat, ugly girl. All I
           could get. All I could get, then. Probably all I
           deserved. I thought she was. . .boring. Nothing
           to say. We drank, she matched me stein for stein.
           Nothing to say. I stared at the dog, stared him
           out. Was it a bitch? Were they both? I'd never
           stared out a dog before. They are easily
           aggravated by a staring match, I found. I won,
           of course. Twice the dog passed the point, twice
           leapt at me, fell back on the lead, frustrated.
           What did the owners look like? (*pause*) No
           recollection. The dog was a black mongrel about
           the size of a. . .badger. It must have disturbed the
           table, a dog that size, caused the beers to shake,
           destroyed any meniscus there might have been.
           (*pause*) Then I forgot about it. I suppose the
           fat fraulein must have made some proposition
           worth considering. I forget. But the dog didn't
           forget. I suppose it had nothing better to do
           than watch for its chance. On the way out I
           walked near its table, and it leapt again at me.
           Providence saved my appendages that day, for
           the length of the dog's lead was such that it
           restrained its teeth by a matter of an inch from
           connecting. It swung round in an arc, snapping
           and nipping, within an inch of my. . .flies. No
           doubt I ducked backwards from the waist, no
           doubt I took steps away, but only when I had
           seen the danger, only when he had committed
           himself. Gnashing he swung, brushing my. . .I
           had nearly said balls.
BELLY:     Ha!
DINER:     Are you still there?
BELLY:     Still here. (*groans*)

| | |
|---|---|
| DINER: | Gnashing. It was a very narrow miss, nearer than an inch, I wasn't measuring accurately. |

*DINER imitates with teeth, swinging his head in an arc in the action the dog performed. Then drinks.*

| | |
|---|---|
| BELLY: | When did you last see Winkle, anyway? (*pause*) Twenty years ago. |
| DINER: | There are mirrors, you know. |
| BELLY: | In the flesh! When did you last see your Winkle in the flesh? |
| DINER: | Does it matter? He still performs one of his two functions. . . . . |
| BELLY: | It's an act of faith, your believing in Winkle now. . . |
| DINER: | He widdles, therefore he is. Winkle. Winkle! Winkle? (*pause*) He used to come at my call. (*pause*) I don't need to see him. |
| BELLY: | But when did you last see him? |
| DINER: | Bratislava? No? Zvolen? |
| BELLY: | Swollen. . . |
| DINER: | Zvolen was where they started, where the idea came from. |
| BELLY: | And ours. |
| DINER: | And ours. But Bratislava. . . |
| BELLY: | Ah. . . |
| DINER: | They'd just built the new bridge over the Danube. |
| BELLY: | Ah. . . |
| DINER: | Bratislava! |

*Enter WAITER with next course; sets it out during following.*

| | |
|---|---|
| BELLY: | Yes, they'd just built the new bridge over the Danube, fine modern design, nothing like it in Europe. . . |
| DINER: | Ah, Bratislava! |

*Pause.*

| | |
|---|---|
| BELLY: | Your last. As the sun went down. (*pause*) In the east. |
| DINER: | (*pause, then starts*) In the east! |
| BELLY: | Sharpen up! Your last true sighting of Winkle! |
| DINER: | I still feel for him. |
| BELLY: | Ha! |

*DINER begins to eat; exit WAITER.*

| | |
|---|---|
| DINER: | What was I doing there? |
| BELLY: | In Bratislava? |
| DINER: | Yes |
| BELLY: | Watching the sun go down. . . |
| DINER: | Ah. . . |
| BELLY: | And feeling for Winkle. |

*Silence. DINER champs away, drinks. BELLY begins to groan: a progression towards the climax.*

| | |
|---|---|
| DINER: | (*suddenly*) There's no conviction about. . .about, any longer. (*pause*) Winkles at Southend, as a boy. And oysters, too. . . |
| BELLY: | (*outburst*) Oysters! The last sod's still not dead down here, bucking and slewing about, my acid's not what it was! |
| DINER: | (*sharply*) What is? (*pause*) Oysters on the front there, was it Nantes, with Zulf, late at night, what a feed, one could see why they thought them such good nourishment long ago, and earlier, poor people's food they were too. . . |
| BELLY: | The bastards! Me hydrochloric's bubbling! |

*All the sounds (slurping, and so on) of a last-ditch stand against the oysters consumed earlier. DINER meanwhile goes on with his steak, lyonnaise, asparagus, regardless.*

| | |
|---|---|
| BELLY: | All those years! Faithfully serving, dealing with all that working-class muck, surviving the lean |

|         | years, pretending I could make do with sandwiches and the occasional rock and chips, ah, I was young then, we all were, weren't we? (*pause*) And the later affluence, the in-between times, when we didn't know where we were, one day taken out to lunch at the Mirabelle, the next back to rock salmon at Bell's by the Angel. . . |
|---------|---|
| DINER:  | Ah. . . |
| BELLY:  | All very well for you! |
| DINER:  | For us! |
| BELLY:  | (*abashed*) For us. And then when it set in, the layers of adipose tissue, I bore the torture, the Pavlonian business of stop-go, in-out, on-off, oaoaoaoaoah. . . |
| DINER:  | (*pausing between champs*) The diets I went on. . . |
| BELLY:  | The diets! |
| DINER:  | My favourite was Slimming the Eastern Way. . . |
| BELLY:  | Just because the exercises were based on belly-dancing. . . |
| DINER:  | The food was good, too, shashlik and. . . |

*BELLY groans piteously.*
*DINER suddenly stops eating, quite dramatically, drops cutlery.*

| DINER:  | Look on the bright side. It has been good. There has been more good than. . .Don't forget the good times. (*pause*) There were good times. (*Brightly*) There are always enough good times to make it worthwhile! That's the secret! No doubt. The reason why one does not actually (*pause*) do it. Look on the bright side! We did enjoy certain things! Don't forget the good times! |
|---------|---|

*BELLY continues to groan, ignoring him.*

| BELLY:  | The blood! Untreated blood! And the vicious pepper! Aaoooooh! I give up, even your |
|---------|---|

361

|       |                                                                                 |
|-------|---------------------------------------------------------------------------------|
|       | shirtfront spattered with blood, how can you, how could you, slobbering outside and in, think about your. . . |
| DINER: | (*fiercely*) Why should I? |
| BELLY: | I am you! You are me! |

*DINER breaks into sudden wild laughter, for say ten seconds; then BELLY joins in. Sudden stop. Pause.*

DINER:      (*soberly*) I don't know why I was born with an appetite. Or, if you like, I don't know why I was conditioned to think that my appetite was the most important thing in my life. I do know I have suffered from my appetite, my grossness, my peculiarity. The thought of death even, of shortening my life itself, has been no deterrent. I was digging my grave with my teeth! Many have been those who have quoted that cliché to me. It has not mattered. I am what I am. I have done what I have done. I have followed, followed. That is what I am. That is what I have been conditioned to become. Who can argue with those laws, those. . .(*pause*) Good teeth they are, too, those I have used to dig my grave. Would I have been given such good teeth if I had not been meant to dig my grave with them?

*Enter WAITER. He begins to clear away, though the course is unfinished; this occasions some flicker of surprise; nothing more.*

WAITER:    (*challenging, seeing the state DINER is in*) And now, sir?

DINER:      What? Ordering, yes, so long. (*ignores proffered menu*) Profiteroles, of course. Sauternes with them, what else? No, rich champagne, not Sauternes, what am I thinking of?

*Exit WAITER with smirk; for DINER is slumping lower and lower over table. BELLY's moans now continuous, increasing to end.*

362

DINER:           In Zvolen, where it started, I had rich
champagne, but Russian, not bad though not at
all as good as they imagined it was, what is,
aaah, but there also. . . (*pause*)

*Enter WAITER with profiteroles, champagne; opens latter; pours
glass. DINER ignores it!*

*DINER suddenly sits up, all attention, bright.*

DINER:           There was the baby, sitting up, with that
unbelievably stupid look of *hope* upon his stupid
face! (*pause*) There was Mahler on at the time,
*Das Lied von der Erde* if I remember rightly, I
objected to that, too. And the baby with this look
of expectancy, the baby expectorant, ha! (*pause*)
And she said, she said as though she could not
have meant it to mean more, (*pause*) sincerely,
she said, I shall dry out without you. (*pause*) I
shall dry out without you.

*DINER slumps again; finally.*

*DINER's eyes close.*

*DINER lifts glass.*

*BELLY meanwhile has been reaching towards a climax of distress.
At climax, DINER joins BELLY at pitch of shriek.*

*Both suddenly stop.*

*DINER's hand pauses; spills glass.*

*BLACKOUT.*

# Short Prose

# The Travails of *Travelling People*

*Published in* Smith's Trade News, *20 April 1963*

You must have an agent, they said.

So I have this agent. She has a fabulous Georgian house in this top postal district. She has carpets on the walls, and gives me Fuller's walnut layer cake, China tea, and spiel. Like how she's made ten thousand last year for this writer just like me.[1] So after some thought I agree to let her do the same for me next year. When my novel *Travelling People* is finished I take it along to her. Take it, not trusting the post. Besides, it would cost too much: big, it is, to me, 110,000 words, all my own, I had to put it in a lever-arch file as they don't make anything else that would take that thickness of paper. Very proud of that bulk alone.

Back it comes a few weeks later. It feels very heavy. All this agent will tell me about it is that it is pretentious and unsaleable. According to her Expert Reader. I ask her if I may see the Report, feeling like a schoolboy trying find out what They have said about him to his Mother. She will not tell me. Only that *Travelling People* is pretentious and unsaleable. What is the point, I even say to her, by letter, of course, of our relationship unless you tell me what I have done wrong so that I can try to put it right next time? That would be to betray a trust, she thinks, to show me the Report; so I am answered, at the third time of asking, pretentious and unsaleable, again. I assume the Report is appalling and obviously recommends instant expulsion. But however bad it is, not knowing is worse. I quietly disintegrate into fairly small pieces.

A sweet friend so very kindly picks up most of these pieces and tidies up generally. Then she gives me the phone numbers of two agents whom she has enquired about and found reputed to be sympa-

---

[1] The agent was Rosica Colin (1903–83). Her distinguished authors included Genet, Beckett, Ionesco, Camus and Sartre, but the fortunate client referred to here was Alan Sillitoe.

thetic to first novels. I am sceptical about anyone being sympathetic to first novels which are also wildly unconventional. But what else is there to do?

So I ring number one on my little list. His phone is engaged. I ring number two, the last, and can speak only to his secretary. I tell this dolly my business, and end clearly but cynically by saying that much wasted time can be avoided if she indicates whether her boss is prepared to read the unusual, the unconventional, and to try to understand what I am trying to do in *Travelling People*. This dolly is very put out at this, incensed at my imputation that perhaps her boss does not read every word sent to him. To mollify her I apologise profusely and promise to send the novel.

I do not send the novel. I take it myself, that afternoon, with a letter explaining what I think I am trying to do. This agent has a Georgian house, too, with nice lead-flashed dormers and crummy cream paint. In the Enquiries office there's this fair old dolly who asks me in what I allow to be a good imitation of the Queen Mum voice whether she can help me. Restraining a natural inclination to explain in hardly necessary detail how not half she could, I give her the letter and my lovely 2¼" thick typescript. She smiles and makes me wish I had bothered to wash and shave. I huddle in my Orson Welles overcoat and hope I look eccentric and mysterious.

Then I retire to the Angel[2] and pretend I am anything but a writer. This sweet bird comes and sticks some more of the pieces together.

Within the fortnight a civil letter from this second agent. I am delighted that he has seen more or less exactly what I was trying to do in *Travelling People*, and that he likes it; he makes suggestions for one irrelevant character and one irrelevant chapter to be cut or re-written; and makes it clear that if I am going to be inflexible about it then there is not much that he can do for me.

But I am not like that at all, and I am certainly pleased to know exactly where I stand. So I ring this dolly again and make an appointment to see her boss.[3]

---

[2] The district in Islington where Johnson lived after leaving his parents' home in Barnes at the age of twenty-eight until his death in 1973.

[3] George Greenfield, who also represented Enid Blyton, Sidney Sheldon, John le Carré and James Baldwin.

She's an even fairer old dolly than the one downstairs. And her boss has his carpets on the floor. Very right and proper, I think, wall to wall, too. And he sits me in this splendid green womb of an armchair, next to the oilfilled radiator, under one of the dormers. Mind you, he smokes a pipe, but I try not to hold this against him. I soon learn he knows his kit: not only did he read English under Leavis, but he has been both an author and a publisher himself. He knows *Travelling People*, too, and his objections to Chapter Two are reasonable and valid: I agree to cut it,[4] though it is like cutting out my own liver. Still, a book can live without a liver. He's read *Tristram Shandy*, as well, and thinks it marvellous: one of the more useful divisions of humanity is into those who do and those who don't adore *Tristram Shandy*. By the end of our talk, I am wholly re-integrated.

The first four publishers find my novel full of promise but are unwilling to spend money to see that promise in print. One of them even invites me out for a drink and we spend a couple of pleasant hours discussing my fullness of promise and his unwillingness to spend money to see that promise in print.

Then T. S. Eliot, Herbert Read, Henry Moore, Bonamy Dobrée,[5] and the other Gregory Trust judges make me the recipient of one of the Gregory Awards for the encouragement of young creative writers.

By what I believe to be a genuine coincidence, the next publisher to whom *Travelling People* is offered by my agent is very interested, and invites me to go to see him about it.

I have strange ideas about publishers. I imagine Dickens, for instance, going in to his publisher with a great idea for a book, and being told:

'No, it won't sell, Charlie. Kill her off in the last chapter, and we'll call it *The Death of Little Nell*.'

But this publisher is very different from anything I had expected:

---

[4] The excised chapter was later published (with changes to the characters' names) as 'Broad Thoughts from a Home' in both *Statement Against Corpses* and *Aren't You Rather Young to be Writing Your Memoirs?*.

[5] Herbert Read: poet, academic and art critic well-known both for his anarchist views and his championing of modern British artists such as Moore and Barbara Hepworth. Bonamy Dobrée: distinguished academic, recently retired from the University of Leeds and mainly engaged at this time in editing the influential *Writers and their Work* series for the British Council.

a most charming gentleman, and he has no carpets on his walls either, just lots of lovely enviable books. Nevertheless I am very nervous and more or less demand to have a whiskey forced down my throat before I can talk at all. Then when we do talk it is more about The Novel than about *Travelling People*. But finally he wins me over when he says that he found my novel funny, which of all reactions is the one I find most pleasing. Then he starts talking about cuts: 'flat patches' he calls them, but really he's after my novel's kidneys.

So I take it away, and cut out the kidneys. To my astonishment, *Travelling People* is a better book for being without its kidneys as well as without its liver. And I'm sure you don't find many authors saying that the surgery suggested by their agents and publishers results in a better book. It makes me wonder whether people, too, wouldn't perhaps be better without some of their offal.

Then one day in August we sign a contract and I receive the first half of my advance. The next day I take off for the south of France. It seems the only thing to do. The only thing I can think of to do, anyway, hackneyed and unimaginative as it may sound.

When I come back it is to find that the printers consider certain passages in *Travelling People* to be obscene. I tell the publisher that my first reaction is to refuse to change a single word, he says 'Good for you,' and it is the printers who change their minds. The publisher also lets me have a big say in the typography and production of *Travelling People*, and I spend a day with a compositor going through the typescript with him page by page: the setting being complex, not to say eccentric. This compositor clearly thinks I am right round the twist. I am also allowed to commission my own jacket from John Holden, a painter whose work I have admired for many years.

Next year he is going to publish my poems: and greater love hath no publisher than that he lays out his loot on an author's poems.

I think the best agent in London found me the best publisher in London.

370

# Bloody Blues

*Published in the* Observer, *18 April 1965*[6]

It was because my father used to swear there that interested me in the beginning. He never used to swear anywhere else when I was around. It became a bond between us, something we had together that my mother did not, unlike anything else, his swearing on alternate Saturday afternoons.

This was just after the war ended, and as soon as he was out of the Kate[7] he started taking me and a Pratt's two-gallon petrol tin to Stamford Bridge.

It was the team, of course, which made him (normally restrained to the point of near-inarticulateness) swear with a vigour and comprehensibility which surprised and delighted me: Chelsea.

It was not as though Chelsea had poor players at that time, either. 'Those three cost a bleeding packet,' I remember him saying, as, with Len Goulden and Tommy Walker on either side of him, Tommy Lawton stood waiting for the whistle, rubbing his hands together as if obsequiously, his great shoulders hunched against the cold, shifting his weight and flicking to loosen each ankle in turn.

All three were at the ends of their careers, all three had come from other perhaps more famous, certainly more successful, clubs, but all three were typical Chelsea players of that period. Their heads were small in relation to their bodies, their dark hair was cut short, parted in the middle and swept sharply back on either side, and they ran as though they had thought out and invented the mechanics of the action for themselves without reference to evolution, as though each thought himself the first human being to run.

The other characteristic of the archetypal Chelsea player then was

---

[6] Johnson was working as a football reporter for the *Observer* at the time. The published title of this piece was 'Same Old Chelsea'.

[7] Kate Carney = Army (cockney rhyming slang).

extreme footballing skill accompanied by an equally extreme inability to produce it at crucial moments.

During the kickabout before the start of Tommy Walker's benefit match against Hearts, for instance, I can still see the way Walker killed a thigh-high ball thundering at him with the calmest and most economical of six-inch movements. Yet when similar use of his brilliant control would have brought him an easy goal during the match, he missed a slower ball altogether.

It was at this sort of thing more than any other kind of shortcoming that my father swore. While, by the time I was old enough not to need the petrol tin to stand on, I used to be happy if Chelsea won, he would be happy only if they played well, win or lose. I still find this difficult to understand.

In those days of huge crowds we used to get to the Bridge anything up to an hour and a half before the kickoff. That was the worst part, waiting. I came to know the roofline from the top of the main banking by heart: flats, acres of chimneys, a green copper dome, the asbestos whaleback of the Earls Court Exhibition, and quaintly fretted decorations on the great grey and rusty gasometers over towards the river. In a gap at the back of the main stand steam occasionally fluffed as a train went along the single-track line, its pace oddly unrelated to that of the steam and smoke.

This roofline is not visible from the press box at the Bridge, which is set so high up under the main stand that only the bottom quarter of the great terrace opposite can be seen. It's not the same, watching a match from the press box, as from that terrace. But, there, the team isn't the same either: a largely home-produced side with no stars has replaced expensive buys from other clubs, but after their most successful season for ten years my father is still dissatisfied. Perhaps he's right, too, they are basically the same old Chelsea: out of the Cup in the semi-finals, and faltering in their challenge for the League after leading most of the season. True, they won the League Cup, but, cruelly, hardly anyone noticed.

The first match I reported this season happened to be a major one at Stamford Bridge (Arlott was still doing cricket, Ferrier and Pawson were god knows where) and immediately after I'd phoned my early report through I met my father for a few moments. Chelsea had won well and easily, but he was still pessimistic and cast severe doubts on the parentage of two of the forwards.

I left him to go back and write another report for the later editions. From the unpopulated terraces came the strange undercurrent of scratchiness caused by plastic beakers blowing about. By the time the preoccupied evening dog racing crowds had begun to straggle in, I'd finished what was my longest and to me most important report so far.

When I saw my father a week later, he hadn't even read it.

# A Fishing Competition

*Published in the* Observer, *30 May 1965*[8]

Some came into the Cornamona pub on the night of the competition meeting with the familiarity of daily visitors, others with a deferent sureness that the occasion broke down barriers inherent in their positions as teachers or doctors, and yet others with that shyness which comes from day-long contact with stock and fields rather than with other men, their faces burnt by two days' April sun; one in a tubular aeruginous suit, looking strangely like Beckett's Murphy ('Word went round among the members of the Blake League that the Master's conception of Bildad the Shuhite had come to life and was stalking about. . . .in a green suit, seeking whom he might comfort.')

Most drank as they canvassed for the exact number of boats and engines available. Then the competitors' names went into a flat cap, and those of the boats into a wet ('I've been fishing all day') trilby. Two men to a boatman, laughter and consternation at some of the coupling brought up by chance in the draw, a little diplomatic rearrangement, fears about the weather (last year the competition was held in a storm, and two men were drowned), and the meeting went out into the Guinness-dark night.

Nowhere wider than half a mile, the Doorus peninsula runs four miles out into the northern end of Lough Corrib from Cornamona, in Joyce Country, Connemara. The boats were drawn up on the lakeshore at a point where it meets the road about halfway down the peninsula, and parked cars narrowed the road for half a mile on the Sunday morning of the competition. The lake was calm, but heavy, vertical rain fell, complicating the starting arrangements: some keen competitors were out promptly at half past eleven, others had to be fetched from the pub at two by impatient companions or boatmen. All seemed agreed that it was a poor day for fishing.

[8] Or to be more precise, 'published but slaughtered' (by the subs) according to the note on Johnson's typescript.

374

The Corrib trout is a brown trout: that is to say, he has a silver belly shading to bronze on the flank and deep olive-black on the back, and the whole length is spattered with inkstain-like splodges, mostly sepia but towards the tail blood-red, about the size of an Irish threepenny. The biggest ever caught weighed 21½ pounds, and the average fish is about a pound and a half; they generally fight very hard, particularly when they see the boat, and their flesh is a salmon-like delicate orange-pink. He can be taken in a variety of ways, but on this Sunday the rule was artificial flies (sooty olives, black pennels, and grand invictas being amongst the favourites) fished wet.

Trout and salmon fishing on Lough Corrib is free, and the Irish Inland Fisheries Board is trying to improve it by re-stocking with a quarter of a million trout a year and making it solely game waters by removing all the perch and pike. Traps rather similar to lobster-pots are used for the perch, and large sprays of twigs for them to spawn on are placed in the shallows and later removed. Pike are caught on fixed, buoyed lines baited with perch: one 45 pound monster caught in this way two years ago glares viciously from a glass case in the Cornamona pub, and 'Let's go and see the Pike' is a pleasing euphemistic invitation to local conviviality.

At six the muffled crackling of outboard motors was heard out among the lake islands, and the boats began to return. The rain held off briefly as the tailboard of a red lorry was dropped, and the officials climbed up to enact the weigh-in before a crowd of a hundred or so. Competitors with sagging landing nets pushed their way through to pass up their catches, and watched edgily as the needle of the kitchen scales deflected, bounced and settled: two fish weighing 1lb 12ozs, five weighing 3lbs 14ozs, a single half-pounder, half a dozen catches under the top so far, and then four fish just reaching four pounds. But with melodramatic suddenness someone on the edge of the crowd noticed a latecomer just climbing out of his boat with a landing net weightily distended by a single fish larger than anything seen yet, and everyone turned to watch his approach.

There were those who thought at first it was a salmon, others who thought it some weird throwback or cross and yet others who agreed with the man who correctly thought it was a sick fish and who later said 'I asked him if he was going to eat it, and he said his wife liked fish, and I told him if he thought anything of his wife at all he'd per-

375

suade her not to like this one.' But it was a trout, and it had been fairly caught during the competition at the mouth of the Cornamona river on a black pennel, and (despite the fact that it would have gone nearly double had it been in good condition) it did weigh 5lbs 12ozs: and it therefore won prizes for both highest total weight of fish caught and for the biggest fish.

Fifty competitors caught 32 trout that day weighing 46 lbs together. Some caught nothing and had not even a sunny day on Lough Corrib to compensate them: but all of them (and many others who had not fished) saw the Pike that evening.

# Writing and Publishing: or, Wickedness Reveal'd

*Published in* Socialist Commentary, *June 1965*

Americans sometimes refer to English publishing as a 'cottage industry'. This is not quite true, for publishing in this country has evolved
to a somewhat later stage than that, is in fact in economic terms
closely comparable with very early capitalism. That is to say, the
basic producers of the wealth are not paid even a living wage and are
exploited by secondary producers and non-productive entrepreneurs.

Every person employed by a publisher, printer, or bookseller
makes a living from the publishing of books: not many make a fortune, certainly, few make a very good living compared with other
jobs, perhaps, but nevertheless all make a living. But not the writer,
not the basic producer, not the prime mover, not the one factor without whom all the others would not be in business at all.

English publishing must surely be the only industry which is still
at this antediluvian stage of evolution. How can such a situation exist
in 1965? The reason lies in the nature of the labour force. Never can
any workers in any occupation have been faced by so many black-
legs. The fact is that everyone, but everyone, thinks they can write:
and many of them do, and most of those that do, submit their work.
And all of them would be glad to see themselves in print for no pay-
ment at all, and such is the (to me baffling) prestige of mere print that
some even themselves pay the less scrupulous sort of publisher to
bring their work out. There is therefore no hope whatever of any
union being formed that would be at all effective: the writers' organisations that do exist, with their collaborative acceptance of the *status
quo* and insistence, when pressed, on the myth that all writers are
lone wolves, are demonstration enough of that.

Publishers maintain this situation by producing large numbers of
books, and paying little to many rather than at least a living wage to
fewer (and better) writers. To say that well over ninety percent of this
output is rubbish can be confirmed by simple statistics. Those papers

377

which review novels, for instance, find on average four or five a week worth notice: say 250 a year. This is roughly one-tenth of those published: yes, no less than about 2,500 novels a year are published in England. And that figure is for new novels: it does not include reprints. Most of these, of course, are never even noticed in the first place, so can hardly be said to be forgotten; it is as if they had never been. And any reviewer who has had to sort through them will tell you that the chances of a masterpiece going unrecognized by every paper are nil. Of the 250 which are reviewed, perhaps a tenth receive good notices and will still be in print five years later, or at all remembered.

Let me make myself clear: I am not against people writing, obviously, such intolerance would deserve condemnation. But my attitude is rather similar to that of the National Association of Schoolmasters over equal pay for women: the reward must be commensurate with the higher level of needs, not the lower. In other words, the quantity of books published should not be allowed to depress the earnings of the better writers, the serious writers, the professional as compared with the amateur. And there is no doubt that it is this thundering cataract of rubbish which is responsible for the situation at the moment, and which also engulfs bookbuyers and literary editors.

All real writing has its origin in some strongly personal need to express emotion or redress a wrong: this is all the excuse I make now for discussing my own experience of publishing.

I have accepted that to become a writer is a long and hard task, and that while I was learning I had to subsidise myself by means of other activity. I decided seriously to become a writer when I was nineteen, and it was ten years before I had learnt enough about writing to complete my first novel: this was published when I was thirty. Having served my apprenticeship, therefore, and moved on to the journeyman stage, it was all the more bitter to discover that publishers paid so badly. I had thought that to learn to write well was the difficult part, and it seemed (and still seems) a gross insult to this difficulty, to the very skill laboured so long to acquire, to the profession of writing itself: but perhaps this insult is a reaction on the part of that majority in publishing who are writers *manqués*. Anyway, for my first novel, the reading public paid some £2,000. Of this I received £200, which was reduced to £180 when I had paid my agent:

who earned every penny of his share, I hasten to add. Of the rest of the £2,000, the bookseller took over £660 (one-third), the printer over £300, and the remainder went to the publisher.

Now I don't suppose any one of the other three involved made much out of *Travelling People*: but at least they did not make a loss, at least they covered their expenses, at least it contributed in due proportion to maintain the living they are all making from the sale of the books. But £180 did not even recover for me my *rent* while I was writing it, let alone the cost of food and clothing during the two and a half years it took: and any sign of profit from the writing of it must be far away.

Of course, they say, you didn't write it for money: of course, I didn't, but since £2,000 has been paid for it, why should not my share at least equal what it cost me to write it? It seems obvious to point it out again, but it is necessary since the whole of publishing does not seem to acknowledge the fact: that £2,000 would not have been made at all without me, the basic producer. Some publishers even trot out that old myth about people writing best whilst starving in garrets, too: and they believe it, despite never having heard an author agree. And, though it almost passes belief, one person engaged in this 'occupation for gentlemen' even assured me that I was lucky things were now somewhat better than in the eighteenth century, when writers had to fawn before patrons to get published!

It is the proportion, then, of the price of a book received by the writer which is too small. When I suggested to another rich shark that he pay me an extra two shillings a copy, this publisher said that could not be done without adding six shillings to the price of the book. My naïve failure to understand the economics of this was met with arguments which merely showed that everyone concerned automatically reacted to keep differentials more or less the same. And there was displayed, too, that sanctimonious concern to keep book prices as low as possible, for the public good, which is largely hypocritical: ask them to take a smaller share themselves, and see how readily publishers keep prices down!

All writers accept this situation, it seems to me, out of sheer conceit and pleasure at being published. Some publishers agree the situation is inequitable, yet they refuse to act unilaterally. I found it intolerable, as should be obvious, but rather than merely bitch about

379

it I decided to do something. I asked my publisher to pay me as much as he did his secretary (putting myself on no higher financial level, conceiving myself at least worth as much to him as she is) for the next five years, in which time I should write three novels. He refused to value me at even this level, did not value me enough to keep me alive to write these next three novels. Nor did several other publishers: but one, Secker & Warburg, has been enlightened enough to acknowledge in practical terms that this system is unfair, and has entered into such a contract for three years and two novels. The salary is still an advance against royalties, the proportion of which remains much the same, but the risk has been transferred from the writer, I shall no longer have to subsidise the publisher, and at least I shall be able to live during the next three years (albeit only at the level of a secretary) doing what I am best able to do.

A Marxist would of course point out that publishing is a classic, fossilized example of a capitalist industry in which the basic producer is exploited to the point of not being paid a living wage. And of course there is a classic Marxist answer, too: the basic producers should combine to form a co-operative.

Is this possible for writers? I think it is. A group (say ten) of established writers could undertake jointly to employ a printer, buy paper, and so on. Obviously new selling methods would have to be found: it would be difficult to persuade booksellers to take less than the grossly disproportionate third they take at the moment. But this would be no loss, since booksellers are in general ludicrously inefficient and bookshops are largely an anachronism anyway: new selling methods, like direct mail (already very effectively exploited by Paul Hamlyn) and completely new ways of promoting books and reaching people who would read if given the slightest encouragement could be discovered by market research. It is yet another indication of publishing's nineteenth-century outlook that no market research has been carried out. Every other industry has been at great pains in the last twenty years to discover why people buy, in what circumstances, and how often: but not publishing.

All profit from a book published by such a co-operative, once costs were covered, would go to the author. One drawback would be that administrative work would take one or more of the writers away from writing: but this could be resolved by employing a manager, providing one could be found with sufficient enthusiasm for the project. Relatively little initial capital would be needed: enough to pay the printing bill whenever it fell due. The real capital would be the talent of the co-operating writers: if ten established authors were to form such a co-operative, it would take only one best seller to demonstrate the attractiveness of the idea to other writers.

And it would knock hell out of publishing as it is now within five years.

# Censorship by Printers

*Published in* Censorship, *Summer 1965*[9]

If it is true that the degree by which any censorship is concealed makes it in that proportion more pernicious, then the one exercised in Britain by printers (which is generally known only to authors and publishers) must be considered amongst the most dangerous.

The most notorious case of this was the first edition of James Joyce's *Dubliners*, where objections by the printer led to a delay in publication of ten years. The three passages at which 'The British Printer raised his Moral Thumb, blew his Moral Nose and lifted his Moral Eyebrows,' as Gorman puts it in his biography of Joyce, were:

'. . .a man with two establishments to keep up, of course he couldn't. . . .'

'. . .Farrington said he wouldn't mind having the far one and began to smile at her. . . .'

'She continued to cast bold glances at him and changed the position of her legs often; and when she was going out she brushed against his chair and said 'Pardon', in a cockney accent. . . .'

Joyce's witty and dignified defence of his work, in which he pointed out amongst other things that far worse was published every day in newspapers, is contained in a correspondence with his publisher, Grant Richards; in another letter he says of the printer:

'I do not seek to penetrate the mysteries of his being and existence. . .how he came by his conscience and culture, how he is permitted in your country to combine the duties of author with his own honourable calling, how he came to be the representative of the public mind. . .But I cannot permit a printer to write

---

[9] The published title was 'Pi Printers'.

my book for me. In no other civilized country in Europe, I think, is a printer allowed to open his mouth. . .A printer is simply a workman hired by the day or by the job for a certain sum.'

The passages in *Dubliners* to which the British printer objected appear ludicrously innocuous today, of course, but the production manager of any publishing company will be able to provide evidence (though almost certainly he will not name names) that many printers are still allowed to open their mouths, still try to write books for authors, and still, in fact, operate exactly the same form of censorship today as they did in 1906.

I had experience of this myself over the printing of my first novel, *Travelling People*, in 1962. The printer considered that certain passages (mainly love-scenes which would really have been obscene if they had been less explicit) in it would lead to a case for obscene libel being brought by the Director of Public Prosecutions against the book. I knew at the time that the 1959 Obscene Publications Act required that any book thus prosecuted should be considered as a whole,[10] and therefore for the printer to object only to parts was either to reveal his ignorance of that Act or to show that despite it he was determined to exercise the power of censorship that he had had before it was passed. The same Act also provides that expert (in this case literary) evidence can be submitted in defence of a work: as *Travelling People* had recently won a literary prize the printer was told that if necessary the judges of the Gregory Award (who were T. S. Eliot, Herbert Read, Henry Moore and Bonamy Dobrée) could be subpoenaed to give presumably favourable testimony as to its literary merit. The publisher resolutely supported my case, being prepared to look for another printer if necessary: at this point the printer capitulated and agreed to set the book as it stood. Had it not been for my stubbornness, however, and (almost fortuitous) knowledge of the 1959 Act, then my book would have been quite unnecessarily emasculated. It was my impression that many first novelists have given in

[10] This Act, based on a draft bill submitted to the Home Office in February 1955 by a Society of Authors committee, had reformed the law relating to obscenity by introducing exceptions for artistic merit or the public good, and abolishing the common law offence of obscene libel.

to such pressure out of a natural desire to see their work in print and to cause their publishers no trouble.

The following year the same printer refused outright to set my second novel, *Albert Angelo*, which contains perhaps a dozen uses of swearwords known to everyone and, I am sure, used in a printing house every time a case of type is dropped on someone's foot. Fortunately, not every printer felt the same about the book, and another was found who was prepared to accept the work: but the first printer was quite willing to bind the book once the second had printed the sheets, since then his name would not appear on it! Had the decision been mine and not my publisher's, I would not have given him the chance to make money from this piece of gross hypocrisy.

There was not the slightest indication by anyone at any subsequent time that either of these two novels was liable to be prosecuted for obscene libel, and this points up the most serious aspect of censorship by printers: for a printer must always err on what he considers to be the safe side, must always be governed by what has been permitted in the past, and is therefore always against experiment and always against any extension of limits. Printers are rarely, I would suggest, good enough judges of literature to know whether a defence of expert evidence is likely to be successful, so they must class literary work which they believe to offend together with pornography. A printer may, of course, choose what he will or will not print, and no one is attempting to deny him this freedom: but when in so doing he sets up criteria which are clearly beyond his province, then, as I suggested in my case, he is either ignorant or desires to act as a moral censor.

And of all those engaged in the book trade – authors, publishers, booksellers as well – it is the printer who takes the least risk financially: his only real risk is that a publisher will go bankrupt, and this does not happen so often that it is more than a comparatively remote eventuality. The power he exercises through his censorship is therefore without true responsibility. I can understand that there is nothing for a printer in pornography – the high price this can fetch goes mainly to the author and the publisher, and the printing is no more profitable than it is in the case of a straight book – but unless he will accept the authority of a reputable publisher capable of telling the difference between this and literature, then interference by printers will continue to be bitterly resented.

The 1959 Act did make some attempt to exclude the printer from prosecution, and he is not mentioned by name in it: but the wording had to be such as to include anyone in any way involved in the dissemination of matter considered obscene, and this must obviously include the printer.

The wider issue is, of course, the law itself, which seems based on faulty premises: no one, to my knowledge, has ever produced any definitive evidence that anyone has ever been corrupted or depraved by a book. An equitable law would state that if a Director of Public Prosecutions was to maintain that a book was liable to deprave or corrupt, then he should be made to produce a significant number of persons that it had depraved or corrupted. This would be difficult, defenders of the current state of affairs reply to this eminently reasonable argument: of course it would, but if such defenders agree they have never known persons corrupted, then how can they support the present law? For the law is based on the certainty that people are corrupted and depraved by books, and will continue to be. Obviously, the whole question of obscene publication should receive the attention of those recently appointed to consider law reform in Britain.

The particular concern with the censorship exercised by printers, however, is that another *Dubliners* may be prevented from reaching its audience for a decade, or that it may be caponized out of its true identity, and that only its author and potential publisher will know anything about it.

## Holes, Syllabics and the Succussations of the Intercostal and Abdominal Muscles

*Lecture given to students at Belfast University. Written in August 1965, subsequently published in the* Northern Review, *vol.1, no. 2 (1966)*[11]

I want to start by asking myself two questions: why do I write at all? and more specifically, why do I write novels?

I write because I have something to say that I fail to say satisfactorily in conversation, that I fail to communicate to most people personally, as a person: I recently went to a wedding where the bride's father thought that, because I was a writer, I could make witty speeches: he seemed disappointed to learn that it was exactly because I could *not* make witty speeches that I was a writer.

There are other reasons, many other reasons: conceit, stubbornness, a desire to get my own back on people who have hurt me, a desire to repay in some indirect way those who have helped me, a great sort of humanistic religion-substitute desire to create something that may live after me, the sheer technical joy of forcing wretched intractable words into patterns of meaning and form that are uniquely, for the moment at least, mine, a need to make people laugh with me in case they laugh at me, a desire to codify experience, to come to terms with things that have happened to me, and to try to tell the truth, to discover what is the truth, about them.

All these are reasons for writing, for me, and there are others, too, I'm sure, that I don't know about consciously, all adding up to a compulsion to write, for me, a quite irresistible compulsion.

But why write a novel? Here I make a distinction, maintaining that there is a conscious decision made to write everything except

---

[11] The editors have followed Johnson's typescript of the lecture, rather than the published version, but some cuts have been made to remove extended passages later repeated verbatim in the 'Introduction' to *Aren't You Rather Young to be Writing Your Memoirs?*.

386

poetry: poetry just comes, writes itself through me. But my conscious decision to write a novel was governed by a number of things.

I was at the time very interested in the theatre, but became dissatisfied with the conditions under which writers work there, with the status of writers compared with actors and directors. I saw that, before the writer could reach his audience, he had first to go through the censorship of the Lord Chamberlain,[12] then through the dictatorship of the director, and then through the egocentricity of the actors: all of whom could at worst twist his work into something quite different, or at best filter it. Until we have a theatre where the writer is the absolute authority on the production of his play, let alone one where he actually produces it himself, as Brecht did, then the theatre must, I think, remain a highly unsatisfactory medium for a writer.

Even so, I might have written for the theatre had I not come to another conclusion at about the same time: that the theatre audiences in London are just not worth writing for, neither the popular one which regards a 'good show' as on a par with the dinner they have before it and the Babycham they have after it, nor the pseudo-intellectual cult audience which will obediently see whatever it is smart or fashionable to see, and which will remain soggily unmoved to action by the revolutionary writing or ideas.

Television was out for similar reasons, and so was the cinema, though I consider film to offer potentially the widest scope to a writer as a pure form: but at the moment it is still so hedged around with economic and pseudo-moral limitations that it is one of the most frustrating media to work in.

The next most free form was the novel, gloriously free of almost any form of censorship, capable of enormous variations within its compendiousness, a great ragbag of a form in which I could make my own shapes as I liked. Furthermore, it needed no equipment other than a pencil or paper, no entrepreneurs, before I could reach at least a small audience of friends. And, from a practical point of view, there

---

[12] The Licensing Act 1737 awarded the Lord Chamberlain statutory authority to veto performance of any new plays or request any modification to an existing play, for any reason. The Theatres Act 1843 restricted these powers so he might only prohibit a performance where in his opinion 'it is fitting for the preservation of good manners, decorum or of the public peace so to do.' This authority was finally abolished under the Theatres Act 1968.

was more chance of what I had to say reaching a larger audience: there were 2,352 novels published in England in 1961, and I doubt if more than 200 new plays ever reached a stage that year.

Since this lecture is being given at a university there is one slight digression I should like to make at this point. It seems to me likely that the majority of writers fall into that section of the population which has been since 1944 (and will continue to be) exposed to a university education. This gives the university a new responsibility which I do not think has been generally appreciated. Certainly it was not at my college, where my English year were told 'If you want to be a great actress or a great writer or something like that, then wait until you leave. You're here at college to get a degree.' This active discouragement of writing – for which I had decided at the late age of 23 to go to university, imagining that the best way to learn about writing was to find out how others had written – this discouragement came as a great surprise, and I believe it to be common to many universities, though I hope not here. I repeat, the university has despite itself acquired a special responsibility towards potential writers, and this is not generally realised, I believe.

So, after the cramping idiocy of a degree course which gave me a quite useless knowledge of Anglo-Saxon – the time spent on which I still bitterly regret as time utterly wasted – I began to read contemporary novels by writers whom I understood to have considerable literary reputations. None of these appeared to have read Joyce, let alone Beckett, for they were using techniques and conventions as dull and as oldfashioned as ever. Nor were they paying attention to language. It is not their subject-matter that I object to – this is often both new and interesting. John Wain, for example, has, rightly, a reputation for having introduced new subject matter into the English novel; but his technique and the literary conventions he accepts are certainly not new. Wain, and most other novelists writing today, are working in a traditional novel form which was spent, exhausted by the early part of this century in England. A similar thing had happened with poetic drama a hundred years earlier – Keats, Shelley, Browning and Tennyson all wrote blank-verse plays which are thumping failures. But they are failures not because they were written by bad poets, obviously, but because the blank verse form was finished, clapped-out.

But it would be wrong of me to base the whole of my case on

388

writers like Wain, Amis and their school as I don't think serious critics imagine they are any more than mediocre. I would not criticise William Golding's use of language, for example, but his book *Lord of the Flies* seems to me faulty in one very important aspect that I want to use as an example of another failing I find in contemporary novels. Apart from the fact that if you don't believe in original sin then you can't take Golding's book seriously – for on those actual occasions when children have been removed from civilizing restrictions, have they reverted to being savages and killed one another? – apart from this, the point I want to make is that the ending of the book is a pure *deus ex machina*: the arrival of the naval officer just in time to prevent the main character from being killed seems to me a completely false ending, and typifies the harmful effect of narrative conventions on those novelists who seem unable to conceive a novel without a story. A novel may tell a story; but it equally may not, if the writer so choose. And, as far as I am concerned, in attempting to convey my truth it is necessary to avoid telling stories. The child's euphemism for telling lies makes my point for me: Telling stories is telling lies.

You may object that there is no reason for reading a novel which does not provide some impetus, some forward notion. To which I retort that it is impossible to write two sentences having the same subject without creating a narrative progression, and it is this narrative progression which provides a reason for the reader to go on reading, whether or not there is a story: if he is interested in the character or subject he will go on reading. And I believe, if he is not interested in either of those things he would not go on reading the piece even if it were telling a story, either.

I believe, therefore, that not only is storytelling unnecessary, but it also involves a fatal falsification, a fatal movement away from truth in literature.

So when I came to write my first novel *Travelling People* I had these two negative things in my mind – dislike of the technical limitations and uncarefulness of most contemporary writers, and their dependence on the crutch of telling stories. But I also had positive elements, which all added up to 'what I wanted to say'. I had a theme – the conflict between illusion and reality – in a particular example, the refusal of an old man to accept that he is no longer young; a setting: the Lleyn peninsula in North Wales; and a mass of minor subject

389

matter (observed, amalgamated and worked-out), which I had acquired over some years.

From these elements I re-thought the novel form for myself. I also re-read the chief novelists of the eighteenth century, during which period the form itself was new in English and all kinds of ideas and possibilities were being tried. The main result of my re-thinking was complete dissatisfaction with the convention of using only one style or literary technique for a novel. The range of my subject-matter was so wide and so varied that no one style I knew was capable of accommodating it while yet maintaining that truth to reality that I believe to be essential. From this dissatisfaction grew naturally a technique of allowing the subject-matter to dictate the style in which it was to be conveyed, and thus to determine it organically. This meant that sections of subject-matter would begin and end themselves naturally and not arbitrarily; and could correspond to chapters, each with its own style or convention. This, I remembered, was similar to the method of *Ulysses*. But I had approached it from the opposite way round: Joyce chose his style and imposed it on his material, whereas I was allowing the material to dictate the style.

*Travelling People* employs eight separate styles or conventions for nine chapters: the first and last chapters share one style to give the book cyclical unity within the motif announced by its title and epigraph. This is the shape of the book, a circle, this is its unity, its reason for the reader going on reading: it is not a story. [...] There are interludes between the chapters which serve various functions usually connected with reminding the reader that he is reading a book and deliberately attempting to destroy his suspension of disbelief; rather in a way that Brecht constantly reminded his audiences that they were in a theatre, watching a play. I also use various visual devices to heighten or point certain events and effects. Thus when a character has a heart attack a random pattern grey section indicates this visually; a regular grey pattern indicates recuperative unconsciousness; and when the reader reaches a section completely black then he should not have to call on his knowledge of Sterne to know what has happened.

In this novel, and in all my later work, I was grateful for the advice and constructive criticism of Anthony Tillinghast, a contemporary of mine and later an academic at Liverpool University until his death last November. At first I showed my work to Dr Tillinghast as it was written, in a spirit of testing a critic to see what use he was in down-to-earth, practical terms. And the experiment worked surprisingly well: *Travelling People* would have been a worse book but for his interest in it, and it is appropriately dedicated to him and to his wife. I miss his help.[13]

The result of all this re-thinking is a novel which is in that minor tradition that runs from Petronius and Apuleius through Rabelais, Cervantes, Burton, Nashe and Sterne to James Joyce, Samuel Beckett and Flann O'Brien in this century. The tradition of the stupidly misnamed anti-novel, in fact, which may be anti-conventional but which should really be acknowledged as the tradition of the ultra-novel, the essential novel, the novel for the novel's sake and not for the story's sake. The approach in this minor tradition is anti-conventional, and its spirit is primarily that of the man who realises the futility of the human condition and can bear it only by laughing at its ludicrousness. Sterne put it best:

> . . .'tis wrote, an' please your worships, against the spleen! in order, by a more frequent and a more convulsive elevation and depression of the diaphragm, and the succussations of the intercostal and abdominal muscles in laughter, to drive the *gall* and other *bitter juices* from the gallbladder, liver, and sweetbread of his majesty's subjects, with all the inimicitious passions which belong to them, down into their duodenums.

Anyone who can make anyone else laugh about any subject at all is on the side of humankind against a chaotic and callously indifferent universe. When *Travelling People* does not follow all my theorizing, it is invariably for the sake of the comic. I also tried to keep its complexities well this side of obscurity, and to make it as readable as possible.

In technique, my second novel *Albert Angelo* is a logical progression in the direction taken by the first one. That is to say, subject-matter and function are allowed organically to determine

[13] Tony Tillinghast's premature death from cancer would later inspire Johnson to write *The Unfortunates*.

391

form and style. But this is one of the few resemblances between the two novels. Since their respective subject-matter differs so much, then their respective forms are correspondingly dissimilar.

This time, I found the problem impossible of solution, and on one level *Albert Angelo* is a dramatisation of this near impossibility of conveying truth in a vehicle of fiction. The problem, and its solution or avoidance, are epitomised in the quotation from Beckett's *The Unnamable* which forms the epigraph:

> When I think, that is to say, no, let it stand, when I think of the time I've wasted with these bran-dips, beginning with Murphy, who wasn't even the first, when I had me, on the premises, within easy reach, tottering under my own skin and bones, real ones, rotting with solitude and neglect, till I doubted my own existence, and even still, today, I have no faith in it, none, so that I have to say, when I speak, Who speaks, and seek, and so on and similarly for all the other things that happen to me and for which someone must be found, for things that happen must have someone to happen to, someone must stop them. But Murphy and the others, and last but not least the two old buffers here present, could not stop them, the things that happened to me, nothing could happen to them, of the things that happened to me, and nothing else either, there is nothing else, let us be lucid for once, nothing else but what happens to me, such as speaking, and such as seeking, and which cannot happen to me, which prowl round me, like bodies in torment, the torment of no abode, no repose, no, like hyenas, screeching and laughing, no, no better, no matter, I've shut my doors against them, I'm not at home to anything, my doors are shut against them, perhaps that's how I'll find silence, and peace at last, by opening my doors and letting myself be devoured, they'll stop howling, they'll start eating, the maws now howling: Open up, open up, you'll be all right, you'll see.

Why 'invent' characters when you know yourself much better? How can an invented character stand exactly for what you want to say unless he *is* you?

So, *Albert Angelo* sets up a character who is an architect *manqué*

392

and who has to earn his living as a teacher and has lost most of his sense of direction as a result of a broken love-affair. Then, after some 160 pages of this situation, I, as author, suddenly and violently break through this character to speak in my own voice and say directly what I had been trying to say less than successfully through this objective correlative.

It is no accident that my hero, Albert, is an architect, for I believe that my aims have much in common with those of many contemporary architects. [...] In this century architects have been presented with radical new techniques (ferro-concrete, plastics, new finishes) which they are painfully, with many bosh-shots, learning how to use. Similarly, Joyce presented writers with new techniques and concepts which – infinitely more slowly than an architect – a handful of people are trying to learn to use.

Various unconventional devices are used in *Albert Angelo* for effects which I felt I could not satisfactorily achieve by any other means. [...] These methods are adopted solely to solve my problems, the problems of saying what I believe to be true as nearly as possible, and for no other reason. The point is that there are writing problems today which just did not exist even fifty years ago, and to attempt to solve them with the methods and techniques of Dickens and the nineteenth century is like trying to make new discoveries in physics without taking Einstein into account. I think particularly of a writer like Angus Wilson, a brilliant observer of contemporary *mores*, but whose style is directly comparable to Dickens – to Wilson's great loss, I believe. Where I depart from convention it is because convention has failed, has proved inadequate. Each of my books is a specific solution to a specific set of problems. They are not exemplars for anyone else; by definition, no other book could or should be written like them.

To turn to poetry. And first of all to make an elementary distinction which experience has taught me has to be made whenever I speak about the subject, if there is not to be a danger of being completely misunderstood. The distinction is between poetry and verse. Poetry is the art-essence, the thing that hits you in the pit of the stomach, a physical feeling that shouts *yes*! A moment of recognition of some sort of truth. Poetry can be found in all arts: it is, I repeat, the art-essence. Verse, on the other hand, is the mechanical putting

393

together of elements of speech into patterns. Different languages take different elements: the Greeks and Romans used quantity, the length of syllables, and arranged them in patterns of longs and shorts. English verse since Chaucer's time has taken the element of stress or accent, and arranged patterns of stress and non-stress.

Verse can be taught; poetry cannot be taught.

Some verse contains poetry. There is more which does not. In the work of Pope, for instance, there is much wit, intellect, discussion and satire in verse: but there is very little poetry. This is *not* to disparage Pope: it is merely to describe his work.

Whether there is poetry or not in my work is a matter of opinion: I think there is. It does not seem to me that one can usefully discuss it.

One can usefully discuss verse technique. I have already said that blank-verse is clapped-out, after centuries of honest toil and excellent service. My own problem was to find a verse form – that is, a pattern of speech elements – that was suited to what I had to say. What I had to say was largely anti-heroic, anti-romantic, and I was determined to say it in the language, the colloquial language if necessary, of the mid-twentieth century. This could not be done in blank verse nor in any other combination of sing-song iambics. Colloquial speech just does not run in patterns of de-da, de-da, de-da, de-da, de-da. Not real speech, that is.

My solution, which I came to independently though I later found that many Americans had been experimenting with it for a number of years, was to make patterns by using syllables as the speech element of my verse. With this system of prosody, the stresses in a line could fall exactly where they did in natural speech.

Furthermore, it seemed to me that since most poetry reaches its audience in printed form, a metre which is easily apprehended visually, as any syllabic one is, would seem to be more appropriate than those metres which depend on sound, like stress or quantitative ones. Syllabic metres can also be recognised by ear easily enough, provided the audience is not expecting a stress metre or is prepared to pay sufficient attention to a different metrical element.

I recently heard Nathalie Sarraute[14] speaking about her work, and she compared literature to a relay race in which the baton of each

_____

[14] Nathalie Sarraute: author of *Portrait of a Man Unknown* (1948), famously described by

generation's new discoveries was handed on. Not only did pre-war novelists in England drop this baton, but now they don't even admit they're in a race. Even now, of writers in English apart from Samuel Beckett, I can think of only Rayner Heppenstall, Philip Toynbee and Christine Brooke-Rose[15] besides myself who are attempting, in different ways, to do something new in the novel, who are accepting that their starting-point is where Joyce left off.

Some rhetorical questions from *Tristram Shandy* are in order here:

> Shall we for ever make new books, as apothecaries make new mixtures, by pouring only out of one vessel into another? Are we for ever to be twisting and untwisting the same rope, for ever in the same track, for ever at the same place?

And of course critics and reviewers are even further behind conventional writers. They measure anything new up against a set of criteria which are largely invalid, and by which, by definition, anything different cannot be judged. I do not wish to seem ungrateful to those reviewers who have praised my work. But my character is something like Shandy's father, who had

> . . .such a skirmishing, cutting kind of a slashing way with him, in his disputations, thrusting and ripping, and giving every one a stroke to remember him by in his turn – that if there were twenty people in company – in less than half an hour he was sure to have every one of them against him.

I would rather have understanding of what I am trying to do, than praise. And I have had little understanding. Many reviewers regard

---

Sartre as an 'anti-novel'. Her essay *The Age of Suspicion* (1956) became a key manifesto for the *nouveau roman*.

[15] Rayner Heppenstall: working-class English experimental novelist, born in 1911, who from the early 1960s associated with a British avant-garde set that included Alan Burns, Angela Carter, Eva Figes, B. S. Johnson, Ann Quin and Stefan Themerson. Philip Toynbee: experimental writer and influential reviewer for the *Observer*, born 1916. Johnson had favourably reviewed his novel *Pantaloon* (1961). Christine Brooke-Rose: writer, critic and French-based academic, best known at this stage for her experimental novel *Out* (1964).

my technical devices as in some way making the books worse: how, I cannot see, for at worst the devices could have only a negative effect, neither detracting nor improving. Similarly, they did not like my changing styles in *Travelling People*, but not one of them examined the validity of my reasons for so doing. Many objected to my breaking off *Albert Angelo*, but not one attempted to suggest another way of solving the problems of conveying truth in a vehicle of fiction – or even so much as acknowledged that it was a problem.

Most critics just would not consider my works in terms of its own basic premises, and not those of other, dead writers. Critics are backward-looking in the extreme. Why – in a radio interview I spent nearly five minutes justifying to one critic my abandoning of punctuation for two pages because I needed to convey that a character was speaking breathlessly, incoherently. That I should have to do this forty-two years after the publication of Molly Bloom's soliloquy is quite incredible, quite ludicrous.

The weight of prejudice against anything new is enormous and deeply rooted. 'Experimental' is the dirtiest of words, invariably a synonym for 'unsuccessful'. The latest evidence of this is a collection of short pieces called *Statement Against Corpses* which I published with the poet Zulfikar Ghose.[16] Critics have tried to discuss this as though these were conventional short stories, in spite of a declared intention – which incidentally has itself been heavily attacked as pretentious – that they were not to be regarded as such. At least two of these pieces employ techniques never before used in literature, and yet not one critic has yet mentioned or noticed that fact. I know that it is not done, tasteless, undignified to attack one's critics, and I do so rarely, but it does seem to me necessary, if we agree that literature can be talked about at all. It does matter. But what use is criticism? How dare anyone say that something I have written does not work when they are simply not in a position to have considered the alternatives? What use is such a criticism? Rilke said it all in twenty-nine words, Rainer Maria Rilke:

[16] Pakistani-born poet, novelist and close friend of Johnson. They had previously collaborated on the editing of *Universities Poetry*, and the writing of an unpublished satire, *Prepar-a-Tory* (1960).

'Works of art are of an infinite loneliness and with nothing to be so little reached as with criticism. Only love can grasp and hold and fairly judge them.'

So to conclude.

When a national newspaper returns its review copy of *Travelling People* saying that it must be a faulty one because some of the pages are completely black;

when the Australian customs seize *Albert Angelo* and will not release it until they have seen the obscenity they are sure must have been excised by cutting holes in the page;

when a printer refuses to print *Albert Angelo* but is then hypocritically prepared to make money out of it by binding it since his name will not appear on it;

when the best thought-of but actually the most conservative of paperback publishers refuse to print a book with holes in it;

when reviewers attack work for not doing what it was not trying to do;

when these, and many other signs, indicate that same kind of bourgeois and reactionary discontent and outright rejection which has always greeted innovation, then I am certain that I am a member, however humble, of that relay team which is moving forward in a significant and meaningful manner in literature.

# London: the Moron-Made City, or Just a Load of Old Buildings with Cars in Between

*Published in* London Life, *23–29 October 1965*

*'We live in moron-made cities. We wish to see towns and buildings which do not make us feel ashamed, ashamed that we cannot realise the potential of the twentieth century, ashamed that philosophers and physicists must think us fools, and painters think us irrelevant. Our generation must try to produce evidence that men are at work.'*

This statement of belief and intention was made in 1954 by two young architects, the husband-and-wife partnership of Alison and Peter Smithson,[17] and it echoed the manifestoes of the previous generation's *avant garde* while at the same time announcing that a new generation was still not satisfied with such progress as had been made. The Smithsons have acknowledged their debt to the Modern Movement as a whole, to its painters, sculptors, writers, composers, philosophers and scientists: to Picasso, Klee, Mondrian, Brancusi, Joyce, Le Corbusier, Schönberg, Bergson, and Einstein. But they have also pointed out that 'Modern Architecture' is now a historical term which describes a certain period in architectural development.

Though the Smithsons originally came from County Durham, they live and work in London.

'The English don't ever seem to have set out to build a city as such,' they say, 'let alone formed the concept of a city as a work of art, which is of course what we see it as potentially; a collective work

---

[17] Alison (1928–93) and Peter Smithson (1923–2003) were leaders of the New Brutalism movement in British architecture. Inspired by the work of Mies van der Rohe (one of Johnson's own heroes), their first notable design had been Hunstanton School (1954), and they were considered by many to be at the forefront of architectural and urban theory. Johnson became friendly with them during the failed campaign to save the Euston Arch in the early 1960s, and saw many parallels between their values and his own. His 1970 BBC film, *The Smithsons on Housing*, documents the design and construction of the controversial Robin Hood Gardens estate in East London, their third and last major public building in the UK.

of art, that is. And if a city is not a work of art then really it's a nothing, it's a load of old buildings with cars in between. . . . [But] if a
city is this kind of work of art you live in, then the living there itself
takes on a marvellous sort of extra quality: you are suddenly made
aware of very ordinary things like entering or moving or being quiet,
things which suddenly become positive and not residual. That's the
trouble with Londoners: they see the city merely as a mechanism
with which you can tinker to make it all right: they don't see it as a
work of art, a live thing, a living organism, which could make life
marvellous. You don't have to start building London all over again:
this sort of life can be achieved by symbols, just as you can transform
an unpleasant room by a pleasant picture in such a way that you
really don't see the room at all.' [...]

The Smithsons see the demolition in 1963 of Philip Hardwick's
Arch at Euston Station as a symbol of the jealousy of London, of an
unhealthy domination.

'What the hell did they do it for? Who were they? The Euston
Arch was a monument to the Railway Age, to an age when for the
first time for centuries the power which had traditionally resided in
the Court and the south suddenly came to depend on the industrial
energy of the north, on men like George Stephenson, born in a cottage at Wylam, near Newcastle, who invented the whole thing from
nothing: a man who could survey a line, organise the men, design the
track, the engines, the signals, the lamps, name the places, design the
lettering, do it all, everything. One envies him his force: no one really
has the will to operate on that scale now. These men suddenly were
the power: they put up this monument in London, a simple, marvellous piece of architecture, which just sort of thundered away there,
standing for what these men had done. All over London there are
monuments to the others which have lasted for centuries, some of
them. And since the 1914–18 war the power has come back to the
south, largely because all decisions had to be made from one place
then, and later London got a stranglehold on the new power, commu-
nications. And so they seized this opportunity to destroy the Arch,
which was a kind of imposition on London, a reminder that what was
the Empire was based on men working in the dirt up north. Obviously
the Prime Minister didn't refuse to act because he knew this consciously, but surely when he was making up his mind or not making

up his mind to save it, he must have felt certain that to knock it down was somehow the right thing to do, as if to wipe out the fact that there was a time when the south wasn't dominant. If it had been a monument to Marlborough or someone like that then they'd have found a reason for keeping it, because he was part of the southern economic power, he came from where the wealth was manipulated.' [...]

The Smithsons have what amounts to a reverence for anything into which effort and trouble have been put. This shows particularly in the care with which they made sure that their first London building, for the *Economist* in St. James's, took into account, blended with, and even flattered the eighteenth-century Boodle's Club on an adjacent site. The Smithsons designed a group of three buildings standing on a plaza to replace the corpus of obsolete Edwardian buildings which had solidly filled the site before. On the St. James's Street side they placed a bank building, conforming in scale and achieving great compatibility with the other buildings on that side of this most conservative of streets; behind this a tower block rises, still conforming in general to the scale of the St. James's area though it is in fact its highest building, which houses the *Economist* offices; and an exact half-size copy of this tower stands behind Boodle's and contains flats, chambers, and services for the Club. Below the plaza on which these three building stand is an underground car park and various services.

The demolition of the building next to Boodle's left a long flank wall of the Club exposed, and it is in the architectural treatment of this that the extreme, almost loving care of the Smithsons' solution to the problems of this site is seen at its most original. They studied Boodle's from what they call an archaeological approach:

'From the bones and other objects an archaeologist finds, he has to comprehend through interpretation the whole culture, what it was, what made it tick, everything he can about it. Similarly, we had to try to think what Boodle's was to its architect, to its time, and then think what it had become, as well.'

This examination in depth revealed information that led to the solution, the blending and neutralising of the lines and proportions of Boodle's with those of the Smithsons' buildings. The feature which most closely links the two is a new three-storey bay window on the exposed wall of the Club, which appears to be constructionally the same as the *Economist* but which actually parodies its Portland stone

400

facing by being carried out in the modern equivalent of Coade artificial stone, just as the Club imitates in Coade the masonry facings of buildings of its own period: a delightful, if rather recondite, architectural joke.

Not only does the *Economist* group of buildings embody almost didactically the architectural theories of its designers and fit beautifully into its surroundings, but it has also provided improved civic amenities: it is now possible to walk across the plaza, an area bounded on three sides by roads, and quite immune from traffic; it is also possible to stop and rest there on seats. Compared with what was there before, the Smithsons have added light, air, space and public amenity besides providing better accommodation for a bank, offices, and Boodle's Club. This is in marked contrast to most developments, which live off built capital and close in every available site rather than attempt to add new values.

The *Economist* is a magnificent example of what can be done in urban renewal, a practical, successful demonstration of how to preserve the better buildings by re-stating them in terms of relationships with new buildings. It has obvious applications to St. James's Street itself: the whole of the east side could be developed organically in this manner, and once, as something of an architects' office joke, the Smithsons imposed on an air photo of the whole St. James's area photographs of the model of the *Economist* on half a dozen other sites: it worked well. Such a redevelopment would make the area architecturally as aristocratic as it likes to think it is historically.

But even the redevelopment of St. James's would solve only a small part of London's problem.

'At the moment they're trying to do something to alleviate the conditions of traffic congestion which already exist, making huge investments at places like Hyde Park Corner which serve only to attract more traffic to them and make conditions worse than they were before. Whereas it would be more sensible if they were to say, Let's leave Piccadilly as it is and concentrate on taking the traffic some distance away from it on a proper road designed for that traffic. Piccadilly would then revert to something more like its former condition. This would shunt off energy – energy meaning money and people and everything – away from the existing congestion. You find the same thing in principle right throughout the country: the local civic engineer is constantly tinkering about with his High Street, putting bus shelters up, erecting railings, concreting some areas, ripping up cobbles somewhere else, setting aside parking places, and so on. Whereas a couple of streets away it's derelict, or of very little value, and if he was to build a new shopping street there with shops properly serviced from the rear, accessible by bus, with off-street parking, then the big multiple shops would be attracted to it and the historical High Street area could go back to its Saturday market, the camera shop, the small grocer, and so on. Maybe part of it would die, and then you could open up spaces, or some houses which had had shopfronts bashed in them could revert to being houses again.' [...]

The Smithsons believe that the only thing capable of pulling London together, structurally, to make the scattered city more like an entity, is a network of motorways. These urban motorways would also serve to move traffic at the present centres of congestion, and bring new life to areas which are now depressed in one way or another. They have prepared a plan for such a network of new roads, on routes which exploit cheap land adjacent to railways (or if necessary over railways), previously unusable land like marshes, and the 'backlands' or wasted land sometimes left in odd pockets. Junctions for these roads are sited on or over railway sidings and cheap property: where land is not available exactly where it is needed, the roads merely cross without intersecting and interconnection is made elsewhere, always with the object of avoiding present areas of congestion to divert traffic away from them. Architecturally the roads are intended to present a clear pattern in themselves, and as the same principles apply throughout, it is hoped that the pattern would be apparent in spite of the many versions of junctions, takeoffs, and so on which are necessary to meet the complex conditions of an already existing city. When two roads have to cross, the junction is so designed that only one decision can be made on each approach road: the decision to turn the other way has either been made further back in the system, or will be made further on in the system. The motorways are routed to provide a series of identifying fixes, or places where a relationship to the city structure could be observed: for example, the route along the Embankment provides fixes on Westminster and the City, and the route across Hyde Park does the same for the central area. The existing raised portion of the M4 at Chiswick is a built example of what the Smithsons mean by such a road re-defining places in relation to each other, such places as Osterley Park and Brentford Football Ground now being able to be seen in relationship to each other and to the road in a way which was not possible before.

Routing these roads through the 'backlands' is intended to regenerate old areas by increasing land values: this would happen especially round takeoffs, where increased accessibility and new facilities for garages, hotels and so on would provide new incentives to redevelopment. To serve these takeoffs, the existing street net has been organised in 'Stop' streets (mainly shopping streets which are also bus routes, two-way, with picking up and setting down permitted, and metered parking provided where possible) and 'Go' streets (often the present 'taxi' routes, which have been organised into a system of one-way streets feeding into the takeoffs with no stopping and no parking whatsoever). The 'Stop' streets, which are really those in which the route itself has no function, would then serve the buildings and the functions of the street itself: there would be frequent pedestrian crossings, lay-bys, and car park entrances. Intersections on the 'Go' streets would be controlled by lights, with filters wherever possible to keep the one-way system flowing.

This London road plan, the Smithsons feel, should be supplemented by a public transport survey, but in any case they envisage a rapid transit bus system to serve the whole central area: the buses would never leave the motorway network, there being alighting points at suitable takeoffs at that level about a quarter of a mile apart and also at railway stations and Green Line termini. Such a system of rationalised, subsidised mass transit facilities already works well in Philadelphia, where two lanes of the urban motorways are reserved for high-speed buses.

There is nothing unfeasible about this plan: it would be expensive, but so is the congestion existing at the moment and which becomes inexorably worse each month. But such a system of urban motorways introduces into the city an element on an entirely new scale, the Smithsons believe, a geographical scale which seems to make the old sort of building totally inappropriate and which implies a new kind of interlocking town-structure/architectural-form about which they have spent much time evolving theories.

These theories have found their most complete expression in a plan for the rebuilding of the city of Berlin made in collaboration with Peter Sigmonde, a plan which won third prize in a competition organised by that city, and was the only non-German entry to win a prize, incidentally. In this plan the function of urban motorways to unify and define a city rather than merely to relieve congestion is seen in its most convincing form. A ring of them serve a central area of access roads, upon the net of which is superimposed a pedestrian platform net some thirty feet above the ground, from which it is reached by escalators. The shape of this city is the reverse of a conventional one, having an inverted profile: that is, the centre is flat, with a single symbolic identifying fix (somewhat like a navel), with a 'wall' of high office buildings on the outskirts linked to both roads and the pedestrian platform. Green zones define but do not define the parts. Growth and change are built into this city concept: each sort of development has its rules by which addition and variation are controlled in an organic manner.

Such a plan was evolved from many years of continuous objective analysis of the structures created by man and the changes which take place in them in an attempt 'to uncover a pattern of reality which includes human aspirations.'

This analysis has also led to the formation of a series of 15 Criteria for Mass Housing, criteria which have that sort of simplicity which makes them appear obvious until it is remembered that no single dwelling in the country measures up to them:

1) Does the housing liberate the inhabitants from old restrictions or straitjacket them into new ones?

2) Can the individual add identity to his house or is the architecture packaging him?

3) Will the lampshades on the ceilings, the curtains, the china dogs take away from the meaning of the architecture?

4) Is the means of construction of the same order as the standard of living envisaged in the house?

5) Are the spaces moulded exactly to their purpose or are they by-products of structural tidiness or plastic whim?

6) Is there a decently large open-air sunlit space opening directly from the house?

7)   Can the weather be enjoyed? ('The English climate is characterised by changeability: therefore a house should be capable of grasping what fine weather it can get: south windows in all rooms and easy access to sheltered patios, roof gardens or terraces which can be arranged in a moment to catch the pleasures of our climate and then closed up in a moment so that we can ignore it.')

8)   Can the extension of the dwelling (garden, patio, and so on) be appreciated from inside?

9)   Is there a place in the open air where a baby can be left?

10)  Where do 3–5 year olds play?

11)  Can the houses be put together in such a way as to contribute something to each other?

12)  Is the house as comfortable as a car of the same year?

13)  Is there a place where you can clean or wash things without making a mess of the whole house?

14)  Is there enough vital storage: that is, storage not of a purely residual nature like lofts, built-in fittings, and so on?

15)  Is there a place for the belongings peculiar to the class of the occupant: poodles, ferrets, motorbikes, geraniums, and so on?

That these reasonable criteria are not those of every form of housing erected in Britain is a condemnation of every responsible authority or private builder.

Only in painting, sculpture and (to a lesser extent) music have the pioneers of the Modern Movement become the establishment in their respective arts. In literature and in architecture the reactionaries who use the techniques of Dickens and put up Shell Centres are still not only in the majority but even represent these arts to many people. Thus Alison and Peter Smithson are faced with a multiple problem: not only to overcome the opposition of reactionaries to a previous generation, but also to have ideas accepted which are an extension and development of those of that generation. Just to come by the requisite experience is difficult enough:

'Really, if you talk about it strategically, dealing with London as it now exists and thinking what's going to happen between now and 1980, say, then you speak of something we've simply not had any experience of. No one can say much about it because you have to be given the responsibility before you can think about it meaningfully, that is, you have to say, what is it that you could actually do?'

With so much theoretical work of obvious validity and importance done over the decade and more since their manifesto, and with one practical example of it built showing what could be done with London, is it not time that the solutions to urban renewal and mass housing put forward by the Smithsons were given urgent, even desperate, consideration? It may not be so disastrous that advances in literature fail to be consolidated: but those in architecture involve more serious and fundamental elements determining the basic quality of living, and we simply cannot afford to ignore anyone who has anything to say as practical and original as Alison and Peter Smithson.

# [On football]

*Unpublished article for* Sunday Times Magazine, *World Cup Issue. Typescript dated 8 February 1966*

The first organised soccer team I played for was formed by a youth club, when I was about eleven or twelve. This club was a church one, and after playing other youth club teams on Saturday afternoons we were morally bound to go to church the next morning. Few of the team did, however, being interested only in the club for the opportunity it provided to play football with a real ball on grass pitches. The Vicar resented this, and one Monday clubnight summoned the team into this little office he had, called us all a lot of little heathens quaintly, and said there would be no more football unless we went to his church: for good measure, and partly for other reasons, he also expelled three of us. But such was the loyalty the team had built up, playing together for over a year, that the rest left, too, and we played friendlies for the rest of that season until we could enter a junior league. We called ourselves Little Heathens F.C.

But it is difficult to remember a time before this when I did not play improvised football of some kind or another. As soon as we were through the school doors at break or lunchtime, someone would say 'Out with the pill!', and a tennis ball would be unsocketed from a trouser pocket and we would then pass and dribble our way across the playground until we came to our goal: which might be between a window and a downpipe, or one section of the bicycle sheds, or just two discarded jackets: such goal being the focal point of just one of many such areas laid claim to by three or four kids who habitually played together.

A tennis ball would fit remarkably neatly into a trousers pocket: perhaps such pockets were thoughtfully designed with this in mind, but in any case those which were not were quickly distended to accommodate the ball, the result being perhaps a quarter of the school was apparently afflicted by a great wens on their thighs: all except

Strickmore, I remember, a brilliant natural footballer, on whose body a tennis ball would disappear as though he had an appropriately-sized hole in him.

Playing with a tennis ball on asphalt taught one good ball control, as it was so small compared with a proper ball (and indeed with the fullsize plastic balls schoolboys use in playgrounds now), and it bounced on asphalt with a higher degree of accuracy than a football on grass. But it did not help with dead-ball kicking, as a tennis ball on the ground always had to be kicked with the toecap rather than with the instep. Thus it was that later, playing on grass or mud with an uneven surface and probably a slope as well, with a much larger ball and what looked like a prairie of open space, organised football seemed almost a different game.

We played as Little Heathens in a junior league until we were all about eighteen, when the team broke up: some took jobs which involved working on Saturday afternoons, one or two became so disheartened by their own failure to improve that they took to the vicarious satisfaction of watching professional games regularly, and yet others became involved with girls who resented the competition from anything as interesting as we found soccer. For the team was for many years our passionate interest, a complete, self-sufficient interest: the week was one long irrelevance from Saturday night to Saturday morning, the summer hardly bearable with no match play and only desultory, overheated practice to be had.

For all this dedication, however, we never won anything, did not finish higher than third in our league and never reached even the semi-finals of our cup. Not that but we wanted to win, for we did: there was none of this guff about the important thing being to compete, or to be a sportsman, for us: we just liked winning, however we did it.

Football so dominated our lives that we could not play enough of it: four games in a weekend was not unusual for some of us, and three games quite common. Several of us would play for the school on Saturday mornings, Little Heathens in the afternoons, and one or two of the scratch Sunday teams the next day.

The Sunday league teams were the weirdest, were made up of the most bizarre combinations of players: a thirteen year-old winger might find himself up against a fullback of fifty-odd, wing halves

408

would be playing in goal, centre halves on the wing, all given a game at the last minute to make the side up. The play was equally unortho-dox: top goalscorers would be defensive inside forwards, goalkeepers would be brought up to take penalties against their opposite numbers, and centreforwards would often be found heading off their own goal line. As far as results went, form simply did not exist: and matches would finish with comic scores like 10–1, 8–7, or, on one disastrous occasion, 22–0.

Some of the players were, or seemed, of epic, even supernatural stature: the great hairy centreforward I once had to mark, called Beetlecrusher by his team-mates on account of his studded Army boots and who had not, it was said, washed since Dunkirk, who bat-tered his way past me to score four times that afternoon; and the unbelievable speed of recovery of one player, perhaps a pro anonym-ously enjoying a Sunday game, who just once I beat in a tackle in midfield to then hit the ball immediately high down the centre where, incredibly, there he was to head it away again.

Looking back, some of my most enjoyable football was played in those Sunday matches, on pitches which invariably sloped, or were bald of turf and thick with mud, or had great clumps of something like esparto grass growing here and there: all or any of which turned football into more a game of chance than it could be. But most of all there was the piquancy of knowing that if the FA came to hear about you playing on Sundays, then you could be banned for life from ever taking part in organised soccer again.

My father had supported Chelsea for years, standing out in all weathers on that great high banking, the Popular Terrace, which has only just this year been converted into a covered stand: indeed, it was on that terrace that I first learnt those swearwords most beneficially applicable to soccer, from hearing him and others effing and beeing at the way Chelsea played, for years the most infuriatingly talented and inept team in London to support. So it was to Chelsea that I applied when I considered that I ought to have a trial for a professional team: more to confirm that I was not missing anything I could possibly obtain than from any real desire to live the life of a professional foot-baller. I travelled on the top deck of a trolleybus all the long way up the straight length of the Edgware Road to the Welsh Harp at Hendon, where I changed in the pub and then played badly and dispiritedly on Chelsea's practice pitch at the back. They talked to one or two of the better players, and told the rest of us we would be hearing if they wanted us. I never heard.

Some sixteen years after this, however, I still support Chelsea, still try to go to Stamford Bridge whenever I can. This lays me open to the often-levelled charge of following the fashionable interest intellectuals now have in soccer, but in my case what amounts to a love of football came years before I was elevated to the rank of intellectual, and so I think it must have done with many others of my generation: the 1944 Education Act may in fact be responsible for this apparent change in the choice of relaxation of those whose occupations qualify them as intellectuals. As one university lecturer who taught me said, in a perhaps unguarded moment, 'No work of art has ever moved me so much as a good football match.'

In any case, I never know whether I ought to consider myself an intellectual or not: I write novels which for want of better terms are called 'experimental' and 'avantgarde' (I call their techniques organic, solving each writing problem in the best way I can find: which may sometimes be a way no one else, or few others, have tried), if that is an intellectual activity. But my wife laughs at my being called an intellectual, says I am far too instinctive for that: which probably involves another definition.

But simply, I am a writer and I enjoy watching football: combining the two, I saw soccer reporting as an opportunity to be paid for watching matches from the best seats. And I enjoyed it, too, both the soccer and the writing: it was what appeared in print that was usually such a pain. I would take great trouble to try to make my copy as good a piece of writing as anything else I might do, as good as a poem written under the same conditions, even (imagining anyone would want to write a poem in half an hour in a cold, windswept football stadium), and the sub-editors would almost invariably ruin it not only by cutting it, but also by re-writing to some faceless sub-standard of their own: I would go to great lengths to avoid the use of clichés, and the subs would go to equal trouble to put them back in again. And they won in the end, of course: all I could do was resign.

There is no valid reason why the sports pages should be any less well written than the rest of a newspaper: but all of them noticeably are. One of the chief reasons for this is that heresy believed in by even the posh papers as well: that because a man played a game well, he must therefore be able to write about it equally outstandingly. Nothing could be less true: the evidence is that few of them can write at all, let alone professionally, and one of the sadder sights of the press box is one of these players of yesterday haltingly speaking his thoughts to a young lad who puts them into English for him.

But there are a few soccer reporters one can read without feeling insulted. Easily the best of these is the *Times* Association Football Correspondent, Geoffrey Green: he alone provides what I want from a soccer report, which is something of the feeling of what it was like to be there, the nearest possible substitute for not actually having been watching, and not just who scored from whose pass in which minute. Green's erudition, his wit, his really skilful (as if poetic) use of imagery, are always a pleasure: even his frequent overreachings are themselves delightful in their preposterousness. Hugh McIlvanney of the *Observer* writes with a kind of sinuous intelligence about the game, sparing of imagery but exact of effect. Brian Glanville (*Sunday Times*) has great fluency, but his reports read like written-down talk rather than worked-out writing: interesting, well-informed talk, to be sure, but not writing.

Apart from these three, there are really only the sportswriting stars of the popular papers, the so-called Heavy Mob, who can sometimes be seen moving down Fleet Street as a solid phalanx in their heavy mohair overcoats and heavier jokes, their fur hats and ludicrous images, short arms swinging and shorter parts hanging, red of face and 'colour' at the ready. What kind of a hell of a mess they are going to make of writing about the World Cup makes me despondent, almost as much as do the recent performances of the England team itself.

After all, the World Cup is not likely to be held again in England this century.

# A Hard Glance at the Poetry Business

*Published in* London Life*, 16 April 1966*

If the state of poetry is to be judged by the quantity actually being written now, then it must be said to be flourishing. Never, it seems, have so many people written what they call poetry, but which others might think worthy only to be called verse, and far more of which is just. . . not even prose. And they submit it, too: the editors of those journals and magazines which publish poetry (and those which don't, as well, for that matter: there is a considerable body of enthusiasts who imagine they will be the first poet to publish an epic in the *Daily Mirror*) receive upwards of two hundred poems every week.

And never before has it been so easy for a poet to achieve publication of some sort or another. The number of 'little' magazines has increased enormously over the last five years, and there now seem to be far more publishers willing to take the risk of a small loss on a hardback volume of poetry in return for the prestige such publishing apparently brings.

The public reading of poetry, usually by the poets themselves, has also gained noticeable ground over the last few years with groups all over the country holding regular meetings. The best of these in London is held not in Chelsea, or Soho, or Hampstead, but in SE22 by the Dulwich Group. The meetings take place in the upstairs room of an enormous, friendly pub, and audiences of over a hundred (on one sweltering occasion, three hundred) are common. It is no doubt the fact of being held in a pub, where the atmosphere is informal and where the audience can meet the poets down in the bar afterwards, that accounts for the success of the Dulwich meetings compared with all other poetry readings in London. Those held by the Contemporary Poetry and Music Circle in Kensington, for instance, are very disappointingly attended, and those organized by the literary magazine *Ambit* and the weekly *Tribune*, usually in public libraries, attract

412

nothing like the Dulwich crowds: and Dulwich is far from being the easiest place in London to reach by public transport.

These readings are certainly a welcome development: there is no poetry which does not gain something from being heard read by the poet himself. Poor readers as many poets are, and in spite of the fact that their interpretations may very often not be definitive ones, their own words in their own voices provide a direct experience of poetry unfiltered by the intervention of another sensibility and unmarred by the 'Poetry Voice'.

But nevertheless poetry is still not primarily a spoken medium, and this to me was the one thing cogently demonstrated by the Albert Hall jamboree organised by the Beats last June.[18] The poems spoken there, when read on the page (as they can be in *Wholly Communion*, a published version of this so-called International Poetry Incarnation), make a far greater impact and indeed seem far better poems than they did heard in the weddingcake architecture of the Albert Hall. It is in fact a myth that poetry demands sound: it has been addressed to the eye since Caxton's time, and whichever way it is moving (and I think it is indeed moving slowly towards more aural acceptance) print is still by far the most common way in which poetry reaches its audience.

No, to me the International Poetry Incarnation did not seem to herald a new interest in poetry: it was a highly-publicised non-event by a group of performers-in-public, one or two of whom were good poets (Adrian Mitchell, Lawrence Ferlinghetti), which happened to take place at a very favourable moment. It was in many ways a sad, pathetic occasion, too, for I believe it marked the demise of the Beats: the Incarnation was in fact their Wake, their Elegy for a generation passed into middle-age, the Funferall (Joyce's brilliant neologism describes the occasion exactly) of the Hipsters. Nowhere was this demonstrated more clearly than in the lack of opposition from the audience, for words which have never before been spoken in public in the Albert Hall raised not a murmur, poetry which was patently absolute rubbish was greeted with reverence during and applause

---

[18] The International Poetry Incarnation, a live poetry event which took place at London's Royal Albert Hall on 11 June 1965. It attracted an audience of 7,000 and featured readings by, among others, Allen Ginsberg, William Burroughs, Alexander Trocchi, George Macbeth, Michael Horovitz, Christopher Logue and Adrian Mitchell.

after it, and almost the only heckling came as a result of boredom or not being able to hear certain speakers properly. No, this audience was on the side of the Beats: they were not there for the poetry but for what the readers stood for as rebels, outcasts: and which is now so quaintly passé.

However much anyone who writes poetry would wish to read at a public meeting, it is still print which has the authority and status chiefly to attract them. The typical successful poet first appears in weeklies like the *Times Literary Supplement*, the *Spectator*, the *New Statesman* and the *Observer*, and later has a collection (usually only about 56 pages long) published in a hardback volume by a reputable publisher: that is, one who publishes a wide range of other books besides poetry.

Space in journals like those mentioned is naturally limited (some of them one suspects use poetry to fill up awkward column-ends) and usually the literary editors, quite justifiably from their point of view, prefer to print poems by poets who have already made some sort of a name for themselves. Like everyone else in poetry, they too have what appears to others as eccentric taste in their choice of which poems to print: some even appear to have no policy at all. It is inevitable therefore that anyone unknown should be rejected very often, however good he is: but at the same time every literary editor wants to discover superb poems by an unknown, and this at least keeps them reading through everything they receive.

After rejection by the national recognised weeklies and magazines, the great mass of those now writing what they call poetry are faced with three alternatives: to pay for publication themselves in one form or another, or to stop writing, or to write only for themselves.

There are many organisations of one sort or another which exploit the vanity of writers and the apparently desperate need of many of them to see themselves in print. A glance at the small ads column of several of the weeklies will discover two or three often cunningly-worded requests for poems. Enquiries in answer to these advertisements usually reveal that they are inserted by jobbing printers who want the author to pay the complete cost of a limited edition of varying degrees of sumptuousness, or magazines which will print every poem sent to them provided that the poet pays a fee and takes out a year's subscription to their usually-duplicated organ. Rather

414

more subtle is the advertiser who asks for your poems, writes back enthusiastically for more, and then says that he will prepare a tape-recording of them for submission to editors and radio companies all over the world: the poems to be read by a professional actor, who will, of course, require a fee of three guineas. . . .

All these organisations take money out of poetry, feed off it, rather than contribute towards its wellbeing, and are in the same class as those poetry competitions which take far more money in entrance fees than are required to cover the cost of prizes and judging. Yet every edition of the *Writers' and Artists' Yearbook* contains a warning to authors never to pay for publication of their work: admittedly, until this year, this warning appeared side by side with advertisements which were nothing if not attempts to extract money from authors by means of an appeal in one form or another to their vanity.

For the writer who does not want to pay someone else to print his work there is what might be regarded as the last resort of the unpublished: starting his own magazine. This can apparently be regarded by the poet's conscience as not exactly paying for his own work to be published, and this method, sometimes the way many good 'little' magazines have started, now seems very popular indeed. Usually it is not print the contributing writers see themselves in first, but duplicated typewriting. The cost of such a magazine, perhaps at first as thin as eight pages, is relatively cheap, and by his third issue the editor might feel confident enough (and possess enough backing from poets similarly frustrated by other magazines) to go to a small printer and have perhaps a twenty-four page edition indifferently printed for about sixty pounds or so. Whether all the five hundred copies he receives for this will ever reach readers depends on the size of the circle of his friends and acquaintances, and also on the stage at which it becomes too embarrassing for him to sell to strangers.

The country is dotted with little groups of friends who have started magazines in this way. Each group believes fervently that it alone represents the way English poetry is going, and that within twenty or at most thirty years copies of their little magazine will be eagerly sought by collectors as rarities: and each poet imagines that it will be for his one poem that each issue will be sought as the fascinating and revealing early work of a great writer who was then unknown and neglected.

They may be right, of course: a number of examples of this happening can be found in the history of English literature. And a small proportion of the magazines do go on to become something very good. But there is a paradox here: they only really become good when they start to solicit contributions from established writers from outside their own small circles. Otherwise they remain narrowly parochial, and their editors are forced to print poems for the very reasons for which they (with far less justification) viciously attack the editors of larger magazines: partiality, namedropping, or slavish following of fashion: publishing friends or allies for reasons which are nothing to do with the quality of the actual poetry.

And the greatest paradox of all this jostling and scrambling to get into print is that, of all writing, poetry is the one field where the satisfaction lies in the writing itself rather than in the publishing or in being paid: no great audience reads poetry, no poet has ever made a living out of his work. By definition, once a poet makes communication with an audience more important than expression of his own self, then his work becomes something different which, whatever else it deserves to be called, does not deserve the name of poetry. True poetry is written for the poet's sake, and for no other reason: though of course he is pleased if it later finds an audience, this must be incidental to him. Young poets who are discouraged from writing because they are not published are neither true poets nor deserve encouragement.

# [On Beckett]

*A review of* **Happy Days** *(Faber) from the* Spectator, *20 July 1962*[19]

> What does it mean? he says —What's it meant to mean? – and
> so on – lot more stuff like that – usual drivel. . . . And you, she
> says, what's the idea of you, she says, what are you meant to
> mean?

This exchange is from Samuel Beckett's latest play, in the first act of
which the main character, Winnie, is embedded up to above her waist
in a scorched, grass-covered mound on a desolate plain. Her husband,
Willie, very occasionally speaks to her from behind the mound, usually to read titbits from *Reynolds News*. It is so hot that Winnie's
parasol catches fire. There is no night, and times to sleep and wake
are indicated by a bell. There are doubts about the earth's gravity and
atmosphere being what they were. Death no longer exists, it seems,
nothing grows and a live ant is a source of great interest. The remarks
quoted above were made by the last people to stray past the mound,
some time in the indefinite past. Winnie's optimism is indomitable:
every day is a happy one for her.

In the next and last act Winnie is buried up to her neck and can
move only her eyes; every time she shuts them the bell sounds to
wake her. Her optimism is hardly less (though she has abandoned
prayer) and her husband's appearance in front of the mound and his
abortive attempt to reach her make this another happy day for her.

*Happy Days* occupies a place in Beckett's dramatic works somewhat similar to that of *The Unnamable* in his novels. One could, if
one needed to, believe in the predicament of Hamm, the blind and
paralysed old man in *Endgame*, just as one could believe in those of
the bedridden Molloy and Malone. The apparently arbitrary immobil-

---

[19] Editorial cuts have been made to these pieces where Johnson was reviewing authors
other than Beckett; and to avoid repetition.

417

isation of Winnie in the mound, however, is as difficult to accept as that of the limbless Unnamable in his jar of rags and sawdust. The difference is that in this latest play the real situation is not made explicit, whereas in *The Unnamable* Beckett makes it quite clear that he is speaking about the writer's condition. Whatever wider applications to the human situation this novel's characters and symbols may have, they are primarily used to convey a statement about the writer's constant struggle to embody truth in a vehicle of fiction and by means of the imprecise tool of language: 'Saying is inventing,' as Molloy says. [...]

The writer's condition is clearly what *Happy Days* is about, to anyone who knows *The Unnamable*; but to anyone who doesn't it is just about a woman stuck in a mound. Quite properly (within his form), Beckett does not provide links in the play for his levels of meaning. This confirms again for me that drama is not the best form for Beckett's own peculiar vision, particularly not for dealing with those processes of the mind in which he is especially interested. And really his reputation as a dramatist is out of all proportion to his achievement as a novelist, for which latter I believe him to be worthy of the most serious consideration and the highest praise.

This said, it is not too much to conclude that *Happy Days* is interesting mainly as a gloss on *The Unnamable*. It is also a refinement of some of the ideas in that novel, and unusual in Beckett's work in that it has a woman as its leading character.

*Happy Days* seems as well to be an answer to those who have mistaken Beckett for a pessimist: Winnie goes on saying what she has to say, considering optimistically how much worse things could be, just as the writer went on working in spite of all difficulties and lack of initial encouragement. Beckett's is not a literature of despair: as Camus pointed out, even to say that everything is meaningless is a meaningful statement, and a real literature of despair would be a silent literature and therefore a contradiction in terms.

*

*A review of* **Murphy** *and* **Watt** *(Jupiter Books) from the* Spectator*,*
*13 December 1962*

Some explanation (but certainly no excuse) is needed for reviewing
two novels written respectively twenty-five and twenty years ago:
*Murphy* was published here in 1938, but only a few hundred copies
were sold before the rest were destroyed during the Blitz, and *Watt*
has only been available here in a limited edition printed in France.
The importance of the republication in paperback of Samuel Beckett's first two novels is that this should now make general the
conviction of most of those who have already read all his novels that
Beckett is the finest prose stylist and most original novelist now
living, and that, interesting as his plays are, they are no more than
dramatised footnotes to the novels.

*Murphy* is the most nearly conventional of Beckett's novels, and
the best introduction to his work [...]. It is set chiefly in London,
where Murphy is part of a ring of lovers, each of whom loves someone who does not return the love: 'Love requited,' as one character
observes, 'is a short circuit.' Murphy short-circuits to Celia, a prosti-
tute whom he persuades to give up work in exchange for a promise
that he will look for work. This he does very reluctantly, for his real
desire is to live only in his mind (Murphy tries to act according to the
philosophy of Geulincx, a follower of Descartes, who believed that
the mind was quite separate from the body) and Celia all too tangibly
reminds him of the existence of the body. Eventually he finds a job in
a mental hospital where he lives alone in an attic and can transcend
his body by sitting naked for hours strapped by scarves to a chair:
only then can he come alive in his mind.

By no means a difficult or obscure novel, *Murphy* does demand
close, attentive reading and occasional reference to a good dictionary
(often this is comically rewarding, as when, for example, the second
element of *triorchous* is found to mean 'testicle'). It is one of the funniest novels ever written, and many of its sequences (the chess game
against a mental patient who plays all his pieces but for two pawns
out and back again without Murphy being able to do anything about
it, the scene where Murphy consumes 1.83 cups of tea whilst paying
for only one) are quite hilariously original.

The style of Beckett's first novel is excellent, but it is not original,

419

not that spare, tense, lapidary use of language which is at once precise and definitive yet easily accommodates the fantastic and the
grotesque. It was in *Watt* that this superb individual style was
evolved, a purification of English diction comparable only with
Eliot's similar service to poetry in the twenties: and it is all the more
remarkable in that it was achieved during the war when Beckett was
in hiding from the Germans in the Vaucluse and had no library to
which to refer.

   *Watt* is the key work for a proper understanding and appreciation
of all Beckett's later novels and plays: in some ways it is also his
greatest. It has a narrative progression rather than a plot. Watt is on a
journey to take up a post as a servant to a Mr. Knott; he arrives, dis-
places his predecessor, serves his term, and is in turn displaced; the
book ends with Watt again on a journey. Like Murphy, Watt tries to
behave according to a philosophic system: this time one based on
Wittgenstein. And, again like the first novel, *Watt* is very funny
("'Larry will be forty years old next March, D.V.,'" said the lady.
"That is the kind of thing Dee always Vees," said Mr. Hackett'), but
there is also a bitterness in the humour which looks forward to the
novel trilogy and to *Waiting for Godot*.

*

**A review of How It Is *(Calder) and* Play, Words and Music and
Cascando *(Faber) from the* Spectator, *26 June 1964***

The work of Samuel Beckett is a vast architecture of exploration,
each part standing on the achievement of its antecedents, each part
starting from the closing premise of its immediate predecessor. *The
Unnamable* took Beckett into an impasse which he has now shown
with his latest novel, *How It Is*, not to be as closed as it appeared.

   This novel is the nearest any writer has ever come to the accurate literary transcription of a man's thoughts in all their chaotic
complexity, with all their repetitions and hesitancies: conscious mind
continually diffused by the inconsequential, illogical, irrational inter-
jections of the subconscious. In order to succeed with this remarkable
technical effect, Beckett has had to limit, simplify, and refine both situation and action.

420

His narrator tells of a journey, crawling through mud, in three parts: before meeting Pim (another old man), with Pim, and after Pim. His repetitious concern with the minimum essential physical acts of moving, eating and excreting are chaotically mingled with random recollections of the past, more or less pointless speculations, and his personal relationships with Pim and some others whom he may or may not meet later.

As in *The Unnamable*, the first-person narrator merges with the author (although not until a much later point in the new novel) and breaks the fiction of storytelling:

> that wasn't how it was no not at all no how then no answer
> how was it then no answer HOW WAS IT screams good
> there was something yes but nothing of all that no all balls
> from start to finish yes this voice quaqua yes all balls yes only
> one voice here yes mine yes when the panting stops yes

*Cascando*, a radio play printed with another, *Words and Music*, in the same volume as *Play*, makes a similar point about the writer's condition (the paradoxical uselessness and necessity of writing) and, by extension, about the human one:

> . . .all I ever did. . . in my life. . . with my life. . . saying to
> myself. . . finish this one. . . it's the right one. . . then rest. . .
> sleep. . . no more stories. . . no more words. . . and finished it
> . . . and not the right one. . . couldn't rest. . . straight away
> another. . . to begin. . . to finish. . . saying to myself finish this
> one. . . then rest. . . this time. . . it's the right one. . . this time
> . . . you have it. . . and finished it. . . and not the right one. . .
> couldn't rest. . . straight away another. . .

*How It Is* is difficult, even exhausting, to read: it is written in short paragraphs, so set that none runs over on to the next page; it is without punctuation of any kind, and it is hard to see what is gained from this. The book is often boring, but this is inherent in the nature of what Beckett is doing. It has been suggested that it helps to read the book aloud, but it added nothing for me.

Beckett seems to me to be exploring a cul-de-sac, and while I cannot help admiring both his integrity and his dedication in breaking new ground therein, I deeply regret at the same time that he has abandoned on the way those incidental qualities of language and intellectual exuberance and wit which so magnificently characterise his first two novels, *Murphy* and *Watt*. But let us be very sure of one thing: Samuel Beckett is out there in front, this is certainly the way the novel is going. No writer need cover this particular ground again, but it is his example (towards truth and away from storytelling) which makes it clear that almost all novelists today are anachronistically working in a clapped-out and moribund tradition.

*

*A review of* No's Knife *(Calder and Boyars),* Eh Joe and Other Writings *(Faber) and* Beckett at 60: A Festschrift *(Calder and Boyars) from the* New Statesman, *14 July 1967*

In 1954 Harold Pinter wrote in a letter to a friend:

> 'The farther he goes the more good it does me. I don't want philosophies, tracts, dogmas, creeds, way outs, truths, answers, *nothing from the bargain basement*. He is the most courageous, remorseless writer going and the more he grinds my nose in the shit the more I am grateful to him. He's not fucking me about, he's not leading me up any garden path, he's not slipping me any wink, he's not flogging me a remedy or a path or a revelation or a basinful of breadcrumbs, he's not selling me anything I don't want to buy, he doesn't give a bollock whether I buy or not, *he hasn't got his hand over his heart*. Well, I'll buy his goods, hook, line and sinker, because he leaves no stone unturned and no maggot lonely. He brings forth a body of beauty. His work is beautiful.'

The writer who inspired such violent, total respect is Samuel Beckett, and Pinter, thirteen years later, has apparently not bettered this description of his feelings since he contributes the quote to *Beckett at 60*, which is in some ways a rather embarrassing volume in celebration of the Irish writer's birthday.

422

Pinter was writing about Beckett's novels in this letter, for at the time *Waiting for Godot* had yet to be staged in England, and this is very relevant to what can now be seen as the dual nature of Beckett's reputation: which reputation has, incidentally, grown from virtually nothing to its present eminence in the surprisingly short time of about fifteen years. The wider reputation, the public reputation it might be called, is based on the plays, particularly on *Godot* and *Endgame*, which have of course become classics of modern theatre: though it is salutary to be reminded by Harold Hobson in *Beckett at 60* just how bad the notices of *Godot* were, his and Tynan's excepted: and the first production of *Endgame* was very badly attended. Those who know Beckett by his plays tend to be only vaguely aware that he has written novels, and would perhaps be surprised to hear that those who do know them regard the plays as footnotes to the novels: interesting and worth while, certainly, but of far less importance nevertheless. John Calder's introduction to *Beckett at 60* mentions 'members of a strange club, each with his favourite phrases of caustic humour or satisfying disgust'. The copies of Beckett's novels belonging to members of this club are defiled or embellished (depending how you look at it) with notes, underscored favourite passages, exclamation marks, and perhaps the meanings of the recondite dictionary words he delighted to use freely in his earlier work, more parsimoniously in the later. [...] Most of us first knew Beckett's work through *Godot*, but probably came across *Molloy* as though it were a dirty book in that beautifully-proportioned olive, turquoise and black Olympia Press edition. We it is who, reading him, feel the urge not for interpretation but for celebration, not exegesis but exultation that anyone can write so well.

*No's Knife* (the title comes from the last of the thirteen *Texts for Nothing*, 'the screaming silence of no's knife in yes's wound') contains all the shorter prose that Beckett is willing to see republished, from the three *nouvelles* of 1945–6 to two short pieces (*Imagination Dead Imagine* and *Ping*) written within the last couple of years, both of which represent the distilled residue of a full-length novel.

The three *nouvelles*, Beckett's first work to be written in French, provide an important link between his second novel *Watt* and his third *Molloy*, and have previously been (scarcely) available in England only in back numbers of *Evergreen Review*. The one called *The*

*Expelled* is about a man who, after being thrown out of his home, spends the day in a horse-drawn cab driving about and looking for lodgings:

> After a few drinks the cabman invited me to do his wife and him the honour of spending the night in their home. It was not far. Recollecting these emotions, with the celebrated advantage of tranquillity, it seems to me he did nothing else, all that day, but turn about his lodging. They lived above a stable, at the back of a yard. Ideal location, I could have done with it. Having presented me to his wife, extraordinarily full-bottomed, he left us. She was manifestly ill at ease, alone with me. I could understand her, I don't stand on ceremony on these occasions. No reason for this to end or go on. Then let it end. I said I would go down to the stable and sleep there. The cabman protested. I insisted. He drew his wife's attention to the pustule on top of my skull, for I had removed my hat out of civility. He should have that removed, she said. The cabman named a doctor he held in high esteem who had rid him of an induration of the seat. If he wants to sleep in the stable, said his wife, let him sleep in the stable.

It is impossible to appreciate Beckett's later work without reference to the earlier, without following his development: like Joyce, he should be read in chronological order. Anyone who thinks they can tackle something like *Ping* as their first example of Beckett is very liable to end up sharing the opinions of modern literature held by Cheltenham colonels. The publication of *No's Knife* makes it possible for the first time in England to follow Beckett completely chronologically, though it should be pointed out that there are two works earlier than *Murphy,* a novel called *Fair to Middling Women* and *More Pricks Than Kicks* (a volume of short stories) which must remain only bloody good titles to most readers since Beckett did not publish the first and will not allow the second to be reprinted.[20] Calder & Boyars published a severely limited edition of *More Pricks Than*

[20] The novel's title was actually *Dream of Fair to Middling Women*. Since Johnson wrote this, both books have been republished and have remained consistently in print.

424

*Kicks* last year to save scholars the labour of doing their own version from the British Museum copy, and anyone who has read it will probably agree with Beckett that, apart from perhaps two or three stories, it does not show up well against the later work.

In *Krapp's Last Tape* Beckett used the tape recorder for the first time in drama and exploited its functional qualities and possibilities as an object to such an extent that no one can write a play about a man and a tape recorder without covering at least some of the same ground. This exhaustive exploration of what is possible in each medium is characteristic: Beckett is interested in doing those things which can be done only in that particular medium. Works written for one medium do not translate into another, which is why he has not allowed either his plays or his novels to be filmed: they are simply not films, not conceived as such. But Beckett has recently written a film called *Film*, the script of which has just been published with the television play *Eh Joe* and a short mime entitled *Act Without Words II*. In *Film* Beckett uses the camera as a character in a beautifully stylized essay on the text *esse est percipi*. I have not seen the film (which has Buster Keaton in the main part, and was apparently shown here only at the London Film Festival a couple of years ago) but it reads marvellously. It is of course a paradox that Beckett should allow a film to be published when he does not allow his books to be filmed, but this script has unusual interest because of a series of notes in which Beckett explains some of his intentions, some of the why. Members recording those strange and as if meaningless elements which recur in the canon (the bicycle, names beginning with M, hats tethered by strings) will note with irrelevant and disproportionate pleasure that Murphy's rocking chair is back and that a description of a photograph of a child at its mother's knee exactly fits the earliest known photograph of the author printed in *Beckett at 60*.

The television piece *Eh Joe* employs the camera in a way related to the technique of *Film*, but in this case the movement of tracking in on the face of an oldish man is controlled by a woman's voice off-screen reminding him of the past: when the voice stops, the camera moves: when the voice resumes, the movement stops. The effect, as those who saw Jack MacGowran in the play may confirm, is an original experience even if the way in which it is specifically televisual is not particularly overt.

Recognition came late to Samuel Beckett (as indeed does the birthday volume: he's been 61 for some months now) and of no one is it more true that he has had to create the taste by which he is enjoyed. Those of us who believe that he is the greatest prose stylist and the most original writer living perhaps cannot reasonably, but do hopefully, look forward to many more years for him as magnificently productive as the last fifteen: to have written as he has, and to be only 61, is remarkable to the point of near impossibility.

# Introduction to *The Evacuees*[21]

It had never been necessary before, and there will not be time for it in a nuclear war: evacuation.

This singular misfortune of the Second World War was experienced by a large proportion of those born between 1924 and 1938. To children of this generation, the more general clonic sense of the word came at some later point in our lives as a surprise; evacuation had other associations for us, though the new one (as one contributor to this book sees and uses to make a point) was not wholly without relevance.

Our allegiances to place may sometimes be curiously divided as between city and village, town and country, even between country and country; our education may have set us differently by its variety or incompleteness in some way or another; we may have somewhat more sympathy for immigrants and other minority groups; for us certain foods, to others ordinary, may still seem luxuries (butter, bananas) because we cannot remember having had them before the war and our appetites for them could not be satisfied, let alone satiated, during the war; in us the tendency to expect the worst from any situation, to cut our losses and accept disappointment (indeed, to feel something near disappointment in any case when the worst does not happen) is perhaps more evident than in earlier or later generations.

It did of course affect everyone involved in a different way, and in an unassessable number of different ways: but all four million who were evacuated in Britain at some time or another during the Second World War must have been marked by the experience.

Anyone who wishes to read a full historical account of evacuation is referred to [...] Richard M. Titmuss's exemplary treatment of the

---

[21] *The Evacuees* was an anthology published by Gollancz in 1968, for which Johnson collected reminiscences, letters, and extracts of writing about the experience of wartime evacuation from a wide range of contributors, including Michael Aspel, Barry Cole, Ruth Fainlight, Jonathan Miller, and Alan Sillitoe.

subject in his volume *Problems of Social Policy* in the official *History of the Second World War*. It does, however, seem appropriate to give a brief general outline, following Titmuss, here.

The evacuation of civilians from cities was seen first only as a counter-move to enemy bombing, to parry the attempt to demoralize the civilian population. This purely military consideration was reinforced by the conviction that there would in any case be a panic flight from bombed cities and that this would greatly multiply any chaos caused directly by the enemy.

In early 1931 the subject was considered important enough for the setting-up of an Evacuation Sub-committee of the Committee of Imperial Defence. Its initial suggestion in relation to the two aspects of the problem was to enlarge the police force and, when bombing took place, to throw a cordon round London and the larger cities to prevent anyone leaving. But when its first report was completed in 1934, the Sub-committee proposed a different scheme. 3½ million people living in central London (fathers, mothers and children) were to be evacuated to billets within fifty miles of the city. Elaborate railway timetables were worked out to move this enormous number of people in the shortest possible time, but less attention was given to their reception: no local authorities were consulted. At no point in the report is the idea of evacuation queried: dispersal is taken as indisputably necessary.

The great increase in the size of the Luftwaffe during 1936–37 led to reconsideration and augmentation of the evacuation plans. By early 1938 they were to a certain extent out of date and in any case had never been fully completed in detail. A government committee, with Sir John Anderson as chairman, reviewed the position and with commendable promptness produced its report by 26 July 1938. The principles laid down, which were to become the basis of the plans actually put into operation in September 1939, were as follows:

1) Except in so far as it may be necessary for military or other special reasons to require persons to leave some limited area, evacuation should not be compulsory.

2) For the purpose of supporting the national war effort and supplying essential civilian needs, production in the large industrial towns must be maintained, but it is

        desirable to provide organized facilities for the evacuation of substantial numbers of people from certain industrial areas.

3)     Arrangements for the reception of persons who become refugees should be mainly on the basis of accommodation in private houses under powers of compulsory billeting. These arrangements will require very detailed preparation in order to avoid unnecessary hardship either to the refugees or to the persons who receive them.

4)     The initial cost of evacuation arrangements should be borne by the government, but that refugees who can afford to contribute towards the cost of their maintenance should be expected to do so.

5)     To meet the needs of parents who wish to send their children away, but cannot make their own arrangements, special arrangements should be made for schoolchildren to move out in groups from their schools in charge of their teachers.

It seems that if in fact war had been declared at the time of Munich (28 September 1938) the arrangements for evacuation would have been far from satisfactory. The London County Council did evacuate some 4,300 nursery and physically defective schoolchildren as a precaution, but the signal for general evacuation was never given. As a result of the scare, responsibility for evacuation was transferred from the Home Office to a new unit drawn from the Ministry of Health and the Board of Education.

One of the first tasks was to decide into which of three zones each part of the country fell: evacuation, reception, and neutral. It is interesting that not one single area asked to be scheduled for reception, and no local authority declared an evacuation area disputed the decision. Thirteen million people were in evacuation areas, eighteen million in reception, and fourteen million in neutral areas.

The size of such totals made an initial thinning-out essential, and the following were declared priority classes:

1)     Schoolchildren evacuated as school units with their teachers.

2)   Younger children accompanied by mothers or guardians.
3)   Expectant mothers.
4)   Blind adults and cripples who could be moved.

The preparation and execution of evacuation plans was greatly complicated by the fact that evacuation was to be basically voluntary, since this made the numbers involved a variable and unknown factor. In the words of Richard M. Titmuss:

> Assumptions had to be made about the probable mental reactions of over 10,000,000 individuals living in, and conditioned by, widely differing environments who, historically, had shown a marked affection for individuality.

Various forms of government propaganda exhorted parents to send their children to safety, and there were other pressures operating: it was, for instance, enough for many workingclass mothers that there would be no school for their children to attend during the working day if they stayed behind.

Billeting was the only practical answer to finding accommodation for the four million people falling into the priority classes: such alternatives as camps or specially-built quarters were impossible to arrange in the time available or with the scale of priorities dictated by rearmament. The billeting yardstick used was one person per habitable room, and a survey was carried out which, given deduction for rooms unusable for various reasons, provided potential accommodation for 4.8 million people in the reception areas. But by February 1939 one-sixth of this accommodation had been 'privately reserved' by the householders for their relatives and friends.

The Civil Defence Bill of July 1939 provided that any additional expense caused by evacuation would be repaid to local authorities by the Exchequer. It also gave compulsory billeting powers and defined the extent to which evacuees should be fed and looked after. Allowances to be made to householders were:

For unaccompanied children (full board and lodging):
   10/6d per week for the first child
   8/6d per week for each additional child taken
For mothers with children (lodging only):

5/- per week for adults

3/- per week for children

For teachers and helpers (lodging only):

5/- per week

A revised scale, somewhat higher and based on children's ages, was introduced in May 1940.

As the threat of war grew, so the emphasis of evacuation (once of the whole non-essential civilian population) fell more and more on seeing that the children, and mothers with young children, would be sent to safety.

From about January 1939 a tremendous sense of urgency made itself felt in the Ministry of Health and those responsible in the evacuation areas, particularly in London, and the detailed plans for dispatching the evacuees by train were brought to as near perfection as possible in the time. This sense of urgency did not, however, extend in all cases to the reception and billeting arrangements being prepared by the local authorities of the destinations at which the evacuees were due to arrive.

It is important to realize that the prior assumption was that the war would start with immediate air attack by the Germans, certainly on London and possibly on other large cities as well. This did not in fact occur, but it is the reason why the actual declaration of war was anticipated by more than two days in giving the order for the by now carefully-worked-out plans for evacuation to be put into effect.

The first evacuees moved out of the cities on the morning of Friday 1 September 1939: by the evening of the 3rd, a few hours after war had been officially declared, 1,473,391 people had been placed in the reception areas. Most of these were children, with some mothers, teachers, and WVS[22] and other escorts. This was the official government evacuation scheme: in the three months previous to and in the first weeks of the war itself at least two million other people had privately evacuated themselves to friends, relatives, or other accommodation.

Not all the children went. Slightly more than half of London's school population stayed, while in Manchester, Salford, Newcastle,

---

[22] Women's Voluntary Services for Air Raid Precautions.

Gateshead, Liverpool and Bootle more than 60% went. Other places were very much less enthusiastic: in Sheffield, only 15% availed themselves of the opportunity to go to safety. In all, the average figure for England was 47%, and for Scotland 38%. These differing responses to the government scheme probably reflect the local conditions and the confidence in the efficiency of their evacuation arrangements conveyed to parents by the various local authorities. In fact, the smaller response (the government had expected to move about three-and-a-half million people) meant that the arrangements in the under-prepared reception areas were not in many cases overloaded; and in all but a few areas the accommodation available was adequate.

The smaller number of evacuees than expected certainly helped the transport arrangements, too, but in any case they were well planned and efficiently executed: there was not a single accident or casualty during the whole three-day operation. Rehearsals of the evacuation movement had been carried out (schoolteachers had been recalled early from their summer holidays on 24 August) and there was an unexpectedly large number of voluntary helpers: the WVS report of 1963 says that many members who took part still regard evacuation as their most arduous task.

As a result of the smaller numbers presenting themselves for evacuation, schedules were brought forward right from the first day. Then, due to an understandable desire to avoid congestion at the main line stations, groups from many different points of origin were embarked on one train: and some groups were split between two or more trains. As a result, many reception areas were sent both numbers and kinds of evacuees they had not made arrangements to accept. Added to the incomplete preparation already mentioned, a state of affairs approaching chaos was inevitable in some areas.

Allocation to billets at random by reception officers, or free choice (either in a hall or in the streets) allowed to foster-parents, were the two most usual ways of settling accommodation for evacuees. Though few of the contributors to this book can remember much about their journeys (which would seem to be evidence of their state of bewilderment, or even of shock), many of them have very eloquent memories of these auction sales of children.

Again to quote Titmuss:

To be torn up from the roots of home life and to be sent away from the family circle, in most instances for the first time in the child's life, was a painful event. This was no social experiment; it was a surgical rent only to be contemplated as a last resort. The whole of the child's life, its hopes and fears, its dependence for affection and social development on the checks and balances of home life, and all the deep emotional ties that bound it to its parents, were suddenly disrupted. From the first day of September, 1939, evacuation ceased to be a problem of administrative planning. It became instead a multitude of problems in human relationships.

A great deal of sociological research was subsequently carried out into these problems, but this is no place to give a summary of the results (indeed, since the problems were on such a vast and varied scale, the results are in many cases contradictory) [...] It was these problems, however, together with the fact that for about a year there were virtually no air attacks to confirm that evacuation had been necessary, which led to the widespread return of evacuees. By January 1940, only four months later, over half of those evacuated had returned to their homes. Those remaining represented 14% of the figure the government had originally expected to have to evacuate. This figure can be misleading, however, since one-third of the children of both London and Liverpool remained in the country.

Much had been learnt from this first evacuation movement, and the result was a virtually complete reversal of policy for the future. Instead of removing evacuees before possible air attacks, it was now decided to evacuate only when bombing had commenced. Furthermore, only limited and gradual movements, rather than mass ones, would be attempted, and mothers with young children under five were now excluded as being impracticable to accommodate. This left only the schoolchildren.

There were of course numerous improvements in detail to these later plans, and in spring 1940 the government made a large-scale attempt, with much publicity, to induce parents to register their children for the new scheme to be put into effect when bombing actually started. But it was a failure: in London less than 10% of school-

SHORT PROSE

children were registered, and in the reception areas only 2% of house-
holds were voluntarily prepared to state they would accept evacuees.
The previous experience, on both sides, had been enough for most
people to want to have nothing more to do with evacuation, and it
took the impetus of actual bombing, which began in September 1940,
to involve them in it again.

The second wave of official evacuees was somewhat smaller than
the first: about 1,250,000 were involved this time. A number of these
were, of course, being evacuated for the second time. Daily or weekly
parties from various bombed districts of London were sent to specific
areas of safety. The arrangements this time were at once more careful
and more complicated. The bombing was far more widespread than
had for some reason been expected, and reception areas were fewer
and in some cases different from those chosen in the previous year.
Furthermore, evacuees were now competing for houseroom with
workers from the new wartime industries which had been started
mainly in the safer and less traditionally industrial zones.

This evacuation was a distinctly different experience for those
children involved in it. This time they were selected over a period of
time and in small groups, and usually they went without their schoolfriends. On the first evacuation, all the children had participated in
what, at least at the beginning, was like an outing with their friends.
Many children on the second evacuation must have been most likely
to feel their parents' action as rejection, or even as betrayal. Their
experience may be compared (perhaps even favourably) with that of
those unprivileged seven-year-olds still sent away to boarding
schools where they usually know no one at all. Several of the evacuees writing in this book declare they would never send a child of
theirs away in this manner.

A similar statistical pattern of return to the cities was followed: in
February 1941 there were 1,340,000 people evacuated under the government scheme, but a year later, when the Blitz was over, the figure
was down to 738,000.

During the next two years, though there was little call for it
and considerable pressure to end it from the reception areas, the government kept the evacuation scheme intact and when the first

434

flying-bomb fell on London during the night of 12 June 1944 it was still functioning. Mothers and children were evacuated within a matter of weeks from that segment of the south-east whose apex was London: 'buzzbomb alley'.

The third wave of evacuation lasted only about two months, and was again different in character in that some reception areas previously considered to be safe were now threatened, and the evacuation authorities in them found their duties reversed. The flying-bomb attacks petered out, but were replaced by V2 rocket attacks which went on throughout the autumn and winter of 1944. Yet again there was the phenomenon of a constant stream of evacuees returning within weeks of their arrival, and the numbers were largest during the first three months of the rocket attacks.

But for areas outside London and the south-east the end of evacuation had come: from September 1944 progressive arrangements delivered the evacuated children back to their homes in much the same manner as they had been taken from them. By March 1945 there were only about 400,000 left evacuated: and they were chiefly Londoners. With the cessation of rocket attacks, and the end of the war obviously in sight, most of these came home without bothering to wait for the government to bring them. When the end of the war did come, only 54,000 availed themselves of the official return scheme.

Three months after the end of the war there were still 76,000 evacuees. They were there mainly because there were no homes for them to return to, or their homes were either too full or equipped with insufficient bedding and so on. A very few, no doubt, were still there because their parents had disappeared or had decided to abandon them for one reason or another. Within six months the figure had been halved, and then the remainder were reclassified with the other homeless and became the responsibility of the local authorities.

For many of the children the return was evacuation all over again. They came back to a mother whom they probably remembered, but she was sleeping with a stranger who insisted he was their father. In some cases they came from a comfortable middle-class home to a crowded flat in slum or near-slum conditions; from friends, again, to an alien society where they had to make friends all over again; from a situation in which they had perhaps been neglected, had learnt independence, to one in which they were petted, fondled, embraced with a devotion perhaps guiltily over-compensating for the deprivations of the earlier years.

> *. . . they got us involved in something we knew nothing about, a game we weren't ready for. We played but we were too young to fight and we didn't know what they were fighting for — we thought they just wanted to win. The fighting stopped and the game went on and they didn't tell us the new set of rules. I'm glad they won but I'd like to know where we were wrong. . . . I'd like to know why they brought me back when I wanted to go on fighting — brought me back safely, I suppose. That's the whole point of being an evacuee. You're hidden away and saved, that's what to evacuate means — 'to withdraw'. I wonder what they saved me for. . . .*[23]

It may be objected that the evacuation of British children was a mild experience compared with that of those in Europe who suffered, say, machine-gunning and dive-bombing by Stukas on the roads of France, or the concentration camps, or even with that of those children who stayed behind to face the bombing of London and other cities. Nothing, certainly, can have been worse than the concentration camps; but it is possible to compare a sudden and relatively short outburst of violence, experienced corporately within the security of the family group, with what happened slowly and over more than five years in many cases, and conclude that the psychological effects of evacuation would in fact be more severe. Even for those who were evacuated with their mothers it was not the same: the mothers, taken from their environments, friends, work, and husbands, were as lost as their children, were different persons.

> *Nothing can overtake these firsts, and the miracle that you know it's a revelation at the moment, knowing nails you to the spot almost crushing the wind.*[24]

[23] *The Evacuees*, p. 114. Writer: John Furse.

[24] *The Evacuees*, p. 248. Writer: Alison Smithson.

436

The effects of maternal deprivation were the subject of certain discoveries in psychological research before the war, but in 1939 they were not widely known and certainly not accepted if they were known by those politicians and educationalists responsible for the evacuation policy. Ironically enough, it was the evacuees who provided most of the raw material for the great amount of further investigation during and after the war by sociologists and psychologists into the importance of security in the early years for the subsequent development of a child's personality. Enough is now known for unaccompanied evacuation to be condemned outright as a way of safeguarding civilian populations. Not that, as I said at the beginning, it will be necessary: you cannot evacuate anyone very far in four minutes — or is it eight we have now?

> *. . . a kind of chameleonism that. . . made it possible to sense what would please, what would make us acceptable, what would dilute our outsiderness, what would not alienate or offend, what would not violate the way of living into which we had been transplanted, or, by being different, imply criticism. In other social contexts such attributes are often akin to insincerity and hypocrisy. Here they were a necessary adjunct to emotional survival.*[25]

> *I thank God I was evacuated: not because I avoided danger. . . but because it changed my way of thinking, it made me love the country: I could never live in town again. . . I found a refuge, quiet and peaceful, after an unhappy home life: I found another family whom I really loved, and still do.*[26]

> *We missed everything. We felt none of the unity that comes from participation and hardship; sentimental songs and snatched weekends were no part of our life. If we were spared the worst grief and anxiety we had none of the wartime thrills, either, and when it was over and we became adults the country was restricted, spent and poor.*[27]

[25] *The Evacuees*, p. 41. Writer: Gloria Cigman.

[26] *The Evacuees*, p. 208. Writer: Mary Owen.

[27] *The Evacuees*, p. 197. Writer: Claire Meltzer.

The accounts which follow are by way of being an interim report concerning the effects of evacuation on what is virtually a random sample of those children experiencing it. All but four of the contributors are between thirty and forty-five now (the others were teachers, and a parent). Some can be measured up against the public achievements of their first years of adulthood; others are unknown to the general public, but the way evacuation affected them is overtly or implicitly evident from what they write. Short biographies are provided as some little indication of what all have since become.

Above all, these are personal accounts: as such, they are more valuable and meaningful, in my opinion, than the impersonality and generalization of sociology: solipsistically, in the face of something as huge and important as this, all you can rely on is the personal, all you are ultimately left with is the subjective. It is a truism that anyone can write well about their childhood: when that childhood included evacuation, the quality of writing from people who do not primarily consider themselves writers can be very high indeed, as several of the pieces in this book confirm.

Most of the contributors were children during the war, but the three teachers included have their own important experiences of evacuation to relate; and one mother, who surely speaks for all the parents in her conviction that she was doing the right thing at the time, that she acted for what she imagined to be the best.

Evacuation undoubtedly did result in the saving of life. The figure of 60,595 civilians who died in the bombing of British cities would certainly have been increased without it. Whether the number of lives saved was worth the psychological damage to several million school-children is one of those unanswerable questions of balance which war throws up. The full cost of this evacuated generation's suffering has yet to be counted: we have not yet come fully to power, and the next thirty years will be ours. Those who ordered our saving and suffering are already dead or dying.

438

# The Professional Viewpoint

*Published (abridged) in* 20th Century Studies, *November 1969*[28]

*'Incidentally, I doubt if the act of love, with its permutations, has ever been described with such detailed freedom in a modern novel.'*

It is the date of this pre-publication trade reference to my first novel *Travelling People* which brings to my attention how much and how remarkably quickly the situation has changed: it was as recent as 1963.

I have already written[29] of how an attempt was made by the printer to censor this novel, and re-reading the passages in question for the purposes of this article I am still unable to understand how anyone (unless psychologically unstable) could have found them objectionable. Technically, the problem with writing about the sex/love correlate in *Travelling People* was the old and basic one of vocabulary: whether to use clinical, Latinised English or Anglo-Saxon derivatives compromised by use as expletives. I cannot at this point remember how much trouble the passages cost me, but I do recall being very pleased with them when I had finished: that is to say, they said all I wished to say in the way I wanted to say it. I avoided the naming of private parts, and I excluded euphemism and the sentimental velleities of flatulent imagery: the only images used are (if I may be permitted) organic to the situations. The result seems to me, some eight years after writing *Travelling People*, rather too careful and studied: I avoided the obvious traps only at some loss of precision and explicitness.

*Albert Angelo* had little about sex in it: but the point of breakdown between fiction and truth which I came to and dramatised in my second novel very much influenced the treatment of sex in the third,

---

[28] Johnson's full text is restored here.

[29] In the article 'Censorship by Printers' (see above, pp. 382–5).

439

*Trawl*. Since I was trying to write absolute (that is, solipsistically absolute) truth within the novel form, explicitness and completeness were necessary as much for sex as for any other part of the material. The chief problem here was the embarrassment first of facing the truth and then of writing it down, exposing it for other to see. This was particularly acute in the sexual passages, and re-reading them today I still feel the same embarrassment (amounting to pain) nearly as much as when I wrote them.

The problem of vocabulary was not as difficult in *Trawl*, since the whole novel was an interior monologue and it was appropriate for the nearest word to hand, so to speak, to come tumbling out. Where necessary, two or more alternative words for the same thing could be used successively as the mind strove for accuracy. Attitudes towards sex in a particular situation were also distinguishable by use of either the cant or the clinical word, cunt or pudenda, John Thomas or penis.

It has always seemed important to me to mention contraception, or lack of it, in descriptions of heterosexual lovemaking: and in *Trawl* I took this concern so far as to mention branded products.

*The Unfortunates* (completed 1967, published 1969) was similarly an interior monologue, but there was (like *Albert Angelo*) comparatively little about sex in it. What there is seems to me as successfully written as I could wish it to be given its own terms of reference. And it is a source of some relief to me that I can now write about similar material far less self-consciously than in *Travelling People*, though I of course recognise that I am nearer to *The Unfortunates* than to my first novel. But there is still for me the problem of self-consciousness in writing about onanism: and this I am facing at the moment in writing a short story provisionally entitled 'Instructions for the Use of Women'.

At the age of the nineteen I was lent (by what I now know to have been a poodle-loving lesbian of indeterminate years and motive) the four limp volumes of Frank Harris's *My Lives and Loves* in the Obelisk Press edition. It is to that library borrowing that I trace my interest in trying to write down everything, my whole truth: and I particularly remember his observation that one-third of anyone's life is passed in the bedroom but is ignored by unbalanced novelists. That Harris was himself a great liar in print I discovered only much later, when I was both too far committed and had moved on anyway.

The present freedom of expression, which from my point of view is absolute (that word again) in that I feel there is nothing to stop me publishing about anything I choose, is really the only part of my youthful concept of what the future would be that has actually been realised. More objectively, I see such freedom as being for nothing but good for the novel form: since at the very least no other medium has such freedom at the present time.

# Soho Square[30] [On British Cinema]

*Published in* Film and Television Technician, *August 1971*

One day very soon (next Wednesday?) it will become possible for the definitive history of British cinema to be written. It will become possible because British cinema will have ceased to exist in any meaningful sense.

And the first question to be asked will be whether it ever did exist in any meaningful sense, the sense of leaving a lasting impression, of having produced films which have stood the test of time.

Look at what it must be compared with in the other arts during the same period (say roughly from the end of the first world war and thus mercifully exclude the infantilia). During that time Britain has produced Henry Moore and Barbara Hepworth in sculpture; Robert Graves, W. H. Auden and Ted Hughes in poetry; Benjamin Britten and Peter Maxwell Davies in music; Samuel Beckett and Graham Greene in the novel; British acting has produced Gielgud and Olivier; British painting has produced Francis Bacon, Ben Nicholson and David Hockney; and British theatre has produced Samuel Beckett (again) and Harold Pinter.

And what has British cinema produced in the same period? *Oh! Mr Porter* and *Carry on Puking*. There is not one British film which could scrape into the world's top one hundred, judged from an artistic point of view, unless the judges were grossly chauvinistic. You know which film the French generally believe to be the only British one worth considering? *Brief Encounter*! That comically distorted view of what it was like to be here and at war: indeed, the French must like it exactly because it represents a cardboard cutout of what they think Britain and the British are like.

No, there is not one British film which can compare with our high

---

[30] This was the generic title of a column to which Johnson made regular, anonymous contributions.

achievements in all the other arts. And the very selective list I have jotted down is only a sample of the top of the cream. These are all world figures, they command respect everywhere for their contributions to international art. It seems probable that British art in general has never been at a higher peak: we have never before had a sculptor of the stature of Henry Moore, for instance, nor a painter like Bacon.

But why has cinema been so poor in this country? Obviously it is not because the acting and writing talent has not been available. Nor is it because British technicians have been inferior to those of other countries, for they have not. But their contribution to a film is one of craft, not art: most British films are full of beautifully lit and shot rubbish. The fault lies with the moneymen, the producers (in the widest sense) who have treated writers, actors and technicians with a disregard amounting to contempt. As a result, none of them have taken the medium seriously enough: writers have accepted large fees for scripts (which were sometimes not even properly read, and often not used for the most arbitrary reasons) and with the money subsidised other more important and more properly appreciated work in the novel and so on; actors took even larger sums for the trivial performances demanded by ignorant producers, while reserving their real work for the theatre; and technicians equally responded to a moneysick situation by laughing or crying, according to their insight, all the way to the piggy bank with as much as they could squeeze out of the conmen.

It was a failure of artistic nerve on a really disastrous scale. After all, artists know more about art than anyone else: and not to give them freedom to exercise their skill and instinct but to make it subject to the barbarism of the counting-house (the anachronistic term is used deliberately) is crass philistinism. Indeed, it might be possible to formulate a Law of Increasing Philistinism: the more money involved in art, the more it is adulterated, and the less real art is produced. At least such a law would explain why as a nation we're so good at poetry.

And now on television we see the last throw, the final deal of the goldlichened moneylovers: there the British film industry is really shown up (not in quite all its dishonour, for someone in television has had the bright idea of chopping them slotwise and thus making them better, since it is impossible to make them worse), shown up for the stinking crap it is. Displayed are fatuous stories about sexless lovers, quaint old trains, action pictures which move the stomach to retch and not the heart to feel, the classriddled setpieces of a dead culture, desperately unfunny double-entendre comedies, all forming a Victoria Falls of cesspool effluent. Only the purer water of the British documentary tradition prevents complete pollution of the environment.

Whoever does sit down next Wednesday to write this definitive history of British cinema should name these men, the barren producers, describe their criminal irresponsibility (where they have not cunningly covered their webfooted tracks), attempt to discover why it happened, to prevent anything similar happening again. For these men have denied us the opportunity of being able to say 'This is our cinematic equivalent of a Moore, a Bacon, a Beckett.'

They have thus diminished and impoverished us all, the bastards.

# The Gregynog Press and the Gregynog Fellowship

*Published in* The Private Library, *Spring 1973*

I had not heard of the Gregynog Press before the poet Zulfikar Ghose rang me up one morning to say that he had been sent some forms from the Welsh Arts Council about a Fellowship to be established at Gregynog; it must have been July or August 1969. Zulf was off to America shortly, to teach at the University of Texas; I had just moved into a senescent London house of which perhaps the best thing that could be said was that it was my wife's and mine. Next morning, forwarded from my old address and also forwarded by Zulf, came two sets of application forms for the Gregynog Fellowship in the University of Wales. I had had a certain amount of contact with Wales; my first novel *Travelling People* is set there and partly based on the experiences of three summers working at a country club in Caernarvonshire, and this was what had prompted Zulf to contact me about the Fellowship.

I read the details and I think sent the spare set on in my turn to another writer. Almost totally absorbed in trying to staunch the trauma caused by moving into a ruin, I mentioned the Fellowship to my wife, saying: You don't want me to apply for this, do you? You don't fancy another move after this one? They were rhetorical questions expecting, even demanding, the answer No. But Yes, she said, I would enjoy six months in Wales.

So I put the application forms in a pile of correspondence and forgot them. What other business took me through the pile I cannot remember though I can guess it was an unpaid bill; but I did apply, only just in time and so hastily that I did not think it worth giving references: thinking, if they know my work I shall not need references, and if they do not know my work then I have no chance anyway.

But they did indeed know my work, and some time in September I received an invitation from Dr. Glyn Tegai Hughes, Warden of Gregynog, to go for interview in October together with five other

445

candidates on the short list. The interviews were a very civilised affair; we candidates were invited to dinner with the eight or so members of the selection committee on the Friday night, and the interviews took place the next morning. I arrived before daylight ended on the Friday, having been driven from the station at Newton by Ted Walters (who had been chauffeur to the former owners of the Press and house, the Misses Davies) in the Gregynog Volkswagen minibus. As we approached along about a mile and a half of drive, Gregynog itself appeared through the trees, an enormous black-and-white house, finely impressive: so much so that it actually brought the traditional tiny gasp in exclamation from me. As we drew closer it was clear that the house could not really be of timbered construction: it was four storeys high. Shortly afterwards I could see that the black-and-white effect was stucco. But it must have been very early imitation Tudor: the present house dates from the 1830s. And of course Montgomeryshire and the neighbouring counties have many genuine black-and-white buildings. So it was possible very early on for me to forgive the house its deceit, and I shortly became very fond of it; and later, as a sort of compliment it would never be able to appreciate, I included a description of it in the novel I wrote in its Small Library. Gregynog has two possible etymologies: either it may come from *grugin*, the old form of the Welsh word for *heather*, or from the personal name *Grugyn*; but in both cases with the place-name *–og* added.

So convivial and civilised was it that October evening that I was not sure who the candidates were and who the committee. Certainly Peter Porter I knew and liked, and had been introduced to the sculptors Michael Pennie and Jonah Jones. The girl must be the painter Gillian Ayres. By coincidence I also knew the Professor of English at Aberystwyth, Arthur Johnston, who had been at Birkbeck College when I was an undergraduate there for a year. But not long after dinner, when the committee went away to take the opinion of one member who could not stay overnight, Peter Porter and I were joined at the unaccustomed port by the highly-respected and senior novelist Richard Hughes. After perhaps the second glass I asked him, following some writerly chitchat, if he should not be in the Main Library with the committee. No, he replied, he was one of the candidates.

446

This came as a surprise to Peter Porter and to me, and I could not help myself (for the second time that day) exclaiming that this seemed to be unfair competition. But we all took it very well.

As part of the preliminaries that evening Dr. Hughes took the candidates all round the houses and outbuildings. In the stables we saw where the Gregynog Press had been, and, indeed, what was left of it. The machine room still had the original Albion on which the first of the Gregynog Press books had been printed; a great hand-operated guillotine; a proofing press; and rows of wires with pegs on them across the ceiling over long benches. Next to this was the composing room, upper and lower cases displayed, old type, dirty, all largely neglected, disused. Upstairs had been the bindery, and part still contained some of the original equipment since one of the few surviving from those days, Mrs. Gwen Edwards, continued to work there binding books for the library maintained by the University at Gregynog. But most of the machinery had been removed to the National Library at Aberystwyth, together with the tools, dies and stamps used for the bindings. A few whole hides remained, and a symbolic tool or two, to show visitors.

And the smell of the place was entrancing.

The idea of showing the candidates all this was really that one of the upper rooms with a ceiling light could have been converted into a studio for a painter, and one of the lower rooms could have been adapted as a studio for a sculptor.

We were also shown copies of the Gregynog Press books; the university kept complete sets of both special and ordinary bindings on the premises. I had never seen anything like them, printing and binding so fine, as perfect as it was possible for me to imagine. The content, however, in many cases seemed to me to fall short of the standard achieved in the form.

You are not interested in my interview; nor in the reasons (whatever they were) why they chose me as the first Gregynog Arts Fellow; nor in my own writing during those idyllic (not a word I have ever used seriously before, I believe) months, but, this being a learned journal, only in my relationship to that historical Gregynog Press whose books are so highly regarded and which fetch so much today. Suffice it therefore to say (as they say) that they did choose me, and that I moved there for six months the following February, that of 1970. And it is also relevant that they appointed Michael Pennie to follow me as the second Fellow later that year.

Gregynog is now used, and much and usefully used, as a residential study centre for students from both inside and outside the University of Wales. They come, about fifty at a time with their staff, on short courses usually of two or three days' length, covering most disciplines. The first course that came to Gregynog after I arrived that snowy February was, as it happened, from the College of Librarianship at Aberystwyth, and part of their course was to see and have demonstrated to them how things were actually printed, on the Albion and other bits and pieces. I very much enjoyed talking to them, the students, but even more to the staff, who included Dorothy Harrop: she was then writing the chapter on the Press in the official University history of Gregynog due to be published in 1974.

After that first course, however, I had little to do with the Press, becoming absorbed in my own work; during the time I wrote about a dozen poems, a novel, three short stories, and edited my selected shorter prose, besides talking about writing and film-making to hundreds of students, formally and informally, in the pleasant course of the other part of the reason I was there. The Press was always at the back of my mind, however, as one of the things I could especially do at Gregynog; I have always thought that the way a book looks and feels to the reader is as much my concern as the choice of the actual words, and have almost always had a major say in the design of my own books. The other day I heard a rumour that I had once been a compositor; it was not true, but who am I to discourage the thought? Ever since I was a student, editing the college magazine, I have been seriously interested in typography and book production. Mrs. Edwards bound a book of mine, with a special label indicating her part in it; she and Ted Walters also talked to me about the Press and its relationship to the Agent for the estate, some of which information I used in the novel. For both of these reasons I used to pass the Albion on my way up to see her, hoping to find time to print something; but it was like fishing in the Bechan and the private reservoir Gwgia, and learning Welsh, and taking advantage of the library to fill in some of the acres of gaps in my reading, and finding out what stu-

448

dents were really like now; none could be done properly except to the exclusion of most of the others.

It was towards the end of July when I was confronted by the fact that if I did not do something on the Press within the next four weeks then the chances were that I never would. Michael Pennie's tenure approached. I could either spend the last month of mine typing the fair copy of my novel, or I could postpone it to London for a rather hairy deadline and toy with the Gregynog Albion instead.

Mrs. Edwards showed me how to use the Albion. She had originally, she told me, wanted to be on the printing rather on the binding side, but when she had joined (as a teenage girl from the village) there had been a vacancy only in the bindery; by such things were one's life determined in a community where there were few alternative sources of employment. But she had retained the interest in printing; and the Albion on which the first book had been printed had been left, not raped by the National Library as a museum piece, because Gwen Edwards needed it to print paper titles for the spines of the books she bound for the University. So she was able to use it to her own satisfaction now, towards the end of her working life, and she only too gladly, it seemed, made me free of it, showed me where everything was, the rules, the chart of a typecase she had made for herself, the shelf of tins of inks from the thirties, the stone, the cracked rubber roller, all that was left there of what the Gregynog Press must have been.

Glyn Tegai also joined me, and together we arrived at various rationalisations of the way the equipment must have worked; though he did have the advantage of a book on the subject. What quickly became obvious was that there was an enormous amount of work involved, work requiring a combination of physical and mental energies which I had come across before only in filming on location. That is, at the same time as one was physically humping heavy metal about one was also having to make aesthetic and formal decisions of an excruciatingly difficult kind as well. The physical labour of it, and the limited amount of time I had available, convinced me that I should not be too ambitious about what I intended to do; and the fewer characters there were to set and print, the less there would be to go wrong. During my Fellowship I had been tinkering with various kinds of the Welsh verse form called *englyn*, trying to see if it were possible in English. Anyone who wishes to know about the form will find it where I did, in Gwyn Williams' excellent *An Introduction to Welsh Poetry* (Faber). The first I chose to print was the first of three I had written:

> *FERN:     englyn penfyr*
> Hookheaded hairy young fern, springy, curled,
> coy greeny thruster set on
> its own spread revelation

It was to be, of course, a limited edition. Quite how severely limited became apparent as I went on: four days' work, perhaps a hundred trial pulls, and much shortness of temper produced an edition of three copies. At the end of was it the third day, late in the evening, I found that the *f* in the first line had disappeared, presumably broken off somehow. It finished me for the day; I signed the last pull for Glyn Tegai *With Greetings from Hairy Young Ern*, and went home to watch television; what was I doing bothering with this obsolescent medium anyway?

The paper was difficult, too. I was using (with the permission of Glyn Tegai and the University) some stray quarto sheets of handmade paper that had been there since the thirties, perhaps since the twenties; and the dogma was that these had to be dampened before an acceptable impression could be made. I tried dampened and undampened pulls and was damned if I could see the difference. Nevertheless, I continued to sprinkle as though it were some religious rite.

Then there was the bloody ink; not that I ever used red. It had thickened almost solid, the ink, having been sitting there congealing since the last book was finished in 1940. On the stone next to the Albion there were at the head two conical canisters: one marked P, and the other B. Petrol and Benzole, I thought, sniffing for vaguely related smells. So I went down to Dilwyn at the garage in the village, who had no B but plenty of P, and filled up one of them. This I sprinkled on the stone with a slice of ink and worked them about with a spatula in a curiously satisfying manner until a consistency was reached which stayed on the roller in a state which was neither lumpy nor wishy-washy. Some months later, when I told Asa

Benveniste[31] of Trigram Press what I had been doing, he told me P stood for paraffin. Was I wrong, then? I asked him. Not wrong, only dangerous, he said, you could have blown yourself up.

The actual setting I enjoyed, for it was like a simple linear cross-word puzzle to which I knew every answer in advance. Once I knew which way up each character went, by the nick on one side, it was childsplay; though I would not have liked my living to have depended on my speed. The more I worked with Baskerville the more I appreciated it; I had thought it very ordinary up till then, but physically touching it led me to prefer it to the small choice (Perpetua, Cloister) of other faces available.

The morning after the birth of Young Ern I went back, replaced his *f* and finished the edition. Then I did another, similar but on paper watermarked GG. I was pleased enough with these, and began to form even more grandiose plans. Why not a collection of all three *englynion* I had written? Why not a title page, too? On foolscap? And make the move into mass-production with an edition of five copies?

It did not satisfy me quite as much as my first attempt, but it still pleased me a lot. It was worth all the neckbending, squinting, the moments of despair which could be relieved only partially by destroying what I had done by a thunderous juddering whirl of the guillotine flywheel.

About the time I was finishing this second undertaking, there came to stay with us for a few days the poet Philip Pacey and Gill. Philip had been trained latterly at the College of Librarianship, Aberystwyth, and had been to Gregynog briefly before. In partnership we evolved a project which was so breathtaking that I would never have attempted it on my own: an eight-page sheet folded to four printed sides devoted to one each of our poems, a title page, and a credits page. Furthermore, such was our hubris, this was to be an edition of no less than twenty copies and was to be on green-tinted paper of an unknown dampening quality.

It was inevitable that such effrontery would be punished. It was the nineteenth pull when I noticed that (on the title page, too) the

---

[31] American-born poet who had settled in Britain in the 1950s. Variously a printer, a typographer, and book designer, from 1965 he managed the Trigram Press, which published work by George Barker, Ivor Cutler, Gavin Ewart, B. S. Johnson, Jeff Nuttall and J. H. Prynne, among many others.

second *O* of my surname was not in the same font as the first *O*. Since this is a scholarly journal in which only the truth may be told, it must be recorded that it was Philip who set the title page; and he had not, by several days, as much experience of typesetting as I had, of recognising the faces, the bodies, the *O*s. It is also probably necessary to state that we were not under the influence of alcohol at the time, neither Philip at the time of setting nor myself at the time of not noticing during machining. As if it were relevant.

At the time, it did not seem to me to make a curiosity of the edition; it made a cock-up of it.

But there was no time to start again. We both signed the edition, and divided it equally between us; the chances of its being held against us we were prepared to accept.


But now, more than two years later, I still do not know what to do with the work of those weeks. The second edition is still complete; one copy from the first, several from the third and fourth have been given to friends. Should I keep them for (as if I were an optimist) three hundred years to give possible amusement to my posited descendants on Mars? The cost of keeping them in the bank might be excessive, while the risk of keeping them at home is uninsurable. Should I offer them for sale at fourpence each in the public gazettes? Should I destroy them, and allow only the myth to survive in this highly respectable place?

Does it matter? It passed the time more enjoyably than typing; though time being what it is it would (of course) have passed anyway.

# Opinion

*Published in* Poet, *2, Summer 1974*[32]

What (as I subject my tastebuds to English fishgum) what (as I over-activate them with American variegated flavours) what, yet again, (as I perform those other acts of clerical drudgery I thought myself freed of at the age of twenty-three) what (is there no end to this?) what do I imagine I am doing in my capacity as Poetry Editor of *Transatlantic Review*?[33]

So fond am I of the opening of David Hume's essay 'Of the Standard of Taste' that I shall paraphrase it here. The opinions even of one's closest friends are noticeably different; though with these friends one may have been brought up from infancy, had a similar education, and been subjected to the same forces of prejudice. But step outside one's own community, let alone country or language, and then the differences are even more marked. So much so that (and I feel sure you can do without Hume's own words no longer) '. . .the highest arrogance and self-conceit is at last startled, on observing an equal assurance on all sides, and scruples, amidst such a contest of sentiment, to pronounce positively in its own favour.'

So there I thought we all were; but are we?

On at least two sides in contemporary poetry (those mentioned in the 'Opinion' of the last/first issue of *Poet*) there are displayed opinions which are arrogances and self-conceits which are even higher than the highest; so much so that one can only say they aspire to sublime stupidity. For both sides (and there are others, sides, that is,

---

[32] The date of composition was late December 1972.

[33] Influential literary magazine, founded by Joe McCrindle in 1959 and published both in London and New York. Johnson was the poetry editor at the London end. His New York counterpart, George Garrett, later wrote that Johnson's role made him 'closely in touch with what was happening in English-language poetry; more so, probably, than any other poet in England or America at the time'.

though I am not concerned to align them here) pretend to act as though they were right, and as though no one else could be right. And, what must indeed be the very height, they do not in the least scruple to act as though they were right for other people, too.

Now it is sometimes necessary for a poet who is interested in originality (rather than in the act of imitating being a poet) to believe that his way of writing is the right way, the only way, and that everyone else's ways are wrong; because if he did not commit himself to this belief then he would not be able to write in his own special, original way. But if he is honest he believes this only for himself, and for his own purposes; he does not say that this is the only way for others to write.

So what, then, do I imagine I am doing as Poetry Editor of *Transatlantic Review*, setting myself up as an arbiter of other poets' work?

I try very hard to suppress any feeling of power in making decisions about accepting or rejecting; though it is, in all honesty, difficult to do so on some few occasions. Simply, given the amount of space I have for poetry in a quarterly, I take those poems which move me in some way or another, purely subjectively. I can find no other reasonable criterion. There are no other standards that seem to me relevant. So that the appearance of a poem in *Transatlantic Review* means that it moved me in some way that resulted in my wanting to be the instrument of its being made into print and therefore having the chance of a little wider currency and (possibly) permanency. There are no schools to be discerned, no fashionable trends, no axes being ground. There are advantages in this catholicity, of course: I have never once been invited to any sort of literary function as Poetry Editor of *TR*, nor am I part of any faction to be manipulated this way or that by the cultural bullyboys. It also seems to me an important advantage that the editorial policy of *TR* in general is to carry no reviews or criticism whatsoever; the furthest we stray from actual writing is to have interviews with writers in which they talk about what they have done or are doing. The opportunities for publishing criticism already vastly outnumber those for publishing real writing, anyway, and they continue to increase. That this is remarkable in a magazine is indicated by the number of publishers and poets who send *TR* review copies of their books, insulting us by revealing they have not done so much as glance at an issue; one might have special pleasure in selling such copies at Gaston's[34] if that was the sort of thing one did.

Every few weeks, as I go through the two or three hundred poems which have been submitted to *TR*, I feel. . . .but this is not going to turn into the usual Poetry Editor's piece on his job, full of sneers at those who are no poets, at their daring even to send in their work, categorising their ineptitudes. For I do take the job seriously; so seriously that it reduces the tiny amount of money involved to a matter of pence per hour, if I was bothered to work it out. Why do I do it? Because I believe it would be worse done if I were not doing it; and (I think it could be demonstrated, perhaps) am sure it was being worse done before I took over some eight years ago. It means that I have to read a great many boring poems, and I have to find time out of that in which I might be writing myself to read those boring poems. But even they keep me in touch with what a lot of people consider to be poetry; and if only by aversion help me in defining what I think my own ought to be. The habit of reading a lot of contemporary verse can in itself be no bad thing. At the very least it is concerned with the problem of writing poetry now; which no poetry of the past is, obviously, whatever else may be said of it.

And there are compensations. This is not going to be the usual piece about who published whom before whom in what, either; but I have published my share of unknowns who went on to become known as well as my share of unknowns who have remained so, deservedly or undeservedly, in all cases. If that is relevant. I would certainly not claim to have published all those who have become known in the last eight years; which magazine could? And I am also aware that there are poets who simply would not submit poems to *TR* even if I asked them; there is an animosity that initially depended on some overheard slight, perhaps, or secondhand condemnation out of malice or ignorance, or sheer class warfare. I find such petitions dismaying, sapping energy and patience, sad.

Perhaps I am being naïve; perhaps it has always been like this; perhaps that brings us back to David Hume again. For while I agree

---

[34] Booksellers in Bishop's Court, Chancery Lane, much favoured by professional reviewers who knew that they would be offered 50 per cent of the cover price for pristine review copies.

with him that there is no more absurd figure than the man pretending to certainty, especially in aesthetics, we now have numbers increasing at least in proportion with the population. Ian Hamilton,[35] to name nearly one.

Let me say at once that Ian Hamilton may well be adopting absolutist attitudes at least partly in order to provoke reactions and have notice taken of him; and I am very conscious that I am serving that end at this moment. But it may also be useful for each generation to have a Hamilton-figure there to hate (it used to be old. . . .er. . .whatisname, remember?) without going to the extreme of saying it would be necessary to invent him. It is good to have something against which to react; that is about as much as is worth saying about him generally. As a poet, I have thought him quite good ever since I first saw his work as Advisory Editor of *Universities' Poetry Four* in 1962. There seems more of the literary politician in him than the poet, however; he is a perhaps typical lame dog of our time, tragically (even pathetically) caught between real work and criticism, the two opposites, synthesis and analysis. If only Hamilton could direct all his energies into writing poems he might develop into a minor poet of real interest. Provided always that he had the necessary luck, too.

Poets in general might concentrate on the business of writing poems, and have as little to do with criticism as possible; they might, simply, do it and not write about someone else doing it. The only important use of criticism would be if it helped poets to write better; yet how many critics try to do that? I cannot offhand think of any who would not find the idea laughable as a prime concern in any definition of their activity.

Anyone's opinion is really only as good as anyone else's; when the desire to express such opinions is combined with an urge to impose them on other people, then the danger is that such absurdity is not seen but overwhelmed by the politics of publishing and academicism.

But perhaps this piece was so difficult to write because the whole problem is not apodictic in any case.

[35] Oxbridge-educated biographer, editor, poet and publisher: a key figure in the London literary circles of the '60s, '70s and '80s. His collection *The Visit* had come out in 1970, and for most of Johnson's tenure at *Transatlantic Review* he was poetry and fiction editor at the *TLS*, making them natural antagonists.

456

# Soho Square [On the Angry Brigade]

*Published in* Film and Television Technician, *January 1973*

It may be by the time you read this that the Angry Brigade[36] trial will be already forgotten; certainly the way the newspapers ignored it for all except the last couple of weeks of the six months it took seems to indicate that they want you to forget it.

As well they might. For it smells very nasty indeed, and raised some crucial issues about what British law and order now mean which the establishment would prefer to remain undiscussed.

In case you think this is going to be another political piece unrelated to ACTT[37] activities and members, let me explain. On January 12th 1971 Robert Carr's house was the subject of a bomb attack. It was also the day massive protests were taking place against the then proposed Industrial Relations Bill. I was amongst those who were working anonymously on part of ACTT's protest, Freeprop Films, at the time. I say 'anonymously', but a week before some generous-hearted brother had blown a number of our names to *The Times*; immediately after the Carr bombing my telephone was (I am as certain as I can be) tapped. After the first amused and flattered surprise

---

[36] A loose-knit British militant group which undertook a series of bomb attacks in London from 1970 to 1972. Targets included banks, embassies, the BBC's coverage of the 1970 Miss World event, and homes of several Conservative MPs including the then Secretary of State for Employment, Robert Carr. The trial of 1972 became a *cause célèbre*.

[37] The Association of Cinematograph Television and Allied Technicians. As a working film and television director Johnson was a paid-up member of this union, made regular contributions to its journal *Film and Television Technician*, and found its hard-line politics far more to his taste than those of that other, more genteel writers' organisation, the Society of Authors. For Freeprop films, the union's production wing, he made a satirical propaganda film, *Unfair!*, attacking the Conservative government's Industrial Relations Bill. The Bill proposed to limit wildcat strikes, introduce prohibitive limits on legitimate strikes and establish a National Industrial Relations Court. It provoked widespread opposition, and the General Secretary of the TUC, Vic Feather, organized a nationwide 'Kill the Bill' campaign which included a 'day of action' on 12 January 1971.

(they think *me* worthy of surveillance?) I became annoyed not because anything I said on the telephone could get me into trouble, but because my telephone service became appalling: crossed lines three times out of four, wrong numbers, silence with the sound per-spective of a huge hall with occasionally a whistling phantom, no dialling tone until someone presumably threw a switch, and a perhaps paranoiac feeling someone was listening. Several times I rang up my telephone manager and complained about the poor service. At length I suggested to him that the cause might be that my phone was being tapped. The conversation then went something like this:

'We do not tap telephones in this country, sir,' he said.

'But it came out in court recently that Rudi Dutschke's[38] phone was constantly tapped. We know that from the papers.'

'It can only be done with a Home Office order, sir.'

'And is there such an order on my number?'

'No, sir.'

'But that's just what you'd say anyway, isn't it? And I've just caught you out in one barefaced lie.'

A lot of people reading this must know from similar personal experience that the Carr bombing (which was only one of a series; news of earlier ones had been suppressed by the media) sparked off a massive police hunt which covered anyone who had anything to do with opposition to the Industrial Relations Bill. It was (of course) denied at the trial that this had happened at all, let alone that someone at Cabinet level had ordered it. What it now seems to me must have happened is that the police just did not know where to look, so there was blanket surveillance of everyone connected in the slightest with opposition to the Bill. Panic in the copshops, in fact.

Why am I telling you all this?

I am not here concerned to debate whether it is right to seek to change democracy violently; nor even with the hypocrisy of the media in condemning it in this case while supporting it institutionally in Ireland and elsewhere.

What I am concerned about is that justice should be (at least more

[38] German leader of radical student protest, who fled to the UK in 1968 after an attempt on his life. Despite having been accepted to study for a degree at Cambridge, he was expelled from Britain as an 'undesirable alien' by the Conservative government in 1971.

or less) what we teach our children it is: if there is a reasonable doubt, then you do not convict people. And in the Angry Brigade trial there were many reasonable doubts. The senior police officer in charge of the case, Commander Bond,[39] was caught out (like my telephone manager) in at least one barefaced lie. The police evidence in general was riddled with inconsistencies, and chopped and changed too. The harassment of one of the accused, Stuart Christie, by the Special Branch was prolonged, crude, and (one would have thought) basically illegal. Repeated requests by virtually all the accused for a solicitor to be present at interviews were blatantly ignored by policemen from Bond downwards.

How (you must be asking yourselves) since the media hardly reported this trial, can I know all this? Well, first of all I was concerned enough to go along to the Old Bailey on four occasions; and then each week *Time Out* carried an excellent report of the main points. *Time Out* (whatever else one may think of it) may be said to have come of age during this trial: it really showed up the national newspapers. *The Guardian*'s attitude, for instance, was transparently demonstrated on one occasion during the last few days of the trial when it gave more space and prominence to a report concerning the possible prosecution of Princess Anne for speeding.

Even so, I (no more than you or anyone else) do not know whether those on trial were guilty or not; what I am sure of is that there was a reasonable doubt. And (once more) at the risk of seeming naïve, I want British justice to be as it says it is; otherwise we really do have anarchy, and there are no standards, and it is all chaos. But those who engineered the vicious change from unanimous to majority jury verdicts must be congratulating themselves that they would not have convicted the four in this case without having altered this basic tenet of centuries of British justice. They are themselves the cause of disorder, of disregard of the law; and they wish to make further changes so that it is even more heavily against anyone accused.

British justice cannot afford many more Angry Brigade trials; or,

---

[39] Ernest Bond, Commander of the Metropolitan Police Bomb Squad, and later Deputy Assistant Commissioner (Operations). In 1976 on retirement he was awarded an OBE, and was later revealed to be a freemason (from the 2003 Masonic Year Book).

for that matter, any more *Oz* trials.[40] The one hope (as in the *Oz* case) is the Court of Appeal, the last defence against overzealous police and biased courts.

Meanwhile, there is Commander Bond. If there were any justice (ha!) he should of course have been required to resign; as it is he may well have been discomfited privately by his bosses for his failure to convict more than four of the twelve he arrested, and for the revelation of police incompetence and unscrupulousness during the trial. But what he should really be asked (loud, publicly, and often) is: who bombed the Post Office Tower, then?[41]

---

[40] The satirical magazine *Oz* was the subject of a celebrated obscenity trial in 1971, when editors Jim Anderson, Felix Dennis and Richard Neville were prosecuted for an archaic offence, 'conspiracy to corrupt public morals'. The 'Oz Three' were found not guilty on the conspiracy charge, but were convicted and imprisoned on lesser offences – though on appeal this was overturned, and it was found that Justice Argyle had grossly misdirected the jury on numerous occasions in the original trial.

[41] The Post Office (later British Telecom) Tower was at this time open to the public, with a revolving 34th-floor restaurant. A bomb exploded in the men's toilet on 31 October 1971, with the Provisional IRA claiming responsibility. The restaurant was closed to the public for security reasons in 1980, and all public access to the tower ceased in 1981.

460

# The Author's Plight – the Need for a Union

*Published in* Tribune, *June 1973*

In 1965 the Society of Authors took a survey amongst its members to find out how much writers earned; the answer, it turned out predictably enough, was Very Little. Then last year the Society repeated the survey, and found that writers were now even worse off; not only relatively, because of seven years' inflation, but the earnings themselves were actually markedly lower.

If the Society of Authors is not to blame for this remarkable failure to defend the incomes of writers, then who is? Surely it is its job to see that such things cannot happen?

But no, that is not how the Society of Authors sees itself at all. The truth is that it is a weak, reactionary, badly-led organisation with a rigid, undemocratic structure that reduces its effectiveness to virtually nil. It is not a trade union; it is a limited company, yet probably in breach of the Companies Acts in that its members do not have the right to dismiss its board of directors. Trying to change anything by democratic means at the Society of Authors is desperately hard work, and certain of the leadership react to the term *trade union* with an oldfashioned class fury that would be comic if it were not to do with the serious business of seeing that writers earn a living from their job as everyone else in the book world does.

And the onus should be on the Society to prove how writers benefit from its not being a trade union, since musicians, actors, film-makers and others concerned with the arts have all formed themselves into trade unions and are affiliated to the TUC. As such they gain enormously in strength and expertise; they are part of something much larger than themselves, and have a shared interest in so much more.

Since Colin Davis, Lord Snowdon and Lord Olivier are prepared to be members respectively of the Musicians Union, ACTT and Equity, I fail to see why any writer should be toffeenosed about joining a union.

461

Furthermore (to nail that old one about writers being impossible to organise) there is a union for writers in film and television: the Writers' Guild,[42] which despite being only a quarter of the membership size of the Society of Authors is very effective in seeing that screenwriters are adequately paid.

The Society of Authors by all logic should turn itself into a trade union. The first benefit would be that publishers would start to take the Society as seriously as the television companies do the Writers' Guild. Another immediate benefit would be that it would be able to go to other trade unions in the publishing industry for help; think of the difference it would make to the Society's position if it could suggest to a publisher with whom it was in dispute that he would have difficulty finding anyone to print his books in future because of our friendliness with the very important printing unions. Such co-operation is happening all the time within the trade union movement; the Society as it is at present constituted and run has no right to ask for or expect any such help.

It might then have some strength to apply in solving the basic cause of writers' financial problems: that they do not receive a fair proportion of the money available from the sale of books. Everyone else in the industry (publishers, printers, booksellers) earns a living from the same source, the bookbuyers' money, but not writers. This is because the writer receives on average only ten percent of the price of his book compared to (for instance) the bookseller's thirty-five per-cent. Does any bookseller think that his part in society is more than twice as important as Graham Greene's? Put like that, it seems absurd: but financially that is exactly how he does think of himself in relation to Graham Greene; and in relation to less distinguished authors he thinks he's worth three times as much!

Publishers would object, of course, that any increase for writers would put up the price of books; but in the last eight years the price of books has doubled, and yet still more copies are sold every year. That argument must be exposed as the falsity it is. The Society should propose to the Publishers Association that some increase in royalty

[42] The Writers' Guild of Great Britain (WGGB) was established in 1959. Unlike the Society of Authors, the Writers' Guild is a trade union affiliated both with the Trades Union Congress (TUC) and the International Affiliation of Writers Guilds (IAWG).

462

rates be agreed: say by stages of one or two percent a year for the next ten or five years. Such an increase might go some way towards seeing that writers make the living from the publishing industry that others expect and take.

And yet is the royalty scheme the best one for authors? No one would advocate a return to the old outright, lump-sum system that existed in Victorian times, but it should be possible to arrange for a guaranteed minimum advance which would cover what it cost the writer to stay alive to write the book, with a later royalty if the book sold well. It is worth asking, too, in connection with royalties (the very word itself derives from the divine right of kings) why it is that publishers choose to apply it only to writers: they do not ask their editors, warehousemen, or even less their printers to accept remuneration only according to how many copies are sold of the books on which they work.

Yet let us not be naïve. Publishers do these things because they can get away with them; and they can get away with them because the Society of Authors historically has never stood up to them and fought them. All right, so authors could never go on strike (though important authors withholding manuscripts at key moments could cause much the same effect) but there are other forms of action which are possible and practical. And the very least the Society could do would be to draw up its own standard form of contract for the publication of a book, containing the minimum terms it recommended its members to accept. You are surprised it has not even done this? So was I; but it was just one of many surprises about that curious organisation.

The main argument so far advanced for not turning the Society into a trade union is that authors still living who have intimated that they are leaving a bequest to it would not do so if it became anything so common. The amount of such bequests is not generally known, nor how many people would agree to change their wills if asked. The Society says it is able to keep its fee down to ten guineas a year largely because of bequests made to it in the past, notably by the George Bernard Shaw estate. And really money, this money, plays a big part in the doings and outlook of the Society, which is ironic considering that the members themselves see so little of it from their writing. But the Society is, to repeat, a limited company, and tends to behave as such. And how ironic, too, Shaw might have found it to see his money being used to support the reactionary policies the Society now follows!

It has been fighting, it says, the battle for Public Lending Right (shouldn't it in any case be Authors' Lending Right?) for twenty years now; there is every prospect it will continue to do so for another twenty the way it is going about it. It should see that authors should take direct action like any other pressure group; the lesson of such campaigns, from the Suffragettes on, is that only in this way does the government take notice of you, do changes come about. And the scheme it currently backs is both unjust, expensive, and takes no account of books already published. Furthermore, the Society has had the incredible insolence to propose 25 per cent of its members' due from PLR to publishers! Never once has the membership been given a chance to vote on whether it wants this scheme or another; never once has it been consulted over any other of the issues involved, either. Such arrogant autocracy must be challenged, even if it does react with its usual weapons of innuendo, slander and the machinations of the old boy network; even if it does meet reasoned argument with evasion and misrepresentation.

Given its nature, the Society of Authors is not likely to give way to the pressures now making themselves felt from certain writers and groups of writers. But if it does not, it will probably atrophy and die; for there is already the nucleus of another organisation formed in the two hundred odd members of the Writers' Action Group.[43] The Society made a serious mistake in the early fifties when it allowed television writers to go off and form the WGGB; if another organisation begins to represent book writers, then it will be difficult to see any function left at all for the Old Lady of Drayton Gardens.

---

[43] Campaigning organisation led by the novelists Maureen Duffy and Brigid Brophy, spearheading the movement to introduce Public Lending Right. The PLR was finally passed in March 1979.

# The Happiest Days?

*Published (abridged) in* Education and Training, *March 1973*

Usually one can find a pattern in an experience as long as an education, draw the threads together to shape an article like this. I have thought for a long time about my own, but it has not been possible: how can you impose a pattern on chaos?

I started early. It seems that there was some distinction in being sent to Flora Gardens Primary, in Hammersmith, at the age of four, and that I was proud of it; most others went at five. That must have been 1937, presumably September. We had to lie down in the afternoons on canvas campbeds, I competed at whopeeshighestupthewall in the Boys', and was disappointingly too well-built to qualify for free codliveroil and malt. Of the learning process I remember nothing.

On the outbreak of war I was six, and was privately evacuated with my mother and the son of a Westminster publican to a farm that was really only a smallholding near Chobham, in Surrey. I went to the village school, St. Lawrence's I think it was called. Again I can remember very little of it, though my life on the farm has left me with very many sharply-felt memories. But I did learn to read during that time. I can date it no more closely than somewhere between my sixth and eighth birthdays, but it was at the end of some days in bed and I was feeling quite recovered from an illness but still not allowed to get up. The story was in one of the kind of comics which contain both picture strips with speech-balloons as well as stories in words with only a heading illustration, and I read it out of boredom, in desperation almost, after exhausting all the picture strips had to give me. It was a spy story with a boy hero who sent messages across the Channel by means of a petroldriven and radiocontrolled model aircraft; a highly improbable tale, I see now, but that afternoon I read it over and over again, with infinite pleasure, glorying in the fact that I could now read stories.

It would be dishonest not to give the school some credit for that; though, as I say, I can remember no one teaching me there, nothing learnt there. I am reduced to circumstantial evidence.

In 1941, after a brief period spent in London during the bombing, I was officially evacuated on my own to High Wycombe. At some point and at no cost my 'name had been put down' for Latymer school, then in Hammersmith Road; I think going to Flora Gardens was a preliminary to this, and I would normally have gone to Latymer at perhaps seven. Latymer had earlier been evacuated as a school to a small village outside High Wycombe called Sands, and some administrative logic sent me there now I was of age. To accommodate the overflow, the village school had taken over a Presbyterian Church Hall opposite; the Latymer boys still wore their uniforms, were not assimilated. I wept at my first billet, was given another the London side of High Wycombe; and for the rest of the next three years I made the long bus journey there and back to Sands every schoolday.

At some point, perhaps after a year or so, Latymer returned as a school to London; for some reason two of us were left behind at Sands. Virtually the last link with London was gone; from then on my isolation grew, my whole life was dominated by the fact that I was away from everything I had known. I was wretchedly miserable, weepy at the slightest cause (or for no cause), bad company, a thoroughly unrewarding pupil for any teacher, even for the odd saint, I suspect.

In 1944 I sat what I now know to be the eleven-plus. At the time I did not understand what it was about. By post came a promise from my parents (my father an RAOC[44] private in Germany, my mother working as a shop assistant in London) of my first twowheeled bicycle if I passed; so I knew it was important. Two of us took it, in the Headmaster's room; from this I presume it must have been a London paper, for the other candidate was the only other Latymer boy left. Afterwards the Headmaster called me back, pointed with his pipestem at my attempt at one of the questions:

'Couldn't you do even that one?' he said.

I had on a previous occasion been caught thieving fruit from an

[44] Royal Army Ordnance Corps.

466

orchard in a mill; and humiliated when up before him by an offer of fruit from his own garden if that was what I needed. That was not what I needed, at all.

I do not remember being told I had failed; and they still gave me the bicycle, anyway.

The secondary modern they sent me to for the last year of the war and my evacuation was called Highfields, I think, but certainly the Headmaster was called Perfect. Here my form-master was the teacher who meant most to me throughout the whole of my education; and his name, remarkably, was Proffitt. He took us eleven-plus rejects and shook us, restored our confidence, showed us we certainly mattered to someone, to him. He really worked us, worked himself: all my memories have him on his feet, usually marching about, delivering, cajoling, enlightening; a balding, greyhaired, springy little figure of about fifty-five. He really brought something out of me; but he could also be cruel, both physically and verbally. Principally, he made us compete: there were exams from the first week, placings, encouragements to do better, to go up the scale of Mr. Proffitt's esteem.

At the end of the first term I ranked third in the class, which position was physically recognised by his placing me in the back row three from the window; the nearer you were to him, the less well you had done, the more you felt he had his eye on you. It all seems rather oldfashioned now, but it worked with me; I was now being stretched, for the first time in my life I think; no one had ever made me work before, had shown me what I could do, what I had in me.

Before the end of my first year at Highfields the war was over; I suspect they sent us home within weeks, whereas they could have waited till the end of term, July instead of June. But no. I remember saying to Mrs. Bailey, my fostermother, that I would not have minded staying on in High Wycombe to finish my schooling. Whether this was an expression of dismay at the prospect of yet another change I do not know; but I cannot think I meant it.

During the war my parents had moved over the river from Hammersmith and London to Barnes and Surrey. Hence I could not go back to Latymer for administrative reasons, and I was sent to Barnes County Secondary Modern School. All my previous Proffitt brightness was now displayed outside the classroom, in cleverness, in putting people down. This I am sure was because there was no teacher in the school to bring it out, to give me a reason to compete; the other kids seemed to accept they were bound to go on to dead-end jobs (I met one of them again recently: as a conductor on the number nine bus to Barnes). Thirteen years later I was to do four or five months there as a supply teacher; a bizarre and unenlightening full turn of the wheel.

At fourteen after passing some sort of simple examination I went to Kingston Day Commercial School, which was then at Hinchley Wood, near Esher, and a long busride round the Kingston Bypass from Barnes. Doug White was the other of my contemporaries at Barnes CSMS to go with me, and we felt ourselves privileged; for by the standards of Surbiton and environs Barnes was then largely rough and workingclass. At KDCS they taught shorthand (Pitmans for the girls, Gregg for the boys) typing, commerce and book-keeping; besides the usual things. Ted Britton[45] was teaching maths there then. It was a two-year course designed to turn out shorthand-typists and clerks; those able and whose parents were willing could stay on an extra year and take the School Certificate.[46] I did; the Korean War broke out as we sat the papers; in the summer holidays I had a note from Ted Britton saying that he was pleased that White and I had gained Matric Exemption. I knew that this meant I had qualified for university, but no one had ever suggested that I stood any chance of actually going; no one had ever gone to university from Kingston Day Commercial School.

There followed five years of various accountancy jobs. I already knew I was a writer, though I had not actually written anything. I was lazy, cocky, distracted by (in particular) sex, soccer and motorbikes. Gradually I saw that further education, perhaps even a degree in English, were there for the having, but the initiative had to come from me; no one was going to bring anything out. A friend at work showed me the Birkbeck prospectus, explaining the college was part of London University but held its lectures in the evenings for students with fulltime jobs. From it I saw that my Matric Exemption was noth-

[45] Later Sir Edward Britton (1909–2005). Distinguished educationalist, who became President and later General Secretary of the National Union of Teachers.

[46] The School Certificate was the precursor to O-Level examinations for each subject, and, later, GCSEs.

ing of the kind; I had, in particular, to pass O-level Latin. The same West Indian friend told me about Davies's, the crammers in Addison Road. I did O-level Latin from scratch in eight months with them, sitting three different Boards in the hope of passing one and actually getting all three. My tutor was an old man of seventy-odd who was gross, ugly, fat, slobbery; and he overindulged in Dr. Rumney's Pure Mentholyptus Snuff. I loved him; he was a real master/teacher.

He died not long after I started at Birkbeck. I worked for an oil company in Kingsway during the day, and at six most evenings went to Birkbeck for two or three hours. The course was an internal equivalent of A-level called Intermediate BA; I did English, Latin and History. I became secretary of the Literary Society, arranged a visit to and a discussion on the first production of *Waiting For Godot*, made friends I still have. Of the staff, Barbara Hardy ravished me with her intellect, Geoffrey Tillotson bored me with his pompousness, and Arthur Johnson made sense of Chaucer by reading the *Prologue* in the original pronunciation.

In the summer term I applied to go as a fulltime student to two London colleges, King's and University. Both required applicants to declare which they preferred; I was honest and put King's on both simply (and now it seems so asinine, so grossly irresponsible) because I liked the sound of the name better. I made no attempt to determine the respective qualities of the English departments, or to ask for any other help or guidance. I still wince at the naïveté of that choice. Of course I was not even interviewed by University College; but I was promised a place at King's for September 1956, at the age of twenty-three. When I told the Birkbeck Registrar he tried to dissuade me:

'You'll be surrounded by eighteen-year-old girls,' he warned me.

The fact that they were girls worried me not at all, but what did make me apprehensive was that they were all bright enough to have come straight from grammar school, glowing with high achievement, and the roundabout way I had joined them after my failure at eleven led me to believe I should have to work very hard indeed merely to stay in their company, let alone compete with them. Not so. After only a few weeks I found very few to whom I might feel myself inferior; no doubt my five years' greater maturity made a big difference. I edited five issues of the college literary magazine *Lucifer*, I

469

wrote, directed, and acted with the Drama Society in London and on two tours of German and Danish universities. I had a disastrously important love-affair. I read *Tristram Shandy* and *Gawain*.

But the three years were unhappy and painful for me. I think (though there were other personal and emotional factors involved) it was because the course I was following unexpectedly seemed insufficiently related to the reasons for which I was following it. That is, much of what I was obliged to read seemed, by any standards I had and was taught, bad, boring and irrelevant; and the London English degree is notorious for falling between the stools of language and literature. Perhaps it is too much to ask that English departments at least take into account the possibility that they may have young writers amongst their undergraduates. It has always seemed to me strange that teachers in art schools are presumed to know how to paint in order to be able to teach it; but that English teachers are not required actually to be able to write a sonnet in order to teach other people's.

At the end of my second year I was interviewed and told how much they admired my efforts with *Lucifer* and the Drama Society, but when was I actually going to do any work?

I came down with a 2:2. I thought it was very fair. I would have been pleased with any sort of degree at all, in fact. According to their rules, I was a lower-second-class of person; I accepted that, as long as it was clearly understood that it was according to their rules. For the next five years, until I could support myself wholly by writing, it counted (somewhat ironically) as a Good Honours Degree to increase my salary as a supply teacher through dozens of schools in west and north London. I will not say I necessarily knew which ones they were, but I think I saw many of my earlier selves going to waste, waste, in those five years.

All my life I have been underestimated by the educational system, I feel. Now when I win the odd literary or film award it is often against, in spite of those teachers and contemporaries who so misjudged me that I feel I have won them. Not that it matters, of course; no doubt none of them even remember me, and I now know none of them.

Do I sound paranoiac and bitter? Yes, I am, that is indeed the way I feel about my educators, that is the way they made me. No doubt the war was not their fault; no doubt there are worse things than a fractured, fragmented education like mine (David Storey's novel *Pasmore* is about someone who has a breakdown at thirty after a long smooth progression on an educational conveyor-belt); perhaps the usual optimist is already contemplating a letter saying 'Ah, but you did win through in the end, you did get the university education for which your mind qualified you.'

Obviously I was university material, in the end; whether I was or not at sixteen seems doubtful. I tried hard to be an accountant, to be what my education had fitted me for. Even now I have the marginal benefit of being able to touch-type this article; my new novel *Christie Malry's Own Double-Entry* leans very heavily on knowledge I gained in learning book-keeping; and I could have annotated almost every paragraph of this account with page references from my books where I have made professional use of material related to my schooldays.

The point is that very few people are writers and thus able to make some positive use of virtually everything that happens to them, including the disasters, the chaos; what do the others do?

## About the Editors

Jonathan Coe's biography of B. S. Johnson, *Like a Fiery Elephant*, won the Samuel Johnson Prize for non-fiction in 2005. He is also the author of nine novels, including *What a Carve Up!* (1994), *The Rotters' Club* (2001) and *The Rain Before It Falls* (2007).

Philip Tew is both Professor in English (Post-1900 Literature) and Deputy Head for Research of the School of Arts at Brunel University. His publications include *B. S. Johnson: A Critical Reading* (Manchester UP, 2001) and, co-edited with Glyn White, *Re-reading B. S. Johnson* (Palgrave Macmillan, 2007).

Julia Jordan is Lecturer in Twentieth-Century Literature at Cardiff University. She is the author of *Chance and the Modern British Novel* (2010).